Slightly Noble

by

Lilly Gayle

Slightly Noble

Cover Art by *Angela Anderson*

The Wild Rose Press, Inc.
PO Box 708
Adams Basin, NY 14410-0708
Visit us at www.thewildrosepress.com

Publishing History
First Tea Rose Edition, 2015
Print ISBN 978-1-62830-778-8
Digital ISBN 978-1-62830-779-5

Published in the United States of America

She raised her chin. "I am a commoner, but as you have guessed, my father was accepted in certain social circles. Accepted, but not always welcomed."

"Well, you will be welcomed now, Abby. You are a viscountess." His voice softened, but his eyes shone with disappointment. Was it because he had hoped she would confide in him? Or because she had confessed her humble origins?

Pride stiffened her spine. "I am more than just a viscountess. I am a wife and mother, and if I am to be a good wife, at some point, I must act like a wife." This meant running a household, not living on a ship. She did not want to argue or have him ask more questions about her past, but she could not bear living aboard ship indefinitely.

He started, his expression surprised. Then a slow smile spread over his face, and his eyes burned as if he had a fever. He leaned over the table, his face mere inches from hers. "A real wife sleeps in her husband's bed."

Abby's breath hitched. Her pulse jumped. Oh dear! He had taken her meaning all wrong. Heat rushed to her cheeks, and her flesh tingled. "What I meant...That is, I should be running your household."

"We live on a ship." He leaned back in his chair. He still smiled, but it was now more humorous than...amorous?

She shivered, unable to suppress a brief surge of longing. What would it be like to kiss that hard mouth? To feel his lips pressed against hers?

Dear Lord! What is wrong with me?

Praise for Lilly Gayle

"I read this well-researched and engaged novel at one sitting. Just had to find out how the various puzzling strands tied together. Brava, Ms. Gayle."

~Vonnie Hughes,
author of Lethal Refuge and other titles

~*~

"Lilly Gayle does it again with a tender yet sexy historical about two lonely people faced with insurmountable problems that can only be resolved with love, trust, and a bit of understanding. If you liked *SLIGHTLY TARNISHED*, you'll love *SLIGHTLY NOBLE*'s charming romantic duel between two strong characters."

~Amy Corwin,
author of The Bricklayer's Helper,
Outrageous Behavior, and other titles

~*~

"Lilly Gayle writes a sweet and sexy tale full of secrets, treachery, and the promise of love. From an honorable hero and his charming sidekick to his sassy heroine, Lilly pulls you into her world with ease, and you won't want to leave!"

~Andris Bear, author

Dedication

I lovingly dedicate this book
to my first grandchild, Caroline.
Papa John and Grandma GG
love you to pieces and miss you bunches.

Acknowledgments

Thanks to my critique partners
Andris Bear and Amy Corwin
and to beta reader, Vonnie Hughes.
I couldn't have done it without you ladies.
Thanks also to JM Stewart
for reading the first few chapters of the first draft and
pushing me to dig deeper
into Abby and Jack's emotions.

~*~

Thanks also to my friends and co-workers
at GHS for their support
and to Selena N. and Jennifer K. especially,
for giving me a better title for this story.
Last but not least, I'd like to thank my editor,
Allison Byers, for all she does. You're the best.

Prologue

England
Late July 1865

Abigail Halsey sat on a bench in the convent garden, head bowed, trying to find forgiveness in a heart grown cold. Her hands drifted to the taut swell of her belly, fingers twisting together as anger warred with fear. She wore the somber garb of a postulant, but she was neither pious nor forgiving. She hated the man who had done this to her, the man who had forced her loving father to send her to The Sisters of Mercy in disgrace.

But where else did a widowed gentleman send his only daughter when the earl who had gotten her with child was betrothed to a woman of his own class?

"Are you praying?" Sister Mary Daphne asked, her steps so light, Abby had not heard her approach.

Sunlight filtered through the trees, piercing the shadows with shafts of light. Abby held a hand to her brow, shading her eyes to meet the young novice's curious gaze. "No."

"You should be. The reverend mother says you need to learn discipline and humility, and prayer is the only way."

"I pray only for this child." Bitterness welled up inside Abby like venom, slowly poisoning her soul. "My life is ruined."

"I am sure that once the babe is born—"

"The reverend mother will take it from me, and I will still be tainted goods, unfit to wed." She ignored the twisting pain in her chest and the flutter beneath her hands. How could she bear giving her child to strangers? Yet, how could she keep it, knowing it would be an outcast in society?

Her fingers stilled over the tight mound beneath her ribs. *I will do what is best for my child.*

The nun wrinkled her brow, dappled sunlight casting her face in ever-changing shadows. "There are worse things than having to give up a child, greater losses from which the soul cannot recover. Count yourself blessed that you will have a second chance at life."

"Yes. Blessed." She had thought herself blessed when she caught Lord Drury's eye. The handsome viscount did not seem to care that she was just a commoner despite her father's wealth and social standing. He had flirted and danced with her, and she had reveled in the attention, hoping to prove to her friends that she could marry as well as them. Too late, she learned the viscount already had a betrothed, and all Abby's flirting and scheming had led to this.

She rubbed her stomach again and met the nun's intense stare. "Perhaps I will stay here once the babe is born." Though she had no wish to become a nun, perhaps if she remained at the convent, she could continue designing jewelry for her father. If she no longer went about in society, no one should care if she worked at a trade.

"Perhaps you can discuss that with the reverend mother," Sister Mary Daphne said with a soft smile.

"She wants to see you in her office. There is a letter from your father."

Abby rose slowly to her feet. Despite her father's disappointment, he had always done what was best for his only child. Still, not knowing the contents of his letter set Abby's pulse to pounding as she trailed after the novice's rustling brown habit to a small office.

Hope stirred in her bosom. Had her father found a family for her child? Would she get to meet them to assure herself they were kind, loving people, and not baby farmers interested only in the money her father paid them?

The reverend mother waved Abby inside the office and dismissed Sister Mary Daphne. Abby sank slowly onto a hard chair and met the reverend mother's kind eyes. A bittersweet sorrow threated her composure. Doing what was best for her child would surely break her heart.

"Do you wish to keep this child?"

The unexpected question set Abby's pulse to pounding even harder. Of course, she wanted to keep her child, but she could not. She tried to respond, but tears clogged her throat.

"Well?" Pinched lines formed around the reverend mother's lips as silence filled the air between them.

Abby blinked back tears. Her plans to marry above her humble origins and raise a family had fallen by the wayside the moment she learned Lord Drury was engaged to another. What decent man would have her now?

She swallowed her dreams and forced herself to speak without emotion. "I am unwed. It would not be fair to the child."

"And if you could wed? Would you hold the child accountable for the father's sins?"

"I hold myself responsible." Her current condition was not the child's fault. Nor could she continue to blame Lord Drury, lest the hatred eat her alive. If only she had made better choices...

The reverend mother smiled, and the lines in her face smoothed, taking years off her forty-plus age. "Then I believe your father has found the perfect solution, though he may have waited too late. The baby is due within the month, is it not?"

Abby nodded, anticipation freezing her hands. Her father's solution was to send her to the convent for her confinement so she could have the child in secret and then return home as if she had been away visiting relatives. Hope fluttered in her chest. Had Papa come up with a better plan? Or had he finally found a family for her child, a couple who would keep her secret?

Pain lanced her and all hope died. How could she give her child to strangers and then return to London and the round of endless parties as if nothing had changed? She would never wed now. And she would never be a mother.

"Your father has arranged a marriage for you," the reverend mother said, and Abby nearly came out of her chair.

"What!" The thought of marriage terrified her. She knew what men did to women in bed—terrible, painful things. "But I am no longer chaste!" How could her father even suggest such perfidy? "Who would have me?"

"A man in need of an heir."

"An heir not of his blood!"

The lines around the reverend mother's mouth returned. She leaned forward, folding her small hands on her desk, her eyes compassionate and gentle. "Your father wants what is best for you, child, and Lord Ruston has agreed to keep your secret."

Revulsion made Abby shiver. Papa could not possibly know what a horrid little man Lord Ruston was with his grasping hands and greedy eyes. What kind of husband would such a man make? What kind of father?

"I would rather my child have no father than that odious man!"

Her hysterical outburst brought another frown to the reverend mother's face. "Lord Ruston will give you a home and your child a name."

Wally Crumpler, Viscount Ruston, had buried three wives, none of whom had given him his coveted heir. Now at fifty-one, he was growing desperate. Abby was desperate, too, but not so desperate she would marry a man she had previously turned down. It was unthinkable! She could not tolerate his foul breath or roaming hands. "I would rather loving strangers give my child a name."

"Have faith, Abigail. God tests us in many ways, and I am afraid this will be your test."

****

Abby pulled the hood up over her head and hurried after Sister Mary Daphne. What must the reverend mother be thinking now? What would her father think? Would he search for her? Or wait patiently for her to contact him again?

Sister Mary Daphne had promised to deliver the letter she had written, explaining why she could not marry Lord Ruston or return home until much later. Papa was not one of the peerage, but he was accepted in their circle, as was Abby. Still, society would not kindly welcome an unwed mother into their midst. But now, thanks to the kind sister, Abby had a chance to keep her baby and preserve her reputation.

"How much further?" she asked.

"Less than a mile. We will meet my brother at the Hog and Heifer in Banbury, and then his driver will take us to Shrivenham in the morning. There, my sister will put you up in her boarding house and see to it that you find employment after the babe is born."

"I will repay your kindness," Abby said past the lump in her throat. She swallowed hard and hurried to keep pace. "Is the bakery where Lydia lives near the boarding house?"

Sister Mary Daphne had helped Lydia, a serving girl sent to the convent after her lecherous employer, the earl of Westover, impregnated her. According to the good sister, Lydia had delivered a daughter, and both mother and child were happy, living over a bakery where Lydia posed as a widow and worked as an assistant baker.

Abby hoped to find work as a jewel smith's assistant though she was used to creating her own designs. Of course, her society friends did not know of her secret talents. Gloves had always hidden the nicked fingers and cut knuckles she got from working with precious metals.

"You will be Lydia's neighbor." The nun turned to smile at Abby as if this were more important than Abby keeping her child. Abby supposed it would be nice to see a friendly face once she reached Shrivenham, but the chance to keep her child was more important than anything.

Sister Mary Daphne turned back around and continued walking. "I told my sister you were a widow. I tell her all my girls are widows."

Abby nodded, though the nun could not see, and struggled to keep pace. Her back ached and come morning, she still had to travel several hours by coach before reaching Shrivenham. But she would not complain. At last, she had a plan in place that would allow her to keep her child and eventually return to society.

Chapter One

"Damn the bastard!" Captain Jack Norton pushed to his feet, glaring first at his solicitor, Mr. Lambert, and then at his cousin.

"You are the bastard," Morris Flick replied with a sneer. "Your mother may have been married to the viscount, but everyone from Seile to London knows Uncle William is your real father and not his brother."

The painful reminder was like a fist to Jack's gut. Morris' mother had started the rumors, accusing her youngest brother, William, of siring Lord Ardmore's son, and all because she was jealous of Jack's beautiful mother. Jack's striking resemblance to Uncle William had not helped his mother's cause. Neither had the fact she never denied the vile accusations.

Consumed by jealousy and fueled with suspicion, Jack's father, Viscount Ardmore, banished his wife and son to America, and Cousin Morris had taken Jack's place in the viscount's heart. Jack had lived with that knowledge for years, but he would be damned before he let Morris take his inheritance, too.

He turned toward the sniveling weasel, fully prepared to pummel him. When Flick leaned back, his face taut with fear, Jack smiled and relaxed his fists.

"Gentleman, please!" Mr. Lambert raised his voice, drawing Jack's attention. "If I could finish reading Lord Ardmore's will..."

Morris curled his thin upper lip and pointed to Jack. "He is Viscount Ardmore now. A bankrupt viscount."

His obnoxious snicker rekindled Jack's desire to slug the bastard, but Jack would have the last laugh. The viscountcy might be bankrupt, but he was not. Thanks to Uncle William and their adventures on the *Lion's Pride*, Jack could buy Ridge Point if he wanted to. But damn it all to hell and back, he should not have to. The estate should rightfully belong to him.

"I don't want what's left of the old man's money. I want Ridge Point." His jaw clenched. Ridge Point had been part of his mother's dowry. His father had no right to bequeath it to anyone but her, and she wanted to be buried there.

When Jack had returned to South Carolina after his final trip to England for the Confederacy, Charleston had been under siege, and his mother lay dying of consumption in a god-forsaken infirmary. He risked his life and freedom to stay by her side, and just before death claimed her, they received word that his father had preceded her into the afterlife. The old bastard must have died soon after Jack's departure from England.

His mother had smiled at the news, a relieved rather than happy smile. "I can go home now," she whispered before asking Jack to bury her at Ridge Point.

It was the least he could do for a woman who had lost so much. But his father had added a damn codicil to his will, leaving Ridge Point and every farthing not entailed to his cousin, Morris.

"There is no money, just this crumbling estate." Morris smiled, looking around the dark, derelict library of Ram's Head. "And Ridge Point. Which is now mine," he added. *The smug bastard.*

Jack clenched his fists, his stomach a mass of mangled knots. He couldn't keep his mother's casket in the cargo hold of his ship forever. It was making his crew nervous. It was making *him* nervous. The Confederate States of America had issued the burial certificate authorizing transport of her body to England, but the Confederacy was a defeated nation. And he was a fugitive from the Union.

"What if I let you have the title and all other holdings? I just want Ridge Point." He had to bury his mother at Ridge Point because he did not have the documents needed to bury her elsewhere in England. And he could not imagine transporting her remains back to America.

Mr. Lambert held up a finger and shook it at Jack as if he were a naughty boy caught dipping snuff behind the stables. "No. No. No. You are Viscount Ardmore now whether you wish it or not, and Ram's Head is an entailed estate. You cannot sell the house nor any land attached, nor can you bequeath it to anyone you choose. You do not truly own it. The Crown grants all rights to the current Viscount Ardmore to preserve the viscountcy and keep it in the main line of succession. Ridge Point, on the other hand, and most of the remaining money in the estate were part of your mother's dowry. The title transferred to your father upon his marriage to your mother, but it is not entailed. Therefore, the former viscount was able to leave it to his sister's child, Mr. Flick, despite the fact you are his son and the heir to the viscountcy."

Fury roared through Jack's veins, hot and

unrelenting. His father could not deny him Ram's Head, so he had let it crumble into disrepair. Why? To remind Jack he did not consider him his son even if he was his legal heir?

"I've lost Ridge Point. My mother's birthplace. *My* birthplace." There was no reason for him to stay in England, and yet, there was nothing left for him in America. He was a man with a title, but he had no place to call home, and no family he wished to claim.

Mr. Lambert lowered his gaze. "Technically, yes."

Jack's heart thumped against his ribs. "What do you mean, *technically*?"

"Provincial colonial!" Morris snorted. "You have lost, and Ridge Point is mine."

Jack looked from his cousin to the fidgeting solicitor. Mr. Lambert shifted in his chair, raising and then lowering his gaze. Jack leaned forward, hands on hips, his famous lion's scowl firmly in place. "What aren't you telling me?"

Mr. Lambert cleared his throat and raised his gaze to Jack's chest. "Your father added a second codicil to his will shortly before he died. If you can marry and produce an heir before your thirty-fifth birthday, Ridge Point is yours."

"The hell you say!" What twisted satisfaction did his father seek now?

Jack had attempted to visit the viscount on his last journey to England nearly a year ago. His father refused to see him. The butler, however, had asked if Jack had brought his family, and he had admitted to being unwed.

Had his father added the codicil then? Had he known he was dying? He damn sure knew Jack would turn thirty-five in December, just five months from now.

Did he hate me that much?

Even if he could find a wife so quickly..."She would have to be *delivered* of the child?"

"Yes. And it would have to be a son."

"Then I have lost." He turned woodenly and headed for the door.

"There is still the matter of Ram's Head and your duties as viscount," Mr. Lambert said.

Jack whirled on the aging man and snarled. "I don't give a tinker's damn about Ram's Head or the title."

Lambert swallowed. "Then what of your tenants?"

"They can fend for themselves as they have obviously done since my father obtained the title." Slamming out the room, Jack crossed the foyer, snagged his frock coat from the startled butler, and took the crumbling front steps two at a time, nearly tripping over loose mortar and broken rocks as he went.

If he could not have Ridge Point, he would bury his mother at sea. He didn't need any damn documents or certificates for that.

But Mother hated the ocean.

Snarling, he slammed his hand against the side of the rented coach. The driver jumped to attention as Jack ripped open the door and slid inside. "Drive!"

The coach jerked forward, awakening Jack's traveling companion. Quentin Stanley sat up and stifled a yawn with his fist. "Did it not go well, Captain?"

"No, Mr. Stanley. It did not."

Too refined and "pretty" to be a privateer, the dark-haired fifth son of an English earl was nevertheless an excellent quartermaster, despite his tendency to stick his patrician nose in where it did not belong. Yet, strangely enough, Quentin was one of the best friends Jack had ever had. So, it was easier than he thought to share the disappointing news.

Afterwards, Quentin shook his head. "So, what next, oh fearless leader?"

"Hell if I know." Jack slumped in the seat, his long legs stretching out across the floor until his feet bumped up against the other side. "I guess we sail back to America."

"Better wait a few months," Quentin said, his eyes somber in the dim light shining into the coach. "You sail into any port in America now and the Yankees will confiscate the *Lion's Pride* for sure and most likely arrest her captain."

"It is a possibility," Jack agreed.

"It is a certainty, and you know it. The Union army is not going to grant amnesty to the privateer who gave them hell for the past two years."

Despite the direness of his current situation, Jack smiled. His crew *had* given the Union army hell. They had spent the last two years attacking Union ships and slipping past their blockades to keep the Confederacy afloat—not that it had done a damn bit of good. The Confederacy was doomed long before his adopted countrymen fired the first shot on Morris Island. But after four long years, the conflict was finally over.

At times, it seemed as if a lifetime had passed.

Jack sighed and leaned his head back against the wall of the coach. "I guess we return to Seile. I'm not ready to retire with Uncle William, but we can keep the ship moored there until we develop a new strategy."

"I think our next move should be to find a couple of warm and willing women," Quentin said with a smile.

Jack sat upright, leaned forward, and slapped Quentin's knee. "That's a damn fine idea, Quent. Damn fine indeed."

Unfortunately, the women they came across a half hour later were neither warm nor willing.

And one of them was a nun.

Chapter Two

"Beggin' yer pardon, governor, but there be a coach in the middle of the road, blocking the way," the coachman said when he stuck his head inside the conveyance. His cockney accent was so heavy Jack could barely understand him. He looked to Quentin for clarification.

"Can we go around them?" Quentin asked. "We are anxious to get back to Seile."

Anxious to find those warm, willing women.

The driver frowned. "There be women inside, and it looks like they broke an axle."

"Damn." Jack straightened. "I suppose we could offer our assistance and speed things along."

"After you." Quentin held out his hand and then followed Jack from the coach. The driver climbed back into his box, pulled his wool cap over his eyes, and settled in for a nap.

It had better be a short one, Jack groused to himself.

As he and Quentin approached the disabled carriage, a high-pitched scream rent the air. Jack and his quartermaster exchanged glances.

What the hell are we getting into now?

Quentin shrugged but dropped his hands to his side—as did Jack—both prepared to pull their weapons from under the fancy frock coats they had worn to

15

Ram's Head. Jack carried a knife and his Colt 1860 revolver. The six-shooter was reliable and efficient, especially at close range. And damn, if he hadn't been far too close to danger for most of his adult life. He glanced at Quentin, smiling at his friend's preference for the Confederate soldier's weapon of choice, the nine-shot LeMat.

The driver of the disabled vehicle stepped around the corner holding an old flintlock. "We ain't got nothing of value so move on to another mark," he said, taking aim. The single-shot pistol had a short range and best served a man as an adjunct to a sword or cutlass. The coachman carried nothing more than an old hunting knife in a worn scabbard. Jack had to hand it to him. He had guts.

"We are not highwaymen," Quentin said before nodding to Jack. "This is the Viscount Ardmore, and you are blocking the road."

Jack frowned, unused to his newly acquired title and liking it even less. He preferred Captain Jack to viscount. Hell, he preferred highwayman to viscount. If he could not have Ridge Point, he wanted nothing of his father's, including his damn, useless title.

The driver shrugged and tucked his weapon into his waistband. "Can't be helped, milord. We broke an axle, and I ain't got the tools to fix it."

Jack pointed to the carriage. "What's going on? We heard a woman scream."

The driver shrugged and pulled his knife. "They be women," he said as if that answered the question. Then he used the tip of his blade to clean dirt from under his grubby nails as if unconcerned that one of them had just let out a blood-curdling scream.

Throwing caution to the wind, Jack stepped forward and pulled open the carriage door. A woman inside screamed again, but she wasn't being ravished. It appeared that had already happened, and she was now giving birth. She lay against the squabs in a rumpled brown robe, her belly huge and heaving, while a nun knelt between her upraised knees and blood dripped onto the floor.

Jack backed out of the coach so quickly he nearly fell over Quentin.

"What the…" Quentin brushed past him and stuck his head inside, only to back out again just as quickly. "A woman giving birth!"

"I know that!" Jack's heart pounded in his throat. The woman had clutched her distended belly while blood dripped to the floor as if the child had already torn her in half. His stomach churned. Did women usually bleed when giving birth?

"Inside the coach," Quentin added, as if Jack were too stupid to notice.

A young, stern-faced nun stuck her head outside and glared at them as if he and Quentin were somehow responsible for her charge's condition. "Something is wrong. I need to get her to Sheep's Crossing."

Quentin's face turned stark white. "The woman needs a birthing, not a shearing."

"We just came from Sheep's Crossing," Jack added. "There's nothing there but sheep." And Ram's Head. And he did not want to go back. He and Quentin had been stuck in Sheep's Crossing for three months. It had taken that long for Jack to answer Her Majesty's Writ of Summons so he could claim Ram's Head as the rightful heir.

He had sailed to England often over the years, but for the most part, he had stayed with the Earl of Gilchrest, Chad Masters, and his American wife, Nikki. He hadn't actually lived in England since he was eleven, and he had never realized how difficult it could be for a noble to inherit.

In America, a simple reading of the will would have granted him his rightful inheritance. But he was a noble heir, and heirs could not just accede to a title without petitioning the crown for a writ of summons to Parliament. Then the pedigree had to be examined, new patent letters prepared, and the title published before he was even called to Lords. And Uncle William had been away as long as he had.

Thank God, Quentin's father and Gilchrest had vouched for him. Otherwise, he might never have proved his claim. But what good was a noble title if he could not bury his mother at Ridge Point? And now another delay.

The nun drew her brows together, and her angular face looked sharp enough to cut glass. "There is a vicar in Sheep's Crossing. He is a pious man, and his niece is a midwife. Take us there."

"Not bloody likely! Moving the woman might kill her." Quentin held up his hands, his expression as horrified as if the nun had asked them to captain a ship full of lepers.

Jack was just as terrified. "Can you not do something for her?"

The nun's face turned red, and her eyes flashed. "She is losing too much blood. Without a midwife, the babe may die."

Was it already too late to save the mother? There

was so much blood. Jack feared any further movement would kill her for sure. He nodded toward the coachman. He had apparently cleaned all the dirt from his nails and was now picking his teeth with the same dirty blade. "Why didn't your driver unhitch the horses and ride for help after the axle broke?"

The nun cast a surreptitious glance toward the man in question. "Mr. Piebald is my brother's driver. We were on our way to my sister's boarding house in Shrivenham when Abby started bleeding. She screamed and Mr. Piebald panicked. He took a turn too fast and snapped an axle. He knows Abby is gently reared and recently widowed, and he was afraid to leave us alone and unprotected."

Another heartbreaking cry echoed from inside the dark recesses of the coach. Jack cringed and took a step back. "Perhaps I should ride one of the horses to Sheep's Crossing and fetch the midwife."

"There is no time," the nun said as the harsh lines of her face softened into a sad smile. "Please. Can you not take us to Sheep's Crossing? It is less than five miles from here."

Five miles in the opposite direction—a direction in which they had just come.

Jack raked a hand through his overlong hair, dislodging strands from the queue tied at the nape of his neck. Then with a curse, he gently nudged the nun aside and climbed into the coach. The hot, sour air nearly stole his breath.

As his eyes adjusted to the dim light, he took in the woman lying across the squabs, her slender fingers moving in concentric circles over her abdomen as she moaned low in her throat and chanted. "Don't let my baby die. Please don't let my baby die."

Jack offered an encouraging smile, but sweat darkened the ash blonde hair hanging over her face, concealing her features. Then she raised a stubborn chin, piercing him with pain-filled blue eyes—eyes that seemed to tug at his soul. Shaking off a sense of *déjà vu*, he bent forward and scooped her into his arms.

"Put me down. You could jostle the baby," she whimpered, as if afraid the child would drop out onto the carriage floor.

Jack's stomach churned. *Was that even a possibility?* He looked down, praying he would not see a baby dangling from its umbilical cord. He saw blood instead. Lots of blood.

His foot slipped. The woman in his arms gasped, her weakened grip tightening around his neck. "Please put me down." She squeezed her eyes shut.

"Not just yet, madam. Now hold tight."

Turning toward the door, his burden held close, he ducked low so he could step down without bumping his head. Their foreheads knocked together. Her eyes flew open.

"If you are a highwayman, you have chosen the wrong coach." Her words were strong although slightly slurred, as if the nun had given her something to ease the pain. "I have no jewels or money, and I am in no condition to tempt a man."

Jack chuckled and nearly tripped. Most women in her situation would be screaming hysterically, afraid of what a big man like himself planned to do to her. This feisty young woman looked as if she held a reserve of strength at the ready. And from the looks of her swollen belly, she would soon need it.

Shaking his head, he turned as Quentin rushed forward to hold the door open to their rented coach. Sister Mary Daphne followed close on his heels and watched as Quentin helped Jack climb in and settle back on the seat with the widow on his lap. He prayed the bleeding would stop and the baby would not come. He didn't know a damn thing about birthing a baby.

Quentin climbed in after him. The nun paused before following them inside. "Climb aboard, Mr. Piebald," she shouted to her driver.

The coach rocked as Mr. Piebald climbed up top with Jack's driver. Then the vehicle lurched forward as another contraction rippled through the young woman's body.

Crying out, she sat up abruptly, nearly hitting Jack's chin with the top of her head. Then she doubled over and nearly fell forward off his lap.

The nun dropped to her knees on the floor at Jack's feet. "Not much longer." She gently brushed the long, limp strands of hair from the young widow's face. "Be strong for the baby, the sweet innocent little baby."

The widow's answering moan was fraught with such pain it tore at Jack's soul. He looked across the carriage at Quentin who sat stiff and pale on the opposite seat.

"Is she having the child now? Do we need to stop the carriage?" Quentin sounded as nervous as an expectant father.

"It is just a contraction," the nun said calmly, but Jack's pulse raced.

"Maybe we should have stayed until after the birth." Tension eased from the woman's body, forcing Jack to tighten his hold so she would not slump to the floor.

The nun rose from her knees and slid onto the seat next to Quentin. "It will be hours yet," she said. "Perhaps even days, which would not bode well for the baby, and we need to save this child."

And what of the child's mother?

Chapter Three

Jack looked down at the woman leaning against his chest, eyes closed as if she slept. Her hair, though damp with sweat, looked healthy and alive, and though her cheeks were red with exertion, she was not tanned from the sun.

His gaze slid to her still hands as they rested on her abdomen. Tiny scars dotted her fingers, but her skin was neither dry nor chapped, and her nails were clean and neatly trimmed. They did not look like the hands of a woman who labored, and although she was not wearing a ring, that did not mean she was not a widow as the nun claimed.

So how did a gently reared widow, heavy with child, end up traveling in a rundown coach with a nun?

"Does she have family? What of her husband's people?" Though it was none of his business, he would hate it if the woman lost everything she owned because he and Quentin panicked and failed to retrieve her luggage. If she had a father or family willing to take her in, then perhaps the loss of her possessions would not burden her too greatly.

Sister Mary Daphne shook her head. "It is a complicated tale and not mine to tell, but rest assured, I will see her safely delivered of this child."

"And after the babe is born?" He avoided the piercing eyes he felt staring at him from across the coach. Quentin was probably wondering why he cared about the young widow when he was dealing with his own difficulties. But a woman needed a man's protection, and there did not seem to be anyone looking after this one.

The nun shrugged. "If she lives, I will see to her care."

"I can take care of myself and my baby." The young woman's voice was strong and determined despite its low pitch. "My father will assist us."

Jack looked down, meeting her gaze. She flushed, seemingly aware of the incongruity of her statement. If her father cared so damn much, then why was she going to Shrivenham to stay with the nun's sister?

The remainder of their short journey was uneventful, the widow's occasional panting breaths the only sound to break the silence before they arrived at Sheep's Crossing. Outside the small stone church and ivy-covered vicarage, a herd of sheep lazily grazed.

"Thank you for your assistance," the nun said as Jack climbed down from the carriage. The young woman in his arms moaned and stirred but barely opened her eyes.

"It was most kind of you," the sister added, reaching for the woman as though to take her from Jack's arms.

He shifted her weight, holding the widow more firmly against his chest. "I have her. You clear a path through the sheep and warn the parish priest of our arrival."

The nun's dark eyes were as cold as flints, her expression sour. Then she turned on her heels and walked away, her worn brown habit rustling over the grass and frightening the sheep. Bleating and baaing, they scurried away.

Quentin came up beside Jack and nodded toward the departing sister. "That is one cold fish."

"She's a nun." Unlike Quentin, Jack had not been raised in the Church of England. He had never actually spoken to an Anglican nun—or any nun for that matter. After moving to America, he and his mother had attended an Episcopal church. Still, he did not imagine nuns were the warm or fun-loving sort. Poverty tended to make a woman bitter. His own mother had certainly grown bitter after her husband forced her into exile.

Before they reached the cottage door, it opened and the vicar stepped out. Sister Mary Daphne spoke quickly and then turned, rushing back down the stone walkway toward her charge and the man who carried her. "Quickly now! Bring her inside."

When they reached the door, the vicar welcomed them before turning toward the nun. "Go fetch my niece."

Sister Mary Daphne gave Jack a chilling glance before rushing off to do the vicar's bidding.

"I am Reverend Harrison," the aging minister said.

Jack nodded. "Captain Jack—uh, Jack Norton, Lord Ardmore. The young lady in my arms is a widow. Her name is Abby or Abigail. I do not know her surname."

The vicar stretched his weathered face into a grim smile. "Nor do I. The good sister would only tell me her given name."

Odd. Why address her by her Christian name? Did she not know the widow's family name?

Quentin stepped forward and took the vicar's hand.

"Quentin Stanley, fifth son of Lord Willoughby."

Quent did not normally flaunt his family's title. For the most part, he wanted to pave his own way in the world, but Jack knew there were times when he used his family's influence. But why did he think they needed it now?

"I have made the earl's acquaintance a time or two," the vicar said as he led Jack and Quentin inside. He closed the front door and crossed the small living room to a closed door on the other side. "Let's put the young lady in here where she will be comfortable."

He opened the door and stepped back. Jack carried her inside and reluctantly placed his slight burden on a wrought iron bed. Blood stained his waistcoat and the tops of his trousers, but at least the woman was still breathing. With a sigh of relief, he straightened, but before he could step away, she grabbed his hand.

"Do not leave me. Please."

Heart twisting in his chest, he sat on the edge of the lumpy mattress and took her cold hand in his. "I'll not abandon you."

"Thank you," she said, her voice raspy and strained. "You may leave as soon as Sister Mary Daphne returns with the midwife."

Jack squeezed her hand and nodded. The contractions seemed to have stopped, and with a sigh, the exhausted woman closed her eyes.

****

Abby heard voices, but they seemed to come from the bottom of a barrel. She opened her eyes and looked up at the tall, blond captain. Was he a captain in the military? A ship's captain? No one had introduced him, but she had overheard his friend call him captain. Yet, the vicar called him Lord Ardmore.

Was he an American captain or an English nobleman?

Her eyes drifted shut. The searing pains had stopped, but when she tried focusing her thoughts, words jumbled in her head, leaving her exhausted and confused. She remembered the coach jostling her as it bumped along the rutted road. Her back had throbbed and pain twisted her belly. Then she had felt a gush of warmth between her legs. When she looked down, there had been blood between her feet. She screamed, and the coach jerked and nearly overturned. Then...

She could not remember. Had the nun given her something to ease the pain?

"Where is Sister Mary Daphne?" she whispered, too weary to raise her heavy lids.

A large, warm palm covered her hand. "She has gone after the vicar's niece, the midwife."

Abby forced open her eyes. The handsome captain bent over her. Sun bleached strands of blond hair escaped the queue at his nape and brushed his wide shoulders. He seemed as immovable as a mountain and quite formidable with his intense brown eyes, square jaw, and brooding features. Yet, there was a gentleness to his touch that made her think he would protect a woman rather than abuse her.

She closed her eyes again. It felt as if only moments had passed before someone was touching her forehead and talking softly.

"I am Mrs. Sheila Beckman. The midwife. Trust in me and the Lord, and everything will be fine."

Abby opened her eyes. The captain was gone, and a heavy-set woman with brown hair now leaned over her bed. Sister Mary Daphne stood on the other side of the room, a pinched expression on her face.

"The vicar's niece will take good care of you, and so will I." Her smile reached neither her eyes nor her words. Fear chilled Abby's hands. Did the nun not expect her to survive?

The midwife moved to the foot of the bed and raised her robe. Humiliation burned Abby's cheeks. She wanted to clamp her knees together in protest, but Mrs. Beckman gently pried them apart.

"Well?" Sister Mary Daphne asked, impatience tingeing her words.

Mrs. Beckman peered over Abby's knees. "I do not wish to offend your modesty or induce indelicate sensations, but I must insert my hand into the womb to feel for the babe."

Abby's stomach lurched. Ears burning with shame, she turned her head to stare at the flickering wick on the bedside lamp. "Do what you must."

Grinding her teeth, she endured the humiliation and discomfort of the midwife's examination. It was over quickly, but rather than feeling relief, fear washed over her like a drowning tide. The contractions had stopped, but her baby no longer moved.

Silence filled the room as the midwife stood and wiped her blood stained hands on a towel. She met Abby's gaze and sorrow shadowed her face. Then without a word, she hurried from the room.

Biting back tears, Abby rubbed her protruding belly and prayed.

Chapter Four

"How is she?" Jack asked. The expression on the midwife's face sent a chill down his spine. Damn it all to hell. He had seen enough death over the last four years to last him a lifetime.

When he returned to England, he had hoped to escape it, at least for a while. But it seemed as if the Angel of Death followed him. Would the widow and her unborn child be the Grim Reaper's next victims?

The midwife clucked her tongue. "It is not good. The placenta partially blocks the birth opening, but if I try to move it aside, the mother could bleed to death, and both her and her child will perish."

"What are you going to do? You cannot stand by and watch her die." Jack wanted to grab her by the shoulders and shake her. Instead, he clenched his fists at his sides.

The vicar placed a hand on his shoulder. He stiffened, but the man's words were calm and damn reasonable. "We can pray. And trust that my niece knows what she is about."

Mrs. Beckman nodded. "There is nothing more powerful than prayer. And I have mixed some herbal teas that should help. Nettle for her blood, raspberry for her uterus, and comfrey for her placenta. The contractions have stopped, and the placenta could still shift enough for both mother and child to survive the delivery."

"But you must save the child!" The nun stepped forward and gripped Mrs. Beckman's arm as she was turning to go back inside the bedroom. "Can you not cut the child from the mother's womb?"

Jack's heart leapt into his throat. He glanced at Quentin, who looked just as unnerved as he felt. How could a woman of God show such callous disregard for the welfare of another human being, especially a defenseless woman in such a vulnerable state?

The midwife looked no less dismayed by the nun's question. Her eyes widened and her jaw dropped. "I am a midwife, not a butcher."

"But the child—"

"Will either live or not as the Lord sees fit," the vicar interrupted with a stern edge to his words. "It is in His hands now, and we must have faith that all will come about according to His plan."

The nun's dark eyes glinted. "But if we cannot save them both, we must attempt to save the child. The babe is innocent of the sin in which it was conceived."

Jack looked past the nun to the closed door separating them from the object of their discussion. Was the widow in fact, unwed? Or did the nun consider it a sin for a husband to *know* his wife in the biblical sense? Either way, he hoped to God Abby had not overheard the woman's cold and ruthless suggestion.

"Conception of a child is not a sin unless the mother is unwed," the vicar replied in a reproving tone.

The nun meekly lowered her gaze but not before something, dark and unforgiving flashed behind her eyes. "I am sorry for telling an untruth, Reverend Harrison. I was merely trying to protect my charge's reputation."

Quentin gave her a considering look. "Then she is unwed?"

The sister nodded, and a calculating gleam lit Quentin's eyes. It was that same glint he got when formulating a plan to acquire the un-acquirable.

"How long before she delivers?" Quentin asked the midwife in a voice now laced with excitement. Jack tensed and inwardly groaned. His quartermaster had a plan, and Jack knew in his gut he was not going to like it.

"It could be days yet or merely hours. There is no telling in these situations," she said with an uneasy smile. "You will pray for her?" she asked her uncle.

He nodded. "Of course."

"Then if you will excuse me, I must get back to my patient." The midwife turned and headed back inside the bedroom.

When she shut the door, Quentin turned back to Jack. Hope and just a hint of mischief shone in his eyes. "You could marry her and solve all your problems. She is unwed and not a widow. And there is a fifty-fifty chance she will have a boy."

"And an equal chance she will have a girl." Had Quentin lost his mind? He looked sane, but he had obviously been at sea too long. Or perhaps, the three months they had spent in Sheep's Crossing waiting on Jack's pedigree had taken its toll. "This is madness, Quent."

He couldn't possibly marry a woman he did not know—a woman about to give birth to another man's child. Could he? He looked to the vicar. "It would never work. Would it?"

The vicar sighed as if hesitant to answer. "If she is indeed unwed and not a widow..."

Jack's heart thumped, but he quickly tapped down what little hope blossomed in his chest and met Quentin's gaze. "It is unreasonable to even consider such a possibility."

"Why? All you have ever talked about is Ridge Point and how you wished to reclaim your mother's birthright when your father died. Well, the old man is dead, and unless you can marry and produce a legitimate heir in five months' time, you are going to lose it all."

"The child she carries is not mine, and I will not lie and say that it is."

"This is not America," Quentin said.

Jack snorted. "Truly? You astound me with your perceptions."

Ignoring Jack's sarcasm, Quentin continued. "You do not have to claim the child. You just have to marry the mother. Once wed, the child will be legally yours regardless of who sired it or when. All that matters is that she is lawfully wed to you before the child is born."

Jack looked from Quentin to the vicar. Reverend Harrison nodded. "If she has a son, you would inherit everything."

Still, Jack resisted. He had been his father's son and legal heir. Yet, it had made no difference. How much worse would it be for a child who did not carry his or her father's blood? And there was no guarantee Abby would deliver the son he needed to inherit. "The lady is pregnant and unwed. I will not compound her problems by coercing her into a loveless marriage with a stranger in need of an heir."

"Why not?" Quentin challenged. "She does not seem to have a family or anyone to take care of her." To bolster his case, he turned to the vicar. "It must be fate that brought them together. Do you not agree? Lord Ardmore needs an heir, and the lady needs a husband."

"And what of the child?" Reverend Harrison asked.

"He will inherit a viscountcy."

Jack's pulse drummed in his ears. It could not be as simple as Quentin implied, but his words were as seductive as a siren's song. "Even if she were willing to wed me, there is no time to petition the archbishop of Canterbury at a whacking sum of twenty-eight guineas for a special license. And there is no time to post the banns if our petition is denied. Quite simply, it is too late for me and too late for her. The babe will be born out of wedlock, and I will lose Ridge Point."

The thought of her giving birth to a bastard depressed him almost as much as losing Ridge Point to his cousin.

He hardened his heart, ignoring the impulse to ride to her rescue like some medieval knight in shining armor. For all he knew, she was a light skirt with no notion of who the father of her child might be.

The vicar gave him a considering look. "There are other ways to marry."

"It has been years since you lived in England," Quentin added. "Only the poorest classes marry by banns anymore. And only those with new money aspiring to live in good society waste it on a special license. Nowadays, those wishing to marry quickly, obtain an ordinary license."

Could it really be that simple? Could he marry a stranger just to get his hands on his mother's estate?

The cleric frowned. "Before a license can be granted, you or the bride-to-be must have resided within the diocese of the bishop in whose name such license is granted for no less than fifteen days."

"I have been here for three months." Three long, boring months spent in a boarding house as badly in need of repair as Ram's Head, while awaiting his summons to Parliament, only to learn of his father's ridiculous codicil when the solicitor finally read the will.

The vicar smiled. "For a few pounds, the bishop can grant an ordinary license that will allow me to marry you here in the parish church. You will need to give notice of the intended marriage in writing, but only one of you needs sign. Filing the license in the Marriage Notice Book will cost another shilling."

"You are currently a resident within the diocese," Quentin added. "And the bishop resides less than a day's ride from here. If I ride all night, I could be back before noon tomorrow."

Jack's head spun. Why would he even consider marriage to a pregnant woman he did not know?

Because he needed to bury his mother. And he needed to bury her at Ridge Point. "Wouldn't I need to petition the bishop myself?"

The vicar shook his head. "Neither you nor your bride need be present to apply for a license, nor is it necessary to show proof of identity. You could stay here and become acquainted with your intended while Mr. Stanley applies for the license. Any reputable man known by the registrar or by the parties intending marriage can appear before him. Mr. Quentin's application and his word will be proof enough. If Miss

Abigail is under twenty-one, she will need a letter of consent from her guardian." He looked at the nun, brows raised in question.

She looked at Quentin, malice shining in her dark gaze. Or perhaps, it was merely concern for her young charge. "She is three and twenty."

"Then there is no hindrance to this union." The vicar smiled. "Mr. Stanley will apply for the license, and the marriage certificate will be drawn up upon your request by making a handwritten copy and certifying it. You need only wait one day before you can marry."

Did he have that much time? Abby could have the baby before nightfall. What if the child arrived before Quentin's return? Could he still marry her if it would gain him naught? And what if she died giving birth? He would have to hire a wet nurse and nanny for a child that wasn't even his.

Should he take such a slim chance?

"The wedding will be legal and binding, even if she gives you a daughter and not the son you so desperately need," the vicar added, a hard edge creeping into his voice. "Will you still honor your vows if that is the case?"

Jack shrugged, trying to fain indifference. "If a daughter cannot inherit a title, how does it benefit me to take such a chance?" But for some inexplicable reason, he wanted to take a chance with the brave woman lying in the next room.

"She could just as easily have a boy," Quentin reiterated. "A fifty-fifty chance is better than no chance at all."

"Are you a gambling man, Lord Ardmore?" the vicar asked.

Jack snorted. Quentin was the gambler. Then again, Jack was a sea captain. Life didn't get more unpredictable than that. "I live on the ocean. My entire adult life has been a series of gambles."

But marriage to a stranger? Such a gamble would last his lifetime. Then again, knowing one's betrothed offered no guarantees either. His mother had known his father for years before they wed, and their union had led to nothing but misery.

"Two days," Quentin said, interrupting his thoughts. "That is all it should take. A day to ride to the bishop's, apply for the license, and get back so the vicar can make a copy and you can sign it. Then you can get married as soon as the sun rises the next day."

"Are the two of you sure this is legal?" Not that he was considering such an insane notion. But if he were, there could be no legal grounds to contest the union.

"Well, there are rules that must be followed," the cleric said. "Since Mr. Stanley will be obtaining the license, you would have to marry in the parish church here in Sheep's Crossing. And of course, you must get Miss Abigail to consent to the marriage."

Ah. That was the rub, was it not? No woman in her right mind would consent to wed him. He lived on his damn ship, which he could not sail home to America until he was sure the unforgiving Union army would not arrest him and confiscate it.

And if he stayed in England, the only home he owned was Ram's Head, a crumbling estate he did not want. No woman with a grain of sense would have him. He was a privateer turned lord, trying to make a fresh start in a country he had not lived in for more than twenty years.

But at least he had Quentin and Uncle William's support. Abby had no one.

Was she desperate enough to accept his proposal?

Chapter Five

Jack looked down at Abby as she rested with eyes closed, her long, damp lashes forming dark crescents against high, noble cheekbones. Perhaps she was highborn. Not that it mattered a whit to him. His father was proof blood did not make the person.

So, how honorable was it to offer a woman marriage in order to use her unborn child as leverage?

Frightened and alone, she was about to give birth to a child who would have no father if he did not marry her. Yet, if the child was a girl, she would likely have no home. Ram's Head was hardly inhabitable and even if she had a son, it could take months for the courts to award him Ridge Point. So, where would they live? Aboard his ship?

Marrying the woman was insane and still, the prospect consumed his thoughts. It was the most sensible solution to both their problems. And Quentin had already left to apply for the license.

Abby's eyes fluttered open. They were oddly familiar—an intense blue that seemed to see into his soul. Did she see the darkness in it? Or the hope he held so close to his heart? Hope for a normal life and loving family—a hope he refused to voice aloud. A hope he feared would one day turn to bitter disappointment— the same disappointment he had seen so often in his mother's eyes.

Straightening his shoulders, he stood with the same erect, commanding posture he used when addressing his crew. "The nun said you are unwed."

Those lovely eyes narrowed, and her lush mouth firmed with disapproval. "My marital state should not concern you, sir."

He smiled, leaning over her. "Oh, but it does. You see, I am in need of an heir and you, apparently, are in need of a husband."

"I will never marry."

The rancor in her voice took him by surprise. He was not anxious to marry a stranger either, but considering Abby's condition, he had assumed his offer would relieve her fears. She seemed protective of the child she carried. So what kind of woman would not want a husband to care for her and her child? Especially, a titled husband?

He straightened, looking down at her as she glared up at him from a reclined position on the bed. "Why not?"

She averted her gaze, but not before, he saw a flash of panic. "That is none of your concern either."

Damnation and hellfire. Some man had obviously abused her trust. But had she willingly submitted and was angry for being discarded? Or had some bastard forced himself on her?

He sat on the edge of the bed and took her hand. She stiffened, trying to remove her cold fingers from his firm grasp. Her jaw clenched. "Let. Go."

"Hear me out." He softened his grip and his voice in an attempt to be less intimidating. "You need a husband, and I need an heir. It will be a marriage in name only."

"Oh, be still my quivering heart," she said, her voice dripping sarcasm. "What woman would not be thrilled with such a heart-felt proposal?"

Her wit caught him by surprise. So did the rumbling laugh that escaped from deep inside his chest. It had been a long time since anyone had made him laugh aloud. But Abby had done so without even trying.

Her eyes widened. Then she smiled. "You roar like the lion you resemble," she said before clamping her mouth shut.

Unexpected pleasure tightened his chest. "Yes, well, your sarcastic humor was quite unexpected."

Her shoulders relaxed, and a brief smile flickered at the edges of her mouth. "So was your proposal."

"But it makes sense, does it not?" He let out a pent-up breath, hoping he would not have to persuade her with flowery words or silly sentiments. If she were a logical woman, she would see the practicality of becoming his wife without his having to cajole her.

"It would be unfair." She lowered her gaze. "I am no longer chaste."

"Obviously," he snorted.

She raised her lids, humiliation shining in her hurt gaze. "All the more reason to decline your *generous* offer."

Embarrassed heat warmed his cheeks. Only a cad would point out her indelicate state, and he was not a cad. Not normally. His mother had raised him better. But it had been years since he had been in polite society. Between the war and his years spent aboard ship with rowdy sailors, he had forgotten how to talk to a gently reared woman—if she was indeed, gently reared. Nevertheless, he knew better than to speak so crudely to any woman.

Shifting on the mattress, he cleared his throat. "Yes. Well, all the more reason to agree to my proposal. The nun said your name is Abigail Halsey. Is it your real name?"

Damn her if it wasn't. That was the name Quentin was using to apply for the marriage license, and he did not want to give his aunt or Morris any recourse when contesting his marriage and the legitimacy of his heir—if Abby married him—and if she had a son. He had made a promise to his mother, and he would do anything to keep that promise—even if it meant marrying a pregnant woman, he did not know.

A weary sigh escaped and her shoulders sagged. "Yes. Halsey is my family name, but I have not consented to marriage. So, I fail to see how it matters."

It mattered to him, and he would have told her so had the nun not entered the room.

"You must let her rest," she said in a stern voice that would have scared the devil out of Beelzebub himself. Jack wasn't exactly the spawn of Satan, but he was no angel either, and the young nun scared the hell out of him.

He left the room without another word.

****

Throughout the long night, Jack paced the living room or sat by Abby's bed, watching over her while the midwife slept in a chair in the corner and Sister Mary Daphne glared. The vicar retired to the spare bedroom, and Jack eventually nodded off. Then sometime around midnight, Quentin returned with the marriage license and curled up in a corner of the living room to rest until sunrise. Not long after, Abby started having contractions again.

Jack woke the midwife and stepped back, watching as Abby suffered through pains that seemed almost impossible to bear. Sweat beaded her brow and color leached from her face as she panted through the contractions that seemed to come one on top of the other.

Would it make any difference if the baby arrived before the vicar could legally marry them? No. He had given his word, and Abby needed him.

He stepped out of the room long enough for the midwife to check the progress of Abby's labor. Soft snores came from the corner where Quentin slept, and Jack felt a stab of envy. If only he could sleep so easily, but Abby's pitiful moans had kept him up most of the night.

When Abby cried out, Jack barged back into the room, despite the nun's protest. "How is she?" he asked the midwife.

She looked up, her serious expression showing a hint of optimism. "The placenta no longer blocks the birth canal, but it's still lower than it should be. I'm worried about the baby now, but Miss Halsey has lost a lot of blood. If she survives the birthing but does not expel the entire placenta…"

Her voice trailed off, but Jack could fill in the blanks. If that were to happen, Abby might linger for days before succumbing to childbirth fever.

His stomach knotted as another contraction rippled through her body. He crossed to the head of the bed and gently squeezed her hand. "I'm here."

Muscles tensing, she drew up her legs and nearly crushed his fingers in her tight fist.

"Do not push," the midwife said from the foot of the bed. Jack had nearly forgotten she was still in the room. "It is not time yet."

Abby's eyes were wide and frightened. Her grip tightened. Jack held her gaze and nodded. "That's right. Squeeze my hand."

"He should not be here. It is highly improper," Sister Mary Daphne said. "The birthing room is no place for a man."

Jack looked at the midwife and started to rise, torn between his desire to help Abby and the midwife's superior knowledge of such things.

Abby clutched his hand. "Please stay."

He eased back down onto the hard chair, and Sister Mary Daphne's eyes narrowed with disapproval. Minutes ticked by like hours. Was it dawn yet? He looked toward the window. The dark drapes appeared a bit brighter, as if the sun was trying to climb above the horizon. Hope bloomed in his chest, but then another contraction tore through Abby, and he feared the baby would arrive before he could get her to the church.

He turned toward the door, just as Quentin barreled into the room, disheveled and out of breath. The vicar entered behind him.

"Is it too late?" Quentin skidded to a halt before reaching the bed. "Has she had the baby yet?"

"No. But he is getting impatient." Relief eased the tension in Jack's shoulders. Abby had made it to sunrise without delivering the child.

The midwife stood, placing herself between Abby and the new arrivals. "It will not be long now."

The vicar averted his gaze and flushed. "Now or never."

Throwing caution to the wind, Jack stood and bent over his soon-to-be-wife. With a surprisingly light heart, he scooped her into his arms. "I am ready."

****

Pain knotted Abby's insides, and her head spun. It felt as if she had been drugged, but if that were the case, then why did she hurt so much? Had Sister Mary Daphne given her another tonic? She could not remember. Her thoughts were hazy and...

Another pain gripped her. She cried out. Arms tightened around her, and her eyes sprang open. Captain Jack held her in his strong embrace, and the vicar stood before them.

Are we in a church?

"Do you agree?" the captain asked.

Agree to what? She was so confused, and the pain was nearly unbearable. She licked her dry lips. The vicar had asked her something—something important. What was it?

Another pain rippled through her. She tightened her grip on Captain Jack, needing his solid strength as another contraction followed on the heels of the last. They were coming stronger and faster now, giving her no time to catch her breath or collect her thoughts.

"Will you have this man to be your wedded husband?" the vicar asked.

Abby closed her eyes against another searing contraction, shaking her head vigorously from side to side, unable to voice her objection.

The captain's dark haired companion answered for her. "She is in too much pain to respond. Let us assume she would say yes if she could."

"No!" her mind screamed, but a pain-filled screech

tore from her throat as the baby moved lower. She felt as if she might fall, but the captain's strong arms cradled her.

Damn, Simon Weston, Lord Drury, and his pretty face! She should remember that looks could be deceiving.

"Do you want to marry this man?" The reverend sounded impatient.

"You are strong. You can do this. You must. For the baby." The captain's voice was soft. Coaxing.

Abby concentrated on his soothing words and tight but gentle grip. He no longer reminded her of Lord Drury at all. He brought to mind a kindly physician.

"Yes," she said in a raw voice she did not recognize. She could do this. She would safely deliver her child if it were the last thing she ever did. But mere seconds later, it seemed, the vicar pronounced her and the captain, man and wife.

She blamed Lord Drury for that, too.

"Damn you, Simon Weston!" she screamed, not knowing if she said the words aloud or only in her pain-filled mind.

The baby moved lower still. Then the captain was depositing her back onto the bed.

"It is done," the man called Quentin said. "Ridge Point is yours."

"At what cost?" she heard the captain say as the two men faded into the shadows.

Sister Mary Daphne moved behind her. "I am here now, and I will help you bring this child into the world."

The midwife pushed up her robes and forced her knees apart. Abby's muscles bunched. The pressure of the midwife's hands inside her body was almost unbearable.

"I see the head," Mrs. Beckman said in a triumphant voice.

Abby screamed as another pain tore through her, and Sister Mary Daphne pressed against her back. Then Abby drew up her legs and pushed, working harder than she had ever worked in her life to get the precious babe out of her body and into the world. She pushed against the unrelenting pain, screaming until her throat burned.

Gentle hands stroked her belly, and the midwife's gentle voice floated upward from the bottom of the bed. "Stop pushing now. You must wait for the next contraction and then push with all your strength."

"It is too big!" Abby cried, the pain so intense she feared she would die with the baby still inside her.

"Nonsense. I have been delivering babes in these parts for years, and yours is no bigger than it should be."

"It should not be at all," Abby whimpered. She should not be having a baby, not until she was wed, and that would never happen now.

Or had it happened already?

She was so confused, her mind filled with thoughts and words that made no sense. Had Captain Jack held her in his strong arms? Had the vicar asked if she wanted to marry him? Was she married? Or had it all been a dream? *Oh, why can I not remember?*

Sister Mary Daphne and the midwife spoke over her as if she wasn't there, but Abby hardly listened. She focused on not pushing as the midwife instructed, when every instinct she possessed urged her to bear down.

"Get ready," Mrs. Beckman finally said. The pain

moved lower. Abby tensed.

"Now push!"

Pressing down with all her might, Abby pushed. Once. Twice. And suddenly, the weighted pain in her belly slid out from between her legs, taking the pressure with it. Abby cried out in relief and relaxed back into Sister Mary Daphne's arms as blood gushed between her thighs.

Chapter Six

Jack paced outside the cottage, ignoring Quentin. The vicar had promised to come for them as soon as the baby was born—a baby Jack would protect no matter the sex. But what of the child's mother? What about Abby? After the ceremony, she had damned a man named Simon Weston. According to Quentin, he was a married man who had been engaged to another woman when Abby conceived.

How can I defend her honor if she attempted to compromise herself in order to gain a titled husband?

Quentin sighed. "Had I known Lord Drury was the child's father, I would never have suggested you marry her."

"How could you know?" Anger and frustration ate at Jack's self-control like sharks on a wounded seal. "The nun said she was a widow. When we discovered she was unwed, we assumed… Ah hell. I don't know what you assumed. I assumed some man had taken advantage of her sweet nature. But she is not sweet. Is she? She seduced a viscount who was engaged to another. I can only assume she had hoped he would marry her if she became *enceinte*."

"Do you think the nun knows the truth?" Quentin asked.

"What difference does it make?" What the nun knew was irrelevant. What mattered were his foolish

48

actions. He had jumped on Quentin's easy solution without considering all the possible consequences. Unless…

Was he misjudging Abby as his father had misjudged his mother? Or had he truly married a woman who would stoop to immoral measures to gain a titled husband? Damned if he knew. And damned if it mattered. His life was now tethered to a woman he could never trust.

"I am sorry," Quentin said.

Jack turned so quickly he nearly collided with him. "Are you sure Simon Weston is Lord Drury? Perhaps Weston was her betrothed, and she was damning him for not marrying her."

"Weston *is* Drury. His name was in the society column less than a month ago. Apparently, he attended the Radford's soirée with his wife, a woman who was definitely not a pregnant woman named Abby."

"Perhaps Drury wasn't engaged when she slept with him." He was grasping at straws now, hoping his new wife had not knowingly slept with a man engaged to another.

Quentin looked as guilty as a sailor caught wasting water on a becalmed ship. "Drury married Lady Vanessa six months ago, and they were betrothed at least six months before that."

"How do you know?" Abby may not be an adulteress, but after the unfounded accusations hurled at his mother, Jack did not want to condemn her without proof. Still, he was not feeling very charitable now.

Am I too much like my father?

"Despite my six years at sea," Quentin said, his expression now smug rather than sympathetic, "I have

Lilly Gayle

kept abreast of the latest London gossip, and if I knew Drury was betrothed, then surely, your wife would have known if she is a gentlewoman as the nun claims."

Perhaps, even that was a lie. For all Jack knew, his wife was a well-kept courtesan who had learned proper decorum and manners from one of her protectors.

His heart sank like a scuttled ship, but his temper rose like a sail on the main mast, billowing with anger. If Drury was the father of Abby's baby, then she was guilty of a similar sin for which Jack's mother had been accused. The irony fed his ill temper. Despite his mother's innocence, his father punished her for her supposed actions while Abby gained respectability in the form of a husband and title.

She was no different from Annabel.

Before the war, Annabel Beaumont's father had owned a large cotton plantation. Jack met her at a ball while visiting his mother, but she had considered him beneath her notice until she learned he was heir to a viscountcy. Then she was all smiles and friendly banter, but he was no fool. Annabel would have married a blind leper—so long as he were a titled leper. His mother had been no different. She may not have been an adulteress, but she had married his father rather than his uncle, the man she supposedly loved, because his father was a viscount.

Women were all the same, always seeking to marry better than their friends.

"The old man must be laughing in his grave," Jack said with a snort. "In my attempts to best the bastard, it seems I have saddled myself with the very sort of woman he accused my mother of being."

"Your wife may be innocent," Quentin said, a trace

of warning in his voice. "There could be any number of reasons for her to damn Drury."

"During childbirth?"

Quentin's eyes darkened. "Drury could have forced himself on her."

Would that it were true. The perverse thought entered Jack's mind before he could stop it. *What is wrong with me?* What man would wish rape on any woman? Yet he had spent so many years defending his mother's honor, he would rather his wife not be guilty of moral turpitude.

He huffed out a frustrated breath and forked his fingers through his hair. The black ribbon he had used to tie it back fluttered to the ground. "Is the viscount the sort of man who would force a woman?"

Quentin sighed and looked away. "From all accounts, he is a true gentleman. Men emulate him and women adore him."

And one particular woman had apparently adored him more than she should have. Disappointment weighed as heavy as an albatross around Jack's neck. "So, it is unlikely."

"Likely or not, she is your wife now, so it would behoove you not to pass judgment until you have heard the tale from her own lips."

"I do not think she is going to share tales of her sexual exploits with a husband who has never even tasted her charms." He folded his arms across his chest, the fabric of his fancy frock coat bunching across his shoulders.

He preferred the loose-fitting shirts and buckskins he wore aboard the *Lion's Pride*, but Quentin seemed quite comfortable in the confining clothes of an English gentleman, which goaded Jack even more. Quentin was like a damn chameleon, fitting in wherever he went. In comparison, Jack felt like a baboon in a suit. A big baboon with a scheming wife.

"You might want to try a little patience and understanding. In this situation, Captain, I do not think your usual tactics are going to work."

When Jack wanted to attack, Quentin often urged patience. Meeting somewhere in the middle had kept them both out of trouble. But Jack was in way over his head this time. How did a man tactfully ask his new wife if she was a light skirt, or if she had simply made a terrible mistake?

He resumed his pacing until the door to the tiny cottage opened and the vicar stepped out to join them. His heart slammed against his chest with the force of a boom. If Abby had delivered a son, Ridge Point was his.

"Well?" he asked, not showing the patience for which he had just claimed himself capable. Beside him, Quentin chuckled.

The vicar frowned. "You have a son."

"I have a son." Excitement mingled with fear. A tiny person had been entrusted into his care—a son who would look to him for guidance.

But the child is not my flesh and blood.

Would he let that knowledge eat at him the way his father's suspicions about Jack's paternity had? Or would he be the kind of father Uncle William had been to him?

Quentin smiled stiffly. "Ridge Point is yours. You have what you wanted."

Did he? He had wanted to bring his mother's body

home to Ridge Point, but he had also wanted to find a faithful and loving wife who would tempt him more than the sea—a wife who would give him sons and daughters to fill the empty rooms of his childhood home. But would his new wife prove loving and faithful? Or would she laugh at the notion and return to London to enjoy the company of any man willing to entertain her? Ridge Point was his, but the rooms would remain as empty as his heart.

Something dark and resentful coiled in his gut. Upon his death, the title would pass to a son whose veins carried not a drop of Norton blood while any sons of his own loins would be left with nothing—or at least, nothing entailed.

"Would you like to see your son now?" the vicar asked, his stern words more a statement than a question.

Jack squirmed under his censorious gaze and nodded. "Yes."

"Whatever the mother's sins, you will not hold the child responsible," the vicar said with a fearsome scowl that made Jack feel like an ill-mannered child.

Puffing out his chest, he rose to his full six foot five inch height. "I will do my duty by the boy."

"You will do more than just your duty," the little man said with an irritated huff. Then he turned on his heels and marched back into the cottage.

With a resolved sigh, Jack turned to follow, but Quentin placed a hand on his arm and stopped him. "Maybe I should wait in the coach."

"Abandoning ship at the first sign of a storm?"

"Hell, the storm is blowing into a gale, and you are foundering on the rocks. I have no intention of going down with you."

"There is courage and loyalty for you," Jack said dryly. "When your captain needs you the most, you scurry away with the rats."

"I will be with you in spirit," Quentin replied with a smooth smile. "But I do not think you need an audience for what lies ahead."

He nodded toward the door, and Jack glanced over his shoulder. Both the vicar and the nun stood in the doorway. The vicar looked worried, but the nun looked positively scary. The scowl on her face was enough to make the most hardened sinner repent.

"Well?" she snapped. "Don't just stand there. Come in and meet your son."

"Captain," Quentin said as Jack turned to go inside. "After you see the baby, we will get rip-roaring drunk to celebrate your nuptials. We should celebrate, and there is no law that says we cannot do so at the nearest tavern."

"Perfect." Stiffening his spine and trying to bolster his optimism about the future facing him, Jack followed the vicar into the tiny cottage.

Once inside, the nun moved in front of him, barring his entrance into the bedroom.

"I am warning you now; you had best treat that babe with the proper care. Whatever you think of his mother, the child is not at fault. I expect you to raise him as if he were your own flesh and blood, and—" Her voice cracked and tears glistened in her eyes. She swallowed hard and met his gaze. "I expect you to keep him safe. Do I make myself clear?"

"You do." Jack dipped his head, feeling properly chastised. He would do right by the boy, unlike his own father who had treated his son like an unwanted bastard despite the truth. But history need not repeat itself. Whatever his feelings toward his new wife, Jack vowed to be the kind of father Uncle William had been to him.

"Then we should not have a problem." The nun stepped aside so Jack could enter the dimly lit room.

"My lord." The midwife rose from a small bedside chair and held a finger to her lips. "Mother and child are sleeping. The babe is well, but it took some time to stop the bleeding once he arrived, and his mother is quite weak. So, keep that in mind."

Jack nodded as the woman brushed by him and closed the door on her way out. Feeling rather awkward and unsettled, he approached the bed where Abby lay propped on pillows. Her ash blonde hair fanned out around her head like a halo and dark, spiky lashes brushed high, noble cheeks creating an angelic picture so pure it was hard to imagine she had very nearly given birth to a bastard.

He eased down onto a bedside chair, his heart in his throat as he peeked at the tiny, blanketed bundle she held close to her chest. The boy was only half the size of Captain Whiskers, the feisty tomcat and champion mouser who lived aboard the *Lion's Pride*. The bundle squirmed. Jack leaned closer.

A thatch of blond, downy hair covered a tiny skull. Jack breathed a sigh of relief. Dark hair would have made it impossible for him to claim the boy as his own. But what color were the child's eyes? He raised a corner of the blanket. The boy had round cherub-like cheeks and eyes as dark blue as the deepest ocean.

Were all babies' eyes that color at birth? Or were those the eyes of the child's real father?

A tiny fist wiggled out from under the blanket and

into his mouth. Instead of sucking his thumb, the babe latched onto the side of his wrist. Seemingly content, he closed his eyes and drifted back to sleep.

Ignoring the warmth seeping into his chest, Jack tucked the blanket under the child's chin and settled back in the chair. The womanly body on the bed stirred. Then she opened eyes as clear and bright as the Caribbean sky.

"You are still here," she said softly, painting the perfect picture of Madonna and child as her hand brushed the soft head beneath the blanket she held so sweetly.

Her tenderness unsettled him, and his words came out gruffer than he intended. "Where else would I be?"

She shrugged, the rough brown robe slipping to reveal one slender white shoulder. The sloping curve of flesh and the soft spot between collarbone and throat, that tender patch of skin so sensual and sweet against a man's lips, drew his attention. He jerked his eyes away from that corporeal display of beauty and met her gaze.

She regarded him with staid composure. "Surely, you have someplace more important to be."

He laughed, the sound bitter even to himself. "More important than by my wife's side?"

Chapter Seven

Abby stared at the formidable captain, her heart pounding so hard against her ribs she could scarcely catch her breath. *Dear God it is true. S*he had married a stranger—a tall, blond rock of a man large enough to hold her son's head in the palm of his hand. Instinctively, her arms tightened around the precious bundle she held against her chest.

"I do not recall agreeing to marry you." She barely remembered him asking. From the time she had gone into labor in the coach until this very moment was a blur. Distorted words and images filled her head like the remnants of a bad dream. She felt fuzzy and disoriented, and her head was pounding. Was childbirth always so mentally exhausting?

The captain's already stony features hardened, his brown eyes turning cold enough to chill her blood. Did he have a violent nature to match his fierce countenance? Was he a man as prone to changing moods as Lord Drury?

How will I protect my child against such a man? She shivered, pulling her baby closer. Her son whimpered softly. She loosened her grip and patted his bottom. The captain leaned forward in his chair.

"The vicar asked if you would take me to be your wedded husband. You said yes." He ground his teeth as he spoke, and a muscle jumped beneath his ear. Yet despite his harsh features and formidable scowl, there was something vulnerable in his eyes.

"I was responding to something you said," she whispered past a suddenly dry throat. Why could she not remember more clearly? Why did everything seem so fuzzy?

"The ceremony was legal. There will be no annulment." He rose to his feet.

He was incredibly tall and ruggedly handsome. The suit he wore stretched a bit too tightly across his wide chest, and his body seemed as taut as a bow, but confusion seemed to color his expression when he spoke. "I expected some measure of gratitude. After all, I gave you and your son a name."

Despite her pounding heart, she met his fierce gaze. "I had a name, not that it was any of your concern."

"It is my concern, Abby," he growled, never raising his voice. "If the name you gave the nun was not your own, our marriage may not be legal. Do you want that?"

With his wild mane of blond hair, her husband resembled a hungry lion. She inhaled deeply and forced herself to speak, despite her waning courage. "I do not recall asking for your help or your name. And please do not use my Christian name. We are not yet that well acquainted."

"And what do you want me to call you?" His words were calm but the softer he spoke, the more violent his expression. Abby had learned the hard way that a man who never raised his voice could be more dangerous than a man who shouted.

She shivered, suddenly afraid. "I do not want you

to call me anything."

He laughed, a harsh sound lacking humor, but instead of reacting violently, he sat back in the chair. The lines around his mouth diminished, and the next time he spoke, it was without anger. "Be that as it may, I am your husband, and I choose to call you Abby. Unless you prefer Abigail."

The futility of her situation enraged her, despite her exhaustion. She could not possibly stay married to this brute of a man with his unpredictable moods. She had a child to protect.

Could she convince the vicar she had not knowingly agreed to marry the captain? Or maybe she could have the marriage annulled. If it were never consummated...

Thinking of the marriage bed chilled her to the bone, cooling her determination. She closed her eyes and saw Simon Weston—Lord Drury's savage face as he moved over her, nearly suffocating her with his need to sate his lust. She held her child closer. Her son. The precious baby she had delivered *after* the vicar had married her to a stranger.

There was no contesting the marriage. No matter that, her husband was not her baby's father, her son was now his child. Legally, he could throw her out and keep her son. She swallowed, coating her suddenly dry throat. "And what do you get by marrying me? I have no money and no dowry."

Liar! She had a dowry, but she was too ashamed to contact her father now. In any event, there was no contract drawn up between her father and her new husband portioning out what he might claim after he married her.

Regret sat heavily on her shoulders, exhausting what few reserves she had left. What was she thinking, running away with Sister Mary Daphne to forge her own destiny when Papa had already secured her future and found a father for her child? For all she knew, Captain Jack could be a pirate who would lock her and her son in the brig until her father paid a hefty ransom.

The captain shrugged his wide shoulders. "I get Ridge Point, my mother's ancestral home. It was part of her dowry when she married my father. When he died, he tried keeping it from me. I suppose it amused him to think he could dangle it just beyond my reach when he was gone. He knew I wanted that land, and he knew I was unwed. So, the twisted bastard stipulated in his will that my cousin would inherit all real property not included with the patent if I did not produce a male heir before my thirty-fifth birthday. I turn thirty-five in December." He offered a bitter smile. "And lucky for me, you had a son."

"I thought you were a sea captain." His friend had called him Jack, but he had also addressed him as captain.

"I am Captain Jack to my crew. To my family, I am Jack Norton and now, Viscount Ardmore."

So, he got his precious estate, and she was stuck with a husband she did not want. Was every man but her father interested only in his own wellbeing and what he could take from those weaker than himself?

She studied her husband's tanned face. He was eleven years her senior, but he was still handsome despite his sun-weathered skin and harsh features. She wrinkled her brow, trying to concentrate despite the tiredness dragging at her limbs. Something else bothered her besides his odd accent.

Realization sent a shiver down her spine. He was a peer with entailed property. He probably dined with Lord Drury at the Athenaeum club and gambled with him at White's. What if her husband took her to London?

Her chest burned with humiliation. How could she face Lord Drury and the rumors he no doubt would spread about her when he met Lord Ardmore's wife?

She straightened, her courage rising. She had never been afraid of a challenge, and she would face this one for the sake of her child. The good Lord knew her life had not always been easy, but Papa had turned things around. So, why had she wished for more?

Wanting a titled husband seemed so self-indulgent now. Yet, there had been nothing sinister or calculating in her desires. She had just grown tired of never being an equal in the world in which she lived. Now, it seemed, she had gotten exactly what she wanted.

Her father's prophetic words came back to her. *"Be careful with your wishes, Abby. Sometimes we get what we want only to realize it is not what we need."*

Had Lord Captain not interfered in her life, she would have been content living in a boarding house with her child, pretending to be a widow until enough time had passed for her to return to London and her father.

She frowned and looked at her husband. "You are a peer."

He ground his teeth. "I am. Now tell me. Do you have another name besides Abigail Halsey?"

A smile played at the corner of her lips as she thought to bait the lion. "Norton."

"Amusing. But it would be nice to know something about my *wife* besides..." His voice trailed off, and a slight flush stained his cheeks.

"Besides?" Her heart pounded. Did he know who had fathered her child? Did he indeed know Lord Drury? She looked down at her son, sleeping so peacefully in her arms. Her throat constricted with love. Her son had a name and a father. Nothing else should matter.

"Is Abigail Halsey your real name?"

"Yes," she said with a sigh. "Sister Mary Daphne told the truth. My surname is Halsey, and I was never married."

"And I suppose Lord Drury is your baby's father?"

Acid churned in her stomach. "If you already know, then why ask?"

"Confirmation."

"Then you have it."

"And he was betrothed at the time you conceived?"

"Yes." She would not beg his understanding or try to explain when he had already judged her. She could not even tell her father what had happened. That day had been the most degrading, humiliating moment of her life. How could she possibly share something so dark and personal with a stranger who would never understand? A stranger who was probably no different than Lord Drury?

She looked at the handsome captain, surprised at how much it hurt to see such condemnation in his eyes. Grinding her back teeth, she patted her son's back, pretending it did not matter. Her son made mewling sounds and turned his face toward her chest as if even the tiniest bit of light hurt his eyes. Or perhaps he was hungry and searched for nourishment his tiny fist could not provide.

She glared up at her imposing husband. "And what do you wish me to call you? Lord Captain? Or Captain Arrogant?"

He leaned forward, his big hands cupped between his knees, a smile teasing the corners of his wide mouth. "Jack will do. Now, may I ask who your father is?"

Her husband may have given her his name, but she was not ready to trust him. He had married her to gain property. What else might he do for money? Extort it from her father? There was no marriage contract, so her father did not have to give him anything. But he would. If her father knew she was married, he would do the right thing and give her husband his portion, and she could not allow it. Until she knew what sort of man her husband was, she would not let him gain easy access to her father's hard-earned money.

Jack Norton may be a peer, but that did not mean he was solvent or even worthy of his title. His father had obviously had reservations. And Lord Drury was most assuredly not worthy of the title he bore. He had dallied with her despite his betrothal to a woman whose dowry would secure his financial future. And had she not left the Sisters of Mercy with Sister Mary Daphne, Lord Ruston would have married her for money and the coveted heir, and he most likely would have bled her father's accounts dry.

Oh, why had she ever thought a titled man would wish to marry her for herself?

She leaned back against the pillows, closing her eyes. "My father is no one you might know."

"Then I assume you are at least as gently reared as the nun claimed."

She raised her lids, meeting his gaze. "Afraid you have saddled yourself with a loose woman, Captain?"

Until he proved himself as dangerous as the lion he resembled, she would not cower beneath his gaze or allow him to intimidate her. She had learned her lesson well with Lord Drury. He had been able to smell fear like a hound scenting a blooded fox. And he had used it against her. The captain was probably no different.

He sighed but showed no other sign of annoyance. "I just want to be sure you can handle the duties of a viscountess."

Papa's words returned to haunt her again. She had gotten her titled husband, and it was most definitely not what she needed.

"I do not want to be a viscountess," she whispered. Her throat cramped and her eyes burned. She blinked, trying not to cry, but tears spilled over her lashes in a hot flood she could not stem.

Chapter Eight

Jack couldn't handle a woman's tears. He sprang to his feet. The sudden movement startled the baby, making him cry, too. Abby made tear-choked hiccuping sounds in the back of her throat and patted his bottom in an attempt to comfort him.

The baby turned his head toward her chest, pushing his tiny face against the rough brown fabric covering her breasts. Jack blinked and in his mind, he saw Abby nursing her son, her face aglow with love and tenderness, a smile teasing the corners of her mouth as she looked up at her husband.

His pulse stuttered, his heart unexpectedly yearning for the image to become reality. Yearning to be a real family. A sudden desire as powerful as a siren's song. And likely, just as dangerous.

Heart pounding as if the Union navy was after him, he got the hell out of there as quickly as he could. He all but slammed the door closed behind him before taking a deep breath that did nothing to calm his racing heart.

Longing for a real marriage with a woman who had just given birth to another man's son made as much sense as trying to swim with an anchor around his neck. It wasn't worth the effort. His parents' marriage wasn't a love match either, but Jack vaguely remembered them being happy together before Aunt Margery's husband died and she and Morris moved to Ridge Point. Soon after, she started accusing her younger brother, William, of being Jack's real father. Once she planted the seeds of suspicion, Jack's father nurtured them. And not long after that, he sent both his wife and son away.

The hurt no longer showed, but it was no stranger to Jack. The pain was as much a part of him as the birthmark on his shoulder. But he hoped he had learned from his father's mistakes. No matter what sort of marriage he and Abby had, he would not send her or her son away as his father had done. Still, the situation was too similar not to take heed. He may not abandon his wife and child, but he could one day grow to resent the fact that Abby's son carried not a drop of Norton blood.

Could that resentment turn to hatred? He could not take the chance. He was his father's son. It would behoove him to remember that before he got emotionally involved with Abby or her child.

With a sigh, he stepped away from the bedroom door as the nun and vicar came out of the tiny kitchen.

"Is something amiss?" Reverend Harrison asked.

Jack shook his head. "On the contrary. I have a son and heir. There is much to be thankful for, so Mr. Stanley and I are off to celebrate my nuptials at the nearest tavern. I shall return for my wife and son day after tomorrow."

"Do you know where the nearest tavern is?" the vicar asked at the same time the nun said, "Your family will not be ready to travel so soon."

Jack looked from one to the other, his heart rate slowly returning to normal. He stepped away from the door and straightened his too-tight frock coat. "I have been in this godforsaken parish three months now. I know where all the taverns are within a twenty-mile radius."

"The Sheep's Head is just two miles south," the vicar replied with a disapproving frown. "You need to celebrate in Sheep's Crossing."

"I need to get back to Seile, but that will have to wait, I suppose." He turned to the nun. "Two days. That is all I can spare. The midwife said if she does not develop child bed fever by then, she will be well enough to travel."

"No. That is still too soon." The nun's eyes were as cold as granite.

Jack gave her the same stern look that evoked obedience in his crew. "It cannot be helped. If my wife is still without fever in forty-eight hours, we will be on our way." He turned to leave, expecting her to obey with the same alacrity as his crew.

She rushed up behind him and touched his forearm as he was opening the front door. He looked down and met her eyes, which were now soft and pleading. "Can you not wait a week? You said yourself you have been in Sheep's Crossing for three months. What is one more week? Her body needs time to heal."

"I am sorry." He would not let this tiny slip of a woman shame him into doing things her way. She was not his mother.

The nun dropped her arm, her face sad. "Very well. There is a tonic I can give her to speed the healing process, but if you put her in a rumbling coach too soon after she has taken it, it could make her sick. Are you prepared for the consequences?"

Good Lord, no! He had trouble dealing with

seasick sailors, but he was not about to admit it. He had built a foundation of obedience around discipline and his ability to lead. If the nun knew his weakness, she could use it against him. He could not allow it. He needed to bury his mother, and he needed to bury her at Ridge Point. It was his now, and he intended to claim it as soon as possible.

"I will give you four days. Give her the tonic if that is what she needs to travel, but we leave at the end of the week."

****

An hour later, Jack and Quentin sat at a booth in a dark corner of the Sheep's Head Tavern. Quentin was on his second tankard of the thick dark liquid the Brits called barley wine. Jack drank more slowly. The potent brew tasted of caramel, malt, and bitter hops with a hint of sweetness Jack couldn't stomach. He grimaced as he swallowed. He preferred American ales. They had a lighter body and no damn fruity flavor.

"So, after you bury your mother, are you going to make Ridge Point your home?" Quentin asked.

Jack stared into his pewter mug, wishing he knew the answer. He wanted to bury his mother at Ridge Point and sail home to America, but the South was a defeated nation, and the house in Charleston was gone. Mortar fire had destroyed it while his mother lay dying from consumption in an overcrowded wing of what passed as an infirmary.

His heart twisted. His mother had never made it home to her beloved England, but at least she had lived long enough to learn her bastard of a husband had died first. "It's the most logical answer to my problems. Ram's Head is barely inhabitable, and I can't live on my ship forever."

Quentin's smile was sympathetic. "Well, I am glad you are staying. I had not planned to return to America, and I would have missed you."

Jack had known it was just a matter of time before Quentin returned to England to find another wife and settle down. "Will you return home?"

Quentin shook his head and took another long drought of ale before replying. "I will visit my family, but I have no wish to settle at Willoughby. I am but the earl's fifth son so there is nothing there for me."

"No title. No property," Jack said with disgust. It didn't seem fair. Every man should leave his son something. Even *his* bastard of a father had left him a damn title, though if not for British law, he would not have inherited a farthing.

Jack thought of Abby's son, now his. If he had sons of his own, he would leave them everything but Ram's Head and the title. But he would make damn sure Ram's Head was worth inheriting, even if he had to stay in England to do it. He would not leave any child who carried his name a bankrupt title.

Quentin held up his empty tankard, signaling the barmaid. "Don't cry for me, Captain Jack. Thanks to our adventures aboard the *Lion's Pride*, I have amassed a tidy sum."

"And what do you intend to do with it?"

His smile was shrewd, his dark eyes calculating. "I thought I would take over the *Lion's Pride* as her captain."

Not bloody likely! Just because Jack had gained a damn title, did not mean he would give up his ship. "Not that I don't think you are qualified, but I am captain of the *Lion's Pride*." And he intended to stay captain. Lord Captain. He almost smiled.

"Really?" Quentin raised his brows. "And who is going to run Ram's Head and Ridge Point and oversee repairs to the estates if you are sailing the seven seas? Are you going to allow Ram's Head to crumble to the ground? Are you going to ignore it the way your father did?"

Damn Quentin and his logical reasoning. "So, what are you going to do if I sell you *my* ship? You cannot settle down *and* sail the 'seven seas.'"

The barmaid returned with Quentin's ale. He thanked her and took a swallow. Then he looked at Jack and shrugged. "Who said anything about settling down? I tried that once. It did not suit."

Jack pretended not to notice the tension around Quentin's mouth or the sheen of moisture in his eyes. His friend still missed the wife who died giving birth to their stillborn son.

When Jack first met him while visiting the Earl of Gilchrest, Quentin had been deep in his cups and up to his elbows in gaming debts to Gilchrest, who had purchased Quentin's other debts. It was Gilchrest who suggested Jack take Quentin on as his new quartermaster. According to the earl, Quentin could procure icebergs in the desert.

Jack had never needed icebergs, but Quentin had never let him down either. Even during the height of the War Between the States, Jack's crew had never gone without, but that did not mean he owed Quentin his ship. "I am not selling the *Lion's Pride*."

"I do not have to buy her to captain her. I could lease her, refit her, and run a luxury gambling ship along the Ouse and inlet waterways. I could make a good living and maintain property in Seile without settling down."

"You, the son of an earl, wish to run a business?" Jack smiled, knowing Quentin attached no social stigma to tradesmen the way others in society did. But it was still an amusing thought.

"It's as good a plan as any," Quentin said with a casual shrug.

And apparently, one he had been considering for some time. But what would Jack do without his ship? He had captained her for twelve years, loving her and the sea more than any mistress he had ever had. And he damn sure loved her more than his recently acquired wife, whose questionable reputation he was now duty-bound to protect.

"I cannot let you have the *Lion's Pride* just yet. I'm going to need her a bit longer."

"Why?"

"Because I cannot take my new viscountess to Ram's Head. The place is falling down, and my cousin, Morris Flick, has already laid claim to Ridge Point. The Union Army could not get him out of there."

"Ridge Point is yours. You have a wife and a legal heir."

Jack did not feel much like a husband or a peer. He did not even feel much like an Englishman. "But Morris and his mother will contest the marriage and the boy's legitimacy."

"You are legally wed, and your wife has given birth to a son before your thirty-fifth birthday. Your claim to the title is secure, Jack."

"But I would like to at least *try* to protect Abby,"

he said, knowing the terrible names his Aunt Margery would call her and her son.

"There will always be talk about the boy's paternity, but it has no bearing on the legalities of your inheritance. She is your viscountess, and the boy is your heir. Legally, that is all that matters."

Quentin's casual tone did not fool Jack. He was fishing, and Jack was not about to bait his hook for him. If Quentin wanted to know how Jack felt about his wife and son, he would just have to ask. Not that Jack had an answer. He was not sure himself how he felt. He only knew he had to protect his wife from scandal.

As highly as the English prized a woman's reputation, once she was married and had produced the requisite heir and spare, it would be acceptable for her to take a lover—so long as she was discreet. But Jack would not be cuckolded. And he would not allow misplaced jealousy to twist his heart up with hatred the way it had his father. He would not allow Abby to take a lover. Even if she had already taken several.

Had Drury been Abby's lover? He did not know. But if Drury had forced himself on her, would she not have said so? And what of the viscount's character? Betrothed or not, if Lord Drury was an honorable man, he would not have left a lady *enceinte* without offering marriage.

Unless Drury was not honorable. Or Abby was no lady.

Even if she was a commoner, she seemed too educated to be a domestic. So perhaps her father was a merchant or shopkeeper who made enough to educate his daughter but not enough for her to enter society.

So how did she meet Drury?

"No man wants his wife's reputation to suffer," he said at last. "I intend to tell Morris that I met Abby on our last trip to London. The timing is close enough that the boy could be mine."

Speculation shone in Quentin's eyes. "Her reputation will still suffer."

"Not if I can help it." He would protect his wife from scandal the way his father had never protected his mother.

"I am sure you have a strategy to protect the child and your wife." Quentin signaled the barmaid for yet another tankard of ale. He apparently liked the rot better than Jack did. He waited for the barmaid to step away before he added, "Due to the timing of the birth, however, there will always be talk."

Jack shrugged. "As long as people believe the boy *could* be mine; that is the best I can do." He did not want Abby's son to grow up thinking he was a bastard. Legally, he was not.

"Even if your aunt and Mr. Flick believe the babe is yours, someone might still recognize her as Drury's consort."

Just thinking of the woman he had married as another man's consort curdled his stomach. Abby was his. He would not share her.

Tension knotted his shoulders. He was just as possessive and controlling as his father. He did not love Abby, but he did not want anyone taking what he considered his.

He forced his fingers open and calmly reached for his mug, raising it to his mouth and taking a swallow. He would not feed the beast inside. He would not let pride, ego, and resentment destroy him the way it had destroyed his father. He would find contentment in his life with Abby. Even if it killed him. "Once I have established myself as Viscount Ardmore, no one will question the boy's paternity, even if they suspect the child isn't mine."

"Drury might suspect the truth," Quentin said.

"It won't matter." He vowed not to let it matter.

"Then what about your mother's casket? You cannot leave it on the ship while you await your cousin's eviction."

Ridge Point was his and just as soon as he presented his marriage license and the baby's birth certificate, Morris would know it, too. "I'm bigger than he is, and one way or another, I will bury my mother in the family plot with or without Morris' permission."

"And while you are burying your mother and waiting for the crown to recognize your marriage and legitimize your claim, are you going to leave your wife aboard the *Lion's Pride*?"

"I don't have a choice. Uncle William's house in Seile is in sad disrepair after his many years in America, and you saw for yourself what poor shape Ram's Head is in."

"You could take her with you," Quentin suggested.

"No." Even if he thought Abby were strong enough to stand up to his aunt and cousin, he would not subject her to their abuse. "Neither Morris nor Aunt Margery will leave Ridge Point without a fight. They will question the authenticity of the wedding and the legal paternity of Abby's son. I will not put her in a position where she is forced to defend herself or me. This is my fight. Not hers."

No woman should be made to feel like a whore,

especially if she were innocent. And Abby could be as innocent as his mother had been. Until he knew the truth, he would *try* to withhold judgment.

"I don't know." Quentin rubbed his jaw. "If she is as gently reared as the nun suggested, she most likely will not feel safe aboard a ship full of common sailors."

"She will be just fine. Most of the crew went ashore and will not be back." And the rest worked in rotating shifts while the ship stayed anchored in Seile Harbor. If they harmed a hair on Abby's head, they would have to answer to their captain. Jack doubted he would have a problem.

"A ship is no place for a lady. And what about the baby?"

"What about him? There is plenty of room for Abby and her son." Captain Whiskers was bigger than the little mite Abby had delivered.

Quentin chortled. "Babies grow fast, and they go through a lot of laundry. You will need room just for all those dirty napkins and swaddling bands."

Dirty baby napkins. Not just wet ones they could hang out to dry, but dirty, smelly ones. His stomach churned.

"Damn." Jack turned up his tankard and drained it. In four days, he would move his family aboard the *Lion's Pride*, despite the smell of all that dirty laundry.

Chapter Nine

"It is a lovely name," Sister Mary Daphne said, "but his father should have a say in naming him."

Abby held her son to her breast, ignoring the furious flutter in her chest. She had not seen her *husband* in four days, and her son needed a name. Her mind was still fuzzy, but she was not so addle-brained that she could not choose a name for her own child. At least she had not developed childbirth fever, and Mrs. Beckman had already announced her fit enough to travel. But her husband had not returned to fetch her.

Butterflies flitted in her stomach. She was not sure if she feared her husband or motherhood more. Every time she held her son, she felt a tug at her heart and an ache in her soul. If anything happened to him...

Her throat tightened. She cleared it and met the nun's penetrating gaze. "I do not think his father will care one way or the other what I call him."

The nun's brows rose. "Lord Ardmore struck me as the kind of man who would have definite ideas about everything, including the naming of his son."

Unfortunately, Abby suspected her husband did not care a farthing about her or her son. Once Lord Ardmore received his inheritance, she feared he would relegate his newly acquired family to some remote country estate.

With a disapproving sigh, Sister Mary Daphne

reached for the baby. She kissed his downy head and placed him in a blanket-lined basket that served as his bed. "Lord Ardmore promised to do his duty by the boy."

By duty, he probably meant abandoning his wife and child on some isolated estate while he pursued his own interests. Fury at the nobility's callous treatment of their social inferiors fired Abby's blood, fueling her temper. "How noble of him."

Sister Mary Daphne turned sharply, her expression hard. "Don't be ungrateful. Lord Ardmore gave your son a name and made you a viscountess."

"You are right, of course." She did not need the viscount's money and no longer cared about titles, but she *was* grateful for his name. Despite her father's ability to support her, he could not have bought her respectability if her ruse to pose as a widow had failed. And if she had given her child to strangers, she would never have known if they loved her child or had simply taken money from her father and left him to die.

Of course, Papa would not be pleased that she had married a stranger instead of Lord Ruston, but the marriage had taken place, almost without her knowledge. And at least Lord Ardmore was somewhat young and handsome.

Abby met Sister Mary Daphne's gaze and sighed. "Do you still have the letter I wrote my father?"

The nun patted her pocket. "I had planned to deliver it from Shrivenham, but your circumstances have changed."

They had indeed, but she could not tell her father the truth. He would insist on meeting Lord Ardmore, and she could not allow that to happen until she was sure she could trust her husband not to take advantage of her father's generous nature.

Perhaps if she told her father she was safely wed and begged his indulgence while she adjusted to married life, he would not grieve too greatly if she did not specify her location. Not that she knew as of yet where her new husband was taking her, but she could not allow Lord Ardmore to meet her father until she knew something of Ardmore's character. She had to protect her father and her son.

Lord Ardmore had gone to great lengths to obtain Ridge Point. What else might he do to secure the prosperity of his viscountcy? If he proved dishonorable or if matters became too unbearable, she could return to London and tell her father her husband had died. She deemed it unlikely that Lord Captain would search for her if they did not part on the best of terms, and she would not be the first wife to return to her parents' hearth after making a mistake in marriage.

Having a plan for escape, should she need it, made her feel marginally better. She forced a smile. "I would like to discard that letter and write another, please."

The sister sighed. "Very well."

****

Abby awoke again two hours later, her breasts heavy and aching, a sure sign her son would soon be hungry. Again.

She smiled contentedly and stretched her arms overhead just as the door creaked open and a tall dark form filled the empty space. Light from the room beyond cast the man's face in shadows, but his broad shoulders left no doubt of his identity. Then Lord Ardmore entered the room and peered into the basket at her sleeping son.

"The boy is well?" he asked without looking up.

Abby ignored the nervous flutter in her chest and spoke as calmly as she could. "The boy has a name."

Ardmore turned, his face as hard as granite, his eyes just as cold. "Did it not occur to you to wait until I was present to name him?"

He stepped closer to her bed, his dark eyes blazing with heat. She refused to cower despite the fearful quiver in her belly. She could withstand the blow from a man's fist. She had done it before. She could do it again. But she would not surrender to a man's will ever again.

"It has been four days. I had no idea if or when you were coming back, and my son needed a name." She notched up her chin, praying it did not quiver.

His eyes narrowed. "If I do not like it, I will change it."

Abby stubbornly held his gaze, but her eyes drifted errantly downward, taking in his strong shoulders and wide chest. Fear, and some other emotion she could not name, sent heat to her cheeks. She swallowed thickly and raised her chin, meeting his gaze once more.

His eyes sparkled, and a mischievous grin played at the corners of his mouth, as if he knew just how appealing he was. Then the smile slipped from his chiseled face. "What did you name him?"

"William Henry." The name came out in a whispered squeak.

Ardmore's eyes widened a fraction. Then he drew himself up and spoke in a low rumble that sent gooseflesh down Abby's arms. "Why that name? What made you choose it?"

There was something soft and appealing about the way he asked that made the warmth in her cheeks spread to her chest. Ignoring the softening of her heart, she concentrated on the question at hand. She had always liked the name William, and Henry was her father's name. Yet, she could not admit that to her husband, even if she did have a sudden desire to tell him everything, and be done with it.

"I like both names and thought they fit well together."

A pleased smile touched his lips, and his eyes sparkled with satisfaction. "My uncle, a man more like a father than my own, is named William, and my mother's father was Henry." His smile widened, reaching his warm, brown eyes. "And as horrible a name as I think it is, I too, am Henry, so you could not have chosen a better name."

Her heart fluttered with delight. She had unknowingly named her son after her husband. Was it a possible sign from God that she had not made a mistake marrying Lord Captain? She could not help smiling in return. "Jack Henry?"

"Not exactly." He chuckled. "My full name is Jackson Henry Bartholomew Norton."

An unexpected feeling of contentment filled her. "A big name for a big man. Were you also a big baby?"

His eyes twinkled. "So I was told."

"And does everyone call you Jack?"

The light faded from his eyes, and the warmth in her chest rose to heat her cheeks. Her thoughtless words had no doubt proved to her husband she was nothing more than a common trollop with no knowledge of the nobility. Her husband was a viscount and heir. He would have been called Master Jackson or by one of his father's lesser titles if he had one. No one other than his mother or perhaps a younger brother would have called him Jack. The name was obviously one he had chosen to use aboard his ship. Perhaps because he engaged in illegal activities and did not want to besmirch his family name.

"I prefer Jack," her husband said, his voice as harsh as his expression. "Even as a child, I was Master Jack. My father is the only one who *ever* called me Jackson, and he disowned me."

He looked ferocious, but a trace of vulnerability shone in his eyes and tugged at her heart. She wanted to take back the question and see him smile again. He seemed less threatening when he smiled. He seemed more like a man with whom she could make a life.

"I am sorry," she whispered.

He leaned forward, drilling her with those intense, lion's eyes. "Enough about me. It is high time you told me something about yourself for a change. Who is your father, and why did he not protect you from Lord Drury?"

A chill settled over her. His cheerful banter and warm smiles had been a ruse to draw her out so she would divulge information. There had been nothing vulnerable in his expression. No pain in his eyes. He was no different from the rest of the peerage, using his charm to gain her trust so he could get what he wanted.

"Lord Drury is a viscount." Let him figure out the rest. It should not be hard. He was a viscount himself. He understood the value of money and power. After all, had he not married her to gain access to a larger portion of his father's?

"And?" His eyes narrowed dangerously, as if he thought to intimidate her with his ferocious scowl.

But she had faced a more fearsome foe than her lion of a husband and survived. At least the lion had not raised his fists. Yet. "And my father is not a peer."

He spiked his fingers through his thick golden hair, exposing lighter skin at the hairline. Proof he spent time on a ship? Perhaps his estate was not even in Britain. There seemed to be a blending of several countries and dialects in his speech patterns. And just because his father was from England did not mean his mother was or that her family estate was on British soil. His estate could be anywhere in Europe, and he might never even set foot in London, which would greatly diminish the odds of her crossing Lord Drury's path again. "You have an odd accent."

His fingers stilled. He lowered his arm, his fingers curling into fists at his sides. "I am an American."

"But your parents…"

"Were not." He turned as if to leave but then stopped. "We will be leaving for Seile within the hour. Make sure the boy is ready to travel."

"The boy's name is Will," she shouted after he left the room. Then she tensed, waiting for him to storm back inside and shout at her, but the only sound to come from the other side of the closed door was a deep, masculine chuckle.

Chapter Ten

"Drink it," Sister Mary Daphne said as Abby forced down the hot, spicy tea. It had a sharp, slightly bitter peppermint taste that numbed her tongue as it passed over her lips.

"There now." The nun took the cup from her trembling hand. "That should help you get your strength back."

Abby smacked her lips together. Her whole mouth felt tingly and warm, the sensation spreading down her throat and into her chest. The tea helped her sleep, but it made her sick. And this dose seemed stronger than the last. "It burns just a bit going down. Is it supposed to?"

"It hardly matters. You have had a chill since the birth, and the midwife was worried about the birthing fever."

Could she still die, leaving her son alone with a man who was not his father and may or may not care for him? Her heart fluttered, and bile rose into her throat. Had she only dreamed Ardmore told her when he was returning?

"We are leaving today. Are we not?" Her thoughts were still so fuzzy but whether she felt up to traveling or not, she could not stay in the vicar's bed forever. She did not have the means to repay him for his continued hospitality.

"I think it is still too soon for you to travel," the

nun said with a huff. "Mrs. Beckman disagrees, but I think she has an ulterior motive. She wants us out of her uncle's house."

Guilt warmed Abby's cheeks. "I am sure having us here *is* an imposition."

The nun harrumphed again, but before she could say more, Lord Ardmore and the vicar entered the room.

"You appear well, and your son is healthy," the reverend said, his eyes looking everywhere but at the woman in his bed.

Abby smiled, trying to keep the bile from sliding up the back of her throat. She did not feel well, but she no longer wanted to impose on the kindly gentleman. "Thank you. I am feeling much better."

"Nonsense!" Sister Mary Daphne snapped. "It is still too soon. It has not been a week yet."

"I am sorry, but I must get to Seile," Lord Ardmore replied. "And my family is coming with me."

Sister Mary Daphne made a disparaging sound in the back of her throat. "She just took the tonic. Traveling this soon could make her sick."

Abby was already sick. Her head ached and her stomach churned.

"We cannot keep them here, sister," the vicar said in a soft yet firm voice. "The man means to take his wife and son to their new home, and we must assist them in their departure."

She had most definitely overstayed her welcome, but the thought of traveling any further than the washstand across the room made her head spin.

"I am not an ogre," Lord Ardmore grumbled. "But it is time we were on our way."

Abby tried to read his expression, but she was tired, and her lids suddenly felt too heavy to lift. But lift them she did. She had to stay focused. Her son needed her.

"If you insist on leaving, you must agree to mix the tonic and give it to her every morning." Sister Mary Daphne pressed a small drawstring bag into the viscount's big hand. "Drop the tiniest pinch of the peppermint powder into boiling water and make a tea. Give it to her only *after* the baby has nursed. Understand?"

"Yes." Lord Captain shoved the pouch into his pocket. "Now get the child while I help my wife to the carriage."

He leaned over her, his lip curling with distaste.

Abby squirmed under his censorious gaze. Did she really look so terribly bad? She tried smoothing her sleep-matted hair, but her arms felt like lead weights. Her hand dropped uselessly to her side, slapping the tick mattress with a hollow plop.

Lord Ardmore shook his head and without warning, scooped her into his arms. "My wife is still wearing a monk's robe."

"It is the garb of a postulant, not a monk." Indignation tinged Sister Mary Daphne's words. "Had you not whisked us away without our luggage—"

"Yes, yes. I know." Lord Arrogant's stern voice halted the nun's protest. "Now grab the boy."

Will! Abby's mind screamed. But no words emerged.

She groaned, closing her eyes, too tired to fight, argue, or even cling to the mountain holding her in his arms. It would do no good to cling. Eventually, her husband would abandon her, just as everyone else in her life had—everyone except Papa.

But he sent me to a convent.

To protect my reputation.

What if he does not want me back?

Oh, God, she was so confused, and the medicinal tea was not helping. She felt hot and flushed and oh so tired. She dropped her head against her husband's shoulder, and the world faded to black.

****

A shiver snaked down Jack's spine. Abby's face was pale. Her cheeks flushed. Had she developed childbed fever? He lowered his head, resting his cheek against hers. Her skin felt cold and clammy.

He straightened, glancing over his shoulder as he carried her from the room. "She doesn't look well."

The nun followed, carrying the basket containing Abby's tiny son. "She should be in bed and not traipsing across England. I warned you about moving her too soon."

Jack crossed the living room. The vicar rushed forward to open the front door, casting disapproving looks at the nun. "Let them be on their way, sister."

Doubt niggled at Jack's brain. *Am I putting Abby's life in danger?*

He headed for the rented hackney, holding her against his chest. She looked worse than she had earlier that morning. He looked at the vicar, seeking reassurance. "Is your niece sure my wife doesn't have the birthing fever?"

He puckered his brow. "She has no fever, though she does look a bit flushed."

"'Tis all this jostling about," the nun said. "She

should rest a day or two longer before you carry her off to Seile. But if you must take the babe..." She lifted the basket in her arms, staring down at the sleeping child within. "If you must get to Seile to claim your title, then take your son and leave your wife. There is a wet nurse in Sheep's Crossing who can accompany you."

"And what of my wife?" Jack was reluctant to leave Abby behind, despite the nun's dire warnings of traveling so soon after giving her the tonic. It would be too much like abandoning her. And he could not separate her from her child. If he did, he was quite sure his wife would never forgive him.

The nun nodded to Quentin who stood by the door of the hackney. "Your friend can stay with her until she is ready to travel. Then I will accompany them both to your estate in Seile."

His estate wasn't in Seile. Seile was a fishing village on the Wash at the mouth of the Great Ouse River where Uncle William had lived before Jack's father banished him and his mother. Jack had left his ship moored there when he and Quentin left for Ram's Head for the reading of his father's will. Ram's Head was just a few miles from Sheep's Crossing, but the estate house was barely inhabitable. And he could not claim Ridge Point until he proved he had met the stipulations set forth in the second codicil of his father's will. So, he had no choice but to take Abby to Seile. Unless...

Could he leave her with the vicar? Even if it was for her own good? She would surely think he had abandoned her, and he did not want to do to her what his father had done to his mother. He knew firsthand the grief that could cause.

"My wife goes with me. I pledged to care for her in sickness and in health, and I mean to keep my pledge." *But Lord help me if she loses her breakfast in the coach!*

"As you wish," Sister Mary Daphne grumbled.

"Ready?" Quentin reached for Abby, lifting her into the coach.

The moment Jack was inside, he took her from Quentin's arms and eased down onto the seat. He leaned back against the squabs, holding her on his lap.

Quentin reached for Abby's son and just as quickly placed the basket on the floor. He flushed, unable to meet Jack's gaze. "I don't want to drop him."

Jack suspected his aversion ran much deeper.

"May God bless you and your new family, my lord," the vicar said. It took Jack a moment to realize he was talking to him. It would take time to become accustomed to answering to anything other than Captain Jack.

"Thank you," he said stiffly.

"Heed my warning," the nun said. Then she closed the door and the conveyance jerked forward. Abby moaned.

"So tired." She curled against Jack's chest and slept. But fifteen minutes later, she moaned again. "I'm going to be sick."

"Stop the coach!" Jack shouted.

Quentin snatched the baby's basket off the floor as Jack lunged for the door and tried to get it open without dropping his wife. He stumbled outside and nearly tripped. Then he righted himself and slid Abby's feet to the ground as she doubled over, retching.

The smell hit Jack like a physical blow. Bile rose in

his throat seconds before he tossed up his breakfast beside hers.

****

"I am sorry," Abby said a half hour later, her head resting against Jack's arm. He had washed her face, and they had both rinsed out their mouths, but Jack still smelled vomit.

His stomach churned, reminding him of the time he had gotten sick on his own damn ship, no less!

Dark weather and heavy rainsqualls had pounded the *Lion's Pride* all evening and into the night. Jack had clung to the ship's wheel, fighting to keep the stern perpendicular to the oncoming waves. Fighting to keep her from rolling over as his crew trimmed the sails and spliced the main brace to keep the *Lion's Pride* from heeling. But tucking in a reef while heeled over was enough to make even the most hardened sailor seasick.

The ship lurched. Vomit washed over the deck. Jack smelled it over the salty sting of the sea and the gorge rose in his throat. When the sea dipped again, Jack heaved, and the wind blew the vomit back into his face. It was enough to make him stand back and fire into the wind again.

He had kept the ship from going down off the coast of North Carolina, but twenty-foot waves had swept most everything topside overboard. Weeks later, parts of his ship and cargo had been spotted floating southeast of Nantucket. The ship's damage and loss of cargo had been only slightly more humiliating than getting seasick in front of his crew.

He wiped his mouth and turned his head so Abby would not smell his breath. "The nun warned me you might get sick."

"Still..." she mumbled.

"Do not mention it again." *Please do not mention it again!* Just thinking about it made him nauseous.

Quentin chuckled, damn him. He had been on deck the night Jack had gotten seasick. Never mind that he had thrown up as well. Quentin was not the captain.

Jack glared at his quartermaster. "Why are you laughing?"

"No reason. No reason at all, my lord."

The rest of the journey was uneventful, save for the uncomfortable moments when they stopped the coach so Abby could nurse her son. Quentin and Jack waited outside. Those moments were torturous for Jack. He couldn't help imagining what it would be like to see the babe at Abby's breast. Then he wondered what Abby's breasts looked like and whether they would fill the palm of his hand.

He stiffened, his imagination taking a lustful turn that made him uncomfortably aware of her presence when he climbed back inside the coach and took his place beside her.

She leaned her blonde head against the window, her small hands resting in her lap, the shapeless brown robe hiding her assets. What *did* she look like underneath that robe? Was she boyishly thin? Or did she possess a woman's curves? And what had giving birth done to those curves?

He shifted his hips and looked away, staring out the window on the other side. Why should he care what his wife looked like underneath that sackcloth she wore? He was not interested in her as a woman.

But for some reason, he could not stop thinking about the size and shape of her breasts.

Chapter Eleven

Abby held her son to her breast and stared at the tall ship rocking in the harbor. The two-masted, eighty-foot vessel rode high in the water despite the weight of at least ten exposed cannons along its length. The sails were down, but high above the deck atop the mizzenmast, a flag fluttered in the breeze. It was not a British flag or the Red Ensign of a private vessel or merchant ship, nor even an American flag. The ship flew a green flag emblazoned with a gold lion standing on its hind legs and pawing the air. It was not a skull and cross bones but...

"It's a ship," she stammered, nearly choking on the words. A ship flying independent colors and claiming no allegiance to any country.

"For now, it's home," her husband replied.

Beside him, Mr. Stanley chuckled. "I believe that is my cue to leave." He nodded to her and then turned to Jack. "I will locate your uncle and let him know we are back."

Lord Captain grunted. "Tell him we will talk later. I want to get Abby and the baby settled first."

Settled? On a ship? Or was he sending her to some remote estate so he would not have to deal with his common wife?

She lowered her chin, holding her son closer. "Where are you sending us, my lord?"

"I am not sending you anywhere. We will remain docked here in Seile until my affairs are settled."

And then what? They had not discussed their marriage, or what he expected of her. Was she to be his viscountess and run his household? Or did he plan to hide her away on his ship indefinitely? "You expect us to live on a ship?"

"The captain's quarters are roomy enough."

Did he plan to stay with her? To share her bed? She was not ready to perform those duties! Not now. Maybe never.

Swallowing her pride and her fear, she raised her chin and met his gaze. "And where will you stay, Captain?"

He ground his teeth. "It's Jack. Not Captain."

She clamped her jaw shut and said nothing. If she spoke again, she would likely burst into tears.

With an exasperated sigh, he raked his fingers through his hair, his gaze drifting back toward his friend who was still chuckling as he headed down the dock toward the village.

"For the moment, I will stay in the quartermaster's cabin. Quentin can stay in the master gunner's berth or with my uncle. Uncle William has a house here in the village."

"Can Will and I stay with your uncle?" Of course, she could be asking to move from the frying pan into the fire. For all she knew, his uncle was a retired pirate with a peg leg and an eye patch.

Lord Ardmore shook his head. "Uncle William left home more than twenty years ago. His house is barely inhabitable."

"And yet, you would send your friend there."

"Don't argue."

Abby bristled but said nothing more, still afraid of the temper he so obviously held in check. But for how long?

Without another word spoken between them, Lord Ardmore—Jack—took Will from her arms and placed him in the basket without looking at him. He then hooked the basket over his arm and helped Abby board the ship. A roustabout met them at the top of the gangplank.

"You bringing a woman on board, Captain?" the man asked in a slow, oddly accented drawl. A disapproving frown marred his sun-weathered face.

Jack seemed incapable of meeting his gaze. Was he ashamed of her? Most likely. He stared over the shorter man's head. "This is my wife, Charlie."

"Wife! I didn't even know you was a-courting."

Jack continued to avoid eye contact, but his voice remained steady. "I met her on a previous trip to England. When I returned this time and discovered..." He held up the basket for Charlie's inspection. "Well, let us just say we made haste to marry before my son was born."

Abby's face flushed, pleasure tinged with embarrassment. The lie meant to protect her son's paternity painted her as an amoral woman who might have lied about the father of her child to gain a titled husband.

Was that not what Lord Drury would have accused her of doing had he known of her condition?

Charlie looked into the basket and grunted. "A boy, huh?"

Jack smiled. "My heir. I am officially Lord

Ardmore now, and this is my viscountess, Lady Ardmore." He turned to Abby, his eyes dark with warning. "Abby, this is my boatswain, Charlie Hogan."

Abby nodded, her cheeks hot. "Mr. Hogan."

"Mrs. Norton."

"Lady Ardmore," Jack said.

Mr. Hogan flushed. "So, this mean I got to call you Lord Ardmore, or viscount of something? Never could get the hang of that nobility business."

Jack straightened, proudly raising his chin as he surveyed the deck of his ship. Then he looked at Mr. Hogan and smiled with genuine pleasure. "Aboard ship, I am still Captain Jack."

But at the moment, he looked as arrogant as any lord.

So, why had he come to England to claim his title if he wanted to remain a captain? He seemed to take more pride in his ship than his viscountcy. Could it be because he had gained the ship through his own efforts? Despite his aristocratic blood, could her husband be a hard-working, self-made man who took pride in his work? A man like her father?

Mr. Hogan saluted, his weathered face splitting into a wide grin. "Aye, aye, Captain!"

Jack returned the salute. "Back to work then, Charlie."

He hefted Will's basket higher on his arm and took Abby's elbow, guiding her across the bridge and down a set of narrow steps to the lower deck. "The upper deck is the spar deck, and this is the gun deck. The galley is back that way. Forward section." He pointed behind them and then turned. "Captain's quarters are in the aft section. There is a day cabin and bedroom. There is also a private washroom with a tub, washstand, and head. While in port, fresh water is readily available so you can bathe as often as you like. Just let Charlie know, and he can fill the tub for you."

She longed for a hot bath, but Will was not even a week old. Her face burned with embarrassed heat. She glanced at her sleeping son, hoping her husband would understand. "It is too soon. The bath will have to wait."

Jack flushed, apparently comprehending. Then he flashed a dazzling white smile that nearly stole her breath. "I imagine you would still like to freshen up after the ride from Sheep's Crossing. I can have a basin filled if you would like."

Her cheeks flushed warmer still, this time with pleasure. "That would be lovely. Thank you."

Still smiling, he led her past the bilge pumps and capstan. As he pointed out the working parts of his ship, he kept up a running litany, as if he were guiding a tour through the London Museum. It was evident from the warmth in his tone that he took great pride in his ship.

"The quartermaster and master gunner's cabins are on the starboard and port sides. Crewmen sleep one deck below on the berth deck, but most of them have been on shore leave for the past three months."

And what happened when they returned? Would her husband abandon his wife in England and set sail with his crew? Or would Jack choose the life of an English lord and abandon his family on an isolated country estate?

Anxiety tightened her chest as Jack dragged her along, oblivious to her fear and fatigue. He walked at a normal pace with the handle of Will's basket looped over his arm as if her son were as light as a feather.

When she had lifted the basket earlier, it had felt like a lead weight. And she had to quicken her pace now just to keep up with his long-legged stride.

"The orlop deck is below the berth deck," he added, "and below that is the hold and powder magazines."

Gun decks. Powder magazines. Had this vessel been used for warfare? Or was the armament meant to protect a merchant vessel against others who might try to steal her cargo?

It had been years since pirates plagued the seas, but there were still captains whose ships plundered slower vessels. Was Jack such a captain? Was that why he needed powder magazines? Was he protecting his ship from pirates? Or did he refuse to fly a flag of allegiance to Britain or America because he was a pirate captain himself?

"What is on the orlop deck?" She hoped her voice did not betray her growing anxiety.

"Surgeon's cockpit and storage."

Even a merchant ship would have need for a doctor. Still, her pulse pounded as they walked past gun chests and cannons before reaching the back of the ship and an oak door framed by frosted windows.

"The day cabin." Jack nudged open the door with his shoulder and let her pass. It looked to be a combination dining area and library, though the only books on the shelves were of a nautical nature. A skylight in the middle of the ceiling filled the room with sunlight from the open deck above.

"My meals are cooked in the quarter galley and brought here." He crossed the room to a small white door on the other side of the dining table. Taking a brass key from his pocket while juggling her son's basket, he inserted it into the lock and pushed open the door to reveal another room.

"My bedroom. Now yours," he added, stepping aside.

The room was small, but it contained a wide berth with a wooden headboard and drawers underneath. A wardrobe took up the other wall, and a small desk for personal correspondence was wedged in the corner beside the washroom door. It hardly looked large enough for her big husband to sit and write without bumping his elbows.

Jack set the basket on the bed, still not looking at the baby inside. Abby rushed forward to check on her son. Will's eyes were closed, but his tiny mouth suckled, even in his sleep. He was so adorably sweet. How could Jack not steal a glance?

"The head is through that door." His smooth, deep voice pulled her attention away from her son. "Make yourself at home while I find you some clean clothes and bath linens."

His thoughtfulness pleased her, but why would a legitimate sea captain keep women's clothing aboard his ship? And why did he wish her to change clothes so badly? Did he have an ulterior motive? Her eyes drifted to the big bed with its rumpled coverlet. She swallowed, her eyes drifting back to her husband.

He shook his head and grunted. "Stop looking at me like that. I am not going to ravish you. As I said when I proposed, this is to be a marriage in name only."

Her emotions bubbled to the surface in a confusing mix of fear and relief. He was not obligated to explain or to keep his word. She was his wife. He had the legal right to imprison her, if need be, to pursue his conjugal rights. And yet, he chose instead to reassure her.

Tears sprang to her eyes. "Thank you," she whispered, blinking to clear her vision.

Raking a hand through his over-long hair, he sighed. "I am not a brute or a pirate, despite what you seem to think. I am, or was, a privateer."

Mistrust bubbled to the surface once more. She held her head high, forcing a haughty tone to her words to hide her fear. "Pirate or privateer. It is a vague distinction at best. The actual work is the same, and the perceived legality amounts to nothing more than a government's letters of marque."

His face flamed, and a muscle in his jaw jumped, but still, he did not raise his voice. Yet, his low-pitched growl was nearly as terrifying. "I was commissioned by President Jefferson Davis himself. My country was in the midst of a civil war, and that is how I came to be in possession of women's clothing—among other things. I did not pilfer and steal for pleasure. I ran the Union blockades, delivering goods to the South."

"For a hefty profit, I'm sure," she said, unable to keep the bitter words from her tongue. Despite her husband's kindness, she did not trust him. How could she? He was little more than a commissioned pirate, and she had not chosen to marry him any more than she had chosen to live with the sisters.

Men, it seemed, were always making decisions for her, and while Jack might seem kind on the surface, it was obvious from the polished wood and brass fittings of his well-appointed ship that he had not suffered during the war. And it was not even his war because he was not an American. He was an English lord who had married in order to claim the non-entailed property to his father's estate.

Was he a man completely lacking in morals? A man like Simon Weston, Viscount Drury?

His softly spoken reply was a low rumble in his big chest. "I had a crew to support, and they all had families. I fought for the Confederacy, and whatever profits I made, I made off Union ships and the countries that traded with them."

He seemed hurt by her accusation, but she could not take back the words, even if she wanted to. And she was not sure she wanted to. She was not sure of anything anymore, least of all, her emotions. One minute, she felt as if she were teetering over a dark chasm that threatened to swallow her whole. Then she would look at her son and feel such love she could hardly contain her joy. But now, she felt like crying.

Forcing words through a throat tight with emotion, she whispered, "I see."

Jack looked at her, his expression neutral, but his words were cold. "No. I do not think you see at all." And without another word, he turned and left the cabin.

More confused than ever, Abby sat on the bed and nursed her son. And an hour later, the boatswain, Charlie, delivered a trunk filled with women's clothes.

Abby cried as she tried them on.

Chapter Twelve

Later that evening, Jack, Mr. Stanley, and Jack's uncle came to the cabin to eat supper with Abby. William Norton was an older version of Jack—tall and broad with a face weathered by the sun and blond hair yellowed with age. He did not have an eye patch or a peg leg, but he did have a pronounced limp. Otherwise, he looked enough like Jack to be his father.

Feeling more like her old self after a nap and change of clothes, Abby pasted a smile on her face and sat when Jack pulled out her chair. He was still in the process of introducing his uncle when Mr. Crenshaw, a former master gunner turned cook, served dinner.

Mr. Crenshaw had lost several fingers in a powder accident and bragged that the captain had given him another job without complaint. "And I couldn't even cook when I first come aboard."

Abby looked at the unappealing fare, doubting his ability to cook now. The tray he placed on the table contained pork, beans, biscuits, and a bottle of dark liquid Abby hoped was not wine.

Jack caught her eying the bottle. "It's sauerkraut juice."

She started, unnerved by the way he seemed to know what she was thinking. "Is it a sauce for the pork?" The meat looked dry enough to warrant pouring something over it.

"No. Sailors use it to prevent scurvy at sea. It is cheaper than limes, and it does not rot."

"That's because it already tastes rotten," Uncle William said, and he and Mr. Stanley laughed. Chuckling with them, Mr. Crenshaw left the cabin.

Jack shook his head as if they were rowdy children. "Mr. Crenshaw serves it at every meal, but you don't have to drink it. We have water, tea, and a very good port, if you prefer."

"I prefer Madeira, but I will have tea."

"Madeira is a woman's drink," Uncle William said. "Try the port. Better yet, try my rum. It'll put hair on your chest." He reached across the table and snagged a bottle filled with a clear liquid.

Abby smiled. "I do not think I want hair on my chest, but I will have a taste of your rum."

"Are you trying to get my wife drunk, uncle?" Jack raised his brows. "I'm sure she is unused to strong drink."

If only he knew the number of times, she and her friends had sneaked extra glasses of champagne when the mothers and chaperons weren't looking. She accepted the glass. "I promise not to overindulge."

The sweet, fiery liquid burned all the way down, warming her from the tip of her nose to the center of her belly. She coughed until she choked, and her hand shook when she placed the glass back on the table. To her embarrassment, the men laughed.

"My, that is potent," she said, her voice raspy from the burning liquid. One taste was enough, especially since her son would soon be hungry again.

Mr. Stanley smiled. "A bit stronger than the champagne served in society, is it not?"

Abby stiffened. What did Mr. Stanley know of society? Whom did he know? Her husband did not seem to know Lord Drury personally, but perhaps Mr. Stanley did.

Meeting his eyes, she held his gaze, trying to ascertain if she had ever made Mr. Stanley's acquaintance. "Yes. It is."

Was Mr. Stanley using his charm to gain information for his captain? Or perhaps he already knew who she was. Her pulse quickened.

Mr. Stanley's smile widened. "Are you acquainted with Mrs. Robert Stanley or Lady Chelsea? Melissa is my brother, Robert's wife, and Agnes Chelsea is married to my eldest brother, Viscount Chelsea. My father is the Earl of Willoughby. Chelsea is his heir."

Abby had met them all, including the Countess of Willoughby before her death last year, but she could admit nothing without giving away her identity.

She dropped her chin, avoiding his gaze. "I am not a peer."

Jack leaned forward, his knees bumping hers beneath the table, sending a shaft of heat up her leg to roost in the center of her belly.

Fear? Or something much more dangerous? She shivered and eased her leg away from his.

"The nun said you were gently reared," he said, his eyes intent upon her face.

She sighed. "So, it is back to that, is it?"

Jack did not seem to need money, given what he had told her about his ship, but she preferred to decide how much to tell him about her father's identity and fortune later, when she was more sure of his character. For some nobles, there did not seem to be enough money in the world to support their debauchery.

Beside her, Mr. Stanley stiffened. Jack's uncle poured another glass of rum, ignoring the tension in the room, and a muscle jumped in Jack's jaw. "I have told you much about myself. Can you at least return the favor?"

She swallowed, wishing she had not set the rum aside when she needed fortification. "Given the circumstances under which we met, can you blame me?"

"I would just like to know who your father is," he said with a sigh. Then the tension seemed to leave his body, and he no longer looked like a ferocious lion ready to attack. Abby said nothing, but her face heated beneath his steady gaze.

"Is he still alive?" he asked.

Guilt twisted her insides. "Yes."

"Then don't you think I should meet him? You owe me that much, Abby." His words were soft, almost pleading.

Was he sincere? Or was he manipulating her the way Lord Drury often would?

"Perhaps this is a conversation the two of you should continue in private," Mr. Stanley suggested, and to her surprise, Jack agreed and dug into his meal.

The silence that followed was rather awkward, but then Jack's uncle entertained them with tales of the sea to smooth over the tension. One minute, he had Abby in stitches, and the next she was on the edge of her seat.

Mr. Crenshaw returned a short time later with a dessert that tasted much better than the bland fare he had served for dinner, and afterward, the men smoked cigars while Abbey excused herself and went into the bedroom to nurse Will. She returned to the day room a half-hour later. Her husband was alone at the table.

She swallowed her fear and stepped forward. "Your guests have left." She could not bring herself to call them "our" guests. It sounded too...intimate.

He rose to his feet rather clumsily and smiled a bit awkwardly, apparently, as nervous in her company as she was in his.

"Yes." He looked around the room as if he were the stranger rather than she. "Is there anything you need?"

"No."

He made his way to the door and opened it. "Good night, then."

He stepped into the hall and a huge, black tomcat poked his head between his ankles.

Abby gasped. "Dear Lord, what is that?"

The animal's purr sounded a bit like a roar as it rubbed against Jack's boots. Smiling, Jack bent over and scooped the huge beast up in his arms. "This is Captain Whiskers."

The cat nuzzled Jack's cheek, purring even louder. The moment Jack set him down, he ran for the bedroom door and stuck a paw underneath as if to open it and go inside.

Fear chilled Abby's blood. "Keep him out of there! He will smell the milk on Will's lips and steal his breath!" She ran to the door, waving her hands and making "shooing" sounds. The cat looked at her as if she were a bothersome fly and then proceeded to rattle the door with his fat paw.

Jack brushed past her and scooped the creature up as if protecting *him* from her. "Nonsense. The worst

Captain Whiskers would do is get cat hair on the boy."

"And you think that is acceptable!" she screeched, hearing the shrillness in her voice. Will could choke on cat hair, and Jack did not seem to care. He thought more of his bloody cat.

It was just another sad sign her marriage was doomed to fail.

****

Jack sighed, holding the heavy cat to his chest. It purred with contentment and rubbed its nose under his chin. Jack turned his head away from the prickly hairs.

"Captain Whiskers will sleep in the quartermaster's berth." He spoke in a calm voice, hoping to appease his excitable wife. He did not believe the old wives' tale about cats stealing the breath of babies, but Abby obviously did, and he did not want to upset her any more than she already was.

Hysterical women were much more irksome than weepy ones.

Her eyes narrowed. "And where will you sleep?"

"With the damn cat!" Why was she angry? He was being courteous, despite her overprotectiveness. If he did not watch her, she would raise the boy to be a damned pantywaist.

"Good. Because neither of you are sleeping in *this* room." She boldly blocked the door, but her voice shook and her body trembled. His heart sank. Abby was afraid of him.

He leaned forward, arm outstretched to reassure her, but Captain Whiskers jumped from his grasp and ran off in search of a mouse or some dark hole in which to hide.

Abby's eyes widened. She stepped back to stand in

front of the door to his sleeping quarters as if she thought he would strike her. Or as if she thought to protect her son.

"I am still bleeding," she stammered, her body visibly trembling. "But if you must assert your husbandly rights—"

"Don't be a fool." He wanted to take her in his arms, comfort her, and make her forget the man who had put such terror in her eyes. But his wife saw him as the enemy. Gaining her trust would be like navigating a ship through the shoals in the midst of a hurricane. "I am not in the habit of taking a woman against her will, and I'll not make an exception because you are my wife."

Her cheeks flushed, and she relaxed her defensive stance, but the fear never left her eyes. "Perhaps later, when we are better acquainted..."

"Only if, and when you are ready." He stepped away from her, hoping he could keep his word. He found her protectiveness and strength unaccountably appealing. As for her beauty...

He normally chose a partner based on womanly curves and a pretty face. The too large dress he had pulled from a trunk below deck earlier that evening concealed Abby's figure. As for her Caribbean blue eyes, they were a tad too large for her face, but she had porcelain skin and a mouth made for kissing. And her thick, ash-blonde hair called to a man, daring him to bury his face in it. She had piled the wavy locks atop her head in some artful style he assumed was all the rage in London, but he wanted to take it down and run his fingers through it.

He cleared his throat. "I promise not to touch you

unless you wish it." But God how he wanted to touch her hair...and her breasts...and...

She nodded, eyes glistening as if she were about to cry.

"Thank you," she said in a shy and quiet voice. Then she turned and went into the bedroom, closing the door softly behind her.

Pulse thrumming, Jack stood for a moment in the day room, trying to get his raging lust under control. He knew nothing about his wife, and yet, he suddenly found himself drawn to her.

Before he stormed into her life, she had been prepared to raise her child alone. Albeit, she had planned to lie about her marital state, but what woman wouldn't lie to protect her character? Yet Abby seemed more concerned for her child's reputation than her own, which endeared her to him even more.

If only his mother had been so determined...

He remembered standing at the bow of the ship bound for America, tears in his eyes as his father turned away without returning his son's pitiful wave. Jack had been eleven at the time, but not so young he did not realize his father was sending him away or that the hurtful names Aunt Margery called him had something to do with it. He had turned to his mother for comfort, but she would not look him in the eye.

Two days later, Uncle William's ship, the *Lion's Pride*, had pulled alongside the *Andover*. Like Barbary pirates, Uncle William and his crew boarded her with swords drawn and removed Jack and his mother so he could transport them to their new home in Charleston himself. He even moved his home port to South Carolina. And the day Jack turned sixteen, he joined his uncle's crew.

Seven years later, Imperial Russia attacked the port at Sinope, drawing the crew of the *Lion's Pride* into battle. Critically injured, Uncle William retired, and Jack took over as the ship's captain. He and the crew aided the British Navy for the remainder of the Crimean War before returning to America.

Now, Jack was a viscount and landowner with a title, wife, and son but no income. At the moment, he did not need money. But he still had a ship to maintain, and he now had an estate. And Ram's Head was in desperate need of repairs. Then there was Ridge Point. Once he took possession of that estate, he would have three households to run—if one considered a ship a household. What the hell was he going to do?

He knew one thing for sure. He would never make the same mistake his father had. He would never send his wife and son away.

No matter what she did to anger him.

Chapter Thirteen

Abby had just lain down after nursing Will when a knock sounded at the door to the day cabin. She climbed out of bed and slipped into a peignoir. Like the dress and night shift Jack had given her, the loose fitting garment was much too large. So, she belted it at the waist and stepped into the day cabin. Before she reached the door, however, her husband strolled in with Mr. Crenshaw who followed behind with a breakfast tray.

"Morning, Lady Ardmore." Mr. Crenshaw set the tray on the table.

She pulled the sash tighter and nodded, hoping her heavy, milk-laden breasts were adequately covered. Since giving birth, they were twice the size of her hand and tended to leak.

"Mr. Crenshaw," she said, feeling her cheeks warm.

Avoiding eye contact, he nodded to his captain and left.

Jack gazed at her, his eyes raking her from head to toe, his lip curling with distaste. "Does nothing I gave you fit?"

Irritation prickled Abby's skin, and a flush spread down her neck to her chest. "I apologize if my size does not suit your tastes."

"I did not mean—"

"To insult me?"

He smiled despite his flushed skin. "I only meant to say that you are much smaller than I would have expected after having just given birth."

Had he just given her a compliment? She lowered her gaze to hide her confusion. What was wrong with her? Since giving birth, she had been a mass of nerves and conflicting emotions. And she did not understand her husband at all. Despite her boldness, he did not seem angry. Lord Drury's sharp tongue would have cut her to the quick.

Had she actually married a man who would allow his wife to voice her opinions? If so, then he would get an earful.

Notching up her chin, she met his gaze. "Well, if you had not left my trunk on top of the coach when you 'rescued' me, I could be wearing my own clothes instead of a borrowed wardrobe."

If possible, he flushed deeper, looking like a very tall, very blond tomato. "I sent a man around to repair the coach and return it to Sister Mary Daphne's brother, but the horses and luggage were gone. I am sorry. I gave the nun money to reimburse her and her brother for their loss, and I plan to replace your wardrobe straight away."

His thoughtfulness caught her off guard. A trembling smile touched her lips. Lord Ardmore might be a broke viscount, but he was apparently a very successful privateer. And he was much more generous than most gentleman of her acquaintance, save for Papa. He was generous to a fault.

All the more reason to tread carefully where her husband was concerned. Jack may seem unselfish, but lords were notorious for running through their wealth to support their vast estates. If he knew her father had money, he could prove as greedy and selfish as Lord Ansley.

The sniveling Baron Ansley had done all in his power to win Abby's hand so he might gain access to her father's bank account. Fortunately for Abby, Lord Ansley was a physically unappealing man with a prickly disposition.

If only Lord Drury had been less charming and attractive.

"That was very generous of you." She watched the subtle changes in her husband's hard face. His expression softened and his cheeks flushed, as if unused to such compliments.

"Yes, well, it is not as if I did not profit myself," he said gruffly, taking her arm and guiding her to the table. He pulled out her chair and then took his seat across from her.

Abby picked up her napkin and spread it over her lap as she carefully considered his words. "I assume you are referring to Will, your heir."

"And a beautiful wife, well worth the cost of two horses, a wagon wheel, and a sizable contribution to Sister Mary Daphne's charity to help unwed mothers so they do not have to give up their children to baby farmers."

Baby farms were a growing industry for unwed mothers unwilling or unable to care for their children. Desperate mothers made monthly payments for the care of infant children until someone adopted the child or the mother was able to care for the child herself. Often, an unwed mother paid a large lump sum, and more often than not, the infant died of neglect or was murdered outright. Whether the child died from neglect or actual murder hardly mattered. Baby farmers made more money when the infants did not eat up the profits.

Abby shook just thinking about it. Thank God, Papa had sent her to The Sisters of Mercy. Even if she had not met Sister Mary Daphne, the Anglican nuns would have found a proper home for her child; she was sure of it. But once Papa tried marrying her off to Lord Ruston, she had no choice but to take matters into her own hands. Even if Jack had not come along, she and her baby would have been safe with Sister Mary Daphne. The generous nun had provided a safe alternative to baby farms to several mothers and their infants.

Abby's heart lodged in her throat. "You are most generous with your compliments and your money, my lord."

"Jack," he said in a husky voice as he took her hand, sending a shaft of heat from her palm to her heart. She jerked her hand away but continued to stare into his dark eyes. They looked hungry enough to devour her.

She shivered and dropped her chin. Mr. Crenshaw had left two plates on the table, each filled with scrambled eggs and bacon. A hard lump of bread, supposedly a biscuit, sat in a puddle of grease.

"Jack," she mumbled and picked up her fork.

Her husband smiled and wolfed down his food as if he were starving. Abby picked at hers, hoping the biscuit would not float back up on a river of grease once she swallowed.

"A seamstress will come aboard today to measure you for new clothes," he said suddenly.

Abby swallowed a rubbery bite of eggs and looked up. "But the cost…"

"Is not prohibitive. You need decent clothing, and your son needs something besides napkins and swaddling clothes to wear, especially since he has so few."

Her heart twisted. He still refused to call Will by name, but at least he was providing for her son's needs. "Mr. Crenshaw was good enough to pick up the dirty cloths and bring me clean ones last night." Good, but not happy. Last night, he had looked positively ill. "I could do the laundry myself."

"You are still too weak from childbirth. You need rest."

Abby was no stranger to hard work. Jewel crafting was not easy, and before her father became a successful jeweler, her mother had taken in laundry to help with expenses. "I think I can manage. When I was little, I helped Mum with the laundry. I still remember having red, chapped hands from the constant immersion in scalding, lye-soaped water."

"Who did the laundry when you were older?" Jack leaned closer, the hopeful expression in his eyes tugging at her conscience. Still, she did not trust him enough to reveal her father's identity.

"My mother died when I was seven, and my father had the laundry sent out until he could afford servants." That much was true. Until her brief stay at the convent, it had been years since she had performed any manual labor that did not involve pounding precious metals into artistic designs or twisting gold filament or silver wires around semi-precious stones.

Jack frowned. "I take it your father is a merchant or

physician. A lawyer, perhaps? He must be financially solvent and socially accepted among the peerage."

He was still digging, trying to find out about her family. Was it idle curiosity? A true interest in her identity? Or was he trying to discover if he had married a penniless commoner?

Her husband might have spent his adult life as a privateer, but he was the son of a viscount and now a viscount himself. And apparently, he did not need money as she originally suspected. Despite his apparent wealth from privateering, Jack had gone to extraordinary lengths to gain back the property his father denied him so he could make the viscountcy respectable. Would such a man want a tradesman's daughter for a wife, even a rich tradesman's daughter? Such a marriage would be a social disaster.

Lord Drury had made that point abundantly clear when he was rutting over her like a pig. And Lord Drury had never known that Abby herself was a craftswoman. How much worse would it be when Jack learned her secret?

If he learns.

She raised her chin. "I am a commoner, but as you have guessed, my father was accepted in certain social circles. Accepted, but not always welcomed."

"Well, you will be welcomed now, Abby. You are a viscountess." His voice softened, but his eyes shone with disappointment. Was it because he had hoped she would confide in him? Or because she had confessed her humble origins?

Pride stiffened her spine. "I am more than just a viscountess. I am a wife and mother, and if I am to be a good wife, at some point, I must act like a wife." This meant running a household, not living on a ship. She did not want to argue or have him ask more questions about her past, but she could not bear living aboard ship indefinitely.

He started, his expression surprised. Then a slow smile spread over his face, and his eyes burned as if he had a fever. He leaned over the table, his face mere inches from hers. "A real wife sleeps in her husband's bed."

Abby's breath hitched. Her pulse jumped. Oh dear! He had taken her meaning all wrong. Heat rushed to her cheeks, and her flesh tingled. "What I meant...That is, I should be running your household."

"We live on a ship." He leaned back in his chair. He still smiled, but it was now more humorous than...amorous?

She shivered, unable to suppress a brief surge of longing. What would it be like to kiss that hard mouth? To feel his lips pressed against hers?

Dear Lord! What is wrong with me?

After the abuse she had suffered at Lord Drury's hands, she need no longer wonder about such things. Yet her skin flushed and her breasts ached.

It must be childbirth fever. Something was putting mad thoughts in her head, and she refused to admit, even to herself, that Jack was responsible for the low-spreading warmth.

His brow wrinkled with concern. "Are you feeling well?"

"Tired," she mumbled, staring down at the unappetizing plate before her. "Just very tired."

"Then you have no business running a household just yet, even if it is aboard ship." He smiled briefly and then nodded as if settling an argument. "You also need a lady's maid. Even if you were not a member of the peerage, I am sure you are unused to doing without one."

Jack was still looking for answers to the mystery that was his wife, but Abby was not inclined to give him more clues. With the single exception of her secret passion for fashioning jewelry, she had been completely honest with Lord Drury, and she had ended up pregnant and in an Anglican convent. Still, Jack's offer was too kind not to grant him some explanation.

"I did have a maid. Her name was Barbara Kersey." Miss Kersey had started out as Abby's nanny and later became her maid. She was sophisticated and taught Abby how to talk and behave like a lady. She had made it clear from the beginning how important it was for Abby to keep up appearances. She was pragmatic, perceptive, and very persuasive. Unfortunately, she persuaded Abby to set her cap for Lord Drury.

"And what about your father? Does he live in London? Cambridge? Where did you grow up, Abby? Why can't you tell me?"

She lowered her chin in shame, too afraid to trust him with the truth. She no longer feared he wanted her father's money. She feared his rejection. Would a man cast out by his own father want a wife shunned by society? And if he knew she possessed a tradesman's skill, how much worse would it be? She could not risk it. If Jack discarded her, she would be too ashamed to admit the truth to her father.

"I cannot say more. My father has been hurt enough."

His voice hardened. "Meaning?"

She raised her chin and met his angry eyes. "Meaning that having an unwed daughter in my situation wounded him deeply. I cannot bring myself to confess I married a stranger when he thought I was going to Shrivenham to live as a widow. He probably thinks me fickle and thoughtless enough."

"So, you are going to cut off all contact with him? Does he even know you are not going to Shrivenham?" He was angry and with good reason. Her caution made her appear the fool. "He must be worried. Doesn't that bother you?"

"I sent a letter by Sister Mary Daphne telling him I had married. But I do not want him knowing to whom I am wed until we have worked this out between us." Even if Jack accepted her, she was afraid he could never be a father to her son. And if he could not love Will as his own, she would go home to her father, despite the embarrassment.

"What is there to work out? We are wed. That is the sum of it."

And that too, terrified her. In marriage, a woman had no rights. Her husband could legally force his way into her bed or discipline her any way he deemed fit to correct what he saw as unacceptable behavior. A husband gained control of his wife's money and property the moment he wed her, and he was free to spend that wealth any way he chose, even if he chose to spend it on mistresses, prostitutes, gambling, and drink. If Jack wanted, he could cast her and her son aside the way his father had done his wife and child, and he would still retain the rights to his precious estate.

Her pulse pounded as she dared meet his gaze.

"What if you decide our marriage is a mistake?"

Jack leaned across the table and took her hands again, his hold tight but gentle. "I am not my father, Abby. I will provide for you and your son. You can depend on me. I swear it."

His eyes held hers with the promise of everything she had ever wanted: security, stability, wealth. But that was no longer enough. She wanted mutual respect and honesty. Could she expect to find those things with a stranger? Could she expect to find those things when she held so tightly to her own secrets?

"I want to believe you are sincere, but I need to be sure. Give me time?"

He sighed and released her hands, leaving Abby cold and bereft. Then he rose to his feet, staring down at her with such disappointment she wanted to hide her head in shame.

"If I wanted to find your father, I could hire an inquiry agent," he said, sounding annoyed. "I know his last name, and I assume he must live near London, but I would rather you trust me with the truth. Until that time comes, I will give you the time you need."

Emotion closed her throat. Time could not heal all wounds. Lord Drury had seen to that. He had betrayed her and taken her innocence. Would she ever trust again? Would there ever come a time when she did not feel unclean?

She swallowed bile and forced a smile. "Thank you."

With a curt nod, Jack strode toward the door, leaving Abby miserable and alone.

Bowing her head, she pushed herself away from the table and entered the bedroom. Without waiting for her son to awaken, she bent over his basket and lifted him to her breast, finding solace in his warm little body.

Chapter Fourteen

The seamstress came aboard just after the noon meal. Jack showed her into the day room and introduced her as Norah Gabb. The intense, middle-aged woman took charge the moment he left the cabin.

"Gawd, you must have lost at least two stone after having that baby." She whipped out a measuring tape and wrapped it around Abby's waist.

"I..." Abby flushed and looked down. Her waist was still thicker than before giving birth, but the clothes Jack had given her were all much too large, and Mrs. Gabb had no way of knowing they were not her clothes.

Norah pinched the excess fabric at Abby's waist and shook her head. "And you're not even wearing a corset!"

"I do not have a maid and—"

"A viscountess without a maid!" Mrs. Gabb clicked her tongue against the roof of her mouth. "Well, we will just have to remedy that now, will we not? My younger sister, Gladys, is very dependable, and she can start tomorrow."

For the next hour, Abby stood while Mrs. Gabb measured and pinned and chatted about the best milliners and cobblers in Seile. By the time she left, Abby felt as drained as if she had spent a day shopping with her friends in London. Once she fed Will and put him down for his nap, she felt restless and in need of fresh air.

She pulled the bedroom door shut to make sure the cat did not sneak into the room and then went topside to stare out over the docks. The unpolluted waters of the Ouse lapped gently at the ship's hull as gulls glided beneath a pale blue sky dotted with white fluffy clouds. Abby closed her eyes, breathing in the salty breeze and listening to the sawing of rope against wood as boats of various sizes rocked with the gentle current.

Seile was nothing like London with its noxious odors and crowded port. Seile was clean and peaceful. Sailors went about their daily chores without all the ruckus and noise, and they did not shout obscenities or whistle at the lonely woman standing on the deck of a privateer ship.

"Enjoying the view?" a deep voice asked.

Abby jumped, turning so quickly she lost her footing. Jack caught her arm, steadying her. "Careful."

As gently as possible, she disengaged herself from his grasp. He frowned, not looking very happy with her apparent aversion to his touch. But he could never know how it affected her. It was quite disconcerting, the warmth she felt whenever he was near, as if she could depend on him. Trust him.

Fear niggled at her gut, warning her of what could happen if she came to rely on Jack the way she longed to. Men tended to take the least bit of cooperation as submission. It had happened before, but she would not lower her guard again.

Ignoring the gnawing unease, she spoke in the same dismissive tone she had heard her friends use with servants. "Seile is beautiful—what I have seen of it."

Jack sighed, as if the weight of the world rested on

his very broad shoulders. "It has been a long time since I was in Seile, and much has changed. I know you would like to go ashore, but until I am sure it is the same safe harbor I remember from my childhood, I cannot allow it."

Was Jack trying to protect her? Or was she nothing more than a prisoner?

Not knowing if she could trust him was torture on her peace of mind. Surely, a viscount was not so solicitous of his wife, especially a wife he did not want.

Suspicion hung over her like a dark cloud. "So, am I to live aboard this ship indefinitely?"

"This is just temporary until the crown recognizes our marriage and accepts your son as my heir."

"Then what? Do you ship me off to America while you take your place in society?" Was that not what *his* father had done? Rid himself of a wife and child he no longer needed? She meant nothing to her husband, and Will was simply a means to an end.

He sighed again, this time raking his too-long hair from his broad brow as if she truly tried his patience. Good. The sooner he reached his limit, the sooner she would learn what to expect in the future.

"I went to Ram's Head, the seat of my viscountcy, for the reading of my father's will, and the place was all but falling down. It will take more money than I wish to spend to make it a fit place to raise a family, and my cousin has laid claim to Ridge Point. So, my ship is the only home I have to offer you at the moment."

Was he being honest? Or was he weaving lies and manipulating her as Lord Drury had done? "Ridge Point is yours. It became yours the moment Will was born."

"I am aware of that." He turned to stare out over

the harbor as if unable to meet her gaze. Or as if, he was ashamed of his reasons for marrying her. "My cousin, as of yet, is not, but I intend to remedy that situation soon. In the morning, I am going to Ridge Point. Aunt Margery and Cousin Morris will not leave until forced by the crown. They will contest the will, contest our marriage, and challenge the legitimacy of your son."

"With good reason." Abby lowered her head, and her cheeks flushed with shame. Will had almost been born a bastard.

Jack spun around so quickly it startled her. Then he gripped her shoulders and forced her to look into his intense brown eyes. "The boy is not a bastard. Our marriage was legal, and he is my heir."

But not his son.

"Of course." Emotion tightened her throat. No matter that British law said Jack was Will's father, Jack would always know the truth. And so would she.

"Remember that." He turned back toward the ship's rail and stared across the water. "Uncle William is going with me. Lady Margery is his sister. Perhaps he can persuade her and Morris to do the right thing. But you will not be alone. I'm leaving Mr. Stanley here. He will sleep aboard ship until my return and make sure you are safe. And I will tell Captain Whiskers to stay out of your room."

He smiled, but Abby's heart sank. How long would he be gone? How long before she set foot on dry land again? Although the ship remained docked, she still felt the rolling beneath her feet. "I need to set foot on dry land and stretch my legs. I am still a bit weak, and this constant rocking does not help."

Jack turned toward her once more, true concern shining in his dark eyes. "Are you still taking the tonic the nun gave you?"

"It made me sick, and I cannot stomach the taste." Or the way it made her pulse pound and her skin flush.

"But it made you sick because of the rocking of the coach."

"And this boat's rocking will not have the same effect?" Just thinking of that foul-tasting tonic and the way it had numbed her limbs made her queasy.

"It is a ship. Not a boat," Jack said with an impatient huff. "And what of your son? He needs you to be strong."

Your son. Not our son. Jack had yet to address the child by name, and that angered her almost as much as it saddened her. "*Our* son will be just fine, thank you!"

She turned to leave, but Jack placed a hand on her shoulder and stopped her. "I'm sorry if I sound unsympathetic, but I am concerned. Nevertheless, if the tonic makes you sick, do not take it."

Taken aback, she blinked. Jack was sensitive enough to know she was upset and supportive enough to allow her to make her own decisions, and yet, he still did not understand *why* she was upset.

Abby did not know whether to laugh or cry.

****

Jack left the next morning without saying goodbye. After breakfast, Abby fed Will and then paced the confines of the day room, wondering what she would do with herself for the rest of the week. Heavens! She did not even know what she was going to do for the rest of the day.

Biting back a most unladylike curse, she glanced

skyward, catching a glimpse of four crewmen as they passed by the skylight overhead carrying a large box. She took a step back, trying to see through the small opening. Jack walked behind them, his words muffled by the thick glass. He had supposedly left for Ridge Point at dawn. So, why was he still aboard ship? More importantly, what was in the box?

Fear battled curiosity. Curiosity won. After a quick check on Will, Abby slipped out of the day room and down the corridor toward the narrow steps leading to the upper decks. By the time she reached the spar deck, the seamen were hauling the long box down the gangplank. Jack scrambled after them.

"Careful!" he shouted.

Abby crossed to the port side of the ship and looked over the rail as roustabouts loaded the box onto a flatbed wagon. Her heart fluttered in her chest. That was no ordinary box. It was a casket. She had been sleeping aboard ship with a coffin!

Jack's American war had been over long enough for the dead to have been buried, and a sailor would have been buried at sea. So, who was in the casket, and why was Jack sneaking it off the ship?

"What are you doing?" a voice said at her ear. Abby jumped and nearly screamed as she whirled around to find Mr. Stanley at her elbow.

When the initial shock and momentary fear diminished, she straightened her shoulders and glared. "It is unseemly to sneak up on a lady."

"It is unseemly for a lady to spy on her husband," he replied, making her feel like a naughty child.

She notched up her chin, trying to recover her dignity. "I was not spying. I heard a ruckus overhead and came topside to investigate. So, can you explain why my husband is off-loading a casket from his ship?"

Mr. Stanley smiled, but his voice was ripe with sarcasm. "Because there is no cemetery aboard."

"Don't be ridiculous." She almost snorted with relieved mirth, despite her irritation. Surely, if her husband and crew were disposing of a man or woman who had died at their hands, Mr. Stanley would not jest.

He lost his smile, and his eyes hardened. "Then do not jump to ridiculous conclusions. Jack did not murder anyone. His mother died, and he is taking her mortal remains home to Ridge Point for burial. It was her dying wish."

Abby flushed at his accurate assessment of her initial thoughts. Then sympathy—and some other emotion she did not wish to examine too closely— quickly covered her embarrassment. Jack was keeping a promise to his mother.

Lord Drury could not even mention his mother without his lip curling in distaste, and she doted on her son. From what little Jack had said about his mother, she did not sound at all doting. Despite that, he was honoring her last wishes.

Hope flitted briefly in her chest. She quickly stifled it, least another man disappoint her. Jack was honorable, but he did not trust her any more than she trusted him. Just because he kept a promise to his mother, did not mean he would keep his promise to Abby.

"It is a shame my husband did not tell me the truth about his mother." Would trust be forever lacking in her marriage? Or was it something worse that had kept him from confiding in her? Her pulse hitched. "Does he think me so unfeeling that I would not wish to be by his side at a time such as this?"

Mr. Stanley arched a brow. "You did jump to all the wrong conclusions when you saw the casket."

"Only because he did not confide in me."

He folded his arms over his chest and tilted his head. "Any more than you have confided in him?"

Flushing, she lowered her chin. Trust was most assuredly lacking in their marriage.

Mr. Stanley nodded as if she had spoken her thoughts aloud and took her elbow, guiding her back toward the steps leading to the lower decks. When they entered her cabin, Mr. Hogan was depositing a trunk in the middle of the floor.

"Here 'tis," he said before backing out of the room.

"What is this?" Another confiscated treasure from some unsuspecting union ship? Or a gift from her husband?

Mr. Stanley smiled. "It was among some items taken from a Union ship we overtook as we left port headed for England. Jack...Uh, Lord Ardmore wanted you to have it."

She stepped forward and unlatched the leather straps with nervous fingers. Inside the trunk were bolts of fabric, several volumes of poetry, and two small jewelry cases. Her heart leapt as she envisioned twinkling gems and the intricate curves of artistically twisted metal. She loved jewelry, not for its value, but for its beauty and the care put into its creation. It did not matter if it was Egyptian lapis lazuli amulets from the Ptolemaic period or hair jewelry, given as sentimental keepsakes when someone died.

Her hand shook as she lifted one of the cases and

raised the lid. Gold brooches and jeweled lockets decorated with delicate enamel work and serpentine designs winked at her from velvet cushions. Seed pearls and floral motifs dated most of the pieces to before America's Civil War when gold was not so scarce—a time before the Queen's beloved Prince Albert's death. Nowadays, jewelry designs were darker and more somber, but Abby preferred older, brighter pieces.

She palmed an amethyst locket. "It is beautiful."

Mr. Stanley smiled. "Your husband is most generous."

He had not purchased the gift for her, but the gesture touched her heart nonetheless. "Yes. He is."

Mr. Stanley lifted a pearl ring from a velvet-lined box. "The Confederacy would have removed the stones and melted the pieces down for the metal."

The ravages of war broke her heart. Nothing was safe. Not people. Not property. Not even art. "Why would anyone destroy something that had taken such care to create?"

He shrugged. "There was a war going on, and the Confederacy needed bullets more than they needed baubles and beads. Jack, uh, Lord Ardmore had turned several such cases over to the Confederate Navy, but toward the end of the war, he knew their cause was hopeless. So, he kept this stash of jewels for the wife he hoped to have one day."

Jack had not chosen them for her, but for some nameless, faceless wife he had not yet met—a wife he had thought to choose freely. He had not selected the pieces from a jeweler. He had confiscated them from a Union ship by cannon fire.

A moment of ingratitude hardened her heart before

guilt twisted her gut. The jewelry was a gift. Just because Jack had not hand-selected the pieces and given them to her personally did not make him any less generous. And she did love jewelry. She missed working with her father at Halsey's on Patton Street. She missed creating fabulous designs for her own pleasure and seeing those designs on the necks of her society friends. Invariably, the moment was usually ruined when her "friend" would then brag about how much her father had paid Abby's father for a brooch or pendant, reminding her that his business thrived on the taste and generosity of a capricious society.

Would her husband prove just as fickle? Would he treat her any differently if he knew she had practiced a trade? She lowered her chin, trying to hide her fears. "I shall thank his lordship for his gift when he returns."

****

Things did not go smoothly at Ridge Point. The solicitors each conceded points, which enraged Jack. Ridge Point was his, but Mr. Lambert agreed to let the Flicks remain in residence until Jack's marriage and the birth of his heir could be authenticated.

"I have met all conditions of my father's will," Jack groused.

"It is a formality to be sure," Mr. Lambert replied, "but you and your wife did marry rather quickly, and Mr. Flick is not convinced there is a wife, much less a child."

"And I will not take *Mr.* Stanley's word for it. He can sign all the papers he likes. It means nothing. He is no more a peer than I am," Morris said with a sneer.

Jack surged to his feet and nearly came across the desk at his cousin. It was his office and his desk, damn it! "Quentin Stanley is an honorable man, and you know it!"

"Jack!" Uncle William rose to his feet and gripped his arm above the elbow. Mr. Lambert came to his feet and took the other arm. The two men pulled him back. Had they not, he would have knocked Morris' teeth from his head.

Trembling with rage, he shook them off. Both men released him. Neither stepped away or returned to their seats. Morris turned chalk white.

"So you say," he said in a high-pitched whine. "But for all I know, you are not even my cousin so it does not make any difference if you are married or not. You could be an impostor."

"Even if you did not already know the truth, *cousin*, the Earl of Willoughby vouched for me as did the Earl of Gilchrest. Gilchrest knows me personally, as does Uncle William, who is your uncle as well." Jack's nails bit into his palms, and the muscles in his thighs trembled. Fury threatened to consume him.

"Calm down," Mr. Lambert said. "These things take time to sort out, but at least you shall have the opportunity to bury your mother on Ridge Point land."

Margery Flick had not attended the proceedings, but she had convinced her son to grant Jack permission to bury his mother in the family plot, despite Morris' insistence that Jack bury her next to her husband. But Bartholomew Jackson Talbot Norton, fourth Viscount of Ardmore, was buried at Ram's Head, next to his predecessors and their spouses. Jack refused to bury her anywhere near the bastard.

Uncle William clapped him on the shoulder and sighed. "It is the least my sister could do for *our* brother's widow. The very least."

****

The funeral itself was brief, a service attended by Jack, Uncle William, and a few elderly Ridge Point staff and tenants who remembered Lady Ardmore from the days before marriage and disillusionment turned her bitter. Jack stood by the grave, head bowed, heart lodged in his throat.

His mother had never been the affectionate sort, but she had loved him in her own way. Despite her banishment, she had never blamed Jack—at least not to his face. But he had often wondered if she wished he had never been born. Had he been a daughter or had he not looked so much like his uncle, both their lives would have been easier. It was one reason he wanted a real marriage with Abby. He did not want his wife to question if her life would have been better if her son had not been born. And he never wanted Will to question his mother's love. He would not wish such doubts on his worst enemy, much less a child who carried his name.

"She was such a vivacious girl," Mrs. Hogsley said as Jack walked away from the cemetery, leaving Uncle William behind, his chin lowered as if in prayer. Mrs. Hogsley had hung back after the other mourners departed, as if waiting for a private word with Jack. "He must be heartbroken to have lost her again."

"Who?" Jack looked down at the plump little woman.

"Mr. Norton," she said with a frown. "First he lost her to his brother and now to death. It must break his heart. But they were together in America, were they not?"

Jack's heart slammed against his ribs, stealing his breath. The old woman was senile. She did not know of which she spoke. "Do not let your tongue get the better of you, old woman. I would not wish those old rumors to resurface now. William Norton was never more than a dutiful brother-in-law to my mother."

Mrs. Hogsley snorted. "Pishaw! Your mother and I were friends from the time we could put together a sentence. Mr. Norton loved her, but his brother, the viscount, decided he wanted her, and he made it a competition. The younger Mr. Norton did not stand a chance because your grandfather wanted her to marry a title, and your mother was always the dutiful daughter. She loved your uncle, but she was faithful to your father. She was too much the lady not to be."

But was she always faithful?

It was a question that plagued him and not one he could ask his uncle. Uncle William had never claimed to be more than Jack's uncle, despite being more of a father than the former viscount had ever been. Still, doubts lingered. Uncle William had followed them to America, and he had relocated his shipping business to remain near them. And when he retired after the Crimean War in 1856, he had stayed behind in South Carolina while Jack took over as captain of the *Lion's Pride*. William Norton had not returned to sea until Jack nearly lost his life fleeing the Union blockades in 1863.

Had he become more than a friend to Lady Ardmore during those seven years? Or had he always been more than just Darcy Norton's friend?

Would the truth set him free? Or was it something he would rather not know?

Chapter Fifteen

A week later, Jack stood in the doorway, watching as Abby nursed her son. Contentment settled over him. This was what he wanted—a home and family. No more roaming the seas searching for a place to belong. No more wandering. Even if he could not make a life for them at Ridge Point, he wanted this.

He took a step forward, and a board creaked beneath his feet. Abby looked up, eyes wide with surprise before a brief flash of fear made him feel like a voyeur aboard his own ship.

"I didn't mean to startle you." He tripped over his tongue and his big feet as he stepped into the cramped cabin.

The fear faded from her eyes, and she managed to smile. "For a swashbuckling pirate, you are not very graceful."

"I'm a privateer. Lord Privateer to you, ma'am." He wanted to see that smile again. He wanted it to reach her eyes and her heart. He wasn't disappointed.

She laughed, and those lovely eyes crinkled at the corners. Damn if he didn't find her the most irresistible female to ever grace his bedroom. But resist her he would. He had given his word.

"I thought you wanted me to call you Jack?" Mischief danced in her eyes, and heat rushed to his groin.

He cleared his throat and shuffled his feet, hoping she would not notice the evidence of his rising desire. "I can think of other things you could call me."

A mischievous twinkle danced in her Caribbean blue eyes. She raised her chin in a haughty fashion. "So can I, but a lady should never say such words aloud."

His laugh was both genuine and unexpected. It startled the baby and Abby. She looked down at her nursing son as if having just remembered he was nursing at her partially exposed breast.

His gut tightened. So did his trousers. The smile slipped from his face, and her cheeks flushed crimson. She raised her chin, and their gazes locked. His heart pounded. His palms grew damp, betraying a nervousness he had not felt since he was a schoolboy.

The laugh lines around her eyes faded, and her expression cooled. Without a word, she turned her back to him and adjusted her gown, hiding the curve of her lush breast from his gaze before tucking her son against her chest. Then she rose to her feet, cast him a frosty glare, and crossed the room. Jack's heart cramped as the temperature seemed to drop at least ten degrees.

Damn his traitorous body. He had scared her. And just when they were starting to make progress. He watched, eyes transfixed on the lush curve of her bottom as she leaned over to put the baby in the basket. Damn. His son was sleeping in a basket. What the hell was wrong with him? He was a randy, thoughtless fool.

"The boy needs a cradle."

"What boy?" She turned to face him, her eyes earnest and sincere despite the stupidity of her question.

"Your son of course." What was the matter with her? Had he waited too long to recognize his oversight?

Was she one of those women who expected a man to read her mind and then pouted if he misinterpreted whatever subtle hint she stingily decided to give?

She stepped around him. "Keep your voice down. *Will* needs his sleep."

Why did she emphasize the boy's name? Did she not think he remembered it? He followed her into the day room, closing the door softly behind him.

"Did you take care of whatever business you had with your cousin?" The chill had left her eyes, but there was no longer any hint of warmth in them either.

Jack wanted to feel that glow again, but speaking of his cousin would only fire his blood with anger. He did not want to talk about Flick, his inheritance, or his mother's burial. "I have done all I can. My solicitor will handle the rest."

Abby nodded, her eyes sad instead of angry, as if he had somehow hurt her immeasurably. She turned her back to him, and his heart twisted. They could not go on like this. Not if he wanted to establish a more cordial relationship with her. They needed to spend time alone together without Uncle William, Quentin, Mr. Crenshaw, or the baby anywhere near. They needed time together without distractions. And she needed time ashore with her feet on terra firma.

He touched her shoulder. She stiffened, visibly forced herself to relax, and turned, meeting his gaze with a wary expression. His stomach lurched as if the ship had just dropped over a cresting wave.

When had seeing Abby smile become so important? "Would you object to Uncle William watching the baby for a few hours?"

Her eyes sparked at the mention of her son, but

then she simply sighed and raised one delicate shoulder in a half-shrug. "I do not suppose so. Why?" she added, sounding suspicious.

Jack ignored the pang of hurt her mistrust caused and smiled. "Then put on your finest new dress. I am taking you ashore."

****

Abby's heart drummed in her ears when she stepped from the cabin in a pale blue poplin walking dress trimmed in dark blue velvet that Mrs. Gabb had delivered earlier in the week. She rubbed her palms over her skirts and hesitantly raised her chin.

Jack smiled as his appreciative gaze washed over her, warming her skin. "You look lovely."

Was he being sincere? She did not know her husband well and was unsure if she could trust him or her judgment. She had thought Lord Drury honorable. Believing his lies, she had allowed him to seduce her, and it was not even in a bed. Jack was her husband. He did not need to seduce her to get her into his bed. It was his husbandly right. Yet, he had been most solicitous toward her despite that.

Can I trust him?

She touched the pearl-encrusted, gold locket at her neck. "Thank you for the clothes and the lovely jewelry. You have been most generous."

"You are most welcome." He took her arm, leading her away from the captain's quarters to the upper decks. The touch of his warm palm against her bare wrist sent a tingling shock up her arm.

Oh, why didn't the man wear gloves? Why had she not thought to tug her sleeves down to meet the lace trim of hers? Jack had much to learn if he was to become a viscount. He was barely civilized.

She held her tongue as he helped her down the gangplank and onto the docks. His palm lightly cupped her elbow as they walked away from the pier and toward the quaint seaside village. Sounds from the dock drifted on the breeze and gulls screeched overhead. An awkward silence stretched between them and nerves flitted like butterflies in Abby's stomach. She nervously toyed with a button on her jacket. "How long has it been since you were in Seile?"

"A long time."

"That is not really an answer." Why must the man be so contrary? She was making an effort to get to know him better, and he was not cooperating. Most men jumped at the chance to talk about themselves. Her husband, however, was more reticent.

His mouth hitched up on one side. He turned his head just enough to look down at her from the corner of his eye. "And you have been so very forthcoming with the answers to *my* questions."

Her cheeks flushed. She wanted to tell him the truth, but how could she face him again if he knew what Lord Drury had done to her? What she had enticed him to do? How would he treat her if he knew the sordid, ugly truth about the woman he had wed?

"You know you want it. You were all but begging for it with your forward behavior."

Nausea roiled in her gut. She stumbled, but Jack's strong grip kept her from falling. "Careful."

Shame burned her cheeks as she continued alongside him, her eyes transfixed on the sandy lane beneath her shoes.

"*Seil* is a German word for cable or high wire,"

Jack said, distracting her from her turbulent thoughts. "A German explorer sailing through the area in the early 1400s discovered several tall ships anchored off shore and decided to build a dock in the area. He named the village that grew up around the area Seil. Later, English settlers added an e to the name and took over the town the way they are wont to take over everything else they covet."

Bitterness tinged his voice. Was it because he believed his uncle had coveted his father's wife? Or did he believe Abby had been so covetous of a British title that she had attempted to seduce a proposal from Lord Drury?

They walked no more than fifty feet further when Jack stopped and nodded. The harsh lines had faded from around his mouth, and he actually smiled. "This is Uncle William's house, Sea Gate. The caretaker who has looked after it for years died last winter. Then a storm tore shingles from the roof. Quentin and Uncle William replaced them, but there is still a significant amount of water damage on the inside, so it is not quite habitable yet."

The cottage was small and weathered, the porch in sad need of repair. Abby shaded her eyes with her hand, squinting into the sun as she looked up at the roof. New shingles stood out in bright contrast against older, graying ones, proof Jack had told the truth about the condition of his uncle's house.

Her face flushed. Jack had not "settled" her and Will on board his ship to hide her away, and he had not planned to send her to some isolated estate. Despite his desperate reasons for marrying her, he had been honest from the beginning.

Ignoring the tug at her conscience, Abby kept her tone casual and steered the conversation away from the uncomfortable fact that she was still keeping secrets. "I hope Uncle William's bedroom is on the west side of the house."

Jack looked down at her upturned face and frowned. "And how would you know which end of the house is east and which is west?"

"I am not a nodcock. I know the sun rises in the east and sets in the west, and since it is before noon and the sun is to my left, then that is east." She pointed to the glowing ball in the sky. Then she pointed to the older portion of the roof. "Since that is the side of the house away from the sun, it is the west side of the house. No shingles were replaced. So, it is logical to assume the roof did not leak there, and if he slept under that portion of the roof, then he would not have gotten wet if it rained before he replaced the tiles."

Jack threw back his head and laughed, startling Abby as well as a flock of nearby seagulls. The birds took flight, screeching their displeasure. Abby stared at her husband, her heart pounding. His eyes danced with merriment, his laughter a rich, soulful rumble that took years off his face.

"Brains and beauty. I am indeed fortunate."

Her pulse jumped with remembered fear and humiliation. Lord Drury had issued a similar compliment once. She had responded with coyly lowered lashes and a flirtatious thank you. His response had been most inappropriate, and she had been too shocked to respond with the outrage society demanded of a true lady.

No wonder Lord Drury had felt justified in his

treatment of her. She had acted the wanton, and he had treated her as such.

She looked away, staring out over the dock and the ships rocking in the harbor. "I am no beauty."

Jack snorted. "You know exactly how beautiful you are."

Her breathing hitched. She stepped away, pulling free of his light grip to meet his gaze.

He turned, giving her his back. "A beautiful woman can gain much if she knows how to use her charms. There is no need to practice your wiles on me, Abby. You are my wife. I will grant you whatever is in my power to give."

Her heart sank. She was not trying to charm or manipulate him for trinkets or compliments. But she had played flirtatious games to catch Lord Drury's eye, and he seemed to know it. "Have I not been punished enough for my sins?"

Jack jerked his head around, a stunned look on his face. "Ah hell. I didn't mean to imply..."

He turned completely, raking a hand through his hair. "We have both made mistakes, and I have no wish to dredge up the past."

Her pulse quickened at the vulnerability in his gaze, but she felt safer with her secrets. She offered a wobbly smile. "Neither do I."

"Then let us be honest with one another from here on out. I'll not ask you again about your past. But I think I have figured out some of it on my own." He smiled, and her heart fluttered. "I imagine you were accepted in high society because of your father's position and wealth, but you most likely felt the sting of disapproval for being born a commoner."

He did not know her father was renowned jeweler, Henry Halsey, but he had accurately guessed the foundation of Papa's social success and society's reaction to a middle class merchant challenging the social order. The very idea that a man could achieve success through hard work and self-reliance alarmed most nobles, but Jack seemed different. He seemed to understand a man's desire to rise above his station in life. Perhaps time spent in America had given him such a unique prospective, despite his noble heritage. Or, maybe he was more like her father than he was Lord Drury.

Abby wanted so badly to trust him. She wanted to tell him about her father and her desire to be accepted by those who saw her family as a threat. She wanted to confess her every sin, her every naïve, stupid mistake. But fear stilled her tongue. She did not want to make the same mistake trusting Jack she had made in trusting Lord Drury. Simon Weston had battered her body, damaged her trust, and injured her heart. But Jack had the power to cripple her soul.

She took a deep breath and let it out slowly. "That is an accurate enough assumption."

"And did Lord Drury accept you as an equal?" Wariness crept into his voice, setting her nerves on edge.

If she answered honestly, she would have to admit she had fancied herself in love with Simon. Thus, she had turned a blind eye to the truth, refusing to believe her eyes and ears, believing instead, the whispered lies he murmured when he caught her alone.

Humiliation burned her cheeks, but caution tempered her response. "To my face, he applauded social mobility. In truth, he believed the middle class should be content with their lot in life and cease their attempts to rise above their birth rank."

Simon had made it clear the day he took her innocence that he believed she had plied him with her feminine wiles in an attempt to marry above her station. He had felt justified in taking what he claimed she had offered. With his derisive laugh still ringing in her ears, he had ridiculed her for believing he would have married her—a commoner—even if her father had caught them in a compromising position. Abby had felt so reviled, humiliated, and ashamed, she had kept silent about his abuse. Only after she had twice missed her woman's time had she gone to her father. Even then, she had not confessed everything.

A sad smile touched Jack's face. "We have much in common, you and me."

Despite his noble birth, Jack had lived most of his life in America or aboard his ship. Had he felt like an outsider, desperately seeking acceptance? Was it possible he might understand her motives for wanting to marry a peer? Or would he think her perfidious and shallow?

Her heart knocked against her ribs. "How so?"

"Neither of us are what we seem. At first glance, I am nothing more than a ship's captain, and you, a noblewoman."

His words pierced her. She may have been born a commoner, but she was his viscountess now. Did he make the comparison because he thought she had manipulated him into believing she was gently reared?

Battling disappointment and hurt, she shielded her heart with anger. "And what does a closer inspection reveal?"

A salty breeze blew a wisp of hair into her eyes. Before she could raise her hand to tuck it behind her ear, Jack's fingers grazed her skin as he gently brushed it aside. Warmth shivered over her, threatening to melt her anger.

"That you are a true lady, despite your common birth."

Her breathing hitched. She leaned closer, seeking his warmth and the glowing acceptance in his eyes. "And you are the noblest viscount, nay, the noblest peer I have ever met."

"Then I, madame, am at your mercy."

Bending forward, he touched his lips to hers. Cold fear froze her blood, and she could not breathe. He leaned closer, pressing against her the way Simon had done before shoving his hands beneath her skirts.

She raised her fists, palms flattening against his chest to push him away. Her fingers encountered hard muscle. His heart beat against her gloved hand, sending warm tingles racing up her arms. He moaned, deep in his throat but gentled his touch, soothing her rising panic.

Warmth seeped into her chest, and a curious longing pierced her heart seconds before he released her.

Abby blinked, her pulse pounding from the unexpected kiss and aftermath of conflicting emotions flooding her senses. Seemingly unaffected, Jack took her arm and continued walking as if he had kissed her a thousand times before—as if it were his right and meant nothing. She tried to behave in a like manner. It *was* his right. She was his wife. He could kiss her whenever he wanted, but not on a public street. Unless...

Had he done so to humiliate her? To prove how common he believed her to be?

Nausea roiled up from the pit of her stomach. She inhaled through her nose and exhaled slowly, concentrating on each step and each subsequent breath.

Sand shifted and whispered beneath her feet, and the wind soughed through the trees carrying the salty scent of the sea. Abby pushed dark thoughts aside and tried to regain her equilibrium. Overhead, a gull screeched, but Jack said nothing as he led her inside his uncle's cottage.

Large windows let in enough sunlight for her to see several new planks in the floor, evidence some of the repairs had already been made. Was that why he had brought her here? To prove his honesty?

He looked about the room, his face cast in shadows. Even in the dim light shining through the windows, Abby could see the pain on his face and the sadness in his eyes. And when he spoke, his words resonated with sorrow.

"When my father banished my mother and me to America, Uncle William sailed after us. He hailed the ship on which my father had booked our passage and boarded. He wanted to take us back to Ram's Head, but my mother refused to go. She stubbornly believed my father would see the error of his ways and eventually bring us home. Uncle William held out no such hope. So, he settled in South Carolina with us, and my mother died on America soil, still waiting for absolution for a sin she did not commit from a husband who did not want her."

Abby's heart twisted, and tears sprang to her eyes.

His pain was real. It touched his soul. It touched hers. She raised a trembling hand to his sleeve. He did not seem to notice. Sorrow slowly turned to anger. She saw it in his eyes and heard it in his voice.

"At least the bastard provided a nice home for our banishment, and we had Uncle William to look after us. He had been a tradesman for years, transporting goods to and from the Americas to Europe. He kept this home in Seile but opened another warehouse in Charleston. He stayed with us when he was in America, and his business thrived. When I turned sixteen, I joined his crew."

"That must have broken your mother's heart," she said, still clutching his sleeve. She did not want to sever contact. She feared he would pull away if she did, and she would never feel this growing closeness again—a closeness that banished her earlier dark thoughts and made her feel safe. But safe enough to share her secrets?

She could only pray that it were so.

Chapter Sixteen

Jack met Abby's gaze, but he didn't seem focused on her. The warmth she'd felt earlier faded, and Jack now seemed distant and cold. He grunted, his mouth turning up on one side in a slight sneer. "My mother's heart was broken long before then. But she rallied quickly when we reached America. She became involved in her women's charities and was invited to the most fashionable parties. She and my father were still married, so she was still his viscountess. Despite the alleged American dislike of titles, she became the toast of Charleston.

"Uncle William and I visited often until he was injured during the Crimean War. Then, he made me captain of the *Lion's Pride* and retired. He still visited Seile once or twice a year, but he settled in Charleston."

Something dark flashed behind his eyes, a deeply haunted look he quickly masked. "After the Confederacy commissioned me for service as a privateer, Uncle William returned to the sea. He promised my mother he would keep me safe. Neither of us realized she was the one in danger. While tending the wounded, she contracted consumption."

Memories of her own mother's death brought tears to her eyes. Her chest cramped and her throat tightened. "Oh, Jack. I am so sorry."

Sadness shadowed his eyes when he lowered his

gaze and seemed to notice her hand clutching his sleeve. Her pulse leapt. She released her grip and slowly lowered her arm back to her side.

Jack looked from her lowered hand to her eyes and held her gaze. His expression was no longer readable. It was like staring into the face of a handsomely chiseled statue, and his voice took on a monotone quality that lacked emotion. "Uncle William and I were with her when she died—the day after we received word that my father had passed. That same day, she made me promise to bury her at Ridge Point."

She watched as he visibly tried to distance himself from the pain, but a muscle in his jaw jumped, and he was unable to hold her gaze.

The former viscountess had died in a foreign country, and everything Jack had done since then had been for her. He had returned to England to claim a title he did not want so he might bury his mother in the country of her birth.

Sympathy nudged at her heart. "So, you and your uncle were finally free to come home."

He jerked up his chin and curled his lip. "Home? England had not felt like home since I was a child, but there was nothing left for me in Charleston either. Mother was gone, the Confederacy was defeated, and I was a wanted fugitive from the Union Army. So, I came back to bury my mother and claim my inheritance, only to learn of my father's latest treachery."

Poor Jack. In his efforts to keep a promise to his dying mother, he had married her—a woman who had committed a similar sin for which his mother had been accused. That alone must feel like salt in an open wound. She could not imagine how they were to bridge the gulf that lay between them, especially when she could barely forgive herself for her idiocy in trusting Lord Drury.

Jack took a deep breath and seemed to shake off his hurt. Abby found it more difficult. As he showed her the rest of the small cottage, dark thoughts twisted her stomach into knots. At last, Jack led her onto the back porch, ending the tour and her self-flagellating thoughts. No matter what lie ahead, she would make the best of her situation. She would do what she must to make a better life for her son, even if that meant facing Jack's anger and telling him the truth about her son's conception.

Would knowing she had acted the wanton and seduced Lord Drury make a difference in how Jack treated Will?

He toed a rotten plank with his boot. "The war in America kept us away too long this time. We should have come back to Seile the moment we learned of Mr. Higgins' death."

Was that his only regret?

A bone-deep need filled her. She wanted to know more about the man she had married. Before she confided the truth about her relationship with Lord Drury, she needed to know if Jack was the sort of man who could forgive. She looked at her husband, resolute in her desire to understand him better. "During any of your trips to England, did you ever visit your father?"

She bit her lip, bracing herself for his anger. The pain in his eyes caught her by surprise.

"Once. A year ago. He refused to see me." He turned to pull the door closed.

Abby stood beside him on the porch, an ache in her

chest. Once again, the wall he had built around his emotions was firmly in place. She could no longer read his expression, and he no longer looked like a lost, hurt boy. He looked like an invincible sea captain who could weather any storm—alone. He looked like a man who expected loyalty from his crew—a man who would not tolerate deception or cowardice.

And she was both a liar and a coward.

They walked away from the cottage in silence and turned left, heading toward the heart of the village. Dark thoughts waned as Abby walked beside her husband down the sandy lane. There were no cobbled streets, no vendors hawking their wares. In fact, it was difficult to tell the businesses from the homes as each building had a rustic charm that infused her with a renewed appreciation for the simplicity of life.

She had grown up in the city and save for her brief stay at the Sisters of Mercy and her time aboard the *Lion's Pride*, she had never lived anywhere else. Yet, something about Seile called to her.

What would it be like to live in harmony with the sea? What would it be like to live, love, and work in a place where the ebb and flow of the ocean tide set a constant and abiding pace? Those who called Seile home heard the background whisper of the pounding, never ending rhythm of the surf every day. It was a reminder of the constancy of life—the ever changing, never ending promise that no matter what, life would go on.

No wonder Jack loved it here. It was nothing like London. Did it remind him of South Carolina? Did it make him homesick for his adoptive country? "What a beautiful village. And so peaceful."

A smile chased the shadows from his eyes. "I have always thought so. I guess that is why I liked spending time here as a child."

"Perhaps it was not just the village but also the company that drew you to Seile."

"Perhaps. Uncle William has always been like a father to me."

She smiled, thinking of her father back in London. She missed his love and support. Jack had never known that kind of love from the man who had sired him. Had his uncle been an adequate substitute? Would Jack know how to be a decent father to her son?

He took her arm, leading her through the small seaside village. On every corner, people stopped Jack to welcome him back to Seile, and he introduced her as if proud to call her his viscountess. But she was a coward, unable to face the truth. Lord Drury was right. She was unworthy.

****

Abby had just put Will down when Jack entered the day room. Mr. Crenshaw followed, carrying a tray with their supper. "Dinner be served."

He nodded to his captain and left. Abby closed the bedroom door and crossed the floor to join Jack at the table. He pulled out her chair, and as he leaned forward, his warm breath fanned her neck, sending a warm shiver down her spine.

"Thank you," she said, her voice raspy. She felt as if he had touched her, but his strong hand curved around the back of the chair inches away from her shoulder. She released her breath on a shiver and raised her eyes from his strong tanned knuckles to his intense gaze. She could hear her pulse beating in her ears, feel it in her neck.

Jack uncurled his fingers and straightened. His dark gaze shone with some emotion she could not identify. He continued to stare as he made his way around the table and took his seat. "Tomorrow I must return to Ridge Point," he said after a brief moment of silence.

She waited before responding, wanting to feel confident enough to control the nervous quiver in her voice. Then she raised her eyes as high as his strong chin. "Have you heard from your solicitor?"

"No, but I do not wish to leave Aunt Margery and Cousin Morris in control of Ridge Point any longer. The estate is mine whether they like it or not, and I intend to see that it is properly managed."

Could she convince Jack to take her and Will with him this time? She had no desire to be left alone aboard ship again, but could she risk being seen by anyone she knew in London?

She forced herself to speak calmly, despite the pounding of her heart. "Is Ridge Point near London?"

"It's near Cambridge. The Great Ouse flows out into the wash near Seile linking the River Cam with Ridge Point land northeast of London. Whenever my family stayed at Ridge Point, I would sail a little boat Uncle William made me downriver to Seile." The memory made him smile, his eyes crinkling at the corners as he held Abby spellbound, making her forget her worries. She smiled back, her heart suddenly lighter.

Perhaps Will would be adventurous like Jack, the influence of his "father" being more powerful than any negative qualities he might have inherited from Lord

Drury. According to the English philosopher, John Locke, "There is no such thing as innate ideas; there is no such thing as moral precepts; we are born with an empty mind, with a soft tablet ready to be writ upon by experimental impressions."

She just hoped Jack would impress moral ideas upon her son and be the chalk to his tablet. Although she wanted Will to be brave and adventurous like Jack, she could not imagine letting her son sail alone before he was out of short pants. "How old were you when you first set sail alone?"

Jack shrugged. "Nine. Ten."

Her fork slipped from her hand and clattered onto her plate. What kind of mother would turn her son loose on a river at such a tender age? "But you were just a boy!"

"A boy who loved adventure." He smiled as if all boys set out on their own at such a young age.

Some parents sent their sons to the Academy at Leeds in York before they were twelve, but a boy of ten was too young to sail alone. She folded her arms under her breasts, appalled that his parents had been so thoughtless. "I should think a viscount would have more care for his son's safety."

The smile slipped from Jack's face. He set his fork aside and leaned forward, carefully and deliberately, as if controlling his motions would give him some control over the anger evident in the harsh lines of his face. "My father was not at all sure I was his son," he said, his words as measured as his movements. "You see, my father had dark hair and wasn't nearly as tall as Uncle William. And by the time I was ten, I was big and broad-shouldered with sun-bleached hair."

Shock and sympathy lanced her. Jack was just like Will. Both were legal heirs by birth to a viscountcy, but neither was truly his father's son.

Was that another reason he could not look at Will? Did seeing him bring back memories too painful to bear in addition to the thought that another man's offspring would someday inherit the title?

She swallowed the sorrow clogging her throat. "You have more in common with my son than I realized."

Jack snorted, his lip curling into a fierce snarl. "You misunderstand. Despite my father's denials, I was his flesh and blood son, and I have the birthmark to prove it."

He stood so quickly the dishes rattled, and Abby jumped. Then he tore open his white shirt, revealing a wide chest rippling with muscle and sprinkled with fine, golden hair.

Abby gasped, all too aware of him standing over her, alone in that small private space.

"What are you doing?" she whispered, her voice raspy with unwanted desire. Her cheeks flushed hotly, but her husband did not gloat. He turned and slipped the shirt from his right shoulder, revealing a purple crescent-shaped mark on his back.

Abby's fingers itched to touch his skin and trace the lines of his birthmark. She clinched her fingers in her lap and swallowed.

"My father bore this same mark on his back," Jack said in a harsh tone barely shy of a growl. "It is proof I am his son—proof he denied despite the fact my uncle bears no such mark."

Heat stung Abby's cheeks, but she could not tear

her eyes away from that perfectly sculpted body as hard and chiseled as marble. Would it feel just as cold? Or warm beneath her trembling touch?

She swallowed again and lowered her chin, ignoring the flutter in her chest and the fire in her belly. A similar birthmark was not proof the former viscount was Jack's father. If it were indeed an inherited birthmark, Jack could just as easily have inherited it from his uncle, despite the absence of a similar mark on William Norton's skin. The same blood flowed through both brothers' veins.

Abby did not have the heart to point out such logic. She lowered her gaze, trying to ignore the heat rising in her cheeks. "So, you believe your mother was innocent."

He pulled his shirt together and buttoned it, leaving the tails trailing over the waistband of his trousers. Then he sat back down, a faraway look in his eyes.

"My mother was in love with Uncle William, but my father was very competitive. He wanted my mother for himself, and her father wanted her to marry the viscount. Being an obedient daughter, she married my father and became an obedient wife. But Aunt Margery hated her. My mother was beautiful and all the servants loved her. Even my father loved her. Or so I was told."

He smiled, but a deep sadness shadowed his eyes. "I suppose things were good when I was first born, but then the sun lightened my hair, and I grew taller than Cousin Morris who was three years older. Aunt Marjory was the first to point out my resemblance to her younger brother, and it did not take much to convince my father that I was Uncle William's son."

Jack was nothing like Lord Drury, but she had

allowed her fears and prejudices toward nobles to cloud her judgment. Jack had not lived a privileged life of excess and decadence. He had been too young when his father sent him and his mother away.

"Do you remember your father treating you differently?"

He shrugged his wide shoulders and picked up his fork. He pushed food around on his plate, fastening his eyes on a point just beyond her left shoulder. "For as long as I can remember, Morris called me Lord Bastard or the bastard heir. By the time I was ten, my father believed the lies, so I don't remember a time when I was treated well by anyone other than my Uncle William."

"What about your mother?" Surely, no woman would punish her own child for his father's beliefs.

Again, he shrugged those massive shoulders, which no longer looked as if they could carry the weight of the world on them. They sagged just a bit, looking as if they needed support. Abby ached to slide under his arm and be the comfort he needed, but she did not dare, not before she had a chance to be as honest with him as he was being with her.

He leaned back in his chair, staring up at the skylight and darkening sky overhead. The ship gently rocked on the current, ropes and wood creaking to the rhythmic soughing. He sighed deeply and then lowered his chin, meeting her gaze. "I don't think she meant to blame me, but she did, especially after my father banished us to America. She was bitter for many years after that, but eventually, she embraced her new life. By then, I do not think she would have returned home if he begged her. I am just thankful she never learned of that damn codicil."

The former viscount had been a cruel man undeserving of his son's love, and Abby was glad she had played some part in helping Jack regain what was rightfully his. "My mother used to say that everything works out the way it is meant to."

Jack's dark eyes turned as black as coal. "Perhaps, but now, Morris is living at Ridge Point, thinking he can somehow wrest it from my grasp."

"But you are married, and you have your heir."

"Ironically enough, when the solicitor said I could not inherit Ridge Point unless I produced an heir before my thirty-fifth birthday, I asked if my wife had to be delivered of the child. So, it was easier than I thought to convince Morris I had met you on a previous trip and was planning to marry you *before* the reading of my father's will. Whether it matters from a legal standpoint or not, I wanted Morris to believe your son is mine. That is why he is now claiming I am an impostor."

Abby tried not to flinch at his refusal to call her son by name. Instead, she pointed out the obvious. "But two earls vouched for you before you were called to Lords. And you met the terms of your father's will when *our* son was born."

She watched his face to see how he reacted to her calling Will "their" child. He did not react at all.

"I'm sure Morris and my aunt would like nothing better than to stir up old rumors and create new scandal, but it doesn't matter. Your son is my legal heir, and I want everyone to believe he is my child by birth."

Her heart ached with disappointment over his unwillingness to mention Will by name, but his efforts to protect Will's paternity warmed her soul. "Lord

Drury might guess at the truth," she said, though it pained her to mention Simon's name.

"I will handle Drury, *if* and when the time comes."

"So, how long will it take before Ridge Point is truly yours?" How long would she be stuck on this constantly rocking ship?

"I'm not sure. Morris is not a peer, but his grandfather—our grandfather—was viscount before my father. So, he is not without influence." He sighed. "I fear his case will be heard in Parliament, and it will take much longer than I had hoped to reclaim my inheritance."

Her heart dropped. She was not a prisoner aboard his ship, but that was exactly what she felt like when Jack left the next day to go to Ridge Point without her.

Chapter Seventeen

For nearly a week, the only person Abby saw besides her son was Mr. Crenshaw. He brought her meals three times a day and spoke very little. She never saw him when she ventured topside to stare out over the rail, and she was not allowed to leave the ship without an escort. Jack had forbidden it.

With a sigh, she laid her son down in the basket that still served as his crib and left the room, closing the door behind her to keep Jack's beast of a cat out. Then she went topside for her daily walk around the deck. When she reached the rail, she saw Uncle William directing two strong men carrying a wooden object up the gangplank.

She stepped closer, pleasure flushing her cheeks when they lowered a cradle to the deck. Uncle William smiled. "Jack wanted you to have it."

Emotion knotted her throat as she knelt down to trace the carved headboard with her fingers. In the center of a crowned shield, a lion stood on its hind legs, pawing the air.

"It's the Norton coat of arms," Uncle William said with pride.

She looked skyward, holding her hand to her forehead to shield her eyes from the bright September sun. The crest on the cradle matched the green flag fluttering overhead. The pawing gold lion she had mistaken for a privateer flag was representative of Jack's family crest. Despite his banishment to America, Jack had chosen to fly the Norton coat of arms rather than the flag of his birth or adoptive country.

Was it pride in the Norton name? Or had Jack hoped to one day regain his father's favor?

"It's beautiful," she whispered past the lump in her throat.

"It has been in the family over a century," Uncle William said before telling the deckhands to carry the crib down to the captain's quarters.

Abby rose to her feet and followed them down to the cabin. Once the men had placed the cradle next to the bed, they left. Abby transferred her son from the basket to the bed and smiled when he remained asleep. Then she turned to Uncle William. "Thank you."

"Thank your husband," he said. "It was his idea to send me to Ram's Head to retrieve it from the attic where it was gathering dust."

Her husband was both generous and kind. "I am most grateful for the care and consideration he has shown my son."

"Did you expect any less?" Mr. Norton looked down at Will. "Jack is a good man, and despite his parent's disastrous relationship, he is not opposed to marriage. His friend, the Earl of Gilchrest, has the sort of marriage Jack always envied—the sort he wanted for himself one day." He raised his chin and narrowed his gaze, as if giving Abby fair warning. "This marriage may not be a love match, but that does not mean the two of you cannot be happy. Give Jack a chance."

She wanted nothing more than to find a common bond with her husband, but the specter of Lord Drury hung over her, suffocating her. The feel of him pushing into her and the foul words he spewed in her ear had etched her very soul, tainting her body as well as her heart. Could she get beyond the nightmare? Could she give Jack the chance he deserved? She swallowed her fears and nodded. "The chance is his. He has but to take it."

****

Draped urns, mural tablets, and engraved obelisks adorned the black shrouded funeral monument shop on the corner of Regent and Air Streets. The clerk raised a brow at Jack's lack of mourning attire as he and Quentin entered the macabre shop, but Jack explained that his mother had died six months prior.

Once Mr. Alder dispensed with the appropriate amount of condolences, Jack ordered a simple marker for his mother's grave—a laurel wreath engraved above her name, date of birth, and date of death. Below that, he requested an epitaph that would surely make his father turn over in his grave. Jack was no longer sure if his mother had been "A faithful wife until the end," but he had been unable to resist the parting shot aimed at his bastard of a father.

He did not know what Aunt Margery had engraved on his father's marker. The former viscount was buried in the family plot at Ram's Head, and Jack had yet to visit his grave, even though the estate was his. And now that the crown had recognized his marriage and son, Ridge Point was his too. His aunt and Morris had two weeks to gather their personal belongings and vacate the premises.

Jack wished he could have seen their faces when the solicitor delivered the news, but he would see them soon enough. He intended to visit before the deadline, dressed in clothing befitting his officially recognized title. Even without his father's inheritance, Jack could afford new clothes, but he and Abby both needed an entire wardrobe.

Dresses from Seile were cheaper than from a fashionable dressmaker in London, but Abby was a viscountess, and he wanted her dressed in a manner befitting her title when she met his relatives. He cleared his throat and looked at Quentin as they stepped outside the monument shop. "If I am going to give up my ship to be a viscount, I'll need a proper wardrobe."

Quentin smiled. "Will you sell me the *Lion's Pride*?"

"No. I'll lease her, but only if you help me dress the part of a peer."

"I think I can manage my end of the bargain," Quentin said as they crossed the street to Jack's rented coach. "But dressing you like a peer will be like trying to make a silk purse from a sow's ear."

Jack scowled, tugging at his ill-fitting frock coat. "Do try to contain your wit, Quentin. Gilchrest claimed you could procure icebergs in the desert. I only need a new wardrobe. Can you perform that simple task or not?"

"Of course," Quentin said with a smooth smile. "I shall take you to my tailor and haberdasher while we are here in town."

"Abby will need new clothes, too. I do not want to introduce her to society dressed in clothes from a country dressmaker or an East End sweatshop. She is a viscountess. She should dress the part, don't you think?"

"My sisters-in-law travel to Paris before the season begins to purchase their finery from the only prestigious dressmaker that matters, Madison-Worth," Quentin said with a disdainful air. "But there is a draper shop here in London that sells partially made clothes, and a good seamstress can stitch them into fashionable designs that will appear custom fitted. Chelsea's wife uses Madam Weston when she cannot get to France."

"Then it will have to do. The wardrobe Mrs. Gabb created fits, but it isn't fitting for my wife's new station in life." And he could not wait to see the look on Abby's face when she saw all the beautiful new clothes he planned to buy her. "I have her measurements."

"Do you now?" Quentin said with a smirk. "It won't be the same as having her fitted, but I believe Madam Weston is up to the challenge."

Jack scowled. "For a privateer, you are quite the dandy, are you not?"

"What can I say?" Quentin responded with a laugh. "I am the son of an earl."

****

Several grueling hours later, the tailor had measured Jack for an entire wardrobe. Then he and Quentin went to Madam Weston's shop. If she was going to sew Abby's wardrobe, then she should be the one to go to the drapery shop and pick out the material. Madam Weston agreed. After another hour spent listening to her yammer on about fabrics and trim, she suggested he purchase jewels to match his wife's new wardrobe.

"Castellani is the best jeweler in London. He's located at 115 Piccadilly. And there is another good jeweler on Patton Street."

"Yes. Thank you." Jack rushed Quentin out the door. Never in his wildest dreams had he thought to spend so much time listening to a woman prattle on about fashion. It quite numbed his brain.

"I think I would rather shoot myself in the foot than go through that again," he grumbled as he and Quentin climbed back inside the rented coach. Once he reclaimed Ridge Point, he would use his father's shiny black coach with the enameled family crest on the door.

Quentin climbed in behind him, and the coach jerked forward before he could take his seat. He nearly tumbled onto the floor. "Before this day is out, I am going to thoroughly throttle that driver."

Jack's rumbling laughter filled the coach as they headed toward Piccadilly. As the two settled in, Jack said, "We will try the Italian fellow's shop first. If I don't see anything Abby will like there, we can try the place on Patton. Are you familiar with either establishment?"

"No," Quentin said with a sigh as he turned to stare out the window. "The ring I gave Ernestine belonged to my grandmother. She died before I ever had an opportunity to buy jewelry for her."

Pity and a touch of fear put a hitch in Jack's pulse. He didn't love Abby or her son the way Quentin had loved his wife and child, but he did not think he could survive losing them either. He leaned forward, elbows on knees. "I'm sorry."

"Stop!"

Jack straightened with a jerk. Quentin despised pity of any kind, but the furious demand was unexpected. If an apology was in order, he had no idea how he might give it. Sentiment of any kind made him uncomfortable.

"I—"

"Driver, stop the coach!" Quentin banged on the back wall. Harnesses rattled as the driver pulled on the reins, bringing the carriage to a sudden stop.

Surely, Quentin wasn't going to leap out of the carriage like a deflowered maiden bent on escape. "What the hell?"

"The jeweler." Quentin pushed open the door. "Look at the name on the window."

Jack stuck his head out the opened door to see what Quentin was rambling on about so incoherently. The name on the window drew his attention. *Halsey's.*

He nearly tumbled out the coach and onto the street. "Abby's father is the jeweler on Patton Street."

Heart pounding in his chest, he climbed down and walked toward the shop. A bell overhead tinkled, the tinny sound sending a chill down his spine as he stepped inside. He waited a heartbeat and glanced over his shoulder at his friend. "Wait in the carriage."

Quentin nodded, and Jack wanted to breathe a sigh of relief, but the air caught in his lungs when a man in his mid-fifties entered from a backroom. The leather curtain that divided the sweltering hot work area from the rest of the store slid closed, but the heat had already escaped. The man untied his leather apron and laid it on the counter. Despite temperatures just south of hell, he reached for a charcoal gray waistcoat and slipped his arms into the sleeves before removing a handkerchief from an inside pocket to mop the sweat from his brow.

"Welcome to Halsey's. How may I help you?" He slipped the handkerchief back into his pocket and brushed back his sweat-dampened hair.

Was he the shop owner? An apprentice? "Who are

you?"

The man held out his arms to encompass the array of glass cases that held sparkling gems set in rich golds and shining silver. "I am the owner. I design and sell the finest jewelry in London. You'll find no wax molded pieces here."

Jack didn't doubt it. The jewelry looked like the expensive type only the wealthiest patrons could afford. So, why had he abandoned his daughter at an Anglican convent? He obviously had plenty of money. Then again, maybe he wasn't Abby's father. There could be any number of Halseys living in London. "What is your name?"

The man's graying brows rose. "Halsey. Henry Halsey. My name is on the door."

Acid burned in Jack's gut. This man was Abby's father, but he was more than just a working class merchant. He was a man of obvious wealth and influence. So, why had Abby kept his identity a secret? Was she ashamed because he wasn't a peer? Or did she think Jack cared about such things?

Frustration bunched his shoulders. "And your daughter? What might her name be?"

Halsey came around the counter. Color leached from his face, and fear shone in his eyes. "What do you know of Abby? Please. If you know where she is, you must tell me."

Damn Abby's secrets! They put him at a severe disadvantage, but he wasn't about to introduce himself to her father until he had more facts. "When was the last time you heard from her?"

Fear still shown in Halsey's eyes, but a vein now throbbed in his forehead. "Did Mr. Flanagan send you?

Are you one of his inquiry agents?"

Jack's nails bit into his palms. Abby claimed to have written two letters to her father. The first letter supposedly outlined her plans to move to Shrivenham and pose as a widow. Then after the wedding, she had given the nun a second letter. Yet, her father did not seem to know what had become of his daughter.

Had Abby lied? Or did she still believe she needed to protect her father from Jack?

For all Halsey knew, someone had abducted her. Was that why he had hired an inquiry agent? Jack would have done the same thing. No, he would have looked for her himself. And he would have found her by now. Why hadn't Halsey?

He narrowed his gaze. "Have you heard from your daughter since she left the convent?"

"Left? She did not leave. There were letters. And then...You don't understand," Halsey said with a note of urgency. "She would not have left on her own. Viscount Ruston had made an offer. But when I went to bring her home so we could finalize the details of the marriage contract, she was gone. The reverend mother said she had run away."

Jack clenched his jaw. Had Abby lied about the letters? She had lied about having a betrothed. But even if there were no letters, Sister Mary Daphne knew what had happened to Abby. So, why had she not informed the reverend mother? Unless, the nun never returned to the convent.

Suspicion clawed at Jack's brain. He had given Sister Mary Daphne money to repay her brother for the loss of his horses and to buy a new wagon wheel. He had also made a sizable contribution to her unwed mother's charity. The nun accepted the payment and the donation. Had she kept the money for herself rather than returning to the convent?

"Did you speak with Sister Mary Daphne?"

Halsey blinked. "Who?"

"One of the nuns. She knew your daughter." The nun with the glacial stare had not seemed warm-hearted, but Jack would not have suspected her of not being true to her calling. Had she absconded with the money? Or, had something happened to her?

"The reverend mother did not mention a nun by that name, and she seemed most upset by Abby's disappearance, but I will never believe my daughter ran away. She has always been an obedient child."

Abby? Obedient? Jack did not point out that his daughter had allowed at least one man to take certain liberties that had left her in a most compromising position. Instead, he said, "Obedience is not what landed her in a convent filled with nuns."

Halsey's eyes flashed with anger. "Drury is a rake and a scoundrel. He took advantage of Abby's naïvety, knowing I would never challenge him."

Jack clenched his fists at his sides. "Why not? Does prestige mean more to you than your daughter?"

"No, damn you! Because I am not a peer. Once upon a time, a middling sort like myself was below the aristocracy, but I became as wealthy as any earl. Still, my Abby was not accepted. Not until Lady Chivington agreed to sponsor her." Bitterness tinged Halsey's words. He seemed to resent the aristocracy while courting their acceptance.

Had that bitterness turned to outrage when Abby failed to land a titled husband?

"And Abby disappointed you," Jack said, unable to disguise the contempt he felt. Abby wasn't a peer, and her father had thrown her to the wolves in an attempt to forge societal connections to the aristocracy.

Halsey reeled as if slapped. "Disappointed? Abby did nothing wrong. It was Drury. But I could not denounce him without exposing Abby."

"So, you sent her away?" No wonder Abby did not trust men. Drury had abused her, and her father had abandoned her.

"No!" Halsey wrung his hands. "I sent her to the Sisters of Mercy until I could find a family to take her child or a suitable husband, and now, she is gone."

He seemed genuinely concerned for his daughter, but perhaps he was upset over his failure to link his family to Ruston's through marriage. Society had changed since Jack had lived in England. Middle class landowners, merchants, and entrepreneurs had acquired larger sums of money, and prominent members of the aristocracy had brought them into the social fold.

Common gentlemen of means could marry the daughters of peers if they could afford to replace the family's dwindling coffers. And if sponsored by a member of the peerage, the daughter of a rich merchant, landowner, physician, or lawyer could be presented at court in the hopes of making a good match—provided an adequate dowry was offered.

Had Abby left the convent with Sister Mary Daphne to escape marriage to Ruston? Or her father's wrath? "Did your daughter know Lord Ruston?"

Halsey swiped at his eyes and glared. "What does that have to do with her disappearance? If you know something, you had best tell me."

Jack hesitated. Halsey took a step forward and pulled a small pistol from beneath his frock coat. "Tell me what you know of my daughter or by God, I will blow you to hell and back."

A muscle jumped in Jack's jaw. He disliked being threatened. But Halsey did not know his daughter was married or that Jack was her husband. And Jack did not know if Abby was afraid of her father or if she had lied to protect him. "Put that thing away. I am not here to extort money or otherwise threaten you or your daughter."

"Then why are you here?" Halsey steadied his aim. "Who are you?"

Jack sighed, wishing that for once, he had Quentin's patience. Maybe then, he could formulate a plausible explanation. Instead, he blurted out a partial truth. "I am Captain Jack Norton, and I have come to tell you your daughter has married a viscount and will be contacting you shortly."

The color leached from Halsey's cheeks. He lowered his arm, the small gun dangling by his side. Jack pried it loose from his fingers and placed it on the counter out of reach.

"Who?" Halsey's voice trembled. "When?" He raised his chin, his eyes feverish with fear. "The child?"

"She had a son. They are both safe. But..." Damn if he had not drifted into a cove with no way out.

"Where is she?" Halsey demanded.

Sailing through the treacherous shoals created by his lies was not easy, but he would manage—not as well as Quentin with his smooth tongue—but he would manage. He did not have a choice. He could not let Halsey know who he was until he talked to Abby. After all, Halsey had sent her away. Might he also have bargained with the devil so Ruston would take her off his hands?

Jack cleared his throat and stretched to his full, lofty height. "At the moment, she is on my ship, waiting for her husband to claim his inheritance."

"I am her father! I do not care if she married the Duke of Wellington. She is my daughter, and I will not be kept from her." Halsey reached for his gun. Jack grabbed his arm.

"He is not keeping you from her. He is trying to protect her reputation."

"That is my job!" Halsey said with a quiver in his voice.

"It is now her husband's job." He let go of Halsey's arm. "Now, besides the inquiry agent and nuns, who else knows your daughter is missing?"

"No one." Halsey shook his head. "Her society friends believe she is visiting relatives in Yorkshire. I spread the tail in case I was unable to procure a husband willing to keep her secret."

"And Ruston?"

Halsey's shoulders slumped. "Is getting impatient."

A stiff smile stretched Jack's mouth. "Tell Ruston the deal is off. Tell him Abby married the father of her child and has taken a wedding trip."

Owlish eyes blinked. "But Drury—"

"Will never know the child is his."

Chapter Eighteen

Abby sighed. Jack had been gone for over a month. If he stayed away much longer, Will would be grown. Already, he was cooing and making the cutest little sounds. He was three months old and had recently discovered his hands and feet. Then yesterday, he rolled from his back to his stomach. And Jack was missing it. Not that he would care. Will was not his "real" son.

With another sigh, Abby closed and locked the day room door. Then she went into the bedroom and pulled a box out from underneath the bed. Some of the jewelry in the chest Jack had given her was broken, and while shopping with Uncle William in Seile, she had managed to ask Mrs. Gabb to find her some wire snips, tweezers and other small tools she would need to repair some of the pieces.

"I want to surprise my husband," she had said to the woman whose name implied a great deal about her. Mrs. Gabb did indeed like to gab about the village inhabitants. "He broke a lovely stick pin that belonged to his grandfather, and I would like to try repairing it myself."

Mrs. Gabb had smiled, swearing to keep Abby's secret, and had somehow found the tools Abby needed. Now, every morning after breakfast and before taking her walk around the deck, Abby pulled out the jewelry box and her tools. What started out as a simple repair turned into a great deal more when she discovered a broken brooch peppered with sky blue turquoise from Turkey. The small stones were exquisite. The bulky, misshapen brooch was not. But without a solder, she could only re-cut and re-bend the silver filament wire into a more desirable shape. And the piece was shaping up nicely. So nicely, in fact, it made her homesick.

She missed sitting in her studio at home designing unique, one of a kind pieces for her father. And she missed hiding in the back room of his shop, working at the jeweler's bench, putting the finishing touches on her beautiful designs. The back of his shop was always stifling hot from the smelting furnace, but she loved apprenticing under her father. There was something so incredibly rewarding about manipulating molten gold or silver in her hands and seeing her designs come to life.

It was certainly more rewarding than being a viscountess. But not more rewarding than being a mother.

She glanced at the cradle beside the bed and smiled. Love for her son filled her with hope. She may never have a chance to design jewelry again, but she had Will. If only she could see her father and introduce him to his grandson. But Jack had abandoned her.

Since their marriage, he had spent more time away from her than with her, so she had little opportunity to get to know him. But there had been moments when she had glimpsed someone she liked and respected. Then there was that odd, fluttering sensation she got in the pit of her stomach whenever he touched her, no matter how accidentally. And his eyes. What was it about those lion eyes that drew her attention so? She wanted to trust and confide in him, but she was still afraid.

Tension knotted her shoulders as she bent over the desk and threaded another turquoise bead onto a wire filament. Using the tiny tweezers, she twisted the end of the wire and picked up another bead. With a steady hand, she prepared to thread it onto the silver wire when she heard a metallic click.

She jumped, dropping the bead. It hit the desk and rolled to the floor.

Heart pounding in her chest, she turned. Someone was unlocking the door to the day room. She jumped to her feet, scrambling to gather her supplies and hide them in the jewelry chest. The brooch she had been working on fell to the floor. The day room door opened and closed. Heavy footsteps crossed the floor, and a tall figure filled the bedroom door.

"Jack!"

****

Abby stood, clutching a wooden box to her chest. Loose tendrils of blonde hair escaped the snood at the nape of her neck and brushed her shoulders. Her blue eyes widened, and her cheeks flushed. Jack could only stare.

She had lost weight while he was away. Her stomach was flat, and her breasts were high and firm behind the wooden box. Even with the startled expression on her face, she looked beautiful.

He swallowed to coat his suddenly dry throat. "I did not mean to startle you. When I found the door locked, I assumed you had gone out with Uncle William."

"You could have knocked," she said, a slight tremor in her voice.

"As I said, I assumed you were out." He strode

forward and bent to retrieve the brooch she had dropped. He turned it over in his hands as he rose, examining the loosened silver wires sticking out at odd angles. Had he just caught her destroying the jewelry he had given her? Or had he just discovered a new facet to his wife's personality?

"It was broken," she stammered. "I was trying to fix it."

He smiled, enjoying the flush that spread from her cheeks to her chest. "Were you, now?"

Her gaze slid to the floor. "It did not seem that complicated a task. Anyone can thread beads onto a silver wire."

He had imagined broaching the subject of her father a bit more delicately, but this was as good a way as any. In fact, catching her by surprise could prove most beneficial. Abby's facial expressions were much easier to read when he kept her off-balance.

A smile teased his mouth, despite his best efforts to hide it. "Especially someone whose father is a jeweler."

Her chin snapped upward, and her eyes widened. "What?"

"I met your father." Brushing past her, he laid the brooch on the desk. Then he took Abby's arm and guided her back to the chair. He eased her down onto the seat and turned to sit on the edge of the bed when he noticed the cradle. He stepped closer and looked down at his heir. A smile touched his face and slithered into his heart. "He has grown."

"Babies tend to do that," she snipped.

He turned to his wife. The guilty flush remained, but her eyes flashed with angry defiance. Abby still did not trust him.

Raking a hand through his hair, he walked to the end of the bed and sat down. Fear flashed in her eyes, but she held his gaze, looking almost rebellious.

He sighed and his shoulders slumped. The time for secrets was long past. Abby was his wife, and he would hear the truth and her reasons for keeping it from him. "Why didn't you tell me your father was a famous jeweler in London?"

Color leached from her cheeks. "So you could keep Will and me hidden until you extorted money from him in exchange for our location? I think not."

Had she honestly believed him to be so unscrupulous? Anger and regret twisted his stomach into a hard knot. He had kept secrets, too, trusting her no more than she had trusted him. He had married her for one reason only, but now that he had what he wanted, he wanted more. Was it even possible? Drury and possibly even her own father had misused her. Gaining her trust would be nearly impossible. Yet, what kind of life would they have together if he failed?

"I don't need your father's money, Abby. I am quite wealthy in my own right."

"Only because you married me and got your precious heir," she said, her voice rising in volume.

"I made my fortune as a privateer. I do not need money from either of our fathers," he growled, and the baby whimpered.

He stood, turning toward the cradle. Abby rushed past him, snatching the child up from his bed, and holding him to her chest as if protecting him from a raging lion.

"Don't touch him!" Her body quivered, and he could almost smell her fear.

During the war, he had grown used to seeing fear in a woman's eyes. Whenever his crew had overtaken a ship with women on board, they had looked at him as if he were Black Beard or some other notorious pirate intent on raping and pillaging. He had never counted women as spoils of war and had forbidden his crew to touch them. Yet their fear had not shredded his heart the way Abby's did.

"You have nothing to fear from me, Abby. I do not need your father's money, and I cannot imagine why you did not tell me the truth. Is your father a greedy man? Are you afraid of him?"

She blinked her big blue eyes. "Certainly not."

"Then who, Abby?" He stepped closer and touched her cheek. She flinched. The baby whimpered. "Who hurt you and made you so mistrustful?"

"Why should I trust you?" She took a step back. "You are a privateer, little better than a pirate."

"I'm a merchant sea captain who used my ship to aid America and Britain during times of war. I did not plunder purely for profit, but I was good at it. I make no excuses for that. But I would never harm you or your child. It pains me that you would think otherwise." It more than pained him. It broke his heart.

He did not expect to have the kind of marriage Gilchrest and his wife shared. That kind of love was hard for Jack to fathom. But he had never wanted a marriage like his parents' either. He did not want to live separately from Abby. He wanted a family. The kind of family he had never had.

Abby flushed but held his gaze. "You have given me no reason to trust you. You have hardly been here at all."

She patted the baby's bottom, soothing his whimpers. Jack's heart twisted in his chest. In his efforts to protect his wife and her reputation, he had widened the gulf between them. "I had little choice. I needed to secure my inheritance without exposing you to scandal."

Her eyes widened for a fraction of a second before she schooled her expression. "And I needed to protect my father. You went to great lengths to secure your inheritance, and I had no idea how much further you would go to gain wealth and power."

She was right, of course. He had given her his name, but he had not given her a single reason to trust him. He had been more concerned with finding out about her past than in getting to know her or allowing her to get to know him. And after meeting her father, he suspected there was more to her relationship with Drury than even he had guessed. "Is that what Drury did? Did he use you to get to your father's money?"

"No." She expelled a frustrated breath. "Drury was already engaged to a duke's daughter. He did not need my father's money."

The damn bastard was a rake and a scoundrel, a heartless womanizer who preyed on the innocent. Blood roared in Jack's ears. His rage was a beast he wanted to unleash, but the fear blossoming in Abby's eyes tempered his fury. Exhaling slowly, he forced himself to speak softly. "But you did not know he was engaged. Did you, Abby?"

The softening of her features made Jack's heart pound against his ribs. She ducked her chin. "No. I thought he loved me. He was so full of compliments. So very gallant."

177

"And you believed his lies."

She nodded, avoiding his gaze. "He seemed sincere, and he was very respectful."

"I'm sure he was—in public." If Jack ever got his hands on the bastard, he would beat him to within an inch of his life. He forced down the fury and tried to rein in his temper.

Abby nodded but kept her eyes lowered. Jack wanted to pull her into his arms and hold her. Instead, he sat on the edge of the bed and patted the mattress. She raised her chin and visibly swallowed, the wary expression in her eyes twisting his gut into tighter knots. Then she took a shuddering breath and bravely came forward to sit beside him, leaving at least a foot of mattress between them.

"Tell me what happened, Abby. Tell me how you ended up at the Sisters of Mercy."

She swallowed hard, staring down at the child she held in her arms. At first, he did not think she would answer. Then, she took a quivery breath and spoke in a voice devoid of emotion. "My father was richer than many nobles. He made friends, but he still was not on the same social standing until the Duke of Chivington commissioned him to craft a pendant for his daughter's presentation at court."

She turned her blue gaze on him, and his heart lodged in his throat. "I designed a gorgeous piece with opals the same shade of lavender-blue as Lady Edwina's eyes, but no one ever knew it was not my father's design. The duke was so impressed that he invited my father and me to a spring ball at his country estate the following week."

Her hard gaze dared and challenged. Yet, he did

not miss the flash of vulnerability. She had hidden her talents from society, afraid of being more of an outcast than her lack of peerage already guaranteed. Times had changed, but society still held to the same, old-fashioned rules of conduct that separated commoners from nobles. So, no matter how much wealth Halsey amassed, some in society would never truly accept him as an equal. Nor would they accept his daughter, unless she married above her station. Even then, some might still consider her an outcast.

"Did Drury know of your talents with jewelry?" Envy burned a hole in Jack's gut. Had she shared confidences with Drury that she had never shared with anyone else?

Fury briefly ignited her gaze, and bitterness crept into her voice. "I may have been invited to share in the pleasures of good society, but I did not make the mistake of believing anyone would accept me if they knew I practiced a trade myself. I wanted to be a part of their world, and I wanted to find a husband, but I did nothing unethical. I just wanted to be accepted among the people I considered friends."

"Maybe you should have sought better friends," he said, unable to disguise the disgust in his voice. All his life, he had felt like an outcast. He may have been born to wealth and privilege, but he had never felt like a peer. Aunt Margery and Morris had seen to it. But how much worse must it have been for Abby to have wanted something so badly, knowing she would most likely never get it?

Her heart-felt sigh twisted his stomach into knots. "Perhaps. But I liked Edwina and most of her friends."

"But there were conditions to those friendships,

were there not?" He remembered the rules. And he detested them. "The worst beating I ever got was when I made friends with a boy in Seile. The son of a fisherman had not been an acceptable playmate for a future viscount, and my father made sure Todd Tidwell never spoke to me again."

She tilted her head at an adorable angle, and her voice softened. "I never considered how difficult it might be for someone of your class to befriend a commoner."

"Ah, but money and goods are the best of references," he said, quoting Dickens. "Your friendship with Edwina benefited both families. Todd's family had nothing to recommend him as a friend other than the pleasure derived from his company."

She smiled, offering her own interpretation of Dickens' work. "Yes, and the nobility believe that what cannot be weighed, measured, and priced has no existence." Her smile turned bitter. "My father learned early on to 'do other men before they would do him.' He too was familiar with Dickens, and he learned to play society's game." She sighed, looking down at her son with what looked to be regret. "By the time I was six, my father's wealth had elevated him to a higher social standing that made prior friendships awkward. That is why I started helping him in his shop."

"Did your mother approve?" His mother would not have approved of him captaining a ship if they had remained at Ridge Point or Ram's Head.

But things had been different in Charleston. Americans seemed to respect a self-made man more than one who had inherited his wealth.

But how had Abby's mother felt about her

daughter learning a trade?

She shrugged. "She knew I was lonely. I think she was, too. By that time, she had stopped taking in laundry and spent her days reading or teaching me needlepoint. She believed in a woman having skills. Then I started spending more time at my father's shop than at home. And Mama got sick."

Her voice quivered and once again, Jack wanted to take her into his arms and hold her. "How did she die?" he asked instead.

"In the cholera epidemic of '48." She sucked in a shivering breath and clutched her child more firmly to her chest.

Jack touched her shoulder. She stiffened slightly and then relaxed. He let his hand fall to the mattress between them. "I was grown when my mother passed. I cannot imagine how difficult it must have been to lose yours at such a tender age."

She kissed the top of her son's head, and Jack's chest cramped with emotion.

"It could have been worse," she said. "By then, my father could afford to hire a governess."

"The maid? Barbara Kersey?" She had mentioned her maid months ago when he had pushed for information. But today seemed different. It seemed as if she wanted to talk about her past.

She nodded. "After mother's death, we moved to a townhouse in a more fashionable neighborhood, and Papa hired Miss Kersey."

"And she taught you proper decorum and etiquette."

"It was not as though my mother were uncivilized. She was just unfamiliar with the ways of the more

Lilly Gayle

fashionable set. Miss Kersey was not."

The hurt look she gave him sent his heart plummeting to his boots.

Chapter Nineteen

Jack bowed his head, feeling like an insensitive clod. "I meant no disrespect. But the nun did say you were gently reared." The nun that had absconded with his money. But he would get to that later. Right now, he needed to keep Abby talking. He needed to learn as much about her as he could. And he needed to gain her trust.

"Not everyone is born with a silver spoon in his or her mouth," she said in that superior tone that set her apart from the working class. She may not have been born to wealth, but she wore it well.

No wonder she had fit in so nicely with society. But had she jumped ship only to land in more turbulent waters? The bourgeois middle class had emerged into a new upper-class society with all the outward displays of wealth the gentry had been accustomed to for centuries. Men such as Drury did not like it.

Had the bastard set out to put Abby in her place?

"I assume Drury was not as eager to accept your father into society as Lord Chivington was."

"Apparently not." She rose from the bed and placed Will back in his cradle. Then she straightened her skirts and sat back down, leaving two feet between them. "Once Lady Chivington agreed to sponsor me, Papa and I were invited to a few social events. Edwina's brother, the Marquess of Sherwood, introduced me to Lord Drury." She turned, meeting his gaze, her eyes pleading and sincere. "I did not know he was engaged. I do not recall hearing it, and he did not act as if he were. He flirted and said the most outrageous things when no one else was close enough to hear, but he was never vulgar and always respectful. I confided in Miss Kersey, and she encouraged me to set my cap for Simon."

Fury burned in Jack's gut. Abby had lacked a mother's guidance and both Drury and the maid had taken advantage. "I guess Miss Kersey was climbing that social ladder as well. Better to be a lady's maid to a lady than a household servant of a merchant."

"You cannot blame her," Abby said with a sigh. "If not for Miss Kersey, I might well have blundered my entrance into society. But I did not. And after the initial start of the season, I received fewer invitations and only saw Lord Drury at public events and places like Almack's Assembly Rooms or at the park. Then August came and London was so hot and smelly, everyone with a country estate fled. Papa could not leave the store, so I went with Edwina and her family to their estate in Kent."

"Is that when Drury took advantage of you?" He tried not to growl. Halsey believed Drury had taken advantage of Abby, but Jack feared the bastard had forced himself on her. Every time he touched her, she flinched. And he had not missed the flash of fear in her eyes whenever he lost his temper.

She lowered her gaze to her hands. Her fingers were so tightly laced, her knuckles turned white. "No. It was my fault. I was foolish. I wanted to prove to Edwina's friends that I could expect to marry as well as them, and I encouraged his advances."

His hands itched to touch her, to pull her into his arms and comfort her, but he resisted. She looked so alone and fragile, he feared touching her might cause her to bolt like a frightened rabbit. "You were naïve and innocent, but Drury knew what he was about."

"I should have known better," she said with a shivering sigh. "But he was so dashing, and I wanted to be a part of his world. Even after Edwina told me he was engaged, I thought maybe..."

Another shiver wracked her slim body, and Jack's heart clenched. Unable to stop himself, he placed his big hand on her small shoulder. She stiffened, her body trembling beneath his touch, but she did not spring to her feet or fling off his offending appendage. He took some small comfort in the fact that she seemed to trust *him* not to take advantage.

"What did you think, Abby?" he asked in as soft a voice as he could manage. It took every ounce of willpower he possessed to hold his temper in check. He wanted to set sail for London, find Drury, and take a cat-o-nine tails to the sonuvabitch's arse.

Her gaze dropped lower, her chin nearly touching her chest. "I don't know. He did not seem like a man in love, and I thought perhaps..."

"He would fall in love with you?"

Her flush deepened, and she turned away, staring across his cabin toward the door. His grip on her shoulder tightened ever so slightly. "Marriage is seldom based on love, Abby. The nobility marry to link titles and gain power or alliances."

His mother had married a viscount instead of Uncle William, the man she supposedly loved. And he had married Abby to gain an heir, so he could inherit a title he did not even want. Disgust filled him. He dropped his hand to his lap, balling his fingers into a fist. "Miss Kersey should have explained that better."

She turned and raised her chin, meeting his gaze. "See. It *was* my fault. Even after Lord Drury announced his engagement to Lady Vanessa, I did not give up on love. I still believed in fairy tales and happily ever after because Lord Drury continued to seek me out and pay me outrageous compliments. I wanted to believe he was only marrying Lady Vanessa to please his family. He never danced with me more than once, but each time, he begged me for a smile or a stolen kiss out in the garden."

Envy burned a hole in Jack's gut. "And did you oblige him?"

"No. I did not want to do anything untoward that could ruin mine or my father's tenuous positions in society. So, I politely declined, but I was so incredibly flattered."

Flattered? The bastard was attempting to seduce her, despite having a fiancée, and Abby was too naïve to be insulted. Halsey should have done a better job protecting his daughter.

She sighed and her shoulders sagged. "Then last August, a little over a year after we met, I attended a race at Goodwood. Simon—Lord Drury—was there, and he offered to show me the racehorse he owned. I should not have gone with him to the stables, but there were so many people around—until there were none. And I suddenly found myself alone with him in an empty stall."

Tears flowed over her lashes and down her cheeks,

each one tearing a whole in Jack's heart. He slid closer and wrapped his arm around her shoulders. Her laced fingers never loosened their grip in her lap.

"You do not have to say anything else." He knew what happened next, and he did not want Abby reliving Drury's betrayal.

"He kissed me," she said, as if she had not heard him or as if she were unable to dam the words that flowed from her heart, purging her soul. "He told me we belonged together, but he was engaged, so I resisted. And then..." She took a hiccuping breath. Jack tensed, fearing her next words, fearing what he already knew.

Simon Weston, Viscount Drury had raped her.

"He slapped me and called me horrible names," she said unexpectedly. "I felt so ashamed and humiliated. The next time I saw him, he apologized, but I ignored him, refusing to believe his charming lies again. Then on the Glorious Twelfth, that final social event at the end of the season, he got me alone again. I don't even know how he managed, but once again, I was alone with him in the stables. He begged my forgiveness, and it was just easier to accept his apology than to carry the heavy burden of a grudge. And when he asked for a kiss to seal our friendship, I allowed it. But then he tried taking liberties I had not granted. When I refused him, he twisted my arm and called me those horrid names again. Then he apologized and said it was my fault that he could not control himself when I was around. He said my beauty and wit tempted him beyond all self-control. I do not know if he expected me to feel flattered, because at that moment, I felt dirty and ashamed."

No wonder Abby was so mistrustful. She had been

mistreated and manipulated by a man she considered a friend, a man she considered civilized and refined, a man who had convinced her that her lack of breeding was to blame for *his* abhorrent behavior.

If I ever get my hands on that sonuvabitch...

Abby took another shuddering breath. She looked both fragile and brave, an intoxicating combination that captured Jack's attention. His jaw tightened; his fingers caressed her shoulder, silently encouraging her to continue.

"I avoided him after that," she added softly. "Then on October 26th, we were both invited to a grouse hunt at the Duke of Chivington's country estate. I do not care for hunting, so I stayed behind, and Simon cornered me in the library. His hands were all over me—pulling at my clothes and tugging at my skirts. I fought him, I swear I did, but I could not scream or call for help. I could not stand the thought of anyone witnessing my humiliation. And as he was rutting over me, still dressed in his waistcoat and cravat, he told me *I* had seduced *him*." Her voice hitched and a tear slid down her cheek. "He said I had all but begged for it with my wanton behavior. Then when he was done, he calmly readjusted his clothes and told me I was good for a rutting, but too low class to ever be a decent man's wife."

A wave of blistering fury roared through Jack's veins, but the pain etched so clearly on Abby's face brought the beast to heel. With a groan of surrender, he pulled her into his arms as the tears flowed freely from her eyes.

****

Abby nestled in the comfort of Jack's embrace,

absorbing his warmth and strength. She felt sheltered and...protected. It was as if he actually cared something for her. But how much better would it feel if he loved her? If she loved him?

Would she ever experience the depth of emotion her parents had shared? Would she ever feel truly loved?

With a sigh of regret, she slipped out of his arms and slid over, putting several inches of mattress between them. The caring expression in his eyes when he looked at her melted her heart. Jack did not love her, but she no longer felt as if she had married a stranger.

She sniffed and swiped at her eyes. "How is Papa? Did he look well?"

The kindness faded from his eyes, and a frown marred his brow. "He is worried about you."

Flushing, she ducked her chin, unable to face the censure in his gaze. "I know. I have been such a great disappointment to him. But now that he has met my husband, he must be greatly relieved."

"I did not tell him I was your husband."

Her pulse tripped. "What *did* you tell him?"

"I introduced myself as Captain Jack Norton," he said, watching her closely. "I told him you were married and safely stowed on my ship while your husband secured his inheritance."

Why would Jack keep silent about the truth now? Her father knew she was married. She had sent him a letter. She just had not named her husband because she had been unsure of Jack's character at the time. So, why had Jack misled him? Why had he not admitted to being her husband? Was he ashamed of his reasons for marrying her? Was he ashamed *of* her?

Even if Lord Drury had learned she was with child, he would not have married her. He would never have considered marrying the daughter of a merchant, even a rich one. Lord Drury had wanted a rich wife with noble blood. Did Jack feel the same? Had he been ashamed to learn his wife's father was a commoner?

Perhaps, he would have been more relieved had he discovered she was the daughter of a bankrupt baron or the ruined daughter of a duke who had disowned her.

Hesitant to meet Jack's gaze, she stared at his left shoulder. "Once you met him, why did you not admit to being my husband?"

The mattress dipped as he shifted. His hand moved closer, his fingers not quite touching hers. "You kept your father's identity a secret, and you did not contact him after we married. I thought perhaps you were afraid of him."

Had she not been so confused, she would have laughed. Her father was one of the kindest men she had ever known. "I wrote my father a letter on our wedding day. I told you about it then. I did not mention your name, but I can assure you, there was a letter. I gave it to Sister Mary Daphne."

Relief flickered briefly in his gaze before he beetled his brow. "I do not think she delivered it. The reverend mother told your father you ran away, and he hired an inquiry agent to find you."

A thousand thoughts and fears swirled in Abby's mind. What dire events had prevented the nun from delivering the letter? "Even if Sister Mary Daphne never returned to the convent and Papa never got the second letter, the reverend mother should have known I had not run away. Before Sister Mary Daphne and I left for Shrivenham, I wrote both the reverend mother and Papa a letter."

When her father arrived at the convent to fetch her home so she could marry Lord Ruston, he should have learned of her original plans. He would not have hired an inquiry agent. "Why didn't Papa go to Shrivenham? If he had, the nun's sister would have told him I had married a viscount, unless Sister Mary Daphne did not go to Shrivenham either."

A chill shivered down her spine, and with little thought to her actions, she inched closer to her husband. The fifth finger of her left hand grazed his right fifth finger. Warmth traveled up her arm and settled in her chest. Contentment mingled with confusion. "I do not understand. Even if something happened to Sister Mary Daphne after we left Sheep's Crossing, what happened to the letter I wrote to the reverend mother *before* I left the convent? Why didn't she or Papa contact Sister Mary Daphne's sister. Why didn't someone inquire after me in Shrivenham?"

Jack shrugged his wide shoulders. "I do not know what happened to the letters, but I do not believe the nun returned to the Sisters of Mercy when she left Sheep's Crossing. Most likely, she took off with the money I gave her. Maybe she decided she had had enough of poverty. Or maybe, she went to Shrivenham to take a more active role in her unwed mothers' charity."

"That would explain why my father did not get the letter, but it does not explain why the reverend mother thought I had run away. Unless Sister Mary Daphne lied about her Charity for Unwed Mothers."

Unwed mothers often paid monthly stipends for

temporary placement of unwanted children, but the baby farmers spent precious little on the children. The helpless infants lived in squalid, crowded rooms, unwashed and unfed by those paid to care for them. When the money ran out, the baby farmers stopped feeding the babies or murdered them outright. The rest died of starvation or disease before their second birthday.

Raw emotion tightened Abby's throat just thinking about it. Was the nun's sister running a baby farm in Shrivenham instead of a boarding house? Was Sister Mary Daphne procuring infants for her?

But she did not take money from me.

"Even if she lied about helping unwed mothers, her concern seemed genuine," Jack said, as if reading her thoughts. "Perhaps, she has to keep her charity work a secret. If neither the Church of England nor its clergy support it, she would most likely not want to risk banishment from the convent if the reverend mother discovered the truth."

"Why would the church object to her charity?" Sister Mary Daphne had not mentioned having the church or the reverend mother's support. But Abby had been so desperate to keep her child and avoid a marriage to Lord Ruston that she had not asked many questions.

Jack shrugged again. "I cannot say for sure, but I assume the church would not support any organization that encouraged unwed mothers to lie about dead husbands who never existed so they might keep their illegitimate children."

Guilt flushed Abby's cheeks, but a warm glow settled in her chest. She had been prepared to live a lie in order to keep her child, but Jack did not seem to condemn her for it. "I suppose Sister Mary Daphne could be helping unwed mothers without the church's knowledge. That would explain why she did not give the reverend mother my letter and why I did not know about Lydia before we left for Shrivenham."

Jack shifted closer. His fingers partially covered hers, sending a warm tingle up her arm. Her breath caught in her lungs, but she did not move her hand.

"Who is Lydia?" he asked.

"A serving girl sent to the convent after her lecherous employer took advantage of her. I thought she had run away until Sister Mary Daphne told me she was living in her sister's boarding house in Shrivenham and working as a baker's assistant."

Jack furrowed his brow. "How many other women disappeared while you were there?"

"I am not sure." She thought for a moment. There had been others, but she had thought nothing of it before. "Besides Lydia, Janet Beasley was the only other woman who 'ran away' while I was there. But I had heard rumors of other women leaving the convent before they gave birth. At first, I feared it was because they had been ill-treated. But the nuns were nothing but kind. So I assumed Sister Mary Daphne had helped them, too."

"I guess your mystery is solved then. Sister Mary Daphne took the money to help her unwed mothers. I just wonder if she returned to the convent or not." Jack rose from the bed.

Missing the warmth of his big hand resting on hers, Abby sighed. "Does it matter?"

"Probably not." Jack smiled, but Abby sensed a

dissatisfaction in her response. He seemed to ponder the situation for a moment, and a frown briefly marred his brow before he shrugged and unexpectedly pulled her to her feet.

The warm touch of his palms against her bare flesh sent heat rising in her cheeks. Her skin tingled where his thumbs lightly caressed the backs of her hands, sending an electric shock to her core. Then without warning, he released her hands and took a step back. "How good a sailor are you?"

She blinked, feeling blind-sided and out of sorts. His touch had been so intimate. So personal. Now, he was looking at her with a determination that frightened her. Had he sensed her wanton response to his touch? Did he now wish to rid himself of a most inappropriate wife?

Her heart dropped to her stomach. "Excuse me?"

"I have secured my inheritance. Ridge Point is mine." He held his hands at his sides, his fingers curled into tight fists as if he were trying to restrain himself to keep from shaking her—or perhaps, devouring her.

Heat seared her skin and settled low in her belly, but then, he turned away as if he could no longer stand the sight of her. Her heart sank, and bile rose in the back of her throat.

Why must she always have her head in the clouds? Jack was a viscount. He had an heir, and he had his inheritance. He did not need a common wife with a slightly jaded opinion of men. "Where are you sending me, my lord?"

He had turned toward his wardrobe. His hand froze as he was reaching for the door. He pivoted on his heel and glared. "Knowing how I feel about my father, do you honestly think I would do to you and Will what he did to my mother and me?"

Will. He had called her son by name. She heard nothing else. Just her son's name on his lips.

She rose on shaky legs and stepped toward him. He bristled, his dark eyes flashing with pride and rage. She raised her hand and cupped the side of his face. He stiffened and some other emotion flashed behind those dark eyes.

"Thank you," she said, before standing on tiptoes to kiss his cheek. "Thank you for acknowledging our son and calling him by his name."

Before she could lower her hand or drop back down to her heels, his arm snaked around her waist, and he pulled her flush against his hard, masculine body. That male part of him swelled as it pressed against her belly, causing her pulse to race and her knees to shake.

Would he force himself on her now, the way Drury had? Would he rut over her like a sweating pig, sating his lust and filling her with self-loathing. Or would he take her in a loving embrace that would melt the fear from her heart?

"By God, woman, you tempt me," he said in a raw and raspy voice that raised the hair on her arms. "If I thought for one moment you were ready, I would brand you as mine and make you forget that bastard Drury ever put his hands on you."

How could she forget, when his firm grasp brought back every painful memory in vivid detail? Then, he gentled his touch and loosened his grip. Her heart drummed in her chest, stealing her breath. She was his wife. If he demanded it of her, she would have to submit. It was her duty.

A quivering sigh shook him as he bent his head and lightly brushed her lips with his. Her mouth opened on a gasp. He breathed it in and dipped his tongue between her parted lips. Teetering between fear and desire, she hesitated—unable to move and unable to respond.

Jack released her on a groan and dropped his hands to his sides. "Do not think for one moment that I do not want you." He took a step back, and his voice was as unsteady as the pulse pounding in her ears when he added, "You are not ready. Until you are, I *will* keep my distance."

Disappointment warred with relief, twisting her into an emotional knot. She felt safe and sheltered in his arms, as if he could protect her from the Simon Westons of the world. It was only after she thought of Lord Drury and the awful things men did to women beneath their clothes that her courage failed her. But she did not want Jack keeping his distance. She wanted to be a wife in every sense of the word. She just could not stomach the thought of his big hands on her bare flesh reminding her of Lord Drury.

"Thank you," she whispered once she found her voice.

Blowing out a frustrated breath, Jack turned his back to her, but she did not miss the subtle movement of his hands as he adjusted his clothing. Her flush deepened. She did not want to think about that horrible part of a man that invaded a woman's body, inflicting pain and humiliation.

So why did she tremble just imagining how it would feel to have that part of Jack touching her so intimately?

He took another deep breath and turned back

around to face her. "As I was saying, Ridge Point is mine. I had planned to go there before returning to Seile, but I changed my plans when I met your father."

Ram's Head was the seat of his viscountcy. Now that the crown had recognized his marriage and legitimized his heir, would he settle her in the run-down estate while he moved into Ridge Point? He had promised to keep his distance, but she no longer wished it. She wanted him close. She wanted him to drive away the last vestige of Simon Weston's hands on her flesh.

She swallowed her fears and disappointment. "Do you wish to send Will and me to Ram's Head then?"

"Of course not. Ram's Head needs too many repairs for anyone to live there. I will see what I can do to restore that lumbering pile of rocks after we are settled at Ridge Point."

Warmth flooded her chest. "Then you are taking us with you?"

He tapped her nose, sending a shiver down her spine. "You are my wife. And I keep what is mine. Of course, I am taking you. And just as soon as I evict my aunt and cousin from Ridge Point, I will take you to London to see your father."

She wanted to introduce her father to his grandson, but fear of a chance encounter with Lord Drury dampened her enthusiasm and diminished her joy. As soon as Simon learned she had a son, he would know he was the father. He had taken her innocence and Will had been born nine months later.

Would he risk offending his new wife by claiming Will as his by-blow? Would Lord Ruston gossip about her father's attempt to pass Will off as *his* child?

Nausea roiled up from the pit of her stomach. "Can

you not bring Papa to Ridge Point?"

Jack's face softened, and the sympathy she saw in his gaze made her cringe. He touched her cheek sending a shiver down her spine to curl low in her belly.

"Do not worry, Abby," he said softly. "I am your husband, and as long as I draw breath, no man will ever speak ill of you or our son."

Our son. Jack had called Will "our" son.

Joy took flight as if on the fragile wings of a butterfly and hesitantly settled in her battered heart.

Chapter Twenty

Abby touched her straw hat, which was scarcely more than a diadem fastened with a pink ribbon around the chignon of curls at her nape. Her carriage dress of coral and white foulard had a trailing skirt trimmed with two deep scalloped flounces of coral silk that sloped in front to make room for several flounces and a striped foulard underskirt. Lacy rose gloves, a pink silk parasol, and wrought gold jewelry from the cache Jack had given her topped off her smart ensemble.

Besides the new clothes he had purchased for his family, Jack had also hired Nora Gabb's sister, Gladys Smythe, to be her lady's maid and another young woman from Seile to act as Will's nursemaid. Yet, Mr. Stanley was acting as coachmen.

Was Jack running low on funds?

He smiled as he helped her down from the crested carriage Mr. Stanley had delivered from Ridge Point the day before. Then he raised her gloved hand to his lips, but rather than kiss the back of her fingers as any other gentleman would have done, he turned her hand palm upward and kissed the small patch of bare skin just above the lace edge of her glove. "You are as graceful as you are beautiful."

His flattery should have set off warning bells. Simon had paid her similar compliments while campaigning to compromise her. A month ago, she would have suspected Jack's motives as well, but his sincere smile and hot gaze made her pulse race. Could he feel it? Did he know the shocking thrill that raced up her arm when his lips touched her bare skin? Would that thrill eventually turn to fear?

She had felt a titillating tingle the first time Simon kissed her hand through the lace of her gloves, but the moment his bare lips touched her throat, she had felt sick with fear. It had only gotten worse when he shoved his hands up her skirts. But Jack's lips on her bare flesh made her heart pound with something far more dangerous than fear. It beat with anticipation.

Would he be patient? Would he wait until she was ready before demanding his husbandly rights?

As if sensing her thoughts and fears, he squeezed her fingers. Then in a serious tone, he said, "Just remember to let me do the talking. My family can be ruthless, and I want them to address *me* with their barbs and not you."

She nodded and smiled, despite the sick feeling in the pit of her stomach. She was a viscountess now, and she must act with the utmost decorum.

Jack turned back to the carriage, took Will from the nursemaid's arms, and handed the baby to Abby before helping Miss Parsons alight from the carriage. The moment the nursemaid's feet touched the cobblestone drive, she reached for Will. Abby felt vulnerable and exposed without her son's warm body nestled in her arms, but society expected a viscountess to leave the task of childrearing to nursemaids and nannies. Still, relinquishing her son left her feeling as gray as the overcast sky.

Repressing the need to cry, she snapped open her

parasol and watched as Mr. Stanley helped the maid, Mrs. Smythe, from the carriage. Once she had her footing, Mr. Stanley relinquished her arm and turned to Jack. "Where would you like us to wait, Lord Ardmore?"

"You are not a servant, Quent," Jack said with a scowl. "You are a friend offering assistance because I don't yet trust the Ridge Point staff, and I could not find a man in Seile to drive the coach on such short notice. You also have leave to use my given name so I suggest you do."

Mr. Stanley's smile broadened, showing off fine straight teeth and the symmetry of his almost too handsome face. A shiver raced down Abby's spine. He was dark where Simon Weston had been light, but they were both exceedingly handsome and charming men on the surface. Could Mr. Stanley be trusted?

He clapped Jack on the shoulder, his smile lighting his dark eyes. "You are my friend, Jack, and that is why I will continue to use your title in the presence of others. But I suppose I could be a bit less formal, *Ardmore*." Jack cringed, but Mr. Stanley continued. "Since we are not family, Mrs. Smythe and I will wait here until you have established yourself as lord and master."

"Really, Quent," Jack said in protest.

"If you want your cousin to treat you like a viscount, then you must be a viscount. Mr. Flick will not show you the respect you deserve otherwise."

Jack raised his hand to his head as if to rake his fingers through his hair but stopped, apparently remembering his black bowler hat and the dark ribbon holding his hair at the nape. His fingers curled before he dropped his arm and smacked his thigh with his closed fist. "I did not like all these social rules as a child, and I like them even less now."

"Ah, but you will get used to them," Mr. Stanley said with another broad smile. "It is in your noble blood."

"Damn your eyes," Jack mumbled. He turned, caught Abby's gaze, and flushed.

She was hard-pressed not to smile. Profanity in the presence of a lady was most unacceptable, but Jack was still struggling for acceptance. But, bless his soul, he was trying so hard. It made her that much more determined to be the viscountess he deserved.

Taking a step toward him, she looped her arm through his. "If you are ready to take on the role of viscount, then I am more than ready to be your viscountess."

But can I be his wife?

The thought sent a delicious tingle straight to her core.

****

Abby's gloved hand clung lightly to his arm as Jack led her up the cobbled walkway toward the front door. Miss Parsons followed behind, carrying Will, but before Jack could knock, a liveried servant answered the door. His white brows narrowed over a beak-like nose as he pulled his watch fob from his pocket. He looked at the attached timepiece, his lips firming with disapproval.

Jack almost smiled. It had been years since anyone forced him to follow the conventions of good society, but he remembered that only family paid house calls before three. Formal visits from strangers and acquaintances were permitted between three and four with less formal visits occurring from four to five. Only family and the closest of friends visited before three or after five, and it was just past noon.

The butler stared, his disdain obvious as he extended a silver tray. "Neither Mr. Flick nor Lady Margery is receiving visitors at this hour, but if you would like to leave your card..."

A smile twitched at the corner of Jack's mouth. He reached into his coat pocket and removed a card that clearly displayed his title and placed it on the tray. The butler stepped back as if anxious to shut the door the moment Jack and his entourage were back inside the carriage. He never even glanced at the card, which hardly mattered. Jack did not intend to quietly slink away to await a more appropriate time to call.

He removed Abby's parasol from her vise-like grip and closed it. Then he took her arm and guided her over the threshold, nudging past the startled butler. Behind him, Miss Parsons gasped but followed them inside. After dropping Abby's frilly pink parasol into a brass umbrella stand in the corner, Jack removed his hat and hung it on the coat tree. A vein bulged in the butler's forehead, and his jaw clenched.

To leave one's hat or walking stick in the hall was considered a liberty reserved for family members who resided in the home. It was considered poor taste for a visitor to do so.

Repressing another smile, Jack turned to the obviously annoyed butler. "I am Lord Ardmore, master of Ridge Point, and this is my viscountess, Lady Ardmore." He glanced behind him at the frightened nursemaid. Miss Parson's eyes were round in her pale face. "Miss Parsons is holding my son and heir, William Henry Norton. So, if you would kindly roust Mr. Flick and my aunt, I would like to see them in *my* drawing room."

The butler sputtered, his wide eyes swinging from Jack to Abby and back again. Abby's face paled, but she showed no other outward display of distress. She held her head high and nodded slightly, acknowledging the flustered man.

"I will meet with the staff later," Jack added. "In the meantime, please have a servant prepare the nursery."

The butler raised his chin, staring over Jack's shoulder. "The nursery has not been used in decades, sir."

"Then I suggest you send several servants to see to its cleaning. Now."

The butler bowed and turned smartly on his heel. Jack turned to Abby and expelled a heavy breath. "I think our arrival is about to cause quite a stir."

"Indeed." She wrung her hands together, her eyes darting to Will as if forcing herself not to snatch him from the nursemaid's arms. When he started to whimper, she strained toward him. Miss Parsons patted his bottom, her eyes darting from Abby to Jack and back again.

"He will be getting hungry soon." Abby flushed and nervously shuffled her feet, moving closer to Miss Parsons.

"Then I had best settle matters with my family quickly." Turning on his heel, he led Abby and Miss Parsons into the drawing room.

He did not want his son going hungry, but he was

not about to let Abby out of his sight until he confronted his cousin and aunt. Still, it would be most improper for her to feed their son in the drawing room. It would also be incredibly distracting. Just thinking of Abby's breasts distracted him, sending heat to his loins.

He shuffled his feet and suppressed a frustrated groan. Abby had suffered enough abuse at the hands of Drury. She did not need an impatient husband demanding his conjugal rights. She needed a man who would be patient. And Jack was damn sure trying his best, though it went against his highly impatient nature.

Trying to distract himself from thoughts of Abby and her breasts, he surveyed his surroundings. He barely remembered this room from his time at Ridge Point as a child, but then, he had seldom entered the drawing room. His parents had firmly believed that children were to be seen and not heard, and once he was seen, he was promptly sent upstairs to the nursery or out into the garden with his nurse. Once Aunt Margery and Morris moved in, he had been sent outside with his cousin, who had tormented him. Now, it was time for Jack to torment Morris.

"Well, well. If it is not the prodigal son returned," Morris sneered from the doorway. "Shall we kill the fatted calf?"

Nerves and fury twisted Jack's gut into a knot. He turned. Morris held a glass of amber liquid up in a half-salute and listed to the left. He straightened, turned up the glass, and drained it. "Higgins!" he shouted.

The butler appeared in the doorway behind him. Morris thrust the glass into his hand. "Refill it." Then Morris turned bloodshot eyes on Jack. "Care for a nip, cousin?"

Jack's fury turned to pity. Morris was a beaten man. He had lost Ridge Point, and kicking him when he was down would not bring Jack the satisfaction he craved. He shook his head. "No. Thank you."

"It is the best quality, I assure you," Morris said with a bitter laugh. "Your father would have nothing less." His drunken smile transformed into a sneer. "Pity he did not have better taste when choosing a wife."

The words hit their mark, refueling Jack's rage. His blood ran hot, his body shaking as he fought the urge to ram his fist so far down Morris' throat that it exited through his arse. Since restraint had never been his strong suit, he took a step forward, but Abby's hand on his forearm stalled his steps.

The sweet scent of lavender assailed his nostrils, and his shoulders relaxed. Then she stepped around him, sending his temper through the roof. What the hell did she think she was about! Morris was like a cornered animal, ready to strike at any time, and she was placing herself in harm's way.

"It is a pleasure to meet one of Ardmore's relatives," she said, her voice soft and sweet with just a hint of nerves. "I am his wife, Lady Abigail Ardmore."

"Lady?" Morris snorted. "Ha! Where did he meet you? A brothel?"

Before Abby could stop him, Jack stepped around her and punched Morris in the face. His fist did not exit Morris' arse hole, but he gained a keen sense of satisfaction when he heard bone crunch.

Morris sank to his knees, cupping his face and whimpering like the coward he was.

"Jack!" Abby gave him a piercing glare that did little to diminish his joy. He had been wanting to slug the bastard since he was nine.

"Was that really necessary?" She dropped to her knees at his cousin's side, pulled a handkerchief from the pocket of Morris' waistcoat, and pressed it into his hands. Morris held the cloth to his nose and moaned, but it was not remorse that set Jack's pulse to pounding. It was envy. Abby had never touched him as tenderly as she touched his bastard cousin.

"He insulted you!" Jack cringed at the petulance he heard in his own voice. But what did Abby expect? He had defended her honor, and she had responded by reprimanding him as if he were a child. Most women would have been all atwitter just thinking of a man physically defending her honor.

But Abby was not most women. She was unique. Special. And she was his. And he damned sure protected what was his. He glared. She shook her head and smiled.

"I appreciate the sentiment, but I do not want you upsetting our son." She gave him a meaningful look and then glanced behind him. It was then that he noticed the boy's wails. Will was squalling, and the dumbstruck Miss Parsons was standing with her mouth open doing nothing to soothe him.

Jack mumbled a profanity under his breath and turned. Miss Parson's cringed, wrapping her arms around Will and taking a step back as if she thought Jack would punch her next. He sighed and gentled his voice. "Hand me my son."

She shook her head and took another step away. The woman had more balls than brains, but at least she was prepared to protect his son. He would have to remember she was braver than she appeared the next time she stared at him like a frightened rabbit. "Then please take him back outside and try to settle him. I do not like hearing him cry."

She nodded and ran from the room as if he had issued a vile threat. It was only after he turned back around and saw Abby that he realized the nursemaid had mistook his meaning. Apparently, Abby had too because the fearful expression in her eyes told him she now feared for their son's well-being. Apparently, both Abby and Will's nurse believed him capable of committing violence if the boy cried.

If caterwauling and wails were all it took to spark his temper, he would have strangled Captain Whiskers years ago. When hungry or determined to gain entry through a closed door, that monster of a cat could howl like a banshee. Will's cry was not nearly as loud...or annoying.

"It breaks my heart to hear him cry," he said, hoping the truthful words would erase the fear from Abby's eyes. She visibly swallowed, then nodded before rising to her feet and coming to stand next to him.

Her gloved hand touched his forearm. "Mine too," she said with a tremulous smile.

Blood rushed to his chest, warming his heart before traveling lower to heat his loins. Abby was definitely a woman worth wooing, and woo her he would. Just as soon as he dispensed with this nasty business with his cousin and aunt.

Morris slid backward on his rump until his hips came up against the wall. The handkerchief in his hand sported bright red splotches, but it appeared he was no longer bleeding. Perhaps he had not broken the bastard's nose after all.

"You uncouth, backwater colonial," Morris spat through lips tinged with blood. "How dare you strike me! My grandfather was the third Viscount Ardmore. Noble blood runs through my veins."

"The same blood that runs through mine, you fool. We are cousins, and well you know it."

Morris rose to his feet, stumbled, and leaned against the wall. "You sir, are an impostor. My cousin was banished to the colonies, and there he resides."

Jack inhaled sharply, trying to relieve the tension in his shoulders. "Uncle William, your own mother's brother, vouched for me. As did Lord Willoughby and Lord Gilchrest. I am your cousin, Jackson Henry Norton. Jack. Now, Viscount Ardmore. There is no disputing my claim."

Morris' red eyes glistened wetly. He swiped at his nose and then his eyes, streaking his face with blood. "You left with your mother. I was here, hiding in this room when Uncle William begged Lord Ardmore to reconsider. He said he would take her back if she returned to him, swearing on her father's grave that you were his son. Then Uncle William went after her, but he did not bring her back, and he did not return to Ridge Point. Mother said she had made her choice. She chose Uncle William, the father of her child, over her own husband."

Jack's heart slammed against his ribs with enough force to steel his breath. He felt lightheaded and nauseous. His stomach churned. Fury was the only thing that kept him from tossing his breakfast.

Chapter Twenty-One

Abby laid her hand on Jack's arm, hoping to reach him as she had before. Her touch seemed to have a soothing effect on his temper. Yet this time, he did not seem to notice. His fingers curled into fists at his sides.

"You bastard." He snarled, and his face was a mask of hatred. "My father sent us away. He purchased a home for our banishment and set my mother aside as if she were nothing more than a kept woman. And he denied me, his own son, because your mother spread her malicious lies."

"Is that the lie your mother told?" Mr. Flick sneered. "Did you believe Uncle William came after you to bring you home? He wanted her for himself!"

"You sonuvabitch!" Jack moved as if to raise his fist and nearly pulled Abbey off the ground. He looked down, the fury blazing in his eyes nearly blinding him to her presence.

She clung to his arm, just barely preventing him from raising his fist to strike his cousin again. Her toes scarcely touched the polished marble floor. "Jack, please!"

His vision seemed to clear as if finally seeing her, but his jaw remained clenched. "Perhaps you should go outside and check on our son."

Our son. Any joy she might have felt at hearing him say those precious words faded when she looked into his eyes. Jack was a just man, but his temper was ferocious, and she believed he had inherited that temper from his father. "Please, Jack. Do not let him bait you."

"Go. Outside." His words were a whispered growl that made her cringe. Memories of Lord Drury shivered over her, peppering her skin with gooseflesh. Her skin crawled at the memories of his lips and then his fists on her body. Her stomach clenched.

"Do not be like him," she whispered past a throat constricted by fear, not knowing if the "him" to whom she referred was his father or Lord Drury. "Do not let your anger rule your heart."

Something she said must have registered. Or maybe it was the fear she heard in her own voice that made him listen. The tension did not leave his body, but the rage faded from his eyes. Pity made a brief appearance before he shuttered his expression and stared at her with a face as hard as the marble floor beneath her feet. "Please. Check on Will."

A wife was supposed to obey her husband, but this was one order she could not follow. If she left the room, she feared Jack would beat his cousin to death. Not that he did not deserve a good thrashing, but...

Mr. Flick swayed on his feet, a sneer on his face and a vindictive gleam in his bloodshot eyes. The rustle of silk prevented Abby from disobeying her husband outright.

Jack stiffened and turned toward the door. Abby and Mr. Flick followed his gaze as a plain-faced woman dressed in a lovely emerald visiting toilette entered the room. The butler followed just far enough inside the room to grasp the double doors and pull them closed as he backed into the hall. The soft thump and metallic click of the doors latching together broke the sudden silence.

"Hello, Jack...Ardmore." She smiled stiffly. "It seems odd calling you that after all these years."

The tension returned to Jack's body tenfold. Abby felt it in his bicep as she clung to his arm. "I imagine you never thought to call me that at all. Did you, Aunt Margery?"

Pink tinged the woman's pale cheeks and quickly faded. "I suppose I did not consider it much at all until recently. Out of sight, out of mind, as they say."

She breezed into the room as if skating over ice, sending a chill down Abby's spine. The woman seemed as cold and heartless as a serpent. Then she turned and met Abby's gaze. Regret or some other humbling emotion seemed to pass behind her eyes but was gone just as quickly. "So, you are the new Lady Ardmore." She nodded. "You are just as lovely as Jack's mother."

"And you hated her because of it, did you not?" Jack challenged, all but spitting the words.

Lady Margery turned to face her nephew. Abby could not see the expression in her eyes, but she noted the stiffness in her shoulders and the trembling in her hands just before she curled her fingers into her skirts, gripping them as if holding on to the edge of a cliff. "Yes. I did."

Jack's jaw went slack, as if surprised by her admission. Then, his eyes blazed. "Your lies destroyed her."

A sigh escaped Lady Margery's lips before she turned slightly to stare up at a portrait over the fireplace of a dark-haired man who upon first glance, looked nothing like Jack. But as Abby stared at the man who was most likely his father, she noted the same dark, fathomless brown eyes and broad forehead. The strong jaw and chiseled cheeks were remarkably similar as well. In fact, it was only the difference in coloring and perhaps, size, that set the two men apart. Jack's shoulders were broader and his hair was blond. Jack's father had dark hair, and it looked as if years of exposure to the sun had tanned Jack's skin to a color that seemed more natural on his father. But, there was no mistaking the family resemblance.

"You have grown up to look very much like him," Lady Margery said quietly.

"Pity you did not see the resemblance years ago," Jack snarled.

"Ha!" Mr. Flick staggered forward. "I look as much like him as Jack. It is in the Norton blood, the same blood that runs through Uncle William's veins as well."

Lady Margery turned, regret and disappointment clearly visible in her gaze as she faced her son. "Please, Morris. Do not make this any worse than it already is. You have Ardie's coloring, but you have Braxton Flick's bone structure. You look as much like your father as I looked like mine. Ardie, William, and myself took after him, but William had mother's light hair and complexion."

Mr. Flick harrumphed, and Lady Margery turned to face Abby. "Ardie was my pet name for Jack's father. I was the oldest, and he was like my very own baby doll. I loved him dearly and miss him still."

"And what of your other brother?" She cast a quick glance at Jack, praying her forward behavior would not earn her a public reprimand. He caught her eye, gratitude evident in his gaze before he looked at his aunt as if curious to hear her response.

She shrugged. "William was nothing like Ardie or me. It was more than just his light hair. It was his attitude and temperament. He ignored societal strictures and cared nothing for tradition. He loved his boats and the sea. And he was not at all particular with the company he kept. So, naturally, I was shocked as well as pleased when he made friends with the daughter of a baronet, and I fully expected him to wed Sir Lionel Ridge's daughter."

"Why would you think that?" Mr. Flick sneered as he staggered past his mother and slumped onto one of two matching, richly upholstered, carved rosewood divans flanking the fireplace. "Ardmore held the title and the purse strings. Uncle William was little more than a fisherman."

"He was a successful merchant," Jack said in that harsh voice that sent fear coursing through Abby's veins. "He did not live off of his brother's charity. He forged his own destiny."

The anger in Jack's tone turned to pride, but it did little to soften his cousin's attitude. Mr. Flick may not be a noble himself, but he was the grandson of a viscount and the son of a lady. He was the Honorable Mr. Flick, although, there seemed nothing honorable about his behavior.

Like most others who carried noble blood, Mr. Flick seemed to believe an individual should not be permitted to achieve social or economic success through hard work and perseverance. His kind believed allowing such upward mobility would provide an equalizing principle that could elevate commoners above their betters. And like many sons of second sons or daughters who did not marry nobles, Mr. Flick had relied on his family name to help him feel superior. Most likely because he had not the brains or ambition to achieve any degree of success on his own.

Mr. Flick harrumphed again, sounding like a matronly old woman. "You would think that. You are no better, and your father knew it."

"Enough!" Lady Margery raised her voice, gaining her son's attention. She looked at Jack, her pale face showing so little emotion she may as well have been molded from wax. "William was in love with your mother, but her father did not want her to wed a man without a title. He offered your grandfather a huge dowry to convince Ardie to marry her." She laughed, the sound bitter and sad. "I was so disappointed when Ardie agreed. Apparently, he loved her, too. Everyone loved her. And I grew to hate her."

"And you turned everyone against her, including my father." Jack stepped away from Abby, leaving her cold and desolate in the middle of the room.

****

Aunt Margery's gaze slid to the floor. "For years, I believed William was your real father. And I hated your mother for breaking both my brothers' hearts."

Jack's pulse drummed in his ears as he paced in front of the door, stopping to glare at his father's portrait before turning to glare at his aunt. "So, you fostered my father's doubts, and he believed your lies."

A tear escaped from the corner of his aunt's rheumy eyes and rolled over her cheek. "Only because he knew your mother did not love him. She married him to please her father, but she was still in love with

William."

"You were jealous!" He raised his voice for the first time in recent memory. Uncle William had taught him years ago that a good captain did not lead by instilling fear into his crew, but by gaining their admiration and respect. With his size, he had quickly learned not to raise his voice, for the louder he spoke, the less others seemed to hear. But Abby had heard his shouted words just fine, and it looked as if once again, he had frightened her.

She cringed and took a step away from him as if to cower in the corner. Was it because of the abuse she had suffered at Drury's hand? Or because she was still afraid of her husband's violent temper?

"Please, do not be like him," she whispered again.

"Abby..." He stepped toward her, but she backed away, tearing his heart from his chest.

"No." That one word nearly crippled him. He stopped and stared, ignoring his aunt's gasp and his cousin's vile laughter. But then, Abby raised her chin, challenging him rather than showing him fear. "Do not be like your father and misjudge what you have failed to hear. Listen to your aunt."

"Spoken like a true commoner," Morris said from the couch.

Abby held her head high, meeting his gaze as if she were a born noble woman challenging an inferior's impertinence. "I am a commoner, but my father is Henry Halsey, world renowned jeweler. Men like him and your uncle William are steering the world away from a society based on rank and privilege. The common man no longer needs the aristocracy to govern them or care for their needs. And free enterprise and the entrepreneurial spirit will bring society out of the dark ages and into a world where hard work and merit dictate success rather than the circumstances of one's birth."

As soon as the words left her mouth, Abby paled. Eyes wide with panic, she met Jack's gaze as if dreading the repercussions of voicing her bold opinion. Such forward behavior would have enraged his father, but Jack's heart filled with pride.

Smile firmly in place, he walked toward her, draped his arm over her shoulders, and pulled her close. She trembled beneath his touch, but boldly stood by his side.

"Oh, please," Morris sneered.

Jack ignored him and turned to meet his aunt's shocked gaze. "Rest assured, my wife did not marry me for my title or for my money. So it would behoove you both to still your vindictive tongues. I will stand for no man or woman speaking ill of her." He turned to meet Morris' gaze, staring until his cousin lowered his chin.

"If only your mother had stood up to your father."

Jack jerked his head back around to glare at his aunt. She smiled and swiped at another stray tear. He could not tell if she was holding back a flood or if her eyes were always red and watery. Her taut, pale face held few clues to her emotions.

He thought he saw her chin tremble, but her oddly smooth face never crumpled, and her waxy complexion never changed. Did she still whiten her face with borax, alum, and white lead? He vaguely remembered overhearing an argument between her and his mother over the toxic mixture she applied to her face in an effort to lighten her skin. A pale complexion had been all the rage then, as it seemed to be now. Abby was fair-skinned, but color often bloomed in her cheeks as it did now when he met her gaze. She was both lovely and smart. So, perhaps he should do as she suggested and listen to his aunt.

Stiffening his spine, he turned toward her, keeping Abby close to his side. "She tried, but he sent her away."

A sad smile touched his aunt's face. "No, Jack. When Ardie accused her, she never denied it."

"Can you blame her?" His heart beat like a drum inside his chest. "His accusations were a vile insult to her integrity."

"A less prideful woman would have denied the charges. When she did not, your father banished her in a fit of anger he quickly regretted. William was furious with your father, but Ardie ranted. He had such a temper, you know."

Jack knew all too well. He still remembered the beating he received for making the wrong sort of friends in Seile. But oddly enough, Lord Ardmore had never laid a hand on his wife. Was it possible he actually loved her?

"He truly loved her," Aunt Margery said as if reading his thoughts. "He was just so blinded by jealousy. He knew she was still in love with William, and he knew William loved her. Thinking to test them both, he sent William after her, hoping she would return home and beg his forgiveness."

Jack swallowed a lump rising in his throat, fear eating away at his composure. Had Uncle William, a man he believed noble and honorable, betrayed them both? Had he betrayed Jack? "Uncle William took us aboard the *Lion's Pride* and carried us to America himself."

Had he done so because he coveted his brother's family?

"No, Jack," his aunt said again. "He boarded the *Andover* first and gave your mother the message sent by your father. She refused to crawl to any man on bended knee and insisted your father come for her himself. William knew Ardie would never do such a thing. So, he and his men took control of the *Andover*. He had caught up with them in the English Channel and forced them to dock in Cherbourg. Then William sailed the *Lion's Pride* back to Ridge Point to try to talk some sense into your father."

"My father didn't want us." Jack's heart pounded so hard he could barely catch his breath. If not for the comforting support of Abby's warm body tucked under his arm, he might have crumpled to the floor like a disheartened child.

"Not true," Aunt Margery said. "Ardie was just so stubborn and so filled with misplaced pride. He kept insisting I had been right about your mother all along. I finally confessed my jealousy and told him I thought you were his son. William swore he had never been with your mother, and I believed him. His parting words haunted your father until the day he died."

Jack forced himself to speak as if unmoved by her heartfelt words. His chest cramped, and his throat felt tight. Then Abby's arm tightened around his waist, and the words came more easily. "What did he say?"

Margery smiled and swiped once more at her eyes. This time, Jack was sure it was a tear. "He said he would watch over you and your mother until your father came to his senses or your mother came to hers. And when Ardie asked what he meant by that remark, William said, 'If you no longer want her, then I do. And I will stay by her side until she realizes it.'"

Jack's head ached, and his chest hurt. He stepped away from Abby, turning to face the fireplace. His father's portrait seemed to mock him.

"He did love her," Aunt Margery said, her words barely penetrating the haze of pain and fury.

He turned with a snarl. Morris seemed to shrink against the sofa as Jack stared at him with all the pain and hatred in his heart. "Then why deny me my birthright? Why leave everything not entailed with the damned patent to him!"

Behind him, he heard Abby's soft sob—a sound of heartbreak and pity that tore at his soul. He wanted to take her hand and drag her from the room. He wanted to board the *Lion's Pride* and sail to America with his new family, but first, he had to make peace with his past.

Forcing his legs to move, he took a step further away from his wife and faced his aunt. Her pale face turned ash gray, and her lips tinged with blue. She inhaled sharply as if she had suddenly remembered to breathe. The blue faded, but her face was no less pale.

"Am I truly Ardmore's son?" The words were little more than a whisper.

His aunt visibly swallowed. "Did you ever ask William for the truth?"

"No." That one word was a harsh growl that made his aunt cringe. But she did not cower or back away. Nor, did she question him further. She nodded as if understanding his reluctance to question the man who had become more of a father to him than Ardmore had ever been.

"Ardie was not a demonstrative man," she said quietly. "Our father had groomed him for the viscountcy from the cradle, and Ardie took to it like a fish to water. William wanted no part of the training. He once said he would be no man's spare heir. Had he not been granted a commission in the Royal Navy, father would have given up on him completely." She smiled ruefully and walked to the sofa across from her son where she eased herself onto the cushions as if unable to stand a second longer.

"Uncle William was always the fool," Morris grumbled. When Jack glared, he turned away with a pout, staring once more at the cold fireplace.

Without a word, Jack turned toward Abby, took her arm, and guided her to the sofa where he seated her next to his aunt. Ignoring her curious expression, he turned his back on the three of them, laced his fingers behind his back, and began pacing.

"I do not believe Uncle William fathered me, nor do I believe my father cared one way or the other. But he did believe my mother had been unfaithful, and he wished to punish her through me. He was considerably older and had no way of knowing she would die before learning of the contents of his will. I am sure he thought he would die long before her and that we would return to England the moment we learned of his death. He had no way of knowing she would return in a pine box, but he knew how much Ridge Point meant to her, and that is why he left it to Morris."

A soft sob sounded behind him. Jack turned as Abby handed his aunt a lace handkerchief pulled from her reticule. Aunt Margery offered her a watery smile and dabbed at her cheeks. The anguished look in Abby's eyes when she turned her gaze on him was almost more than he could bear. He hardened his heart, forcing himself to be unmoved by her tears.

Aunt Margery sniffed. "Ardie was proud of you."

Jack normally prided himself on his ability to mask his expressions, but the incredulity he felt must have shown on his face.

His aunt sniffed. "Honestly. He was. He kept up with you through letters from your uncle. William wrote twice a year."

Did father write back? Jack's heart lodged in his throat. As a boy, he had wanted desperately to hear from his father. Even a single letter would have made all the difference, but no letters had come. Surely, Uncle William would have told him if a letter had arrived from England. Then again, Uncle William had never mentioned writing the viscount either.

Was Aunt Margery lying? Or had Uncle William betrayed his trust?

Chapter Twenty-Two

The room spun. Jack gripped the back of a nearby chair, leaned forward, and glared. "There were no letters."

"Oh, Ardie never wrote back, but he treasured every letter, every word William wrote about you. He put them in the safe."

Jack and his aunt both turned to face the portrait hanging over the fireplace. Abby's and Morris' gazes followed.

"So, that is where he kept his safe." Morris gave his mother a sour look. "He could have money or jewels in there that belong to me." He cast a sullen look at Jack and then scowled at his mother. "Why did you not tell me?"

"Because I do not know the combination, and I knew you would tear down the wall and possibly destroy my brother's portrait to get to it."

Morris sneered. "And you do not think Jack will do the same?"

For the first time since setting foot into this room, Jack's smile was genuine. "I do not need to tear down the wall. I *know* the combination."

Unless his father had changed it.

A pang of regret pierced his chest. The combination was his birthday. Or it had been when he was a child. In a rare moment of affection, his father had ruffled his hair and told him the combination. It was one month before his tenth birthday and just a little more than a year before his banishment. It was a rare, cherished memory he had kept safely locked in his heart—a memory he had wanted to forget.

"I did make the viscount proud that day." He smiled, but bitterness welled in his heart. "The day of my first fox hunt, I not only kept up with the riders, but I did not shy away when Father blooded me after the hounds killed the poor animal. I suppose my behavior was a reflection of how well he had groomed me. So, it was really just pride in himself." But had there been other moments he had wiped from his memory?

His aunt shook her head and sighed. "No. Ardie was truly proud of you. He told me that same story after I saw you in London last year."

Jack's fingers curled over the edge of the chair. His knuckles turned white. "I do not recall seeing you when I was here last. And I would have remembered. I met my wife on that trip."

The lie slid smoothly from his lips. More smoothly than he would have imagined. But in that moment, he realized he would lie, cheat, or die for his wife. It was what husbands were supposed to do for those they...for those in their care.

But did he more than just care for Abby? Dear God, had he fallen in love with her?

He met Abby's gaze, daring her to dispute the lie specifically designed to protect her reputation. Her eyes were radiant and not with gratitude. They shone with some deeper emotion he dare not analyze.

His aunt sighed. "I was not referring to that visit. Though, I wish I had been here when you came to see your father. Perhaps then, I could have persuaded him to speak with you. But he believed it was too late. He said you had grown into a fine young man, one as stubborn as your mother, as if that were not calling the kettle black." Another sigh escaped as she sagged against the sofa. "No. I saw you in London months before, when you were on one of your earlier trips. I was in London shopping for another new wardrobe." She lowered her gaze, and color suffused her face. "Your father doted on Morris and me after your mother refused to come back. I must admit that at first, I was glad." She sighed again, the sound rife with pain and regret. "But then, I began to feel guilty. I saw how much your father missed you and your mother. He was so miserable, that I told him you seemed happy."

"You lied to him? Again?" Fury roared through Jack's veins. How could she profess a guilty conscience in one breath while admitting further sins in the next? She would do anything to regain the life she had lived before her husband gambled away his fortune and took his own life, thus forfeiting his wealth.

His aunt rose on shaky legs, reaching for him. "Jack. Please..."

"No." The low growl came from deep down, a snarl filled with anguish and rage. "Get out of my sight and take that sorry excuse for a son with you."

Morris stumbled to his feet. Aunt Margery grabbed his arm, her white-knuckled grip forestalling his protest. "Let us leave your cousin and his family to their unpacking." She sniffed once and bit her lip to stop it from trembling. Then she looked at Jack, the sorrow in her gaze, making him cringe.

Damn her! How dare she attempt to make *him* feel

guilty. After everything she had done to him and his mother, he should not have to put up with her presence in *his* home a second longer. But if anyone should be expected to leave, it was him. The courts had granted her and Morris two weeks. And he had given them but one.

Hardening his heart, he glared. "I cannot legally evict you from this estate for another week, but I expect you or Morris, whichever one of you inhabits my father's room, to remove his or her things from the master suite posthaste. My family and I are moving in today."

His aunt sniffed once more and nodded. "As you wish, milord. I will ensure that Morris moves into the blue room across from mine until we can make other arrangements."

"You had best make those arrangements quickly. You have one week." With those parting words, Jack snagged Abby's elbow and escorted her outside.

****

Bloody hell! Ridge Point was his. But now, here he stood, twiddling his damn thumbs while his wife nursed their son inside a carriage. Until Morris removed his personal belongings from the master suite of the estate, it was the only place she was guaranteed privacy.

Damn, but he felt useless and out of sorts. At least Quentin had something to do. After assisting the Ridge Point footmen with the luggage, he had gone inside with Mrs. Smythe and Miss Parsons to see to the unpacking and to make sure the Ridge Point servants did not snoop through their things.

Would he have to fire every last one of them and find his own staff? He would not even know how to go about such a huge undertaking. Hell, he did not know the first thing about writing reference letters. But if it came to that, perhaps Abby could guide him. It was just too damn bad he could not bring his ship's crew to Ridge Point. Unfortunately, they would not fit in here any better than he did.

What was it Quent had said about silk and a sow's ear? Abby may not have been born into the same class as him, but his common born wife was nobler than he would ever be.

A smile touched his face when she stepped down from the carriage with Will cradled in her arms. She would much prefer to care for the boy herself, but in this world, it was not done. And if he wanted to impress upon the staff that he was indeed, lord of the manor, then both Abby and he would have to behave in the expected manner.

Once inside the house, he summoned Miss Parsons who took Will up to the nursery. With Aunt Margery and Morris still in residence, he could not show his bride the entire house for fear of running into them. So, he showed her the ground floor while introducing himself and his viscountess to whatever staff they ran into along the way. He would deal with the entire Ridge Point staff later. Then, he would learn where their loyalties lay. Until then, he and Abby would be confined to the common rooms and the master suite, which included a nursery and nursemaid's room.

Abby had already seen the large entry hall and the drawing room. So, he showed her the library, salon, dining room, music room, and family salon. The kitchen, butler's pantry, and scullery were below stairs. She would have no need to see those areas until after she took over as mistress of the manor, and unfortunately, he could not show her the five other bedrooms until that time either. As of now, he was a guest in his own home, and etiquette deemed it improper for a guest to see any bedchamber other than the one to which he or she was assigned. But as Lord Ardmore, he was assigned the master suite, and he was damn sure moving his wife into the mistress's room just as soon as Morris vacated the master bedroom.

Abby seemed subdued but suitably impressed with the estate, and Jack was pleased it was still in such good condition, considering his cousin's fondness for fast horses and loose women. Then again, the apple did not often fall far from the tree, and Morris' father had ruined his own life in a like manner. So, he could only assume there was little money left in his father's accounts. He knew for damn sure he had received precious little to maintain that monstrosity of a house, Ram's Head.

"Your family home is lovely," Abby said as he escorted her upstairs.

"It is our home. Or it will be once we rid ourselves of our unwanted 'guests.'"

As they completed the tour of the house, Higgins met Jack in the hall to inform him the master suite was now vacant. Jack nodded and led Abby upstairs so she could see her room.

The master suite consisted of a master chamber and lady's bedroom separated by a dressing room. He carried her in through what would soon be his room, through the connecting door of the dressing chamber, and into the room that had once been his mother's. He made a point of showing her the lock on both sides of the door.

"To insure your privacy," he said, hoping she would trust him enough to leave her side unlocked. He hoped like hell that he would be strong enough to resist her charms and earn her trust.

"It is all very lovely." She wrung her hands together, her eyes darting not to the door separating her room from his, but toward the door leading out into the hall.

"There is a large water closet at the end of the hall." He smiled, wondering if she needed to relieve herself. "There is also a necessary out back, hidden by a large hedge."

Her eyes darted from him to the door again. "But where is the nursery? How far will I be from our son?"

A chuckle escaped, and Jack smiled down fondly at his overprotective wife. "The nursery and nanny's room are just across the hall."

She turned toward the door, and her chin trembled as she looked up at him with those big, Caribbean blue eyes. "I am sorry. It is just that I have never been away from him for this long."

Jack grazed her cheek with the back of his hand, wanting to reassure her, but the soft touch stirred areas of his body he did not wish stirred when there was nothing he could do at the moment to ease the ache. He snatched back his hand and stiffened his spine. He needed to control his lusty nature with Abby if he wanted to gain her trust. Until she was ready, he could not even think of seducing her.

Clearing his throat, he stepped back and smiled. "He is safe. I can assure you. And although I cannot show you the other bed chambers, I can show you upstairs if you would like."

She quirked a brow. "Do you really think it proper for me to see the staff's quarters while I am still little more than a guest?"

She was right of course, but he did not intend to show her the dormitory-like rooms above stairs where the servants slept. "My mother was one of nine children, none of whom are still alive. But when she was a child here, her father built a day nursery above stairs between the men's and women's sleeping quarters. When she and her siblings were older, the room was converted into a schoolroom. Their tutor slept in a small room next to the classroom. I thought maybe you would like to see where Will is going to study until he is old enough to go to Eton or Harrow."

"I would rather see my son," she said with a tremulous smile, as if she thought he could deny her.

He could. But he would not. Had she not yet learned he could deny her nothing? Heaven help him when she did. He would well and truly be at her mercy then. With a shake of his head, he cupped her elbow and escorted her across the hall. He did not know what to expect when he opened the door to the nursery, but he had not expected to find it stripped of all furniture save for the cradle they had brought with them from the *Lion's Pride* and an old rocking chair. The staff had cleaned the room as ordered, and while he had not expected them to locate his old baby bed, there should have been some furniture left in the room besides the rocker. What had happened to the rosewood child's bed he had slept in? Or his dressing table, wardrobe, and toy chest?

Miss Parsons stood in front of the window

overlooking the river, jiggling Will in her arms in an attempt to soothe his grumbling. Jack's heart twisted. He used to stand at that same window, staring out at the river and wishing he could sail his little boat to Seile to see Uncle William.

Had his father always been jealous of his brother? Had he stripped the room of all reminders of his son the moment the *Andover* set sail for America?

Abby seemed unconcerned with the lack of furnishings. She broke free of his light touch and rushed over to take her son from Miss Parsons' arms. She held him close, raining kisses on his tiny head as if it had been days rather than hours since she had last seen him. It was almost embarrassing. If he did not put a stop to her coddling now, she would turn their son in to a pantywaist.

He opened his mouth to issue a gentle reprimand, but the words would not come. A flash of memory stopped him cold—a memory of his father reprimanding his mother for showing "too much" affection. Swallowing his criticism, he led Abby to the rocking chair.

Miss Parsons clasped her hands at her waist. "Beggin' your pardon, milord, but..."

Jack turned to face her. "Yes?"

"After Mr. Stanley brung in the cradle, I asked Mr. Higgins where the rest of the baby furniture was. He said Lady Margery had been using this room as her dressing room, and there weren't no baby furniture."

Well, at least that answered one question. If Aunt Margery had been using this room as a dressing room, there had probably been no room for furniture. When she moved to Ridge Point after her husband's suicide, dozens of trunks and wardrobes filled with clothes had moved in with her, and her shopping habits had most likely not changed in all these years. Even as cold hearted as his father had been, he had not denied his family any luxury. He had lavished both his wife and sister with clothes and jewels, not because he was generous, but because their appearance reflected upon him.

Had his aunt cleaned out this room before or after his father died?

"Do not concern yourself Miss Parsons," he said. "I will see to my son's needs. Now, if you will excuse us?"

The young woman hesitated, glancing at Abby to ensure herself that her charge and his mother would be safe before she quietly slipped from the room, leaving Jack alone with his wife and son.

Locking his arms behind his back, he gazed down at Abby's head. She had temporarily quieted her son by allowing him to chew on her little finger. It would not satisfy him for long. Will may not be Jack's son by blood, but the boy's appetite was just as voracious. Perhaps he would grow as tall and broad as Jack himself.

He smiled and looked down at his wife and son. "I am sorry about the room. If you will make a list, I will see that Will has everything he needs."

"It is quite all right. Will has not outgrown his cradle just yet."

But at the rate he was growing, he would soon. "Still, I will rectify the situation just as quickly as I can. If I had known..."

"How could you have known?" She met his

steadfast gaze. "You have been gone for over twenty years. Even if what your aunt says about your father expecting your mother to come back is true, he would have given up waiting eventually. And your father has been dead for over a year now. Even if he had kept the room the same, your aunt and cousin would not have left it undisturbed."

"I suppose." He hunkered down beside her and gently brushed the top of Will's head. No longer satisfied gnawing on Abby's little finger, he started rooting against her chest. Abby flushed but ignored his thus far silent demands.

Memories of this room and his mother nudged at Jack's brain. He rose slowly to his feet and pointed to where Quentin had placed the cradle. "My bed was over there." He turned. "And there was a bookshelf and toy chest over there."

"Is that a smile I see?" Abby said, drawing him out of his thoughts. "I am glad you have some fond memories here. I would not want you to live in a home where there were only bad ones."

Her eyes shone when he looked into them. Was she holding back tears? For him? He did not need them. Life had not always been kind, but he was stronger for it, unlike his pampered, worthless cousin who had never worked for anything.

"When I was six, maybe seven," he said after some reflection, "my parents had been away for what seemed like forever to a child. My nanny was trying to get me into bed when my parents came into the room. My mother dropped to her knees so I could run into her outstretched arms. And right there, in front of the nanny, my father scolded her as if she too were a child.

233

Apparently, he did not want her to coddle me nor show such common displays of affection in front of the help. So, I suppose my aunt was right in that respect. My father, the viscount, was not an affectionate man."

"Oh Jack. A child needs to feel loved, especially by his parents."

"Too much coddling spoils a child." How many times had he heard that? If nothing else, his father had taught him to be strong and self-sufficient.

"No, Jack. Love blesses a child," Abby said with a sad smile.

Jack did not need her pity, despite his lack of experience when it came to softer emotions like love. He had had Uncle William's affection, even if their easy banter had never included hugs. He was also quite sure no one had ever kissed the top of his head before. And while he knew he cared for Abby, he was unsure what it was he actually felt for her.

Was wanting to ravish her the same as wanting to love her?

Will's grumbling saved him from having to respond. The boy's face turned red, and his fists flailed. Jack cleared his throat, thankful for the timely distraction. "I believe our son is growing impatient. He is ready to eat. Now."

Abby flushed but did not move, and Will's cries gained momentum. Still, Abby stalled. "I..." Her face flamed. "If you could please..."

"Oh!" Disappointment warred with regret as he turned away from her. Apparently, Abby was still uncomfortable in his presence, or perhaps she was just uncomfortable nursing her son in front of him. Shuffling his feet, he stepped toward the door. "I, um, need to see to the unpacking of our things."

"Don't go," she said, her voice shy and quiet. "He is settled now, and I am decently covered."

Pleasure settled over him as he turned. Abby kept her head bowed and did not meet his gaze. She had covered her son's head and her breast with the swaddling blanket, leaving much to his imagination. And imagine, he did.

"It pains me to see you so troubled," Abby said, seemingly oblivious to his fixation on her covered breasts. She continued to stare at the top of her son's head. He continued to stare there as well. "I know it is not my place, but I think it would behoove you to hear everything your aunt has to say."

He jerked, lifting his chin, but Abby kept her gaze lowered. He would do almost anything for her, but he would not do this. He would rather dip his rod in blood and swim naked in shark-infested waters than listen to one more word from his aunt's lying mouth. He bit his lip. He was not angry with Abby. His aunt and her continued lies was the source of his rage.

Trying to hold his temper in check, he knelt at Abby's feet and hesitantly raised his hand to her lap. When she did not cringe or attempt to brush it off, he gently squeezed her knee. "You are my wife, and though I will not bow to your advice whenever you give it, rest assured that you will always be free to speak your mind."

The look she bestowed upon him in that moment was filled with more than just gratitude. Her eyes shone with the prospect of hope and so much more.

"I thank you for that," she said softly. "It is more than I expected from marriage to a noble."

In the blink of an eye, joy turned to disappointment. He had thought they had gotten beyond her mistrust, and yet, she was still comparing him to that bastard, Simon Weston. Grinding his back teeth, he snatched his hand from her knee and rose to his feet. "I am nothing like Lord Drury."

The stricken look on her face made him regret those harsh words. Her hand trembled as she gently touched her son's head. "No, milord, you are not. You manage to hold your fierce temper in check." She raised her chin, glaring at him with such pain and hurt he was unable to hold her gaze. "You have yet to raise your fists to me, despite my forward behavior. Nor have you punched me so hard that I feared my insides would explode. But your temper frightens me just the same."

Heart in his throat, he sank to his knees once more. Fearing her rejection more than he had ever feared anything in his life, he wrapped his arms around her and Will, holding them as tightly as he dared. When she seemed to melt beneath him, his soul rejoiced. "I would never raise a hand to you nor frighten you on purpose."

With a sigh he could not interpret, she leaned toward him, the side of her face touching his forehead. The scent of lavender and woman assailed his nostrils, sending a surge of white-hot desire straight to his groin. His body was so focused on hers that his brain could barely interpret her words when she spoke.

"I do not fear your temper because I am afraid of you, Jack. I am afraid *for* you. I do not wish to see you become your father."

Desire withered and died. His heart clenched. Raising his head, he notched up his chin and glared down at her upturned face. "How many times do I have to tell you that I would never, *ever*, send you or Will away? What must I do to prove my loyalty to you? Slit my wrists and swear a blood oath?"

Her eyes widened and her face flamed, but she did not look away. Settling Will more firmly in the crook of her left arm, she raised her right hand and cupped the side of his face. "Oh Jack. I no longer fear you will send me away. I am afraid you will never be at peace if you do not let go of your rage." She smiled, but a deep sadness lingered in her gaze. "We are much alike, you and I."

He smiled, his heart filling with some emotion he could not quite grasp. He leaned closer, pressing his face into her palm. "Have I not said so myself?"

"You have. And you were right in more ways than you know. We have both been hurt by people we believed cared for us, and we have both allowed pain to dictate our actions. I was so furious over what Simon had done that I was hesitant to give you a chance, even after you so gallantly came to my rescue."

"Ah, so you are now willing to give an old pirate a chance, are you?" Did she know how beautiful she was? Did she yet realize she had been the one to rescue him?

She threw back her head and laughed, exposing the long, luscious column of her throat. "You are neither old nor are you a pirate as you were so quick to point out." The laughter died, yet her gaze lingered on his face. "But I did give you a chance, and you did not let me down. All I ask is that you give your aunt a chance as well. Allow her to explain. Things may not be as they seem, but you will never know if you do not listen."

Hardening his heart, he rose stiffly to his feet. "She had her chance."

"Did she?"

He gave her the same stern look that stopped his crew from arguing when he issued an order. "I have done nothing in response to my father's actions that I regret."

She lowered her hand but held his gaze. "Haven't you?"

Apparently, she did not find him as intimidating as his crew did. "No. And before you ask, I do not regret marrying you either."

She sighed and to his utter surprise, she switched her son to her other breast before his lecherous gaze. The brief flash of dark pink nipple sent heat rushing to his groin, but the sight of her nursing their son held him enthralled. He wanted her. Now. He wanted her to put down their son so he could drag her to his room and make love to her all night. But he was unsure if he could stand, much less walk. He was so hard he doubted he could even move.

His heart nearly stopped beating.

What if he was unable to make her forget the degradation and pain Drury had inflicted?

What if he could not give her the pleasure she deserved?

What if she denied him?

Fear rose into his throat. *Will I be able to walk away with my dignity intact if she does?*

Dignity be damned! If she denied him, he would have no choice but to walk away.

"Well?" she asked, finally gaining his attention. He apparently did not hear whatever it was she had asked.

He raised his chin, meeting her gaze.

"Yes. Whatever you wish, whatever you desire. Yes."

Chapter Twenty-Three

Jack's words set Abby's heart to pounding, but the look in his eye as he slowly rose to his feet sent a thrilling spark to her midsection. Her body surged, and her stomach clenched. Trying to ignore the slow burn spreading through her, she rose on shaking legs and carried Will to his cradle. When she straightened, Jack stood behind her. He leaned in, his front covering her back. Heat radiated through her clothes, sparking a fire low in her belly. Then he wrapped his arms around her waist and pulled her against his arousal.

With his hot breath tickling her ear, he rasped, "I want you."

Anticipation warred with fear. Blood roared in her ears, and her pulse beat against her throat. She wanted to turn and fall into his arms, but the memory of Lord Drury's foul words and groping hands kept her rooted to the floor. Then Jack's lips grazed the side of her neck, pebbling her skin and sending an electric shock down to her toes.

"Say the word and I will make you mine in every sense of the word." His huskily spoken words sent a shocking thrill through her veins, hardening her nipples and making her weak in the knees. She wanted to turn. She wanted to say yes, and still, she could not move.

"Please," came Jack's harsh whisper as his lips brushed the side of her face.

She nearly melted. He did not need to beg. He need not even ask. He was her husband, and he could take what he wanted. Lord Drury had certainly not asked her permission. Yet Jack not only asked, he pleaded. And she could no longer deny him. Whether she felt obligated or thoroughly seduced, however, she could not say. She could barely think.

Heart pounding in her throat, she turned, and his arms banded more tightly around her. As his hands skated up her back, he pulled her closer, nestling her against that male part of him that would cause so much pain. And yet, he made no move to shove his hands up her skirts. Instead, he stood frozen for a brief moment, giving her a chance to remember the pain and fear Drury had inflicted. Nausea roiled in her stomach. Her flesh crawled. She was poised on the brink of denial until Jack's dark eyes burned down into hers, begging. Pleading. Promising.

She met his gaze as boldly as she could, making no promises but denying him nothing.

"Come to bed with me, Abby," he said, his voice low and gravelly. "Let me love you the way you were meant to be loved." His lips touched hers. Once. Twice. As light as a butterfly kiss, making her heart flutter. "Let me make you forget. Let me be the first and last man to ever touch you with real desire."

He lowered his head, capturing her reply in his mouth. His feather-light touch was pleading and then demanding as he sipped and tasted, delving his tongue into her mouth and taking her to dizzying heights of sensual awareness she had never known. His hands were everywhere at once, pulling her closer, sliding down her back, and cupping her bottom in an erotic rhythm that heated her blood.

Gasping for breath, she turned her head, trying to regain her wits, but they scattered like leaves in the wind when Jack scooped her into his arms with a low-pitched growl. "If you do not stop me now, I will carry you to my bed and make love to you until sunrise."

Oh. My. Was that even possible? She glanced toward the nursery window. Weak beams of dying sunlight danced across the floor as the sun set, painting the horizon in shades of pink and gold. It could not be much later than eight. Could a man make love to a woman for so long a time? She did not know. Nor was she sure she was brave enough to find out firsthand. Once again, Jack was holding her in his strong arms, awaiting her answer and this time, unlike on her wedding day, it was not in her heart to deny him. Still, the words failed her, and so she simply nodded.

Pleasure lit Jack's face as he strode across the room and into the hall. Despite his usual grace, he fumbled with the knob as he opened the door to the master suite. Once inside, his grip tightened. So did the hold he had on her heart. Then he kicked the door shut with his booted foot, and her heart nearly stopped beating.

"You are so beautiful," he whispered, his voice low and raspy, sending goose flesh dancing across her skin as he lowered her feet to the floor. Her body slid over every delicious inch of him, making her acutely aware of how hard and stiff he was.

He offered a lopsided smile and held up trembling hands. "I want you so badly, I am shaking. But I will not force you, Abby. If you are not ready, if this is not what you want, I will walk away right now and not bother you again until it is what we both want."

Heart in her throat, she pulled away. Standing before him, she began to unfasten her bodice. Despite her bold determination to be the woman he deserved, her fingers shook. When she reached the last button, she dared to glance up and into his eyes.

He seemed frozen for a moment, giving doubt and fear a stronghold on her heart. Then Jack reached out with gentle fingers. His hot gaze roved over her body, sending a thrill racing down her spine as he stripped her down to her chemise and drawers. Then, he shrugged out of his waistcoat, cravat, and shirt, flinging them onto the bundle of clothes piling up at her feet.

The sight of his naked chest set her body on fire. Her face flamed, and her fingers itched to touch the hard, sculpted contours of his firm muscles. He stood there, breathing heavily, watching her watch him. Then, he reached up to help her finish stripping out of her clothes before dropping his pants and linens.

"Oh. My." She glanced down at the hard, jutting appendage between his legs, and a knot of fear formed in her belly. She had not seen Lord Drury naked, but she could not imagine that part of him being as large as Jack's.

On the verge of losing her nerve, she raised her trembling chin to meet Jack's gaze, but the words never came. Instead of forcing that huge part of him inside her, he pulled her into his arms and held her shivering naked body against his until her quaking ceased. Then he lifted her into his strong arms, kissing her throat and breasts as he laid her across the bed.

The hot press of his body on hers seemed to melt her fear as his lips skated up from her breasts to lock onto her mouth. The kiss was hard and demanding, stirring desires deep inside her she never knew existed. Her body pulsed, and her womanhood thrummed as an ache built between her legs that both thrilled and terrified her. Then he lowered his lips to her throat, kissing her neck and trailing lower until he took one turgid nipple into his mouth. The sensation she felt when he suckled her was nothing like what she felt when Will nursed at her breast. Jack's mouth sent a jolt to her very core, and she very nearly bucked him off the bed.

"You were made for loving, Abby," he whispered as he moved against her, slowly at first, his tongue drawing circles around first one nipple and then the other.

She moaned, pushing her breast more firmly into his mouth. He then laved her chest down to her navel and back up to her throat, moving slowly at first and then faster and faster, rubbing his hard body against her softer one. His fingers slid inside her. Her body arched, flames licking her core at the intimate invasion. His tongue swept into her mouth. His fingers delved deeper, touching her in such a way that she felt every muscle in her body coil tighter and tighter. Sensations spiraling out of control, she thrashed beneath him until he finally raised his head, arched his back, and plunged deep inside her.

She gasped, unable to breathe or move as her body closed around his. He pushed deeper, rubbing all his hard muscled planes and crisp hair—textures she could feel but not see—against her. She wanted him in her and on her, but it was too much all at once. The fear she expected had faded the moment he kissed her, but there were other feelings, feelings she could neither grasp nor explain as her body reacted in the most unusual manner.

"Wait!" she panted, her heart beating so hard she could barely speak.

Jack froze. "Am I hurting you?"

He started to pull out, but she clasped the globes of his firm bottom and held him fast against her. He groaned low and deep in his throat as she held him in place, marveling at the way his body fit so nicely inside hers. "No. Just wait."

Her mind whirled with sensations she wanted to savor, but every small movement of his big body drove her closer and closer to the unknown. A chuckle rumbled through his deep chest, and she felt it down to her toes.

"Hmm." She wiggled beneath him, luxuriating in the way her body responded to his. It was so very different from the way it had reacted to Drury's crass coupling. Jack surely knew what he was doing.

"This is how it should feel, Abby." He arched over her, moving his hips in a slow circle that set her lower half to throbbing with sensations that were addictive and delicious.

She thrashed beneath him, lifting her hips higher, driving his manhood deeper into her as he pumped his hips, pounding her with a ferocity that sent her soaring. Desperate and not knowing exactly what she craved, her hands roamed over his hard back and shoulders, wanting more. Needing more. She wanted to grasp his beautiful hair and pull his head down to meet her mouth, but his back was arched, his head thrown back as if he were a lion about to roar.

His face contorted, and a groan escaped as he lowered his head to claim her mouth in a brutal kiss that drove her to the brink of something wonderful that she feared and craved at the same time.

"Jack. Please!" she cried into his mouth, arching against him, not knowing how to reach that glorious destination hovering just beyond her reach.

His hot breath touched her bare flesh as he nuzzled her neck, licking and sucking, increasing the sense of urgency building deep within her. She arched upward again with an anguished, pleading cry. His hands skated over her breasts and down her sides to slide beneath her bottom and anchor her more firmly against his hips as he drove into her even deeper.

"Hold on, Abby," he said, his voice hoarse and strained.

Her hands fisted in his hair, kissing him deeply, sweeping her tongue into his mouth, wanting to feel joined to him at both ends. He nearly stole her breath. Then suddenly, he arched his back once more, jerking his head out of her grasp, and pushing into her so deeply she feared he would come out the other side. His hand reached between their bodies, his thumb circling the hottest aching part of her until she felt ready to explode. She gasped. He growled and plunged hard and deep one last time as they reached the summit and tumbled over the edge together.

****

Dust motes danced on dappled rays of sunlight shining through an opening in the heavy drapes covering the east-facing window of the master suite. Branches swayed in the early morning breeze casting one corner of the bed in alternating sunlight and shadow. The flickering lights penetrated the fog of Jack's sleep-numbed brain and satiated body. One eyelid cracked open, and his mouth quirked upward in a satisfied smile. Abby lay on her side, nestled beneath the covers, her body curved toward him, her blonde head pressed against his shoulder. Sprawled on his back, he opened his other eye and took note of the tent beneath the covers.

Despite being thoroughly satisfied by Abby last night, he wanted her. Again. And this wasn't just a morning erection either. He wanted her both physically and mentally.

He rolled onto his side and stroked her bare shoulder. She sighed contentedly, bringing an ache to his chest and his groin. He smiled. He could think of no better way to wake a sleeping angel than by making her climax.

Brushing the hair from her face, he kissed her cheek, sliding his lips down the side of her neck. She moaned and stirred, rolling onto her back to give him greater access. His body jerked and his erection pulsed.

Heavy with desire, he groaned and lowered his head to her breast, drawing one, taut nipple into his mouth, suckling until milk beaded on the tip. Then he abandoned her breasts and trailed kisses down to her navel. His tongue dipped inside, and she cried out. But when he trailed kisses even lower, she squirmed beneath him.

"Jack!" She grabbed his hair as if to push him away, but the moment his fingers grasped her feminine lips and spread them, her fingers tightened.

And when he dipped his tongue deep inside to taste her musty sweetness, she jolted. Licking and tasting, he brought her to a sweet shuddering climax before rising up on all fours. Then he rose to a kneeling position and slid his hands beneath her knees before dragging her legs over the tops of his thighs to impale her with his heavy, aching shaft.

"Jack," she screamed again as he held her thighs aloft and pounded into her until she was weak and gasping.

Pleasure fired his blood, fueling his desire. His soul soared. Then with a low-pitched growl, he threw back his head and emptied his seed deep inside her. And with a satisfied moan, he collapsed onto the bed and dragged her on top of him.

Their mingled breaths slowed. Muscles relaxed. But Will's muffled cries soon penetrated their delirium. With a gasp, Abby bolted upright in bed. "Will!"

Before he could stop her, she pulled the covers up over her breasts, threw her legs over the side of the bed, and slid to the floor. "He must be starving!"

She ran toward the door connecting his room to hers and paused to look back. He'd slid back to rest against the headboard, one knee bent so he could rest an elbow against it and stare at his lovely wife wrapped in bed linens with her bare back exposed.

A pretty pink flush stained her cheeks. "I'm sorry. I have to get dressed so I can feed Will."

He nodded. "He does like to eat."

Her gaze strayed to his crotch. His balls and rod were flopped out on the mattress, resting against his outstretched thigh, but the moment he caught her looking, he stiffened and came to attention. Abby flushed crimson, turned, and ran from the room with Jack's laughter echoing in her ears.

Chapter Twenty-Four

Jack had already bathed and dressed by the time Abby finished feeding Will. Once her son was satisfied, Jack filled the hipbath inside the water closet and stood guard outside the door while she bathed and dressed. Neither knew what to expect when they descended the stairs. He assumed his cousin would sleep past noon as many nobles who spent their evenings gaming and drinking were wont to do, but he did not dare guess at what time his aunt might rise.

Would she insist on serving a big breakfast in the dining room as his mother did when guests were in residence? Did she have a servant bring a tray to her room? Or did she and Morris eat breakfast in the smaller, family salon?

With his hand on Abby's elbow, he guided her into the family salon and felt his face flush with embarrassed heat. Quentin sat alone at the table, drinking coffee. The remains of whatever he had eaten for breakfast still sat on his plate.

Upon seeing Abby, Quent rose quickly to his feet and executed an eloquent bow. "Good morning, Lady Ardmore."

She smiled. "Good morning, Mr. Stanley."

Quent straightened, catching Jack's eye. Jack knew the minute he guessed the truth about where Abby had slept. Mischief danced in his dark eyes, and his face broke into one of his best pretty-boy smiles. "Ah, Ardmore. How dashing and...satisfied you look this morning. It must be because you have finally taken your rightful place as...lord and master of Ridge Point."

"Do shut up, Quent," Jack said as he escorted Abby to the table.

She cocked her head to one side and gave him the most adorably confused look. But she would just have to remain unenlightened as to why he was being rude to a guest. He refused to explain that Quent's compliments were double entendres to let Jack know that he knew just what had transpired in the master suite last night.

After pushing in Abby's chair, he reached behind Quent and tugged on a bell pull before taking his seat on the other side of his wife. Her curious expression had turned to one of annoyance. He could tell from the expression on her face that she did not like feeling left out, and he and Quent were speaking as if she were not in the room at all.

After taking another sip off coffee, Quent lowered his cup and arched a brow. "Do let me thank you for telling Higgins I am a friend and not the hired help. Otherwise, I would have had to spend the night in the stables because I was not about to sleep on the third floor with the servants. I cannot imagine how hot it must get up there this time of year."

"I am sure it was even hotter back in the summer, but the house has always been well ventilated, so I do not suppose you would have died. Still, I trust you were allowed to stay in one of the guest rooms?" Regardless of any feeble protests from Morris or Aunt Margery, Quentin Stanley would not have slept with servants. He did not mind sleeping aboard ship with the crew, but servants gossiped, and once on British soil, Quentin behaved with the utmost decorum so as not to embarrass his father, the Earl of Willoughby.

Quent nodded. "I was. Amusingly enough, before realizing I was more than just your driver and valet, one of the servants informed me your cousin was not happy having to move into the smaller room down the hall. Apparently, he had moved into the master suite the day after your father's funeral. And while your aunt never changed rooms, she had ordered the nursery cleared so she might use it as an expansive dressing room." He chuckled. "I cannot imagine how well she slept last night. By the time the servants moved all of her clothes from the nursery and into her room, she probably could not even find the bed."

"Do not expect me to feel any sympathy for her," Jack replied, which earned him another glowering look from Abby. But before either of them could speak, a servant arrived, carrying extra place settings. Behind her came another young woman carrying a large tray containing four covered dishes. She placed them opposite one another on the table, as if it would tip over if not perfectly balanced. When she raised the lids, steam and tempting aromas wafted into the air.

The first maid stepped forward and began serving his and Abby's plates with bacon, ham, eggs, haddock, and toast.

"What is your name, miss?" Abby asked.

The woman froze. Her hand trembled. "Molly." She offered a wobbly smile. "And that be Olive."

Abby offered her own smile. "Thank you, Molly. Olive. Everything looks delicious."

Molly nodded. "Mrs. Lux be the cook, my lady."

"Is breakfast always ready at this hour?" Jack asked, and the one named Olive nearly dropped one of the silver lids as she was putting it back on the bacon dish. They were probably wondering if they would have jobs in the morning. If their loyalties lay with Ridge Point and not whoever happened to be sleeping in the master suite, they had no need for concern. Otherwise, he hoped they were good at what they did because they would soon need a letter of reference.

Molly nodded again and lowered her gaze. "Mrs. Lux has strict orders to have breakfast ready by nine and to hold it warm until after Mr. Flick done eat."

"That simply will not do." Jack looked at Abby and excused himself. He then followed the two maids down to the kitchen.

The large room was the hub of the house, and even at nine-fifteen in the morning, it was a hive of activity. It wasn't hard to tell the scullery maids from Mrs. Lux. The large woman was brandishing a wooden spoon and issuing orders like a captain on deck. The moment he stepped into the room, all activities ceased.

"Good morning. I am the new Lord Ardmore, and I will be introducing my wife to each of you later in the day. Until then, there is one thing we need to get straight here and now. Breakfast will be served between six and nine, as I am an early riser. If it is to be served later, Lady Ardmore will inform Mrs. Lux the day before. I also expect a light luncheon to be served at noon until further notice or at Lady Ardmore's discretion. Afternoon tea will be at four, and dinner shall be served no later than eight, unless Lady Ardmore informs you otherwise. Whatever meals you have planned for the week with Lady Margery will be acceptable, but any future meal planning or questions are to be directed to Lady Ardmore. And unless we have more than two guests, all meals will be served in the family salon."

Not waiting to see the response to his demands, he turned sharply on his heel and returned upstairs. Once again, Abby had that same quizzical look on her face. He smiled, shook out his napkin, and sat down to eat his food before it grew any colder.

An incessant tapping under the table drew his attention. "Well?" Abby snapped. "Where did you dash off to and why?"

"I wanted to meet Mrs. Lux and give her orders about our future dining plans."

Her brows furrowed, but she no longer looked cute and adorable. She looked just a bit angry. "And you did not think that was something I should be included in?"

"I told them when I wanted my meals and to discuss menus and such with you." What more did she want? Total control of the kitchen?

Abby threw up her hands and huffed out a breath as if thoroughly exasperated. "I do not even know what time you like to eat! Perhaps it would have been wiser for you to talk to me first."

Quentin chortled and Jack flushed. Damn if this husband business wasn't going to take more getting used to than being a damn viscount.

****

Later that morning, Higgins gathered all the servants on the front lawn. Abby's knees shook just a bit as she stood beside Jack with Miss Parsons to her immediate left holding Will. Beside Miss Parsons was Mrs. Smythe who was to continue acting as her lady's maid. Once Jack introduced them to the rest of the staff, Mrs. Smythe returned to the house, and Miss Parsons carried Will back up to the nursery. Then Jack led Abby down the front steps, stopping in front of each servant who bowed or curtsied as they walked past.

When they reached the end of the sidewalk and the end of the servants, Jack turned and addressed the crowd as if he had been groomed his entire life to be the next Viscount Ardmore. Only the tension Abby felt in his bicep as she lightly clung to his elbow showed how truly uncomfortable he was in his new role.

"The law requires obedience and loyalty from any servant contracted to the Viscount Ardmore, and I am the new viscount. Any infringements will be dealt with in a court of law and met with a jail sentence or hard labor. So, if you wish to stay on, your loyalty and obedience to my viscountess and me is paramount. Any servant not wishing to stay under those conditions and anyone contracted personally to Mr. Flick or Lady Margery will be given a letter of reference. I will need your decision and your signatures on the new contracts by tomorrow evening. Any questions are to be directed to Mr. Higgins." Jack gazed at the crowd, his bearing and posture as proud as any viscount—or sea captain. He spoke with authority and conviction, and Abby was proud to stand at his side.

Holding her head high, she gazed at each servant's face. Most stared straight ahead, their bearing almost as steadfast and proud as Jack's. One or two shuffled their feet or gazed at the ground. Another two cast shifting glances around them. Abby made a mental note to warn Jack against signing contracts with them. She raised her chin, meeting his gaze. His eyes sparked with understanding, and a slight smile lifted his full lips. Somehow, without exchanging words, he knew exactly what she was thinking.

If only they could communicate so easily when it came to matters of the heart.

With a resolved sigh, Abby allowed Jack to guide her back inside. The moment they entered the front entrance, Jack's demeanor changed. His shoulders stiffened, and a scowl crinkled his brow. Pressing his hand to the small of her back, he propelled her across the wide hall and threw open the drawing room door. His aunt and cousin were huddled beneath the portrait of Jack's father, and they appeared to be engaged in a heated argument.

How had Jack known they would be in here? Had the closed door alerted him? She had been so focused on her husband that she had scarcely paid any attention to her surroundings.

"Trying to figure out the combination to the safe?" Jack growled as they entered the room.

Lady Margery turned with barely a twitch of her oddly smooth, pale skin. Mr. Flick whirled to face them, his face flushing an unbecoming shade of guilt-red. "You are up and about at an ungodly hour, cousin."

Jack arched a brow. "I have been up for quite some time, Morris. The hour is only ungodly to one who was deep in his cups the night before."

Mr. Flick snorted. "I can afford to get corned every night. At least, I could afford to do so before you returned. I must say, it would delight me to no end if you were to set sail on your little ship and never come back."

"Morris, please," Lady Margery said, a faint flush

to her cheeks. She turned, her gaze briefly seeking Abby's before honing in on Jack. "Even if I had known the combination, Jack...Ardmore...I would not have divulged it. The contents of that safe are private. Whatever is in there, Ardie meant for you to have it."

"I don't give a tinker's damn about what my father wanted."

Tension radiated from every pore in his body, making Abby quite nervous. She no longer feared Jack, but she feared what he might do. He was quick to anger and slow to forgive, and she did not want him acting out in anger and living to regret it. And regret it he would. Jack may be slow to forgive, but he had a big heart filled with regrets. "Jack, my lord, please listen to your aunt. I can excuse myself if—"

"No! You will stay here, and they will leave." Rage darkened his eyes.

Mr. Flick blanched, but Lady Margery's pale face fell, and a single tear leached from the corner of one eye. "I never meant to harm you. I swear. I was just so afraid after Morris' father hanged himself. He never told me how desperate his finances were, encouraging me to spend money as I had when I lived under my father's roof. And after his death, the crown seized everything but my clothes and a few precious jewels."

"That has no bearing on your behavior," Jack snarled. "You hated my mother, and you hated me. Why should I believe a damn thing that emerges from your lying lips?"

"Because she is most likely telling the truth."

Both Abby and Jack jumped, whirling toward the door to find Uncle William and Mr. Stanley standing at the threshold. Abby was often taken by surprise, but catching Jack unawares was a testament to the amount of stress he was under.

"What are you doing here?" The usual pleasure etched on Jack's face when addressing his uncle was absent from his expression.

Uncle William gave him a piteous look filled with love and heartache. "Mr. Stanley sent the coach for me last night. He said you needed me."

Abby's heart melted, and in that instant, she decided Mr. Stanley was not only trustworthy, he was a good friend to Jack and much more kind-hearted than she would have guessed. She offered him a smile that sent color to his cheeks.

"Not now, uncle. And you!" Jack pointed an accusing finger at his friend. "Keep your patrician nose out of my goddamn business."

Abby cringed at the use of such foul language until she noted the hurt shining in his eyes. Poor Jack. He felt betrayed by everyone in the room. She nestled closer and gently squeezed his bicep. He did not seem to notice, but then she dared a glance at his face. He glanced down for just a second, his face softening enough to let her know he appreciated her support. Then, every muscle in his body stiffened, and he turned angry eyes on Mr. Stanley.

Shuffling his feet, Mr. Stanley backed toward the door. "This is a family matter. So, if you will excuse me..."

Jack's glare intensified. "Do not go far, Quent, because I *will* be talking to you later."

"As you wish." Mr. Stanley backed from the room, but he did not appear cowed or properly chastised. Jack growled and turned his frustration on his aunt.

"You and Morris still have the weekend, but I expect you gone by Monday. Until then, I do not want to see you or hear even the softest patter of your feet."

Morris sneered but said nothing as he turned toward the desk, removed the stopper from a bottle of brandy, and poured himself a drink. Lady Margery, however, looked as if she were about to cry. Her chin trembled, and her pale face seemed to crumble.

"Hate me if you wish, but please, do not hate your father. He did not write the codicil to his will until after I told him I had seen you with a woman in London."

Jack's expression darkened. His hands fisted at his sides. "So you told him yet another lie. And he believed you. Why should I forgive either of you?"

Uncle William stepped forward, his eyes on his sister's face. "Because she alone is not to blame. I had a hand in this mess, too, and for that, I am truly sorry."

Chapter Twenty-Five

The room spun, and Jack's world tilted on its axis. His aunt had confessed, which wasn't surprising, but hearing Uncle William admit to being culpable was like having a knife plunged into his chest.

"Jack." Abby's voice barely penetrated the haze of fury pounding against his skull. "Please listen."

Uncle William clasped his shoulder. "Your father was a fool, Jack, but he did not hate you."

"He had an odd way of showing it." Jack's throat cramped, but he ignored the burning tightness and reached for Abby's hand, clasping it as if it were a lifeline.

Aunt Margery stepped away from her sullen son, taking a hesitant step closer. "I honestly believed William was your father. He was always so defensive of Lady Darcy. But when she refused to beg Ardie's forgiveness, I began to wonder if I had misjudged her. And Ardie was so miserable after she left I believed it no longer mattered. He loved her. Then, Ardie lavished all of his money on Morris and me, and it was as if my darling Mr. Flick were still alive. Once again, I was being fitted in Paris and attending the most fashionable balls. I soon forgot all about you and your mother."

"I bet you did," Jack growled. He would have said more had Abby not squeezed his hand.

A flush lightly stained Aunt Margery's pale

cheeks, but her skin stretched so tightly over her bones that her face barely registered any expression at all. "I ignored the guilt, living in fear of the day when you or your mother returned and tossed Morris and me out on our ears. So when I saw you in London with a beautiful blonde six months before you attempted to see your father, I told him you seemed happy without us in your life."

Blonde. What blonde? He felt Abby's eyes on him, but he did not dare turn to meet her gaze. He was relieved both his aunt and Morris had readily accepted the fact he had met Abby over a year ago while in London, but he did not remember any blonde. "Where did you see us?"

Again, a slight stain colored his aunt's cheeks. Her gaze darted to Abby and back before she lowered her chin and stared at her shoes. "On Patton Street. Lady Carstairs, Lady Vera, and Lady Emma Ellington and I had spent the day shopping at the Burlington Arcade on Piccadilly. We'd grown quite famished, so we walked to Patton Street to a café that sold Italian ices. As we came around the corner, I saw you. You looked so much like your father and uncle that I knew it was you. You were standing with a beautiful blonde woman, and you were holding her packages."

Jack's pulse hitched. Beside him, Abby gasped. He looked down. She looked up.

"That was you?" she whispered.

He nodded, unable to believe the woman he had plowed into nearly two years ago on the corner of Patton and Oxendon was Abby. No wonder he had been so drawn to her when he saw her in that rundown coach. It was those Caribbean blue eyes. They had mesmerized him then as they did now. "That was the day we met."

She smiled, and it lit her entire face like sunshine bursting through the clouds. "I had just bought new shoes, gloves, and a bonnet for a garden party at Chivington Manor. I was so flustered when I walked into your broad chest and dropped all my packages. But you were so gallant and kind."

"It was love at first sight," Aunt Margery said with a sigh. "And here, I had wondered if perhaps...Well, again it seems, I misjudged."

"You did not even know who she was, and yet, you told my father we were wed?" He did not believe in love at first sight. There *had* been a mutual attraction, but at the time, he had been interested only in the nightly pleasures a woman could offer, and Abby had been off limits. She had probably not even given him a second thought after he had gallantly kissed her gloved hand and walked away. She had still been infatuated with Drury at the time.

Aunt Margery's face flushed a bright pink before fading to snowy white. "I assumed the worst and had no intention of telling your father anything. But when I returned home, he was in one of his moods. He had heard you were in town and despaired that you would never attempt to see him and that you would never wed or give him grandchildren because of what he had done. He was so despondent I feared he would do something rash." She paused, inhaling deeply and brushing a tear from her pale cheek. "So, I told him I had seen you with a woman and that you seemed quite close. I did not know at the time how accurate my assessment was or that you would return to London to marry her. At the time, I just wanted to give Ardie hope."

"Hope for what? He all but disowned me, and he never once attempted to see me! What in God's name had he hoped for? To throw it in my face how little he cared?" His throat closed. So did his fists. But Abby's touch stopped his left hand from closing completely. Her thumb stroked the back of his fingers, soothing him in a way that only she could.

A single tear fell from Aunt Margery's eye, but her oddly pale expression never changed. She looked as animated as a porcelain doll. "Ardie had added that first codicil months before. That was another reason he refused to see you. He was planning to send a copy of the codicil to your mother. He thought if he threatened to leave Ridge Point to Morris, your mother would come home to argue with him, and he would not have to beg her forgiveness. He thought the two of you would come home, and he could convince you to stay."

"There was a damn war going on." Jack let go of Abby's hand and spiked his fingers into his hair. His parents had both been stubborn, manipulative, and damned unforgiving. And he had been caught in the middle of a battlefield that had been their marriage. Was it any damn wonder he had been against the notion of wedlock for so long?

Abby's gaze seemed to draw his attention. Her blue eyes offered compassion, sympathy, and something much deeper that he was not quite ready to acknowledge or accept.

"But that is not why Ardie did not send the letter." His aunt sniffed. "I was so afraid of losing my home, that I told him there was no need to inform you or Lady Darcy. I told him you had adopted America as your home, and you would most likely marry and sail back to America with your wife. I honestly did not believe you wanted anything more to do with England or the estate."

"Only because you wanted Ridge Point for your worthless son!"

Morris drew himself up as if only then realizing that he was part of the conversation. "I beg your pardon!"

"Beg nothing!" Jack snarled. "You will both leave my home!"

He turned to storm from the room, but Abby's hand on his arm and Uncle Williams's firm voice stopped him.

"Jack!" Uncle William raised his voice, as he had not done since Jack was a child. "Stop acting like a spoiled adolescent and listen. Your father was not perfect and neither are you. You are just as stubborn and pigheaded as he was, and it is high time you learned the truth. All of it!"

Jack's heart nearly stopped beating. Was this the moment when he would learn he was not Viscount Ardmore's son by blood? Had his entire life been a lie? He would rather not know the truth. He would rather die believing his biological father had disowned him than learn he was Uncle William's son. Sometimes, a lie was kinder than the truth. And in that moment, he swore he would take the truth of Will's paternity to the grave.

Will must never learn that I am not his father or that his mother was raped. The truth could be devastating.

"Damn it, boy, I am not your father!" Uncle

263

William snarled. "Damn if you are not just as stubborn as Ardmore. Now stop being a jackass and listen!"

Blood pounded in Jack's ears, relief making him weak in the knees. He draped an arm around Abby, tugging her close. Her arms circled his waist, hugging him tightly.

Aunt Margery lowered her chin and stared at the floor. "You had your ship and you had Ram's Head, but Morris had nothing. His father forfeited his estate to the crown when he hanged himself. I knew Ardie would care for us, but Morris does not have your flair for finance."

Morris snorted. "Mother, please! Jack is a disreputable pirate. Where is the flair in that?"

"Do be quiet, Morris." She glared at her son until he flopped down on the sofa with his glass of brandy. Then she turned back to Jack. "I asked Ardie to leave Ridge Point to Morris and he agreed. Then you showed up six months later and told Higgins you were unwed. Ardie was devastated and three months after that, he killed himself."

****

Jack staggered and nearly fell. Abby's arm cinched more tightly around his waist. There seemed to be nothing she could say or do to ease his pain. So, she simply hugged him.

"What the hell are you saying?" His words were strained, harsh, but barely above a whisper. "He could not have taken his own life."

His eyes strayed to the portrait hanging over the mantel. Abby's gaze followed. The stern-faced viscount seemed to stare back, his eyes filled with misery and dark secrets. A shiver snaked down her spine as she huddled closer to Jack. He hardly noticed. His father's portrait held his attention.

Was he thinking about the hidden safe and the answers he might find inside?

His Adam's apple bobbled, and his shoulders sagged. Releasing Abby, he stepped away from her and turned toward his uncle. "Is it true? Did you know?"

William Norton nodded and lowered his gaze, but not before Abby noticed a suspicious glistening in his eyes. "I received a letter from Margery a couple of days before your mother died. It included a brief note from your father. I was going to share it with you, but then Darcy—Lady Darcy—took a turn for the worse. The next day, you received the official letter from Ardmore's solicitor stating that your father had died of heart failure. So, I let the matter rest. Then after your mother died, we had to make haste to leave Charleston before the Union army confiscated the *Lion's Pride*. After that?" He shrugged. "I saw no need in adding to your pain."

"So, my mother never knew?" Jack's voice cracked. So did Abby's heart. She wanted to take him in her arms and hold him, but he pulled away from her and took a step back.

"No." Uncle William sighed. "Ardmore was a fool, but he grew to love your mother. Perhaps if I had not told him I loved her, too, then maybe he would not have been so quick to believe Margery. But I can hardly blame my sister. She knew how I felt, and she knew why your mother was marrying our brother. Then after you were born, Margery warmed up to Darcy, but by the time you were ten, you looked so much like me that the old fears and doubts resurfaced. She voiced her

265

concerns to your father, and he began to believe the worst. I tried convincing him of the truth, but the die had been cast. He confronted Darcy, and she never denied it. She simply refused to dignify his accusations with a response. But I had no trouble denying his claims, and I begged him to accept the truth and ask for Darcy's forgiveness. He refused, and I felt partially responsible. So, I tried convincing your mother to vocally deny his charges and return to Ridge Point. She too refused. She said it was up to Ardmore to beg her forgiveness and ask her to come home. I knew he never would. They were both so damned stubborn. So, I decided to stay in Charleston and look after you both."

Abby's heart ached as much for William Norton as for her husband. Mr. Norton had been caught in the middle of a situation beyond his control. How could he stop loving a woman because a match with his brother had been deemed more suitable? And how could anyone blame Jack's mother? Women were more or less the property of their fathers or the property of their husbands. Had not her own father forced her into a convent until he found a suitable solution for her?

"Did you covet your brother's wife?" Jack's voice was barely above a whisper, the anguish in his words almost palpable.

His uncle sighed and lowered his gaze. It seemed as if he were unwilling or unable to answer.

"Did you?" Jack growled, low and feral, causing the hairs on the back of Abby's neck to stand on end.

"Yes," came the whispered reply. "But your mother was faithful to your father. It was not..." He swallowed hard, inhaled deeply, and met Jack's damning gaze. "It was not until after I was injured in the Crimean war and gave you the *Lion's Pride* that the situation changed."

Jack's face turned crimson. "So. My mother cheated."

Morris Flick snorted as if in triumph. Lady Margery gasped. And William Norton's shoulders seemed to sag with defeat. "We did not mean for it to happen, but we were both lonely, and I had always loved her."

Abby's heart dropped, and her knees began to shake. How could Jack blame his mother? After the false accusations and years of living in exile, how could he blame her for falling into the arms of the man she had loved from the beginning? How could he be so unfeeling and cold?

He may look like his uncle, but he was truly his father's child. What must he think of her and what had transpired between them the night before?

A shiver snaked down her spine. What if Jack was as possessive, jealous, and unforgiving as his father? What if he questioned the motives behind her wanton response to his lovemaking? Worse, what if he began to wonder if she had responded as ardently to Lord Drury?

Rage colored Jack's expression and though he did not raise his voice, his controlled response chilled Abby's blood. "Then Aunt Margery was right all along. My mother was unfaithful."

"No!" Uncle William raised his voice. Jack cringed but did not back down. He glared. So did his uncle.

William Norton gnashed his teeth and fisted his hands at his sides. "Do not blame her. She is the only one who is innocent in all of this. Your father and I both loved her. He later regretted his actions, but he was too stubborn and prideful to go after her, and she was too stubborn to return home."

"And what about me?" Jack's voice dropped, and in that moment, he looked like a lost little boy. Abby took a step toward him, but he jerked his head toward her, his eyes cutting into her, daring her to take another step closer. And so, she did not. She froze where she stood, her heart pounding in her chest.

Lady Darcy Ardmore had been no more innocent than her husband and sister-in-law. She could have voiced her innocence or returned home for the sake of her child. Instead, she had put her misplaced pride before Jack, thus denying him his father, home, and birthright. Jack was the only innocent she saw, but she feared his pain, rage, and resentment would twist his heart as surely as it had twisted his parents'.

Mr. Norton took a hesitant step forward. "Your parents loved you, Jack. This was never about you. Ardmore did not realize what his decisions and your mother's actions would do to you until years later. He wanted so badly to believe what our sister had told him about you and the woman she had seen in London. He believed you were happily married and living in America until you came to Ridge Point last year. When he learned you were unwed, he felt too ashamed to face you."

"He was a coward and a hypocrite." Jack ground his teeth. His shoulders bunched, and it seemed as if he grew two inches taller as he stepped forward to stand nose to nose with his uncle. The two looked so much alike in size and coloring that it was easy to see the family resemblance.

Abby glanced once more at the portrait and then

back at the two men circling one another like roosters in a cockfight. Jack's jaw was firmer and squarer than his uncle's, his lips fuller, and his brow broader. He may have William Norton's size and coloring, but he had his father's bone structure.

Mr. Norton's shoulders slumped. He stepped away from Jack as if refusing to engage him further. Then with a heart-felt sigh, he lowered his gaze. "Hatred can eat a man alive, Jack. Your father learned that first-hand. Let it go, boy."

"I am a full-grown man, *uncle,* and my father was more than just a fool. He should have known better than to believe his sister's lies or assume I had married just because she had seen me with a woman. There had been women before Abby, and I did not marry them!"

Abby cringed. Lady Margery and Cousin Morris turned to stare. Lady Margery frowned. "A man should not boast of his former conquests in front of his wife."

Jack flushed, but he did not meet Abby's gaze. "The fact remains. We were not married when you saw us in London, and yet, you misled my father into believing I had not only married, but had sailed back to America to live happily ever after. It was only after I showed up here six months later that my father learned the truth."

If possible, Lady Margery's pale face lost even more color. "Ardmore wanted you to be happy, and I saw no need to disillusion him when we both thought he would have time to make things right. I thought I had smoothed things over, but the night after you came here, he sent for his solicitor and added the second codicil to his will. He mailed you a copy the next morning. He said you should have the right to decide if you wanted your inheritance or not, but I guess with your American war going on, you never got the letter. When months passed without a word, he assumed you did not care. Then he took his own life. It was his way of atoning for his sins."

"How is that any kind of atonement?" Jack looked stricken, but there was a hard edge to his voice, and his eyes were cold. "Suicide is a cowardly act, and he risked not only this family's reputation, but the entire viscountcy. Why was I not informed by his solicitor that he died in such a manner?"

A tear slid over Lady Margery's pale cheek. "He took care of everything, and for once, his plan worked exactly as he envisioned it, with the exception of your mother's death. He wrote all of us a letter before taking the poison. I found mine under my pillow. Yours and your mother's is in the safe." She looked at William. "He mailed your letter the day before."

Mr. Norton nodded, and Lady Margery turned her attention back to Jack. "Your father assured me in the letter he wrote me that Dr. Jamison would attest that he died of a heart condition so the crown would not consider confiscating anything entailed. His solicitor never even questioned the cause of death." A shiver racked her frail body. "Poison, it seems, is a woman's weapon. Men are expected to hang themselves as Mr. Flick did." She glanced up at the portrait, and all eyes followed. "Your father's way was much kinder and left no mess. He was always generous to a fault, and his dying wish was for you and your mother to return to England." She offered Jack a wobbly smile. "And so you have."

"I brought my mother home in a bloody box!"

Jack's voice rose in volume before he managed to calm himself.

His aunt nodded, tears now streaming freely down her face. "And you buried her at Ridge Point. It is where your father knew she always belonged." She looked at him once more and offered a tremulous smile. "Look in the safe, Jack. You'll never find peace until you do."

Chapter Twenty-Six

It had been hours since Jack evicted everyone, including Abby, from the drawing room. She had looked at him as if he had betrayed her—not that he could blame her. He was having trouble getting his bearings and making decisions. He did not need her softhearted advice or the distraction of her warm, comforting embrace.

Aboard ship, it was easy to think with his head and not his heart or his rod. As captain, he knew a single miscalculation could result in the loss of life or the destruction of the *Lion's Pride*. But ever since meeting Abby, he had allowed lust and emotion to get in the way of common sense. He should have known better.

Years ago, he learned to react quickly and go with his gut. Quentin was the one who thought things through and came up with last-minute plans, just as he had done when he thought of Jack marrying Abby. Had it not been for her, Jack would have taken a different approach to achieving his goals. He would have intimidated his cousin into giving up his claim to Ridge Point. If that had not worked, he would have ruined him financially before buying back the property. But he had not been thinking clearly and had allowed Quentin to convince him to marry Abby. Truth be told, it had not taken that much to convince him. This was reason enough for sending Abby to their room. She distracted him beyond reason. She made him weak.

Had his father had similar thoughts about his wife? Was that another reason for sending her away?

Jack stared up at his father's portrait and then back down at the glass of brandy in his hand. *Bloody hell!* He was not like his father!

With a roar, he hurled his untouched drink at the painting. Amber liquid spattered, and the glass dented the canvas just below his father's be-ringed hand before crashing to the hearth. Cut crystal shattered, and droplets of brandy formed rivulets that rolled over the painting to puddle at the edge of the gilt frame before dripping onto the mantel. Jack's pulse hitched but the brief outburst did nothing to relieve the tension in his neck and shoulders.

Damn if he wasn't going to have to open that bloody safe and read those letters.

With a sigh, he grabbed the whisk broom and wrought iron fireplace shovel. As he was sweeping up broken glass, a firm rap sounded at the door. Jack straightened and turned as Quentin stepped inside. "Your uncle told me where I could find you."

Jack dumped the glass shards inside the cold hearth. Then he hung the broom and shovel back with the other fireplace implements and turned to face his first mate and friend.

Quentin arched a brow. One side of his mouth lifted in a smirk. "There are three more glasses on the tray if you would like to hurl another one at the old man's head. Or you could pour us both a drink."

Jack snorted but stepped toward the desk to pour two glasses of brandy. He handed one to Quentin and downed the contents of his in one swallow before refilling the glass. He snorted again. "I much prefer rum to brandy. I guess that's something else that will change around here."

"Ah. So you are staying." Quentin sat on one of the sofas flanking the fireplace and took a sip of his drink. "I always preferred brandy myself. Then again, I did not take to pirating as naturally as you did."

"Privateering, damn you, and of course I am staying. This is my house." Jack sat opposite Quent on the other small sofa, sipping his second drink more slowly.

Quent saluted him with his glass before taking a swallow. "So... What about the letters in that safe? Are you going to read them, or hold tightly to your hatred and preconceived notions and leave them locked in there forever?"

Damn Uncle William and his big mouth. If Jack had wanted Quentin to know about the letters, he would have told him. His pulse jumped, and his stomach churned, but he resisted the urge to reprimand Quent for overstepping his bounds. They were both, after all, the sons of peers, but more importantly, Quent was his friend and possibly the only person who had his best interest at heart. He refused to think about Abby. Doing so distracted him.

He forced her from his thoughts with some difficulty and took another sip of his drink before replying. "I had thought about putting a bullet in my cousin's brain, beating my aunt, and challenging Uncle William to a duel over my mother's honor, but I now wonder if she had any. So, I will settle for feeding my anger and ignoring the damned letters of a dead man who took the coward's way out."

Evan as he spoke the words, he knew they were a lie. Just thinking of his father killing himself caused an ache in his chest he could not contain.

Quentin exhaled slowly and looked up at the portrait. "That is most harsh, Jack. Perhaps you should consider how very young your mother was at the time she wed. Would you have expected her to defy her father when your uncle had not even made an offer? She was still just a girl, and her father encouraged, nay, demanded she accept your father's suit. Your mother was stubborn, but she was not disobedient. Had William not accompanied the two of you to Charleston, she most likely would have returned home within the year to deny your father's charges, and he would have taken her back."

His chest cramped. Jack rubbed his breastbone and took another swallow of brandy before replying. "So, my uncle is to blame."

"No, Jack. Your uncle did the gentlemanly thing. Your mother was just too bloody stubborn for her own good, and your father was a jealous, unforgiving fool. Do not be like him."

Jack paused, his drink mid-way to his mouth. Had Abby not said the very same thing?

Memories overlapped the daydreams of a small boy until he was unsure what was truth and what was imagination. He had been so young and confused the day he and his mother left England. He remembered his father standing on the docks, not returning his wave, and he remembered his mother not holding him or grasping his hand when he reached for hers. But his perceptions were those of a scared little boy, and he was now a man. In all the years in between, he had never once considered how his mother might have felt that day. Rebellious? Angry? Betrayed?

Certainly, she had been all of those things, but perhaps she had not been as defiant as he once believed. Perhaps, she had been afraid her denials would change nothing, and her refusal to apologize had been nothing more than an attempt to salvage her pride. Even after her banishment, she had held her head high. And she had survived.

He looked into his glass. "You could be right, Quent. My mother grew to love Charleston, but I do not think she would have been so eager to stay and make a new life for herself if she had been alone."

"She was not alone, Jack. She had you," Quent pointed out.

"Yes, but I was a burden. Until I was old enough to fend for myself, she protected me." He smiled as another memory surfaced, one he remembered well. "Despite my affinity for the sea, she wanted me closer to home. She even attempted to match me with Charleston's version of royalty."

Quentin smiled. "Ah yes, the lovely Anabel Beaumont. I remember her well."

"Do you now?" Charleston society was much like London's. Wealthy plantation owners viewed themselves as southern aristocracy, and their upper class daughters sought advantageous marriages. Being a British noblewoman, his mother was invited to every social event, but it was not until she introduced her son as a future viscount rather than a sea captain that he was genuinely accepted among their ranks. And despite his lack of any impending title, Quentin was still the son of an earl and obviously quite acceptable.

Quentin shrugged as if it were a small matter, but a flush stained his cheeks when he said, "Let us just say that she was quite fascinated with all things noble."

Jack raised his brows. "Including you?"

"A gentleman does not kiss and tell."

For the first time in quite a few hours, Jack smiled, but it quickly faded as he looked once more upon his father's portrait. "As much as I would prefer never to open that bloody safe, I suppose I have no choice. I'll never find peace if I do not read my father's letter."

****

Abby felt useless and out of sorts. The nursemaid had all but dismissed her once she had put Will down for the night, and she had nothing to do with her hands. Designing jewelry or creating unique designs in her father's shop had always distracted her from depressing thoughts and painful memories. It was what had gotten her through those dark days following the humiliation she had endured at Lord Drury's hand. But Jack had not thought to pack the jewelry she had been working on aboard the *Lion's Pride*. He had, however, remembered to pack his cat.

Captain Whiskers had not been happy boxed up in a crate that had once contained French champagne. Earlier in the evening, Mr. Stanley told her the cat howled like a lone wolf until he released him from his makeshift prison. The cat had all but flown up into the stable rafters, and Mr. Stanley had not seen him since. But had Jack seen the animal?

Jealousy ate at Abby's composure. She had not seen her husband since he banished her from the drawing room with the rest of the family. He had not even come out for supper.

Lady Margery and Mr. Flick had taken a tray in their rooms, and Abby had eaten in the family salon with Mr. Stanley and Uncle William. Shortly before supper, Mr. Stanley had gone into the drawing room to speak with Jack, but he did not mention their conversation to Abby. Instead, he had prattled on about Captain Whiskers. Uncle William had said very little and quickly excused himself from the table on the pretext of "making peace" with his family.

But would there ever be peace in this household?

Abby turned toward the window and drew back the drapes. A lush green lawn swept down toward a hedgerow and arched gate. Beyond the gate was a cove along the wash at the mouth of the Ouse River that she could just barely see in the fading light. Jack had once sailed his little boat down that river to see his Uncle William in Seile.

Abby smiled, wishing she could sail there as well. She would give anything to be back aboard the *Lion's Pride*. Jack had seemed more at home there than he did here. He had seemed more optimistic. Now that he had what he wanted, he did not seem any happier. Not even with his wife. Even after she had surrendered to him completely, he was once more shutting her out of his life.

A tear slid over her cheek, and she angrily brushed it away. She had given Jack more than just her body. She had attempted to give him her heart, but he did not seem to want it. He did not even want her with him when he read his father's letters.

The door crashed open. Abby jumped and turned from the window with a gasp. Jack's face was as dark as a storm cloud, but his hands trembled. "It is my fault."

She stepped toward him. He backed away, pushing the door shut with the heel of his boots before brushing past her on his way to the window. A sigh shook his wide shoulders as he brushed the curtains aside and stared out at the river. "My aunt was right. He took his own life."

He glanced at her over his shoulder. The anguish in his eyes nearly brought her to her knees.

"It was not your fault," she whispered past the painful lump in her throat.

Jack raked a trembling hand through his hair and turned back to the window. "A poison in a small dose is a medicine; a medicine in a large dose is a poison. He was being treated with aconite for a heart condition, but he took a deliberate overdose." He turned from the window and met her gaze. "He took wolfsbane, Abby. Aconite is derived from it. Do you realize how painful his death must have been?" His Adam's apple bobbled. "He tortured himself because of me, and then he begged my forgiveness while I have spent the past year damning his soul."

Tears clogged her throat as she stepped closer, praying he would not turn her away. His shoulders shook on a quivery sigh, but he pulled her into his arms and held her. The ticking of a porcelain bedside clock and Jack's labored breathing were the only sounds to break the silence. Still, words would not come, and so, she offered the only comfort she could. With a trembling sigh, she stepped free of his encroaching embrace and began to unfasten the tiny pearl buttons at her bodice. And if he should refuse her now, if he turned her away, it would devastate her beyond repair.

He stood frozen for a moment, staring at her as the setting sun cast golden light on her pale skin through the opening in the drapes. Then he reached out to help her undress before shrugging out of his clothes and pulling her shivering naked body against his. His mouth devoured hers, kissing her until she was breathless before lowering his head to kiss her throat and breasts. Then with a low-pitch growl, he scooped her into his arms and carried her to the bed.

****

Abby's maid had just finished the final touches to an elaborate coif that framed her face with wispy blonde ringlets when Jack entered through the dressing room door. Mrs. Smythe straightened and backed away.

"Good morning, Lord Ardmore." She cast a nervous smile in Abby's direction and scrambled out the room.

Abby rose to her feet and faced her husband. "Are you ready to talk now?"

Her heart pounded in her chest. His father's letter had devastated him, but she did not know half of what those letters contained, and she had been too much of a coward last night to risk discussing it. Instead, she had used her body to distract Jack, hoping that in the clear light of day, he would realize he was not like his father.

He smiled briefly. "You look lovely."

"Thank you." Why did he appear so nervous? So guilt-ridden?

"Please." He took her arm and guided her to the bed. "Sit. We need to talk."

Her stomach coiled into a tight knot, but she did as he bade her and sat beside him. His feet touched the floor. Hers dangled over the edge of the mattress.

Jack clasped his hands in his lap and lowered his gaze. "My mother's father was merely a baron. A wealthy one to be sure, but it was not a hereditary title. After his wife and all of his children, save my mother, died, he doted on her. He would have given her anything she wanted except the freedom to marry the man she loved."

The knots in Abby's stomach tightened. "Your uncle."

Jack stiffened. Then his shoulders relaxed and he nodded. "My father was heir to a viscountcy, but it was nearly broke. According to my father, by the time his father inherited it, Ram's Head had already fallen into disrepair, and he needed money to repair it. My mother's father was suffering from consumption, and he did not have long to live. He wanted his daughter to wed a title higher than his own, and she would have done anything to please him. He offered my father a staggering amount of money, and Ridge Point. My father accepted the dowry and proposed. He would have done anything for the money he needed to repair Ram's Head, even if it meant marrying the woman his brother loved."

Abby slid over far enough to place her feet on the embroidered bed steps and turned to face her husband. He stared at his hand and the official ring of the Ardmore viscountcy. "I do not understand. If your father married her for the money, then why did he not use that money to repair Ram's Head?" From what Jack had told her about the estate, it was little more than a crumbling pile of rubble.

The implications increased the painful knotting in her stomach. Had Jack been right all along? Had his father let the estate crumble as a some sort of punishment? Had he so firmly believed that Jack was not his flesh and blood son that he would do something so dastardly?

Jack sighed but kept his head lowered. He twisted the ring on his finger. "He had actually begun repairs on the estate. According to my father, the roof and upstairs interior had been completely renovated. He was just starting work on the downstairs and exterior when Aunt Marjorie's husband died. She had always doted on my father, and he felt he owed her his loyalty and protection."

He heaved another heavy sigh. "So, my father promised my aunt that she and Morris could stay at Ridge Point. My mother did not object until he told her that once the repairs at Ram's Head were complete, we would move there, and Morris and his mother could remain here. My mother was furious. I was still just a young boy, but I remember hearing her storm out of the bedroom one night, hurling insults at my aunt. I suppose Aunt Marjorie heard her as well, which only increased the tension between them."

Abby briefly touched his thigh. Again, he stiffened, but he still did not meet her gaze. "I can understand your mother's anger," she said. "This was her home, and your father had not discussed it with her first."

He cast a sharp glance in her direction before diverting his gaze once more to the ring upon his finger. "She was his wife, and the moment they wed, the house became his. Even if they had discussed it, my father would have expected her to do as he commanded, and he wanted to live at Ram's Head."

"Then why did he not complete the repairs?" He

had the money he needed, and after sending his wife away, there were no more obstacles. So why did he remain at Ridge Point?

Jack shifted his hips and turned just enough to face her. Sorrow filled his eyes. She wanted to soothe away his pain and promise him all the love he had been denied as a child. But she could only sit with her hands clasped tightly in her lap while he struggled to tell her the rest of what had been in that letter.

"He thought she would come back," he said, his voice barely a whisper. "He said he invested the money and let the estate crumble. He wanted to prove to her that he cared more for her than Ram's Head. But she never came back."

Abby touched his arm. "Can you blame her? He accused her of infidelity, and he never apologized."

Jack snatched his arm away as if she had burned him. "She never denied the charges, so he believed his sister's lies. She twisted and manipulated him so she could have Ridge Point!"

"Was that also in your father's letters?" She braced herself for a slap or verbal reprimand that never came.

Jack inhaled slowly and then exhaled sharply. "No. According to my father, my aunt tried convincing him to go after us. But he would not. So, she stayed on at Ridge Point to look after him. He rewarded her by promising Ridge Point to Morris. But he never spent another farthing on Ram's Head. In his letter, he said he never planned to fall in love with his wife, but he did, and when Aunt Margery voiced her suspicions, jealousy ate at him like a cancer. He expected my mother to confess her sins so he might forgive her. When she refused, he was unable to accept the fact that he and his beloved sister might have been wrong. So, he banished us."

A sigh racked his big body. "Then after Uncle William returned, swearing an oath that I was not his son and accusing my father of being a fool, the truth finally dawned on him. He had been wrong. He had allowed jealousy to blind him to the truth. He never left the house after that. He continued to dote on his sister and nephew, but he began eating and drinking far too much and getting out far too little. He accredits his heart condition to too much drink and too little activity. He wrote that second codicil, promising everything to me if I married and gave him an heir after I attempted to see him and he learned I was not married as my aunt had led him to believe. He thought learning of the codicil would force me to come home and challenge him. But when I did not return and I did not respond, he lost all hope of ever seeing either of us again. He did not know I had not gotten the letter."

"But he did not change his will either," Abby pointed out. "He knew you were unwed, and he knew when you would turn thirty-five. So, he knew Morris would inherit Ridge Point." And that angered her far more than it seemed to anger Jack. If she could have, she would have dug up the former viscount and slapped him silly for treating his son so poorly.

A smile touched Jack's lips when he finally turned to face her. "There was also a thick packet in the safe along with bank notes for more money than I have seen in a life time."

"What was in the packet?" She could not care less about the money.

Pain etched Jack's handsome face, nearly breaking

Abby's heart. His big shoulders sagged, and regret shone in his eyes. "An updated will, leaving everything to me and my heirs. It was wax sealed with his ring and witnessed by Dr. Jamison."

Chapter Twenty-Seven

Abby reached across the bed and placed her hands over his. He stopped twisting the ring on his finger. His heart stilled. And when their gazes met, sympathy shone in the depths of her eyes. Jack could not take it. He could not stand the sorrow brewing in his heart nor the tender emotions his wife instilled. He could not stand the raging jealousy that roared through his veins when he thought of her in Drury's arms. He knew they must return to London so he might establish himself and reunite her with her father, but he could not stomach the idea of her running into Drury.

He no longer feared Abby's feelings for the man. He feared what he might do to the bastard if they ever came face to face. It seemed that where Abby was concerned, he was every bit as possessive as his father.

Would he one day allow those feelings to override his better judgment? Was love always such a painful, damaging emotion?

His pulse jumped. So did he. He sprang from the bed as if his crotch were on fire. *Bloody hell!* He could not be in love with his wife. Love weakened a man and made him lose all common sense. Look what it had done to his father and uncle. Both men had lost their heads over a woman who did not have the courage to follow her own heart.

Or had she? Had his mother's refusal to deny his

father's accusations been a deliberate move to force Uncle William's hand?

Uncle William had gone after her, and when she refused to return home, he had moved his base of operations to Charleston. William still traveled, but he always returned to Charleston—and Jack's mother.

Even on her deathbed, she believed she would get well. It wasn't until Charleston was burning around them and she became too weak to raise her head that she was able to face the truth. She had asked for a moment alone with both him and his uncle that last day. She had made him promise to return her body to Ridge Point. But what had she said to Uncle William? He had been too afraid to ask. Now, he suspected the two lovers had exchanged one last kiss and a final goodbye.

"Jack?"

Abby's soft voice startled him. He watched as she planted her feet on the bed step and rose from the high bed. Her eyes locked onto his as she stepped down to the floor and took a hesitant step toward him. His pulse pounded in his ears. He could not think when she was near.

He took a step back. "I'm sorry I did not tell you last night, but I have decided it's time to reunite you with your father. He needs to meet Will, and he needs to know you are safe."

"I agree," Abby said, but she did not look happy. She looked afraid.

Did she fear running into to Drury? Or did she fear her father's reaction to the decisions she had made? Damn it! He might look like a swashbuckling American privateer, but he was a viscount. What English father would not want his daughter to marry a peer?

"Very well. We leave today." He turned, but her soft voice halted him in his tracks.

"And what of your aunt and cousin?"

He spun around, meeting her curious expression. Anger simmered in his veins. Her impertinence was unacceptable. She was much too vocal with her opinions for his taste and not nearly as obedient as a viscountess should be. She should do as he bade her without question or argument. She should...

Be more like his mother? Hardly! His mother's "obedience" and passive machinations had been just as damaging as his father's jealousy and greed. Had they only been as open and honest with one another as Abby was with him now, perhaps his life would have turned out differently.

Yet, had that happened, he would never have met Abby.

She truly was a breath of fresh air and sunshine in his dark life. She brought out the best and worst in him. And his greatest fear was that she would always be honest. His greatest fear was that one day, he would admit he loved her and she would be unable to repeat those words back to him.

In his heart of hearts, he knew she would never lie. And if she did not return his love, he would react no better than his father had done. Best if he kept those tender emotions to himself. Perhaps then, they could live in harmony for the rest of their days.

He gave her his best, indulgent smile. "What about them? Ridge Point is mine without question. I do not even have to allow them one last week to find other living arrangements."

She sighed, and he could tell she was not happy

with his reply. A frown marred her lovely brow. "Surely, you realize your aunt is not as villainous as you once believed."

Wasn't she? He folded his arms across his chest. "And what do you think of my cousin?"

Mischief danced in her Caribbean blue gaze. "He is an arse."

Laughter bubbled up from his chest, erupting in a guffaw that startled Abby. It startled him as well, but it released the remaining tension in his shoulders and brought a smile to his heart. Abby had a way of bringing him out of the doldrums and putting everything into perspective. "Yes. He is an arse and a worthless one at that."

A smile touched her face, and her shoulders relaxed. "But he is your aunt's only child, and once they leave here, they will be homeless."

Arms still folded, he leaned against the bedpost. "And what do you suggest I do? Allow them to continue living under our roof? I would have to sleep with one eye open and lock up the family silver." He frowned as another thought occurred to him. "In fact, I should get Uncle William to inventory the silver and everything else of value before he heads back to Seile with Quent."

"That would not be a bad idea, but I think a better one would be to give your cousin a purpose. He has no direction and no skills, save for his desire to live as a peer."

"He has squandered his life. How is that any concern of mine?" What female flights of fancy were in that brain of hers? Did she expect him to raise Morris as if he were an over-grown child who needed guidance and discipline? He would rather take a cat-o-nine tails to his hide and be done with it.

"Do you plan to restore Ram's Head?" she asked, rather than enlightening him.

"I do." It was his father's dream, and thanks to the bank notes he had found in the safe, he had more than enough money to repair the estate to its former glory.

"Then why not allow your cousin to oversee those repairs? He and his mother could live at the estate on a strict allowance. You could keep an eye on the books and make sure that he does not pilfer any of the money for his own needs. It would give him a purpose in life and a roof over their heads. And," she said with a smile when he looked at her with narrowed eyes, "it would stop him from going to London and tarnishing your good name—or worse. Keep in mind, you and Will are all that stand between him and a viscountcy, and desperate men often resort to desperate measures."

If Morris Flick ever laid a hand on Will, he would kill him and dispose of his remains in the deepest ocean. "All the more reason to wash my hands of the bastard."

A pleading look came over her. "Why tempt him needlessly?"

He sensed Abby's fears, but was there more to her suggestion? Did she believe Morris could be redeemed? Did she think *he* needed redeeming? Bloody hell. He was on the verge of falling in love with her, and she saw him as nothing more than a soul who needed saving. He curled his lip. "And for the record, I have no name in London for Morris to tarnish. I am nothing more than a sea captain turned viscount who hid away from society for the last twenty years."

"Because of your father's heart ailment." Understanding and something more shone in Abby's eyes. "Your aunt told me that is the tale she told her peers whenever she and Mr. Flick ventured out in society."

"And what did she say about my mother and me?" His heart thumped against his ribs. What vile names had she called his mother?

"Despite any snide remarks your cousin may or may not have made in her absence, your aunt had nothing but your father's best interest at heart. She told her peers that your father did not want to saddle his wife with a sick husband. Whenever anyone asked, she told them the two of you were traveling with your uncle or staying close to your father's side. Since Uncle William frequently travelled between America and London before you took over as captain of the *Lion's Pride*, no one suspected the truth. And your father never confessed what he had done."

Warmth blossomed in Jack's chest and spread to his gut. Despite his father's cruel actions, he had never sullied his wife's reputation in public. And neither had his aunt. But what of his cousin? That bastard gossiped like an old hen. But did anyone take him seriously?

"My aunt has made her bed and must now lie in it. As for Morris, he is—"

"A desperate man who may react in a desperate manner if given no other choice," Abby said again. "Extend the olive branch and see if he takes it. He may not be gracious about it, but I bet he will accept your terms and be grateful for it."

"And if he is not?"

Abby smiled. "Then my handsome privateer, you

may make him walk the plank."

With a laugh rumbling in his chest, Jack pulled Abby into his arms.

****

The reunion with her father was everything Abby had hoped for. Henry Halsey doted on his grandson and insisted they take his open conveyance into the park to show off the newest member of his family. Jack thought it a fine idea. Abby had to fight an onslaught of nausea just thinking of the possibility she might run into Lord Drury or Lord Ruston.

When she tried voicing her concerns to Jack when they were alone in her old bedroom, he brushed them aside. He insisted she was his viscountess, and nothing else mattered. And when she tried to talk to him about allowing his aunt and cousin to manage Ram's Head, he brushed those concerns aside as well.

"I am allowing them to remain at Ridge Point for another week, but after that, I do not care where they go, nor do I wish to discuss the matter further."

"Where do you expect them to go, Jack?" she asked, risking his wrath.

He bristled, and his face turned red, but he did not raise his voice when he said, "I do not give a tinker's damn where they go so long as they leave."

"Jack..."

He glared, no doubt, intent on stifling her protests, but she could not remain quiet. Ironically enough, his aunt had shown her nothing but kindness the last day they were at Ridge Point. Whether it was an act or not, she might never know. But she could not rest easy until she knew the elderly woman would have a roof over her head. "I have little sympathy for your cousin, but your aunt has repeatedly attempted to make things right, and you refuse to even listen. Have you no heart? She has nowhere to go. Her husband left her penniless, and if not for your father's generosity, there is no telling what would have happened to her and her son. And while your father did your cousin no favors by pampering him when he would never be viscount, Mr. Flick has lived off your father's charity his entire adult life. How is he going to care for himself or his mother?"

"My aunt manipulated my father. I am sure she can manipulate some man of means to take in her and her worthless son."

"She is not well, or have you not noticed?" Was Jack really so cruel? Or was he still trying to protect himself from hurt? His heart was not nearly as hard as he liked to believe, but in his efforts to protect himself from pain, had he walled it off too completely? Would he ever trust anyone? Love anyone?

He draped her pelisse over her shoulders. "I will consider your request."

She turned into his arms and dared looking into his eyes. "Then I suggest you consider it quickly as your aunt and cousin will be attending tonight's soiree at Lord Chivington's London townhouse."

Jack's eyes changed from smoldering hot to dark shards of ice in an instant. His gaze narrowed. "And how would you know this?"

She swallowed nerves and forced a smile. Jack had never raised a hand to her. She was confident he would not do so now, no matter how angry he might seem. "She promised to champion me and sing my praises so no one will question our hasty union."

Surprise flickered in his dark gaze, but he quickly

masked it and dropped his arms to his sides. "Then I suppose we should bid our son good night and be on our way to this damnable affair before I change my mind."

Hope bloomed in Abby's heart and took root. Jack continued to think of Will as his own, and no matter how angry she made him, he did not revile or ridicule her. And if she had her way, one day, he would love her the way she had come to love him.

Chapter Twenty-Eight

Nerves fluttered in Abby's stomach like butterfly wings as Jack helped her into the carriage. He settled her across from her father before sitting beside her and draping an arm over the back of the richly upholstered seat. The casual brush of his fingers on her shoulder sent warmth to her chest, chasing some of the butterflies away. Then the carriage jerked forward, and the butterflies returned.

Her father leaned across the carriage and patted her knee. "Do not fret. Lady Edwina cannot wait to see you again, and I am sure that despite your prolonged absence and sudden return, your friends will welcome you and Ardmore with open arms and few questions."

The butterflies in Abby's stomach flitted into her chest. "There is sure to be gossip, Papa. Besides my mysterious absence, I have returned home with a husband and a child."

"No, no," her father added in that soothing tone he used to placate her whenever she disagreed. It was the tone an adult used on an unreasonable child, and Abby was neither a child nor unreasonable. "I told everyone you were traveling abroad and visiting friends. Perhaps we can even say you met Ardmore in Paris or Spain. No, you have no reason to fret. I will handle everything."

"I am her husband, and I will handle whatever

needs handling," Jack said, in a low, firm voice that normally brooked no argument. But alas, her father was too busy plotting his own strategies to pay much attention.

"Yes, we will just say you met your husband during your travels, had a whirlwind courtship, and married post haste."

"And who was my chaperon while I was doing all this traveling?" Abby asked when she felt Jack bristle beside her. "Did you send me off to visit relatives alone? Did I travel with the nuns? Circus performers?"

Papa frowned. "Do not be so impertinent."

Jack snorted, and she could not tell if he was holding back an unexpected chortle or if he were snarling like the lion he often resembled. She feared it was the former, and if she turned to meet his gaze, she would collapse into hysterical giggles that might unduly embarrass her father. Her sharp tongue and "impertinence" had no doubt annoyed him enough already.

"You need to trust me," Papa added, his frown deepening. "Had you but trusted me before, we would not be in this fix."

Had she trusted him before, she would have been wed to that lecherous old fool, Lord Ruston. She arched her brows. Her father flushed.

"Surely, you see the wisdom of my words," he said in his most arrogant tone. "What is the harm in telling a little white lie? If you will not do it for your own sake, then think of Lord Ardmore. We must protect your reputation before his peers."

Her reputation had suffered the moment she left home to live at an Anglican convent, despite whatever lies her father may have told to protect her. Now that she had returned home with a child, just nine months after Lord Drury's abuse, he might even guess the truth about her hasty marriage and do irreparable damage to her reputation. Then there was the matter of Lord Ruston...

"Father, you offered Lord Ruston money to marry me and give my child a name. Do you think he has forgotten that already? Or that he did not spread malicious gossip when you could not produce his compromised bride and hefty dowry?"

Jack sat forward with a scowl. "I trusted you to handle things with Ruston. I assumed you had done so."

Her father blanched and leaned back against the seat. Despite the look of annoyance that briefly flickered in his dark gaze, he nodded. "Of course I handled it. I told Ruston the father of Abby's child had planned to ask for her hand before he was called away on business, but I did not trust him and that is why I approached Ruston with my offer. I also told him Abby refused because she had more faith in you than I did." Her father's eyes narrowed slightly as he leaned just a bit closer. "And I told him this before I knew Captain Jack and Lord Ardmore were one and the same."

"Good," Jack said before glancing in her direction. "And if we happen to run into Lord Drury, I will ensure that he treats you with the utmost respect and decorum due any viscountess."

Her father rubbed his hands together as if everything was properly settled. "Splendid! Tonight shall be a most enjoyable evening then."

His obvious joy did not bring her pleasure. The fact she had wed a peer who did not need his financial backing seemed to please her father more than her happiness or his grandson. Granted, he had doted on Will the moment he laid eyes on him, but that was most likely because he was heir to a viscountcy. Especially since it was not a viscountcy he would have to support financially.

The ungrateful thought was unexpected. Her father had given her everything and though he craved social acceptance, so had she. Then again, if her father had not been who he was, she might not have cared so much about marrying above her station.

She glanced at Jack. Had he and his friend not happened along when they did, she would not have married Lord Ruston, no matter how high his rank. She would have followed through on her plans to live in Shrivenham until after Will's birth. Then, she would have returned to her father's townhouse as a widow. No doubt, her father would have pawned her off on a baron or some other lesser peer who would not mind saddling himself with a widow—so long as she were rich or her father provided an adequate dowry—which he would have done. He was a parvenu, desperate to climb the social ladder despite his lack of a pedigree. She did not doubt his love, but she could no longer be a part of his plans, whatever they might be.

Heart in her throat, she straightened her shoulders and met her father's gaze. "I met Jack—Ardmore in London nearly two years ago. Ironically, it is true. His aunt, Lady Margery, saw us together, and she will attest that she met me then, even though she did not. She will also attest to the fact Jack returned to London some six months later, which is also true, but she will say the war in America prevented us from getting married earlier."

Despite Jack's sharply indrawn breath and the tension radiating through his bicep, she continued. "As for my prolonged absence from society, I believe the reasons will be quite obvious once people learn I am a mother. But I will tell anyone curious enough to ask that while I waited for Jack to return from America, I stayed with a spinster from a good family."

"And who is this spinster?" Jack asked before her father could pose the question.

"Daphne Dupree." She smiled. "I was traveling with her when we met, and she is most definitely a spinster."

"Sister Mary Daphne?" Her father's eyes widened. "Isn't she the nun who was supposed to send letters?" He folded his arms over his chest, resting his clasped hands on his slight paunch. "What ever happened to her? To her sister? I am outraged no one told me you had concocted your own plans until after they were underway and had already gone awry. The reverend mother was concerned as well. She knew nothing about you going to Shrivenham, and she never mentioned Sister Mary Daphne or any letters you were supposed to have written."

"I do not understand myself." She had been so consumed giving birth and adapting to life with Jack that she had little time to ponder what might have happened to the kind nun. "Sister Mary Daphne seemed so dedicated to her cause. I wonder what happened to her." She looked at Jack.

He shrugged. "I assume she absconded with my money and had no more use for the convent or her vows of poverty."

"Jack!" Surely, he did not believe that. "What if

something bad happened to her? Do you think we could go to Shrivenham later this week and pay her sister a visit?"

"I do not see why not. If Sister Mary Daphne did not return to the convent, I would like to know what she did with the money. I would most assuredly like to know that she gave an adequate amount to her brother so he does not suffer the loss of his horses."

"What about the other women and their babies, the ones she said she helped? What if there is no boarding house? What if her sister is running a baby farm?" Fear raked icy fingers down Abby's spine. She dared another glance in Jack's direction, and the compassionate gleam in his eyes set her fears to rest. No matter what had happened to those women, Jack would make things right. He would no more abide by the farming of babies than he would the mistreatment of a woman. "If I could just visit with Lydia and make sure she and her child are safe, I will be most grateful."

"I do not need your gratitude, Abby." His palm curved over her shoulder, drawing her closer. "If the nun lied about her charity for unwed mothers, she might very well have lied about your friend Lydia as well. But we will get to the truth. I promise."

Abby's chest tightened. She had to believe the nun had kept the money and not returned to the convent, so she could devote her time and resources to her unwed mother's charity. It was the most logical explanation. It was also the only one Abby could consider without bursting into tears.

Squeezing her eyes shut, she prayed for Lydia and her child, and she prayed she would not have to face Lord Drury or Lord Ruston.

****

Abby stood between Jack and her father outside Lord Covington's townhouse on Upper Grosvenor Street in Mayfair. Liveried footman stood on either side of the iron gate, and gas lamps set every window in the sprawling brick mansion aglow. Her stomach churned. Jack looked up and whistled.

"This place would put Ram's Head to shame, even in her better days."

"You should see his country estate." Abby swallowed her nerves and glanced at her father.

He patted her shoulder. "Everything will work out swimmingly. Just follow my lead."

"Where you might lead is as terrifying as the thought of running into Lord Drury," she mumbled.

"I am right here beside you." Jack placed his hand at the small of her back and nudged her forward. She glanced up. He looked down. And winked!

Heat shot to her cheeks and flared lower. She stumbled on a loose cobblestone, but Jack's firm grasp held her upright.

"Breathe," he said with a smile. And the next thing she knew, the butler was announcing their arrival.

Clinging tightly to Jack's arm, she walked in between him and her father, moving forward inch by painful inch in the receiving line. Lord Chivington stood next to his wife. Beside her was their oldest son and heir, the marquess, Lord Sherwood. All three greeted Abby with cool reserve until her father stepped forward to shake Lord Chivington's hand. Then, he turned to introduce Jack in such a pompous way that Abby wanted to hide her face in shame. Jack, however, took it all in stride.

He offered a gloved hand to the duke and then the marquess. "A pleasure, your grace. Lord Sherwood."

He then turned to Lady Chivington and raised her gloved fingers to his lips. Her face flushed crimson, and a girlish giggle escaped.

Lord Chivington smiled. "It is good to meet you, Lord Ardmore. I knew your father well at one time, but I hear he had been quite ill before his passing. May I offer my condolences?"

Abby stiffened, fearing how Jack might respond. He patted her gloved hand as if to reassure her and nodded to the duke. "Thank you."

"I understand your mother passed recently as well, in America," Lord Chivington added, a curious glint in his eye. "Such a tragedy. I had not seen her in years either."

Abby did not suppose he had. She had been living in Charleston for the past twenty years. No doubt, Jack's cousin had spread as many rumors as possible, not that she had ever heard a whisper of scandal. In fact, she had never heard of Lord Ardmore or his family before meeting Jack. So perhaps, his aunt had not lied about the former viscount becoming a recluse and not telling anyone he had banished his wife.

"It was difficult on us all." A nerve visibly twitched in Jack's jaw, and tension radiated from his bunched muscles through the sleeve of his frock coat. He was as tightly wound as a jungle cat preparing to pounce on unsuspecting prey. Abby feared that if someone else mentioned his parents, he would snap.

She thrust herself into the conversation to take the focus off Jack. "I wish I could have met her. The former Lord Ardmore's sister, Lady Margery, told me that after her brother became ill, neither he nor his wife ventured out very often, except when she traveled to America to visit friends."

Jack glanced sharply at her, no doubt concerned over how easily she had lied. But she would lie, cheat, or steal to protect him as he had protected her. With a vapid smile and flutter of her lashes, she prattled on about Charleston and society as if she were some empty-headed debutante who had personally attended a southern ball.

Lord Chivington smiled politely but looked rather bored. "Indeed."

Lady Chivington reached over and patted her shoulder, all aflutter with the possibility of some new scandal. "Odd, that the late Lady Ardmore never mentioned friends in America. But I am sure she would have adored you, Miss Halsey. Oh! I mean, Lady Ardmore." Her tinkling giggle was as phony as her smile. "Your new title *will* take some getting used to."

"For me as well," Abby replied with her own fake smile.

"And I would love to hear about the former Lady Ardmore's adventures. We were great friends at one time, but after that awful scandal with Lord Ardmore's brother-in-law, Mr. Flick, she became less sociable." She pinned Jack with curious eyes, and Abby could almost see the wheels spinning in her devious mind. "Despite the scandal, Lady Margery became quite active in our little social circle, until recently. Has she taken ill too?"

"No." Jack's expression was as readable as a block of ice.

Abby forced another smile. "She did accept your

invitation for tonight's soiree."

An unpleasant glint flashed behind the duchess's pale eyes. "Really? I must confess that I never check with my housekeeper on such mundane matters. And as I had heard she and her son would be leaving Ridge Point, I did not expect her to accept my last-minute invitation."

Before Jack could respond with some remark sure to put her in her place, Abby once again intervened. "They will be staying at least another week until other arrangements can be made. You see, my husband is as generous toward his relations as his father was." She looked up, and despite Jack's glower, it would have been impossible for him to miss the pleading look she cast his way. He shook his head and his expression softened. Then, he smiled and...

Did he just wink? Again? A flush shivered over her, warming her cheeks.

****

The marquess snorted behind his glass, drawing Jack's attention away from his softhearted but scheming wife. "I say, Ardmore, it is a jolly good thing you returned home when you did. Your cousin was making himself quite at home in your absence. A word of advice?"

Jack leaned closer. Lord Sherwood lowered his voice. "Keep an eye on Flick and on the family silver if you intend to let him and his mother stay on at Ridge Point. He is quite the gambler and not a very good one."

Morris Flick was a useless waste of skin, and despite Abby's pleas, he would never let that bastard oversee the repairs at Ram's Head. He would rather leave Lord Gilchrest's twin brother in charge of the estate. Edward Gilchrest had been left brain damaged by a fever when he was a child, and he still had more sense than Flick. Jack nodded. "I'll keep your warning in mind."

"Do come and sit with me later in the evening," Lady Chivington said to Abby with a calculating gleam in her eyes. "We simply must catch up."

Abby flushed but boldly held the older woman's gaze. "Where is Lady Edwina? I have missed her so."

The duchess laughed, a tittering sound that grated on Jack's nerves. "Oh, you know our dear Eddy. Her dance card is full, and she is enjoying every minute of the attention. See?" She nodded and Abby turned her head to follow the older woman's gaze. "She is dancing with the Earl of Glamorgan, he is the Marquis of Worcester's heir, and Worcester is heir apparent to the Duke of Beaufort."

Abby smiled, but it did not appear genuine. "I am sure she could have any man *she* chooses."

Jack nearly laughed aloud. Despite her need for acceptance amongst the peerage, Abby was quite the rebel, a polite rebel, but no less rebellious.

A disapproving frown marred Lady Chivington's powdered face. "True, but she is also an obedient daughter who will one day be a duchess. I expect nothing less."

Enough was enough. Jack could no longer tolerate the vapid woman's condescending remarks and veiled insults. He smiled as politely as he could, although he was sure it looked more like a snarl. "If you will excuse us, I believe I owe my wife a dance."

Before another word could be spoken, he nodded to

Lord Chivington and the marquess and swept his wife onto the dance floor. The look of surprise that briefly flashed behind her eyes was almost worth the reprimand he was sure to get because of his rude behavior. Despite her rebellious streak, Abby had been a most obedient daughter, but unlike his mother, she did not quietly do as she was told. She protested and argued every step of the way, and she would, no doubt, argue with him for many years to come.

He chuckled and pulled her close as he waltzed her across the floor.

"What is so funny?" she hissed under her breath, though her eyes danced with merriment.

He dropped his mouth to the side of her face, grazing her ear with his lips. A delicate tremor shook her, and his rod stood up and took notice.

"You, my spirited little rebel. You stood up to that old bat with the utmost decorum and class. What happened to the scared little monk I married."

"Damn you, Jack," she whispered as he pulled her flush against his chest. "It was not a monk's robe. How many times must I tell you?"

He smiled, all the way down to his toes. "As many times as I have to tell you that I am no pirate. And watch your tongue, my lady. You are my viscountess now."

"I am not just a viscountess," she whispered, her tightly corseted belly brushing against his erection. "I am Lord Captain's lady."

He groaned and very nearly lost his footing. This time, Abby chuckled, and a mischievous glint shone in her eyes. "I knew it was too good to be true."

"What?" he whispered, once he finally found his

voice.

"I knew my big pirate of a husband was not the graceful dancer he was pretending to be. It was only a matter of time before he tripped over his own big feet."

"Then perhaps I should prove you wrong." Pulling her more firmly into his arms, he swept her across the dance floor.

Chapter Twenty-Nine

Midway through a waltz, Jack stumbled to a stop. Abby would have teased him once more about his big feet, had she not noticed the expression on his face. Jack looked as if he had seen a ghost.

Her eyes followed his shocked gaze to a broad shouldered gentleman with dark hair lightly sprinkled with gray who was talking with Mr. Stanley. Was he surprised to see his friend? He shouldn't be. Although Mr. Stanley had worked as Jack's quartermaster for the last six years, he was still the son of an earl and a notable member of society. But who was the man to whom he was speaking? He was a bit older than Jack and Mr. Stanley but no less handsome. Beside him, a voluptuous woman with reddish-brown hair artfully coiffed and curled to perfection smiled up at him.

"By God, I would not have believed it if I had not seen it with my own eyes." Even as Jack spoke, he pulled Abby's hand through the crook of his arm and dragged her across the dance floor.

Mr. Stanley spoke to Abby and stepped back as Jack let go of her arm and clasped the handsome gentleman's broad shoulder. "Gilchrest, you English dandy, how in God's name did Nikki drag you out of your damnable castle?"

Lord Gilchrest had vouched for Jack when he was called to lords. But who was the woman? She smiled up at Jack as if he were the only man in the room, making Abby's blood boil. Gilchrest glowered. "Lady Gilchrest to you, you disreputable pirate."

Abby froze, her heart pounding in her chest. Until this moment, Jack had managed to behave in a somewhat civilized manner, but now, he was insulting a peer whom she thought was his friend and speaking most informally to his wife. Then Jack pulled Lady Gilchrest into his arms in a bone-crushing embrace that drew curious gazes from the crowd gathered nearest the dance floor.

"Jack!" Lady Gilchrest touched Jack's cheek, and Abby's heart dropped to her silken slippers. "It is so good to see you looking so...noble. But I must confess I prefer your captain persona."

Gilchrest snatched her hand away from Jack's face, and Abby tensed, expecting the men to come to blows. Instead, Gilchrest flashed a dazzling white smile that took years off his face and shook his head at his wife. "Nicole, he is not a salty old sea dog anymore, and you must remember to call him Ardmore."

Jack turned to Gilchrest. "After vouching for me before Parliament, you said hell would freeze before you returned to London. However did Nik—um—Lady Gilchrest convince you to return?"

"What makes you think I did not convince her?"

Jack snorted. "I know you."

"Then you should know I can talk Chad into anything," Lady Gilchrest said, her throaty laugh burning a hole in Abby's chest.

She could not see Jack's face, but she heard an answering smile in his voice when he said, "You could talk the hind legs off a donkey, Nikki."

"It seems you know my wife rather well," Gilchrest said with a stiff smile.

"Wife!" Jack spun around, his face flushed and his eyes, apologetic. "Abby, I am so sorry." He pulled her hand through the crook of his arm, dragging her to his side before turning once more to face Lord and Lady Gilchrest. "Where are my manners? This is *my* wife, Lady Ardmore. Abby, this is my good friend, the earl of Gilchrest and his wife."

"Wife!" Lord and Lady Gilchrest exchanged astonished glances before looking once more at Jack. Lord Gilchrest laughed. "Dear God, man, I had not expected such news from you."

"It did take a bit of encouragement," Mr. Stanley added before turning to wink at Abby. She nearly swallowed her tongue. First Jack and now Mr. Stanley. It was as if this entire evening were a game to them. Only she did not know the rules.

"Do be quiet, Quent," Jack grumbled before clearing his throat and adding, "We also have a son. His name is Will."

Lady Gilchrest blinked. "Oh."

She looked at her husband. He turned to Mr. Stanley, who chuckled. "That did *not* take any encouragement on my part."

Lord Gilchrest and Mr. Stanley laughed. Jack flushed. And heat rushed to Abby's cheeks, setting them on fire. These people were sure to question the expediency of her marriage and the paternity of her child. She held her breath, dreading the knowing looks sure to follow.

Lord Gilchrest reached for her gloved hand and kissed her fingers with nary a raised brow or condemning glint in his ice blue eyes. "Congratulations, my dear. It is indeed a pleasure to meet the woman who could capture the heart of a cantankerous privateer like Captain Jack."

Abby's flush deepened, and a profound sadness filled her. If only she had captured his heart. She forced a smile. "I have heard much about you, my lord."

"Call me Gilchrest. Please," he said with a smile.

Lady Gilchrest reached out a hand and pulled Abby into her arms as if they were long lost friends. "Oh, I am so happy for Jack. You are simply stunning, and I know Jack—Ardmore adores you. I cannot wait for you to bring little Will to Land's End so my children can meet him."

Abby wanted to like the countess, but her continued use of Jack's first name gave her pause. Then, there was her odd accent that sounded so eerily similar to Jack's.

"My husband did not mention you were, um, American," she said, hazarding a guess.

"My mother was the daughter of an earl, but she married an English sea captain as bold and dashing as your husband," Lady Gilchrest said, seemingly unconcerned that her unrepentant flirtations had put a scowl on her husband's face. "In fact, my dear, childhood friend is a loyal member of Jack's crew."

"You remember my boatswain, Charlie Hogan," Jack said, and all Abby could do was nod. Her head spun. She had never seen this flirtatious, social aspect of her husband before. Did all women have this effect on him? Or was it just this particular woman? "Charlie and Nikki—um, Lady Gilchrest are both from North Carolina. Her father used to sail out of Wilmington and

New Bern, ports I frequently visited."

"I assume those ports are north of South Carolina, Lady Gilchrest?" Abby forced a smile. Her throat tightened.

"Yes. And you simply must call me Nikki," Lady Gilchrest said. "My closest friends do. And I shall call you Abby. If that is all right with you."

"Nicole..." Lord Gilchrest shook his head and cast his wife an indulgent smile. "You are overwhelming Ardmore's wife. She looks quite stunned."

Abby was more than stunned. She felt like a shrinking violet next to the bold woman who seemed to disregard societal conventions without a single qualm. "No. It is quite all right, sir."

"Oh, do stop being so formal, Chad," Nikki said. She turned her warm brown gaze on Abby. "Forgive me, but I have never quite fit in with British society, and after seven years of marriage, I have stopped trying." She laughed. "In fact, it is very rare that Chad and I attend society functions at all, but Mr. Stanley insisted. Then I ran into an old friend of my mother's and she too insisted. She said she had happy news to share about her nephew." She looked at Jack. "I must confess that when you asked Chad to vouch for you before Parliament, I was so stunned to learn you were not an American but Ardmore's heir that I never made the connection to Lady Margery before."

Abby felt the change in Jack even before his muscles tautened and his jaw clenched. "It is not a connection I cherish."

"And I regret that more than I can say." Lady Margery stepped forward and placed a trembling hand on Jack's shoulder. He stiffened, and Abby feared he would throw off her offending hand and make quite a scene. To his credit, he remained eerily silent.

Lady Margery sighed and turned to the earl and his wife. "I had hoped to surprise you with the news of Ardmore's marriage and the birth of his heir, but it seems he beat me to it."

Lord and Lady Gilchrest exchanged uncomfortable looks. Abby's nerves twisted her stomach into knots.

"I believe I am the one surprised, madam," Jack said in a tense, controlled voice that sent a shiver down Abby's spine. "I was surprised to learn from my wife that you would be here tonight."

Lady Margery gave Jack a pleading look, and her voice shook. "I had not planned on it, but then I ran into Lady Gilchrest and her husband on Market Street, yesterday. I knew Lady Chivington had invited them, so I begged them to come to tonight's gathering. I thought you and Lady Ardmore could use their support."

Jack's eyes briefly widened before he masked his startled expression. He turned to Gilchrest, brows raised. "Is that true?"

Gilchrest nodded, but said nothing, despite the curious glint in his eyes.

Jack looked at his aunt, suspicion evident in the hard planes of his face and the terseness of his reply. "Why? You had no way of knowing we would attend tonight. It was only at Mr. Halsey's insistence that I agreed to come. And you had no way of knowing that."

"I have never met Mr. Halsey, but we attended some of the same social functions a year or two ago, and I assumed he would want to show off his daughter and her new husband. So, I hoped you would be here, and I knew how fond you are of Lord Gilchrest." She inhaled sharply and cast a sympathetic look in Abby's direction. "You know how your cousin is, Ardmore, and while I know Morris' behavior is not always appropriate, he has been a devoted son. Still, I cannot condone his behavior or the way he has talked about you and your wife since learning of your nuptials and the birth of your son."

Just then, Mr. Flick pushed through the crowd, his face a mask of rage and pain. Jack stiffened and pulled Abby closer to his side. Lady Margery and Mr. Stanley stepped closer as well, as if attempting to form a protective circle around her. Abby's heart thumped with fear and gratitude.

"Why, Mother?" Mr. Flick glared at his mother with sad, bloodshot eyes. His breath reeked of alcohol. "Why have you betrayed me?"

"Morris, please," she said, her voice soft and pleading. "This is neither the time nor the place. Go home. We shall discuss this later."

"Home?" He nearly shrieked and had it not been for the swelling crescendo of the orchestra, Abby was sure every eye in the room would have turned toward him to stare. "We have no home! Jack has evicted us. Or have you forgotten? We are to be cast out on the streets with nary a sixpence to our name."

Abby squeezed Jack's arm, panic welling in her chest. She had feared a confrontation with Lord Drury or Lord Ruston. She had not expected Jack's cousin to create such a spectacle. Jack patted her hand and then released her. He stepped forward and clasped his cousin's shoulder in a firm grip that caused Mr. Flick to flinch.

"Calm down, Morris. You are creating a scene."

Mr. Flick tried to shrug out of Jack's grip, but when Jack did not loosen his hold, his face crumpled. "And you have wreaked havoc on my life."

Jack's gripped tightened. Mr. Flick whimpered. Instead of wringing his neck as Abby feared, Jack steered him toward the glass doors leading out onto the veranda. Fearing Jack would toss him over the balcony, Abby followed. So did Lady Margery, Mr. Stanley, and Lord and Lady Gilchrest. Apparently, none of them trusted Jack's temper any more than she did.

"Jack—Ardmore, please!" Lady Margery whimpered as she slipped outside behind the rest of them and closed the glass doors behind her.

Jack dragged Mr. Flick into a shadowy corner of the veranda and pushed him against the brick wall, his forearm pressed against his throat. Abby touched his shoulder, fear tightening her chest. "Jack, no!"

He cast her a hard glance, but then his eyes softened. "Trust me."

Dare she? Jack had a volatile temper, but would he commit murder before witnesses? Doubtful. But did she trust him not to do something so outrageous that neither of them would ever be able to set foot in society again? Most assuredly not!

She cast a glance over her shoulder at the rest of the assembly. Lady Margery's pale face seemed to glow in the moonlight and terror shown in her eyes. Mr. Stanley merely raised a curious brow while Lady Gilchrest clung to her husband's arm, quietly pleading with him to "do something."

Lord Gilchrest smiled. "Need any help, Jack?"

Jack met his friend's gaze, brows arched. "Oh, so now it's Jack again, is it?"

"You seem to be acting more like a pirate captain than a peer," Lord Gilchrest said with a shrug. "But if you need help, just let me know. I am here for you, my friend."

"Then be a friend and stop him from doing something foolish," Lady Gilchrest hissed.

Abby stood rooted to the spot, her hand on Jack's shoulder. Mr. Stanley and Lord Gilchrest did not seem nearly as concerned as the women. Perhaps they knew Jack better? Or perhaps, they did not care as much.

"Trust me," Jack said again.

Abby glanced once more at Mr. Flick. Sweat beaded his brow and his eyes bulged, but he did not seem to be in immediate danger so she dropped her hand to her side and gave Jack a stern warning. "Do not let your temper best you."

He nodded and turned back to Mr. Flick. He pressed a little harder against his windpipe. Just when Abby feared he would choke the life out of his cousin, Jack released him.

Mr. Flick sagged against the wall, his breath coming in panting gasped. "You nearly killed me!"

"Trust me, dear cousin, had I wanted you dead, I would have taken care of it already, and I would not have done so before witnesses. Now stop sniveling and listen for once in your miserable life."

"How dare you!"

Jack smacked the side of his head with the flat of his hand. "Shut up."

Eyes wide and face aflame, Mr. Flick grabbed his cheek but closed his mouth. Jack nodded as if satisfied and took a single step back. He raked his cousin with contemptuous eyes and sneered. "If it were up to me, you would be living in some dank gutter, drowning your sorrows in cheap swill from a disease infested tavern in the slums of London."

"And what of my mother?" Mr. Flick asked through tears that now filled his bloodshot eyes. "She is old, and she is fragile."

Jack shrugged. "I should not care. You see, I know how much money my father bequeathed to you and Aunt Margery. You received that money months ago, before the official reading of the will. Even after I found the new will and the money he had saved for the repairs to Rams Head in the safe, there should have been enough money for you and your mother to live a modest life."

Lady Margery gasped and looked at her son. "Is this true, Morris? If we have money—"

"Had, Mother! We had money." He stepped away from the wall and turned furious eyes on her. "But there were dressmakers and balls, gaming debts, and travel expenses." He turned glaring eyes on Jack and pointed a shaking finger. "And servants! I had to pay your servants from that money. The very least you can do is reimburse me for that now."

Jack nodded. "It is the least I can do. And if it were not for my wife, it would be the only thing I ever did for either of you. But she has a much more generous heart than I will ever have. So, if you will keep your mouth shut and stay out of my way for the remainder of the evening, I will meet with the two of you tomorrow to discuss your future living arrangements."

"Will I at least have a decent allowance?" Mr. Flick asked in a pleading tone.

Jack snorted. "No. You will have a job. Now get

out of my sight and take your mother with you."

Lady Margery took a hesitant step forward. "Thank you, Jack."

"Do not thank me, madam. Thank my wife. For if not for her, the two of you would be out on the streets."

She turned watery eyes on Abby and smiled. Her trembling hands reached for hers. "Thank you, my dear. Thank you."

****

Abby watched through the glass doors as Mr. Flick and his mother disappeared into the crowd inside the ballroom. Those still gathered on the balcony seemed to breathe a collective sigh of relief.

"Well played, Ardmore," Lord Gilchrest said.

Jack arched his brows. "Make up your mind, Gilchrest. Am I Jack or Ardmore?"

"That was not a Jack move. It seemed more like one of Quentin's tactics—much more noble than a mere pirate." He looked at Quentin, a mischievous gleam in his ice blue gaze. "We just might make a decent viscount of him yet."

"It has been quite the struggle," Mr. Stanley said with a long-suffering sigh. "Although he is much more trainable than I would have imagined."

"Perhaps his wife has something to do with that," Lady Gilchrest added. "What man is not improved by a good wife?"

"I am not a damn dog in need of training," Jack grumbled, but then he stepped closer to Abby and pulled her under his arm. "However, I cannot argue with your logic, Nikki. Abby is indeed the best of wives."

Abby's fears melted under the weight of Jack's

arm. Her heart filled with hope. Was it possible she might get through the remainder of the evening unscathed? Was it possible she might make a real marriage with Jack?

She clung to his arm as their little group trouped back inside the ballroom. But before she could breathe a sigh of relief, she spotted Lady Edwina. Lord Drury and a plain-faced woman followed closely on her heels. Abby's breath froze in her lungs, but her heart nearly leapt from her chest. If not for the weight of Jack's arm pulling her more firmly to his side, she would have been tempted to run back out onto the veranda and hide.

"Abby!" Lady Edwina rushed forward and reached for her hands. Clasping them in her own, she said, "Mother said you were here. Wherever have you been?"

Abby swallowed her nerves and gave her friend's fingers a nervous squeeze before releasing them. "We were out on the veranda, taking in the night air."

"No, silly." Lady Edwina spoke to Abby, but her gaze strayed to Jack. "Where have you been for the last six months? Your father told my mother you were visiting friends in the country, but you did not even write."

When had the duchess asked about her? Tonight? Months ago? What had her father said? He was such an elaborate storyteller, keeping people enthralled with whatever tale he told. How many details had he peppered into the story of her travels to make them seem more real? How could she possibly respond without running the risk of Edwina and Lord Drury catching her in a lie?

Jack's arm tightened around her waist, but her

tongue seemed to stick to the roof of her mouth, and the words would not come. She pressed her sweat-dampened palms against her skirts and took a deep breath. "I—"

"You must be Lady Edwina," Jack said coming to her rescue. "I am afraid I am somewhat to blame for her disappearance. When Abby—Miss Halsey and I met outside of her father's store the year before last, I was completely taken by her beauty, but I had to sail back to America. I returned six months later and promised more than I could deliver. You see, the war in American delayed my permanent return to England, and my dear Abby was left waiting."

"I am sorry I did not confide in you, my dearest friend," Abby added once she found her voice. "But he was gone for so long that I feared he would not return. So, I spent my summer in the country with friends." She affixed her gaze to Lady Edwina, trying to avoid eye contact with Lord Drury or his plain-faced wife. But she could not help squirming under the weight of Simon's stare. She felt his eyes on her, crawling over her like bugs beneath her skin. She wanted to scratch until she bled. She wanted to throw herself into the river and wash the feel of his lecherous hands from her body. She wanted to—

"But I found her as promised and made her my wife," Jack interjected, as if completing the final lines of a fairytale. But this was no fairytale. It was beginning to feel like a nightmare. Lord Drury would not stay silent for long. With or without his wife by his side, he would say something to put her in her place and prove to everyone standing near that she was not welcomed in polite society.

"Oh how romantic," Lady Edwina gushed. But Lord Drury's gaze narrowed, and a smirk colored his expression when he gazed at Jack.

"And who might you be?" He spoke in a droll tone and somehow managed to look down at Jack while looking up to his superior height.

Abby felt the tension in Jack's body as surely as she felt the fear coursing through her own veins. But he simply smiled, a mere quirking of his lips that made him look dashing and noble. "I am Jackson Norton, Viscount Ardmore and Miss Halsey is now my viscountess and the mother of *my* son."

Lady Edwina gasped, as did Lady Victoria who was now Lady Drury, Simon Weston's wife. Lord Drury smirked, but he did not look noble or dashing.

Why did I ever think him handsome or charming? Lord Drury was a disreputable rake posing as a gentleman. Jack had more character in the bottom of his boot than Simon Weston possessed in his entire body.

Lady Edwina flushed prettily and shuffled her feet. "I did not know you were—that you had—I did not know you were a mother."

Despite a maiden's reinforced ignorance on anything related to the marriage bed or childbirth, she was not a complete ninny. Even innocent Edwina would know Abby had not been chaste when she wed Jack. Would she also guess the child was not his?

She knew of Abby's former fondness for Lord Drury. Would she assume the worst? Or would her innocence prevent her mind from traveling in that direction?

Abby held her breath. Lady Drury blinked like an owl, but she did not look wise. She looked confused and quite sad. Lord Drury smirked. Again. "How old is the boy?"

Nausea roiled up from the pit of Abby's stomach, and she nearly wretched. Jack's muscles coiled. She felt it in the arm still wrapped around her waist. He smiled politely and stared beyond Lord Drury as if bored with his company. "Just a few months. He arrived earlier than expected."

Mr. Stanley walked up on the other side of Jack and slapped him on the back. "The boy looks like his mother, but he's growing like a weed. I swear, he is going to be every bit as tall as his father. Do you not agree, Ardmore?"

"I cannot wait to see him," Lady Gilchrest said. She could not know Lord Drury was Will's father, but she could not miss the threatening undercurrents of tension flowing between Jack and Lord Drury. "Ardmore is such a proud new father."

"Embarrassingly so," Lord Gilchrest added.

"What father would not be proud of his son and heir?" Jack drilled Lord Drury with hard, threatening eyes as if daring him to say another word.

Lady Edwina and Lady Drury exchanged confused glances.

"Congratulations," Lady Edwina said after a moment's hesitation.

"Yes. Indeed." Lady Drury's soft words were barely audible.

Beside her, her husband stiffened. Lord Drury looked down at the top of her bowed head. His lip curled in distaste, and he gave her the same look of annoyance he often gave his mother. Then he raised his chin and looked at Abby. "You, no doubt, have met *my* wife, *Miss* Halsey. Oh, forgive me. It is *Lady* Ardmore now." He chuckled, a vile rather than humorous sound that made Abby's flesh crawl. "And this is my wife, Lady Drury. She is the former Lady Victoria, the Duke of Rathbone's daughter."

"I have not had the pleasure," Abby said, though the words hung in her throat.

"Not surprising." Drury smiled, a slick stretching of his thin lips. "She is Welsh, but her father is quite wealthy, not unlike your own, but Rathbone is from an old, noble family with direct blood ties to the Queen herself, a true peer in every sense of the word."

"Quite a fitting match, I'd say." Jack smiled and somehow made his compliment sound insulting. Then he turned sympathetic eyes on Lady Drury. He reached for her hand and brought her gloved fingers to his lips. "It is a pleasure meeting you, my lady." He then performed the same gallant act on Lady Edwina who flushed and fluttered her lashes every bit as much as Lord Drury's wife had. "But if you ladies would excuse us? I would like to dance with my beautiful wife once more."

Mr. Stanley smiled and bowed to Lady Edwina. "If it would not be too forward of me, might I have the pleasure of your company on the dance floor?"

Lady Edwina fluttered her lashes again. "I do not believe we have been properly introduced."

"Mr. Stanley is Lord Willoughby's son," Abby said, finding strength in Jack's firm hold on her arm. "Besides being the son of an earl, he is a dashing sailor and quite the gentleman. A most appropriate dance partner."

"Indeed?" Lady Edwina smiled, and her lavender

blue eyes shone with pleasure.

"Absolutely." Mr. Stanley took her arm and led her onto the dance floor. Lord Gilchrest and his wife followed.

After a final withering look at Lord Drury, Jack guided Abby onto the dance floor as well.

Chapter Thirty

Lies! It was all lies. He was a liar and a fornicator! He had promised to love the boy as his own, but that was hardly a promise worthy of trust. Men seldom loved the children of their own loins. Why would anyone believe a man could love a child he had not sired?

Daphne Dupree snorted. She had not truly believed Lord Ardmore would honor his vows. He had only wanted the boy so he might inherit another estate. That property was now his, but he had not taken his family there. Nor had he taken them to his crumbling estate in Ram's Head. Instead, he had taken them to his ship in Seile. Now, he had delivered his wife and child back to her father's hearth, which proved, he no longer wanted her.

Fornicators! They were all lying fornicators, and women were foolish creatures. Foolish and sinful.

Ah, but blood would wash Abby clean of her sins. As for the baby, it might already be too late. A child born into wedlock at least stood a chance in this wicked world, but Abby's child had been conceived in sin, and now he was destined to live a sinful life.

Oh, if only Ardmore had honored his vows. Perhaps then, the child might never have learned of his wicked beginnings. But alas, that was not to be. Sin always came home to roost. Now, it was her job to set things to rights and make the mother repent. And it was time to send the sweet little boy to Jesus. Jesus needed angels—sweet, innocent cherubs.

But was it too late for Abby's son to become one of Jesus' littlest angels?

Daphne pulled the hood of her dark cloak over her head and peered through the hedgerows. Abby sat on a stone bench inside the garden wall of her father's house, holding her son's back to her chest. The child chewed his tiny fist and cooed. Daphne sighed, and her shoulders slumped as a weight lifted from her shoulders. It had taken some time to find Abby and her child, but she had finally returned to her father's home, just as Daphne predicted.

Had her father taken her in willingly? Or had Abby begged for forgiveness?

No matter. She would beg soon. And she would receive blessed forgiveness through a blood cleansing.

Daphne nodded to her companion, prepared to move forward, but Abby and her son were not alone. There was a young woman with them in the garden. Her words froze Daphne in her tracks. "It is getting cool. Shall I take Master Will inside now?"

Abby pulled the edges of a blanket up over her son's chest. "Not just yet, Miss Parsons. He is full and happy, and I hope he will drift off to sleep without any fuss. He has become so stubborn of late, fighting sleep as if he fears he will miss something." She smiled and stroked her son's head. "He has his blanket, but I am feeling a bit chilled. Would you mind fetching my cloak?"

"No, m'lady." The nurse turned and followed the garden path back to the house, leaving Abby and her son alone in the garden.

Ahh, but she is not alone. Is she?

Daphne smiled, watching from the other side of the hedgerows. The moment Abby began to sing to her son, Daphne signaled her companion once more. They slipped through a break in the hedges, tiptoeing over freshly fallen autumn leaves to flank Abby on either side. It was time for her to disappear. And this time, like the other two times, there would be no letters. There was no proof she had ever written letters to the reverend mother or her father. Sister Mary Daphne had seen to that.

Ha! Sister. Daphne shook her head. She was not a nun. She wore the somber garbs of a novice, but she had never taken her vows. Nor would she. She had a much higher calling. She was a disciple of Jesus, working for him and helping him find new babies to turn into cherubs. And Jesus wanted another angel.

She motioned behind her, signally her accomplice. His heavy footsteps alerted Abby. She tightened her hold on her small son and gasped. "Mr. Piebald! You are the coachman Sister Mary Daphne's brother hired."

He doffed his cap and nodded. "Yes'm."

"But what are you doing here? And what happened to Sister Mary Daphne? Do you know where she is?"

He smiled, exposing snaggled, discolored teeth. Abby started to rise, but he motioned her back down. She lowered her hips, her arms tightening ever so slightly around her son.

"Well?" she snapped. "Where is she? Why did she not return to the convent?"

"It be the babies," he said. "She was thinking of the babies."

As Mr. Piebald spoke, Daphne inched up behind Abby. She pulled a small glass vial from her robe and tipped the contents onto a white cloth.

Abby's shoulders sagged. "Then she is not a baby farmer. I am relieved to hear that. But why did she not give my letter to the reverend mother or my father?"

Mr. Piebald flashed a wicked smile. "You'd best be asking her that yerself."

Before Abby could respond, Daphne covered her mouth and nose with the cloth. Abby gasped. Her body stiffened. And despite a valiant effort to hold onto her son, he slipped from her grasp and into Mr. Piebald's waiting arms. Then with barely a whimper, Abby slumped limply to the ground.

Mr. Piebald held the child at arms' length as if he was a mangy dog. The boy started to whimper. Daphne slipped the cloth and vial into her pocket and reached for him, comforting him as only a loving mother could.

"Hush now. Shhh." She held him to her breast, rocking him and loving the feel of his warm little body. He popped his tiny thumb into his mouth, and his eyes drifted closed. Within seconds, he was sleeping like the angel he would become.

Heart pounding in her chest, she nodded to Abby's unconscious body. "Quickly now, Mr. Piebald. Get her to the carriage before the maid returns. We must be on our way."

The coachman nodded and scooped Abby into his beefy arms as Daphne looked once more into the face of her sleeping angel. A smile spread across her face. Yes, he would make such a beautiful cherub.

****

Damn. I am well and truly under her thumb.

Jack shook his head. He'd been unable to resist Abby's pleas, and so he had agreed to let Morris and his aunt live at Ram's Head. Now, here he sat, with Mr. Lambert and his cousin in the library. His aunt was not in attendance, but Morris grudgingly admitted she was thankful to have a home more befitting of their social status.

"Although, the estate is in sad disrepair." Morris brushed an imaginary speck of dust from the lapel of his expensive frock coat and looked around the room with his lip curled in distaste. "And the allowance you have agreed to provide will not permit me or my mother to live in the manner to which we are accustomed."

Jack arched his brows. He would provide them both with an adequate allowance so long as Morris kept up his end of the bargain, but he would not grant them unlimited access to money. "My generosity does not extend to extravagant excesses and shopping trips to Paris."

Morris harrumphed. "Mother has enough clothes. I, on the other hand—"

"Have more than enough." Jack stared until Morris lowered his gaze. Then he rose to his feet, shook his solicitor's hand and left.

Mr. Lambert had drawn up a fair contract, and if Morris was a successful manager, both he Aunt Margery would receive a substantial bonus at the end of Morris' ten-year commitment. That should be enough time for his podsnappery cousin to either prove his worth or bankrupt the estate completely.

Jack snorted as he climbed inside his coach and settled against the cushions. If he were right, he would have to use his personal funds to salvage the viscountcy

329

when Morris was done with it. But if Abby were right, Morris would come up to snuff and turn his life around, using Jack's money of course. Either way, Morris won.

So, I have no reason to feel guilty. He smiled. *And the generous offer I made to my worthless relatives will make Abby quite happy.*

And making Abby happy made him happy.

"Damn." He shook his head. When had it come to that? When had he fallen so completely in love with her?

He pondered his feelings, trying to make sense of them as the coach turned down a well-worn road that led to Banbury. Abby knew he had gone to Ram's Head to make the arrangements with Morris and his solicitor, but he had not told her he was going to stop by the Hog and Heifer to inquire after Sister Mary Daphne while he was away. According to Abby, the nun's brother owned the tavern. Perhaps, he knew what had become of her.

At the very least, Jack could learn if she had repaid her brother for the loss of his horses. And if the man knew where Jack could find his sister, Jack might also be able to locate Abby's friend, Lydia. And wouldn't that make Abby happy?

He smiled, just thinking about the methods in which his lovely wife might show her appreciation. Still smiling, he entered the tavern. The tantalizing aromas of roasted pork and malty ale assailed his nostrils. Stomach rumbling, he slid into a corner booth and waited for a barmaid to take his order. Then he watched and waited.

A balding man behind the bar issued orders like a ship's captain, demanding obedience and respect. When Jack finished his meal, he left some coins on the table and approached him. "I am looking for Mr. Dupree."

The beefy man with the fly rink of shaved hair circling a polished bald head turned. "I be Dupree."

Jack extended his hand. "I am Viscount Ardmore of Ram's Head. I am looking for your sister."

The man blinked twice. "Millie is dead."

Millie must be the sister who owned the boarding house in Shrivenham. Had her sudden death prevented Sister Mary Daphne from returning to the convent? But why hadn't the nuns at the Sisters of Mercy known of the tragedy? Jack briefly bowed his head. "I am most sorry to hear that."

Dupree blinked again and frowned. "She been gone a good six or seven years now."

It was Jack's turn to blink. His confusion quickly faded, and a knot formed in his gut. It was the same type of visceral warning he often got when his ship or crew were in danger. "I was told just a few months ago that she ran a boarding house in Shrivenham."

"It ain't been a boarding house for years. Millie turned it into a confinement house after her husband died. She wanted to help unwed mothers what couldn't keep their babes." Dupree snorted. "I don't suppose your kind would care, but Millie did. She knew about the dead babies littering the allies and canals throughout the cities. It be so common, it ain't even newsworthy to men such as yourself. But being as she couldn't have her own children, she ached for those what were lost. And she ached for the women who kilt their babies cause they couldn't afford to keep 'em."

Sympathy tugged at Jack's heart. Abby had been one of those unwed mothers, trying desperately to make the best decision for her child, no matter the personal cost. But before he could respond, Dupree snorted again, condemning him with his eyes.

"It be your kind what come up with legislation to deter illegitimate births. But them Bastardy Laws condemn unwed mothers to impossible situations and protect society gents from financial responsibility. Them laws force women out of employment and bar them from the workhouse. They got no choice but to become prostitutes, pay baby farmers, or kill the babes at birth. My sister provided a safer solution. Then that Dryer woman got caught starving babies she took in and tossing their little bodies into the Thames like garbage. She was charged with neglect and only served six months."

His face turned red and his eyes glistened. "Then everybody started looking at Millie like she weren't no different. But she weren't no baby farmer. She helped her girls find real employment so they could keep their babies."

Apparently, Millie had been as dedicated to her cause as Sister Mary Daphne claimed, but she'd been dead for years. So, why had the nun pretended Millie was still alive? Had she been carrying on her sister's good works without her brother's knowledge? Or had losing her sister been more than the nun could handle?

Sister Mary Daphne's sheets might be flapping, but she was sailing in circles.

Jack cleared his throat. "I do not doubt your sister's dedication, but I am actually looking for your other sister. Sister Mary Daphne."

Dupree blinked. "Daphne? She ain't no nun, though she did spend time at the Sisters of Mercy after..." He took a deep breath and let it out slowly.

"She stayed with them several times."

The foreboding knot in Jack's gut tightened. "But she was there just a few short months ago."

"I suppose they are still hopeful they can save her. But she is a lost soul." He glanced around the dimly lit tavern and then nodded toward a back room. "I would rather not say more in public."

The nun had not seemed overly friendly, but neither had she seemed dangerous. Still, a frisson of fear shivered over Jack's skin. Ignoring the chill, he nodded to Dupree and followed him into the back room behind the bar.

Dupree shut the door and slipped behind a small desk cluttered with papers. Jack sat opposite. The old wooden chair creaked as he lowered his hips and leaned back against the slatted back. He affixed his gaze on Dupree. "Do you know where your sister is now? She claimed Millie is still running the boarding house and that the two of them are helping unwed mothers pose as widows so they might find lodging and employment."

"That was accurate enough a few years back," Dupree said with a sad sounding snort, "but the house has been boarded up since Millie's death, and Daphne does little more than tend the graves."

A chill shivered over Jack's skin. "Graves?"

"Millie, her husband, Harold, and the baby are buried in the garden behind the house. The boy, Micah, was Daphne's child." He sighed again and shook his head. "Daphne worked for Sir Bolton. After he took advantage of her, Millie and I sent her to the Sisters of Mercy. Since Millie and her husband couldn't have children, they claimed Micah as their own. Daphne stayed at the convent, but she visited the boy often. A year later, Harold died in a hunting accident and Millie converted the boarding house into a confinement house. Two years after that, Micah drowned in the garden pond while Millie was watching one of her charge's children."

Another deep sigh wracked his body, and his shoulders slumped. "Daphne blamed Millie for Micah's death. She was so angry and despondent, I sent her back to the nuns, but Daphne refused to take her vows. Then after Amelia Dyer was arrested for starving children she had taken in, Daphne became enraged and accused Millie of killing her son and other babies as well. A few days later, she suffocated our sister in her sleep."

Jack leaned forward, gripping the arms of the chair so tightly his fingers throbbed. Daphne had spent hours alone with Abby. She had given her tonics and had tried desperately to get Jack to leave her in Sheep's Crossing. Had she wanted to harm her? Or just separate mother from child as she had been separated from her own child?

His pulse jumped. "Why was she not arrested? Why has she been posing as a nun at the Sisters of Mercy and left to roam free?"

Dupree lowered his gaze. "The inquest was inconclusive. Although Millie's eyes was bloodshot and she had bitten her bottom lip, the constable believed it was because she had been drinking excessively since Micah's death. And since she had been taking laudanum to help her sleep, he did not pursue the matter further. But I weren't sure. So, I sent Daphne back to the nuns for a third time. They offered counseling and guidance, but Daphne is always borrowing my coach and driver so she might visit Micah's grave. I don't know why she would pretend our sister is still alive, but she borrowed my coach and driver again yesterday so, she has most likely returned to Shrivenham."

Jack rose slowly to his feet, his pulse pounding in his ears. "Do you believe she is dangerous?"

Once again, Dupree lowered his gaze. "The constable did not believe she was capable of murder."

"Damn it, man!" Jack leaned forward, slamming his palms on the desk. Papers scattered and Dupree jumped. "I did not ask what the constable thought. I asked what you think!"

"I, sir, believe my sister is quite mad. A year after Millie died, Daphne said Micah had been conceived in sin, and he would have been better off had Millie done like Amelia Dryer and given him to Jesus." A sheen of moisture shimmered in Dupree's gray eyes when he looked up to meet Jack's gaze. "I do not know if she is a danger to others or not, but if she is not at the convent, then she is most likely in Shrivenham."

Fear coiled like a serpent in Jack's chest. Had he not met and married Abby when he did, Daphne Dupree would most likely have taken Will the moment he was born. That would explain why she had not given the reverend mother Abby's letter or contacted Abby's father. It made more sense than her wanting to keep the money Jack had given her for her unwed mothers "charity." There was no charity. Daphne Dupree was not performing good works or helping her sister. Millie had been dead for six years, and her brother believed Daphne had killed her.

Was she now luring unwed mothers away from the convent and keeping the babies? She did not spend enough time in Shrivenham to care for them herself.

But she could be taking money from the mothers and allowing the babies to starve as Amelia Dryer had done. Or was she killing them outright and "sending them to Jesus?"

Yet, she had not taken any money from Abby. So, what was Daphne Dupree doing with the children? And what had happened to the mothers?

Fear rode Jack like a storm at sea, chilling his blood as he raced back to his waiting coach. He had to get to Shrivenham and find Daphne Dupree. Her own brother believed she was insane, and Jack couldn't shake the feeling that Abby was in danger.

Chapter Thirty-One

Her head ached, and her stomach cramped. Was she losing the baby? No. She had already given birth.

"Will..." Abby moaned, and her eyelids fluttered open. She blinked, trying to clear her vision when Sister Mary Daphne came into focus.

The nun smiled. "I see you are finally awake."

"Yes." But why had she been asleep? And where was she? She had been in the garden and...

She was still in the garden. Lush grass cushioned her back and a canopy of colorful leaves sway overhead. Sunlight flickered in and out of her eyes making it even more difficult to focus. She blinked again, noting a slight pounding in her head as her memory began to clear. She had been holding Will in the garden when Mr. Piebald appeared. Now, Sister Mary Daphne was kneeling over her and... Will was gone.

Forcing herself to remain calm, she pushed herself up into a seated position. Bracing one hand on the ground and one on an upraised knee, she took several deep breaths until the world around her stopped spinning. Then she took a deep breath and met Sister Mary Daphne's intense gaze. "Where is my son?"

The nun smiled. "He is sleeping like an angel, gathering his strength for the journey ahead."

"Journey?" Abby rubbed her temples. Her head

pounded as if someone had clubbed her over the head with a mallet. She looked around the garden, a lush green and gold oasis filled with blossoming fall flowers and foliage. A beautiful, secluded garden that was not her father's. "Where am I? We were in my father's garden, and then Mr. Piebald arrived." Fear shortened her breath. Her pulse hitched, and she started to rise. "Did he take Will? I must find him!"

Sister Mary Daphne placed a hand on her shoulder and held her down. "Do not attempt to rise. Your muscles are too weak."

The truth hit home as Abby crumbled back to the ground. Her legs tingled, and her feet felt numb. "I must find Will."

"He is fine. See?" Sister Mary Daphne rose to her feet and pointed behind her. Will lay wrapped in his blanket beside an autumn Damask rose bush. Blossoming pink flowers with darker pink centers gave off a sweet fragrant aroma that normally soothed Abby's soul. But Will lay still and quiet beneath the fragrant blossoms, and Abby could not tell if he was breathing.

She rose up on her hands and knees, determined to crawl toward her son, but Sister Mary Daphne shoved her back onto her haunches. "Leave him be! The boy is resting."

Abby scrambled back to her knees and choked back a sob. "He is too quiet. I must see to him."

The nun hunkered down low enough to cup Abby's chin in a cruel grip. "I gave him the quietness to help him sleep." She smiled, but her eyes appeared glassy and unfocused. "Just a few drops of laudanum to help him rest."

"No!" Dosing babies with laudanum was dangerous. What if the nun had given him too much? What if Will never opened those dazzling blue eyes again?

Her heart slammed against her ribs, and her breath caught in her lungs. She shoved the nun aside, knocking her off balance. Sister Mary Daphne fell sideways, catching herself with her hands as Abby scrambled to her feet and staggered to her son.

His respirations were slow and shallow, but Abby's sigh of relief turned to a cry of pure terror when she noticed the pile of dirt beside him and the gaping hole on the other side of his small body. The depression in the earth looked like a shallow grave.

"No!" Abby cried again as she collapsed to her knees and reached for her son. Before she could scoop him into her arms, Sister Mary Daphne grabbed her from behind and dragged her to her feet.

Tightening her arm around Abby's throat, Daphne pinned Abby's back against her chest. Her lips brushed Abby's ear, and her warm breath sent a chill down Abby's spine. "I said leave him be!"

"Will!" Abby struggled against the nun's stronghold until the woman pulled a knife from the folds of her rough brown robe and held the blade to Abby's neck.

Abby's heart slammed against her ribs, but she ceased her struggles and held perfectly still in the nun's arms. Despite the ache in her throat, she managed to whisper past raw emotion. "What do you want?"

"Your repentance." Sister Mary Daphne gripped her by the chin and forced her to turn. Abby craned her neck to keep an eye on her son but was unable to maintain visual contact.

Struggling for control, fighting fear and fury, she bit the inside of her cheek until it bled. Then she took a shuddering breath and spoke through her tears. "I repent."

The nun squeezed her jaw and shook her face. Abby's neck popped and pain shot down her left arm. "You are a whore and a sinner. Repent for your wicked ways so I might save your soul from perdition." The same note of insanity ringing in her voice loomed in her eyes. "Admit your sin and ask the Lord to forgive you."

Once more, Abby ceased her struggles. "Dear God, please help me," she prayed aloud, "and spare the life of my son."

"No!" Sister Mary Daphne lowered her hand to Abby's shoulder and shook her fiercely. "You gave yourself to a man before you were wed, and for that you must repent!"

No matter how often Jack had told her she was not to blame for what happened with Drury, Abby had always blamed herself. Had she not flirted with him, had she not wished to marry above her station, he might never have taken notice. But she had flirted. She had wanted more than she deserved in life, and for that, she was truly sorry.

Guilt tightened her throat, and the words nearly choked her. "I was naïve and did not know where my flirtations would lead, but you are right. I sinned against God, and I should be punished, but please do not hold my son accountable. He is innocent. You said so yourself in the convent garden."

Sister Mary Daphne raised her hand, and Abby cringed, but the slight brush of her fingers against

Abby's face was as gentle and unsettling as her smile. "He was born innocent, only because the viscount married you. But Lord Ardmore no longer wants you or the boy. So, it is up to me to save the child's soul."

"No." Abby shook her head as tears streamed down her face. "Jack did not abandon us, and my child does not need saving."

"You silly girl." The nun made a tsking sound in the back of her throat. "A child needs both parents to keep him safe, and your husband no longer needs you. He got what he wanted, and then he returned you to your father's hearth. Now, it is up to me to send your child to Jesus before something bad happens to him. You do not want your son to suffer. Do you?"

A shiver snaked down Abby's spine. Had the nun been watching and waiting all this time, waiting for an opportunity to take Will? "I am only visiting my father while Lord Ardmore attends to business matters at Ram's Head. When he returns, we will move to Ridge Point, and I will take my place as his viscountess."

In the blink of an eye, the nun's expression turned bitter, and her gaze narrowed. "Stupid, stupid girl. You no more deserve to be a viscountess than I deserved to be the wife of a knight." She grabbed Abby by the arm and dragged her across the garden to a small pond nearly overgrown with water lilies, their dying blossoms fading in the cool autumn air.

"My son drowned there." She nodded toward the pond. "My sister and her husband locked me in the convent and took him from me when he was born. They were supposed to keep him safe, but then Harold died, and Millie took in whores. She stole my son but helped them keep *their* children. And while she was watching the bastard offspring of one of *her* girls, my son drowned. Without Harold, she was unable to keep him safe." She shook Abby hard enough to rattle her teeth. "Is that what you want for your son? Is it?"

The fear and misery clogging Abby's throat prevented her from responding. The nun snarled and jerked her forward. Half-dragged, half-walking, Abby followed the nun down an even narrower path to a small clearing containing three gravestones. The nun pointed to a small headstone with a carved lamb resting on top.

"My Micah is buried there between my sister and her husband, but he was not their child. He was mine, and they allowed him to suffer. He should not have been anywhere near that pond. But he was, and he entered the water, knowing it was wrong." A sob escaped, but it did not elicit any sympathy from Abby. The nun's anguished cry sent fear coursing through her blood.

"My son should have been made an angel before he had a chance to sin." She swiped at her tears and thrust Abby onto the ground. "Born in sin, die in sin. I was too late to save him. But I have saved other babies." She pointed to the rose bushes planted around the small graveyard. Some were flush with autumn blooms; others had faded with the warm tide of summer. "There are so many babies now; I have run out of room. Your son will be the first angel I bury where my Micah died. He will be special. And I will cleanse you in blood so you might see him again in heaven."

Fear and confusion muddled Abby's thoughts, but they did not dampen her motherly instincts. Scuttling backward, she jumped to her feet and ran toward the pond. Her feet felt weighted and her head spun, but she pushed onward, desperate to reach Will. Sister Mary Daphne was upon her before she made it to the clearing by the pond.

The nun shoved Abby to the ground and then rolled her onto her back. Crouching beside of her, she held a knife to Abby's throat. "I did not explain my mission to the others, but you are special. I saw you bring Will into the world, so I need you to understand that I am doing this for you."

"No!" Abby struggled to sit up, but the nun threw one leg over her body and straddled her hips. Then she pressed the tip of her blade against Abby's throat, pricking her skin. A warm trickle ran down the side of her neck, and cold slithered into her heart.

Fear pulsed through her veins. "Please, do not hurt him. Kill me if you must, but do not harm my son."

"I am not going to hurt him." Sister Mary Daphne smiled the smile of the insane. "I am going to give him to Jesus, just like all the others. Jesus loves his little angels more than their mothers ever could."

Terror settled over Abby like a dark cloud, hovering, and waiting. The oppressive weight made it difficult to breathe. Had Sister Mary Daphne killed Lydia and her baby? "Where is Lydia?"

"Why, she is here." Daphne's smile would have looked radiant had it not been for the madness shining in her eyes. "After I cut the babe from her womb, I cleansed her in the sacred, motherly blood of the afterbirth. Then I stopped sin from entering her daughter's body by holding my hand over her mouth and nose until she stopped moving. And with the mother's blood still running down my arms, I held the baby girl up to Jesus. He took her soul, and I buried their bodies." She looked once more at Abby and smiled. "The world does not need any more bastard children, but Jesus always needs angels. Don't you see?"

Abby could not see anything. Blinded by tears and swamped by terror, she opened her mouth and screamed.

Chapter Thirty-Two

Jack didn't take time to locate his driver. He ran from the tavern and climbed into the box himself. Then with a flick of the reins, he set the coach in motion. He drove the animals hard, forcing them to run at a punishing pace along the rough, rutted path to Shrivenham. He took one curve too fast and nearly lost the coach as it tilted to one side, the wheels briefly leaving the road before he brought the team under control.

When the coach righted, Jack slowed the animals, but his pulse still beat at a punishing rate. He had nothing to go on but a hunch, but his gut told him Abby was in trouble.

The nun had seemed distressed when Jack took Abby and Will away from the vicar's house. She had alternately coaxed and demanded that Jack not force mother and son to travel so soon after Abby had given birth. Then, she had willingly agreed to let Jack take Will, but insisted he leave Abby behind. Why?

Nobles had taken advantage of both Abby and Daphne Dupree, and both had been sent to The Sisters of Mercy. The families of both women had wanted to protect their daughters from scandal. The nun's sister had taken her child as her own. Abby's father had planned to find a family to raise Will until he came up with a better plan that would allow his daughter to keep her child. But that plan had included marrying Abby off to that lecherous old fool, Lord Ruston. Then the nun offered Abby a better alternative. Only, the nun's sister was dead, and the boarding house had been boarded up for years.

So, what had the nun planned to do with Abby and her son? And what had she done with Lydia and the other unwed mothers she had lured away from the convent?

The possibilities were as chilling as they were endless, and it was clear now that the nun had some sort of plan for Abby. But Abby was wed now, and her son was not a bastard.

Still, Jack couldn't shake that gnawing in his gut that told him Abby was in danger.

Then why go traipsing off to Shrivenham after some crazy woman dressed as a nun? If he truly believed Abby was in trouble, shouldn't he ride to her father's house post-haste to ensure her safety?

"Shrivenham is closer," he said aloud as he flicked the reins and set the horses into motion at a slower pace that allowed him to think more clearly.

Mr. Dupree had told him the boarding house was on Ashe Street. If Daphne Dupree was there, he would ask her about Lydia and her baby. If she wasn't there, he would ride as fast as he could toward London, praying all the way that Abby and Will were safe. Because no matter how many times his rational mind told him Abby and Will were not in danger, he could not shake that damn gnawing.

The soft thump of the horse's hooves on the hard ground changed to a rhythmic clip clopping when they stepped onto the cobbled roads of Shrivenham. The town was a blend of old world structures with thatched roofs and newer, stone buildings with slate shingles. To the right were rolling hills and grazing sheep. And to the left was a shady lane with the name Ashe Street carved into a wooden post. Per Mr. Dupree's instructions, Jack followed the road out of town and turned down a long, winding driveway at the end. Ahead, a two-story stone house with a tile roof came into view.

Hidden by large, stately oaks and covered in thick ivy, it took a moment for Jack to notice the windows were shuttered and the doors were boarded over. Despite the quiet solitude surrounding the property, a chill settled over him as he pulled the coach around to the back of the house, climbed down from the driver's box, and hobbled the horses.

His heart in his throat, he approached the house, circling around to the right until he had made a complete circuit around the building. The place looked boarded up tight, and there was no sign anyone had attempted to break in or use a key to get inside. He sighed and his shoulders slumped. His gut might be a reliable indicator of danger at sea, but apparently, he had the instincts of a skittish old woman on dry land.

Abby wasn't in danger, and he was a fool for believing otherwise. A chuckle escaped. If she ever found out what a nitwit he had been, he would never hear the end of it.

"Damn." He shook his head. He couldn't even go back to London yet because he needed to stop in Bandbury to retrieve his driver. The poor man was probably still waiting for Jack in the servants' room at the Hog and Heifer.

Disgusted with himself for allowing his fears to get the better of him, Jack turned toward the horses and bent forward to remove the hobbles. His hand stilled, and his heart slammed against his ribs when a terrified scream rent the air.

He bolted upright, his heart in his throat as he stopped to listen. From which direction had the scream come?

The sound of a softer, muffled cry sent him bounding off down a small, twisting path behind the house. The faster he ran, the harder his heart beat and the shorter his breaths came. His heart all but stopped when he came upon Abby lying on the ground with Sister Mary Daphne straddling her. A trickle of blood ran down the side of Abby's neck, and Jack saw red.

With a roar befitting the lion some say he resembled, he launched himself at the nun, slamming her onto the ground. The knife flew from her grasp, and a crack echoed through the trees as Jack's knee dug into her ribs. She released an anguished cry, but rather than sagging limply against the ground, the crazed woman fought him with a strength born of desperation.

Scratching and clawing, she fought until he had finally had enough. With another roar, he drew back his arm and slammed his fist against her temple. The nun stilled, and color bloomed on the side of her face.

Heart pounding like a violent storm surge against his ribs, he checked for a pulse. The nun was still alive, but she would have one hell of a headache when she regained consciousness.

Knees still shaking, Jack pushed himself to his feet and turned, fully prepared to take Abby into his arms, but she was racing down a path that led further into the woods. "Abby!"

He raced after her, his heart beating in his throat. "Abby!"

After rounding an apple tree ripe with fruit, he came upon a shallow pond. On the other side, Abby knelt by a blanketed bundle, her hand shaking as she reached for it. Jack slowed his steps, fear stalling his breath.

"Will," he whispered. "Is our son..."

She turned a panic-stricken gaze on him. Her mouth opened and closed, but no sound emerged. She turned toward the baby, her hand trembling so much she clasped her hands in her lap and raised her eyes to his once more. "The nun drugged him, and I am afraid..." A sob escaped. She covered her mouth with her clenched hands and cried, "I cannot bear it."

Jack eased down beside her and reached for the swaddling blankets. He peeled back one corner, revealing Will's pale face. His mouth was partially opened, but he was breathing. The relief Jack felt was so pronounced, he could not speak. Fighting tears, he handed him to Abby.

She took him in her shaking arms and rained kisses on his tiny head, jostling his little body as she murmured. "Please wake up. Please open your eyes, little one."

The words were barely more than a whisper, her voice cracking on the last word. Jack swallowed hard and helped her to her feet, pulling both her and the child into his arms. "You're safe now. You are both safe."

Abby raised tear-stained cheeks, and a hiccuping sob escaped. "She cut Lydia's baby from her womb and buried them both here in the garden." Her eyes were wild, her words hurried and strained, as if she feared she could not get them out fast enough. "She was going to kill me and then Will."

"I know." Jack pulled her closer, holding her as tightly as he dared. "She is insane. I spoke with her brother. Sister Mary Daphne had a son. After the boy died, she blamed her sister. Her brother feared she killed her, but the inquest was inconclusive. So, he continued to care for her, letting her come and go as she pleased. I do not think he was aware of just how deeply disturbed she is or to the degree to which she wished to wreak vengeance against those who had what she did not."

"A family," Abby whispered. "She wanted a family for her son. She wanted a family for all children, and she wanted to give babies who did not have two parents to Jesus." She placed a trembling hand on Will's tiny head and choked back another sob. "Jack, she wanted to kill our son."

"I do not kill babies!" The nun shrieked as she staggered into the clearing by the pond. She held a hand to her swollen temple, and her glazed eyes were wild in her haunted face. "I send them to Jesus."

****

Abby clutched her son more closely to her breast, her heart pounding so hard, she feared it would leap from her chest.

"Give me the boy. I must send him to Jesus!" The nun's eyes were glazed, her face feverish. She gnashed her teeth and waved the knife.

Jack stepped in front of Abby and Will, putting himself between them and the nun, protecting them with his big, solid body. "You will have to go through me to get to them, and that is not going to happen. Now, put down the knife."

"I cannot." The nun smiled her crazed smile. "I take orders only from God."

"And I take orders from her." Mr. Piebald stepped from the trees and aimed an old flintlock at Jack's head.

Jack snarled. "You best put that pea shooter away before you hurt yourself."

"You ain't got no guns on ye now, guv'nor. So best you be backing away from the lady and chavy, else I blow a hole in yer head."

Despite the fear coursing through her blood, Abby could feel the rage building in Jack. His body tensed, and he seemed to grow even taller and wider, his body all but hiding her and Will from Mr. Piebald's vision. "You have one shot in that old flintlock, Piebald. One chance. And whether you miss your mark or not, I will take you apart, limb from limb before you can touch my wife or my son."

"How much is she worth to ya?" Mr. Piebald smiled, but Abby noted a slight tremor in his jaw. Jack terrified him.

Jack arched his brows. "Everything."

"Ahh." Mr. Pieblad relaxed marginally, his dark gaze darting to the nun. Sister Mary Daphne ground her teeth and glared. "Miss Dupree pays me to bring her fallen women. How much will you pay me to walk away?"

Jack smiled. "Not one damn farthing."

Mr. Piebald drew back the hammer on his flintlock with a trembling hand as Jack lunged. The gun fired, its sharp retort echoing through the trees, startling Will awake. Abby jumped and screamed. "Jack!"

Had he been hit? Or had the gun fired harmlessly into the air? She wanted to run to Jack and check every inch of his body for injuries, but Will's weakened cries sent terror coursing through her veins. She would give her life for Jack, but not if it meant losing her son. Desperate now, she flung the confining blanket from her son's limp body and knelt to the ground. Placing Will on her knees, she vigorously rubbed his chest, attempting to stimulate his weak lungs. His mouth opened and only silence emerged, but his face was turning blue with the effort to howl. Abby rubbed faster, jiggling her son on her knees, hoping his lungs would open and air would pour in, giving him the strength to cry. Her efforts seemed to be working as Will worked up a good cry, but then the prick of a blade touched her neck, stilling her fingers.

"Stand up." The harsh words emerging from Sister Mary Daphne's voice sounded foreign and feral, and spittle dotted her chin when Abby placed her son on the ground and rose to face her.

She glanced once at her son, who was now crying with renewed strength, and then she sought Jack with her eyes. Blood bloomed on his left coat sleeve as he held his arm and circled Mr. Piebald. Then with an outraged roar, Jack lunged. Mr. Piebald flung his now useless pistol at his head and tried to duck, but Jack's fist slammed into the side of his face. Abby heard the crunch of bone from six feet away as blood exploded from Mr. Piebald's nose, and he crumpled to the ground. Sister Mary Daphne shrieked like a banshee, raised her knife, and charged while Jack's back was turned. Abby screamed, but the nun brought the knife down as Jack was turning and buried it up to the hilt in the same arm Mr. Piebald had shot. Then she pulled out the blade and was about to plunge it in again when Abby hurled herself at the nun and knocked her to the ground.

The nun shrieked again and tried bucking Abby off her back, but before she could make any headway or slash Abby with the knife, Jack pulled her to safety. And when Sister Mary Daphne rose to her feet and lunged again, Jack felled her as he had Mr. Piebald. Only this time, her head arched backward at an impossible angle, and when she went down, her eyes did not close.

Jack had broken her neck.

Epilogue

Abby shivered, hugging Will tighter as the coach slowed. Jack looked down and smiled. His left arm was still in a sling, but he draped his good arm over her shoulder and pulled her closer. She sighed, content for the moment and happy they were finally free to travel.

Following the incident in Shrivenham, the coroner ruled Daphne Dupree's death a case of manslaughter, and the parish constable arrested Jack and Mr. Piebald. Jack's privileged status as a viscount kept him out of county lockup, but neither he nor Abby could leave Shrivenham until the magistrate examined the case.

While a local doctor dug bullet fragments from Jack's arm and stitched up the gaping wound left by the bullet and Miss Dupree's wicked knife, Jack sent for Mr. Dupree. Once the magistrate took his and Mr. Piebald's statements, he dismissed all charges against Jack. And after forty-eight hours of questioning, Mr. Piebald pled guilty to conspiracy to commit murder and was sentenced to twenty years hard labor at Newgate Prison. Had he not pleaded guilty, the barrister assured Jack he would have hanged.

Abby shivered again and buried her face in Jack's side.

"Cold?" he asked, a smile in his voice.

She looked up. "No. Just a bit nervous."

"Come now. You? Nervous?" He chuckled. "You

are the bravest woman I know, and it is not as though you have not already met Gilchrest and his wife."

"No, but so much has happened since then." She straightened, adjusting her son's weight in her arms. When he was first born, she could have held him for hours without complaint, but he was now five months old, and they had been trapped inside the coach for nearly two hours. Normally, Jack could have held him, but his arm was still in a sling.

"Stop fretting. The past is behind us now, and we have a bright and shining future to look forward to." He turned toward her and held out his right arm. "Here, place Will in the crook of my arm. I'll hold him until we get to Land's End."

The rest of the trip was uneventful, but the moment the coach rolled up the cobbled stone walk in front of Lord Gilchrest's home, Abby's heart started pounding again. Lord and Lady Gilchrest lived in a castle perched on a cliff above the sea. There was no drawbridge and only one tower, but parapets edged the roofline.

"Are they royalty?" she whispered as the coach rolled to a stop.

Jack laughed as he turned, and she took Will from his arms. "No, my love, but Gilchrest's title dates back to Cromwell's time and so does the castle. It has been in his family for centuries."

A shiver passed through her as Jack leaned forward and turned so he could open the door with his right arm. Before either of them could alight from the coach, a man approached with a big, sloppy grin on his face. Abby remembered Jack telling her Lord Gilchrest's twin brother had suffered a brain fever as a child and had been left somewhat damaged.

"Cap'n Jack!" He reached for Jack's good arm and shook it vigorously. "How'd ya hurt your arm?"

"It's a long story, Edward. Would you mind assisting my wife?"

He smiled again, and Abby offered her right hand while holding Will cradled in her left, but rather than reaching for her hand, the big man encircled her waist with his long arms and lifted both her and Will out of the coach and onto the ground. He then leaned forward and kissed the top of Will's head. "She's purty."

"She is a he, Edward." Jack looked at Abby and winked, causing her heart to flutter up into her chest. "Don't let the dress fool you. Will is a boy, but he isn't quite old enough for breeches yet."

Edward nodded vigorously. "I 'member when Vonn and Trenton was in dresses." He smiled. "I tease 'em now and call 'em girls when they start to pick on their sister, Charlotte. She's still a baby, but she's wearing a dress 'cause she's a girl."

Stunned into silence, Abby gaped, as Edward talked non-stop. He was the size and strength of a full-grown man, but he spoke with the boyish enthusiasm of a child. And seeing how Jack interacted with him melted Abby's heart. Despite Edward's obvious mental deficiencies, Jack treated him with dignity and respect.

She swiped a tear from her eye and turned as Lord and Lady Gilchrest approached. Two boys, one who appeared to be around six or seven, and another who was possibly a year younger walked beside their father. Lady Gilchrest held a beautiful, dark haired toddler on her hip while a tall, thin young man in his late teens or early twenties walked alongside her.

"Jack! Abby! I am so happy you made it." Nikki

leaned forward and brushed a kiss on Abby's cheek before turning worried eyes on Jack. "Goodness, what happened to your arm?"

"It's a long story," Jack said as he shook hands with Lord Gilchrest.

The earl nodded to Jack's sling. "Well, you will have plenty of time to give me the gory details over brandy and cigars."

Jack smiled. "Still getting drunk whenever you are forced to entertain guests, Gilchrest?"

"Hardly!" He snorted but then smiled. "But you are here to celebrate your birthday and celebrate we shall." He then turned toward Abby and scooped Will from her arms. "Here, let me take this little guy from you."

Without Will, Abby felt naked and exposed until Jack draped his good arm over her shoulder. Then Nikki smiled down at her two sons. "The oldest, Vonn, is almost seven, and Trenton is five."

"He didn't stop wearing dresses until last year," Edward said with a snicker.

Trenton glared. "Be quiet, Uncle Edward."

"Boys." The single word spoken by Lord Gilchrest stilled grumbling tongues. Even Edward bowed his head in silence.

Nikki jiggled the baby on her hip. "And this little lady is Charlotte. She will be two in March."

Abby brushed a dark curl from the child's chubby cheek and smiled. "She is quite the beauty, but I bet you have your hands full."

"Yes, but my mother helps, as does Ralph." She reached behind her until the young blond man stepped forward. "This is Ralph. He's been with us since he was fourteen."

"Ma'am." Ralph nodded shyly and smiled. Then he looked at Nikki. "Do you want Edward and me to take the children into Mother Bea so she can watch them?"

"Mother Bea is what Edward and the children call my mother," Nikki said before calling Edward over. "Would it be all right with you if Ralph and Edward carry the children inside so mother can watch them?"

Edward took Charlotte from Nikki's arms and promptly perched the toddler on his shoulders. She squealed with delight, apparently unafraid of the big man. Perhaps, because he looked like her father, or maybe she felt safe in his care. But Abby did not feel safe giving Will to strangers. Since the incident at Shrivenham, she had not let Will out of her sight for a second.

She glanced at Jack, but he and Lord Gilchrest were huddled in conversation. The earl held Will on his hip as if he weighed no more than a stone. She did not like the earl holding her son, but Jack was right there if Will needed him. But who would be there for her son if she allowed Edward and Ralph to take them inside? "I..."

Concern colored Ralph's expression. "I am quite good with children."

Still, Abby held her tongue as fear ate at her self-control. She wanted to grab her son and wrap him in her arms, never letting him go. Her pulse quickened. So did her breathing. She sought out Jack, her gaze finally meeting his. And just like that, he seemed to know her fears. He reached for Will with his good arm and brought him to her. "He is quite safe here, my love."

He tipped Will forward so she could kiss the top of his head. Then with a smile, he handed the boy to Ralph who then herded Edward, Vonn, and Trenton toward the castle.

Nikki stepped forward and laid a gentle hand on Abby's shoulders. "I'm sorry if I overstepped my bounds. I just thought you could use a break from holding him, but if you prefer—"

"No." Abby's heart rose into her throat. "It is not you. It's just that we have been through so much these last few weeks."

Gilchrest looked at Jack, arching his brows. "Another long story?"

Jack draped his good arm over Abby's shoulder and pulled her closer. "All part of the same story, which I would love to tell you just as soon as you pour me a glass of your fine brandy."

"And perhaps we can split a bottle of Madeira?" Nikki asked Abby.

Jack chortled and pulled her closer. "I bet she'd prefer rum."

"Jack!" Abby punched him in his good shoulder and then cringed when he grabbed his injured arm and grimaced. Both Nikki and her husband laughed.

Gilchrest slapped Jack on the back and grinned. "Then let's break open a bottle of rum and get this birthday celebration started."

****

Once inside the castle, Abby met Nikki's mother, Mrs. Keller, who insisted on being called Mother Bea. Apparently, she was not only the children's grandmother, but their nursemaid and tutor. And Edward was her assistant, or so he claimed, but Abby figured he was just another beloved child in Mother Bea's eyes. She somehow managed to dote on him as if he were a young schoolboy while treating him with the respect due a gentleman. And Edward relished the attention. He also minded her as easily as he had minded his brother when she asked for assistance herding the children upstairs. Ralph stayed in the library with the adults. The men drank brandy, and the ladies did indeed have rum while Jack and Abby filled them in on everything that had happened since Lord Chivington's soiree two months ago.

"Oh you poor thing." Nikki leaned forward to take Abby's hands. "I can't imagine how terrified you must have been."

"It was awful." Abby shivered. "But now that it is over, I can't help feeling some sympathy for Miss Dupree. She suffered untold tragedies."

"Is it any wonder she went mad?" Nikki agreed. "Women can be such fragile creatures."

Jack ground his teeth. "Do not be so naïve. That crazy nun killed a dozen women and infants. She was as dangerous as any man."

"And vindictive," Gilchrest added. "She may have been more malicious than insane."

"Really, Chad." Nikki let go of Abby's hands and glared at her husband. "Do not be so insensitive."

"Insensitive?" He all but roared. "That nun you are feeling so sorry for tried to kill Ardmore's wife and son!"

"And she very nearly killed me," Jack added in his calm, but lethal voice. "She stabbed me in the very arm that had just taken a bullet."

Nikki gasped. "Oh my! What happened?"

Leaving out some of the gorier details, Jack explained how he obtained his injury. "But had it not been for Abby hurling herself at the nun when she did, there is no telling how things might have turned out."

"Very heroic of you, Lady Ardmore," Lord Gilchrest said, but he only had eyes for his wife, as if they had shared a similar experience in the past. "It quite astounds me when women rally their strength and overcome nearly insurmountable odds in defense of their family. It is really quite unsettling."

Nikki arched her brows. "Why do you sound so surprised? Inside every woman is a ferocious mother bear that will go to great lengths to save her children. Whether those children are hers or someone else's, her husband, or her family, most women have within them the capacity to maim and kill anyone who poses a threat to those they love."

Gilchrest lowered his head in humble apology. "How well I remember, my love."

Abby looked at Jack who looked at Gilchrest. "Another long story?"

Gilchrest smiled. "Very long. So, perhaps we should save it for some other time. Because if I am not mistaken, I smell leg of lamb, and I am starving."

Nikki and Abby rose and the men came to their feet as well. Jack smiled. "You remembered leg of lamb is my favorite."

Offering a sheepish smile, Gilchrest lowered his chin as he draped an arm around his wife. "Not quite. Nikki remembered and asked Cook to prepare it for you."

"She's also making you a very special birthday cake," Nikki said.

Abby smiled and looked into her husband's eyes, feeling loved and cherished, not just by him, but by his friends. And for the first time in her life, she did not feel as if she did not fit in. She felt accepted and loved for the woman she was. That feeling of acceptance continued throughout the meal and late into the evening as the two couples adjourned into the drawing room after supper to discuss everything from the toilet training of children to world events. And neither Jack nor Gilchrest reprimanded their wives for voicing their opinions. It was as if they considered their wives equals.

It was more than Abby had ever hoped for in a marriage, and as she climbed the stairs to the guest chambers, her head spun. After Jack made love to her until she was gasping and weak, the entire room spun.

With a sigh of contentment, Jack collapsed by Abby's side as satiated and spent as Abby herself. Yet even before his breathing slowed to a normal pace, he rose up on his good elbow and smiled down at her. His warm, sweat-slick body heated her skin. His adoring eyes warmed her heart.

"Any man can tell a woman she is beautiful," he said, "but I want to make you *feel* beautiful. Always."

Despite the anticipation rising in her throat, she managed to snort. "Not a difficult task. Flowery compliments offered by a stranger can make a woman feel beautiful."

He stopped her protest with his lips, kissing her gently. Sweetly. Then he raised his head, and she could see the love he felt for her shining in his eyes. "But I want to make you feel more than that. I want to make you feel needed." He kissed her cheek. "Wanted." He kissed her forehead. "Desired." He kissed the tip of her nose. "And loved beyond measure."

Her heart soared, feeling all the love he offered and more. There was no containing what she felt for him, or what he felt for her. She could feel his love in the depths of her soul. But before she could respond, his mouth fused to hers, stopping her breath and nearly stopping her heart. Then he raised his chin, his glorious, loving gaze meeting hers. "I love you."

Her throat constricted. She pulled him closer, until their foreheads touched. "Forever. I love you forever."

"Forever," he agreed, and sealed his vow with a kiss.

If you enjoyed *SLIGHTLY NOBLE*, you might also like to meet Jack before he was a viscount, in Lilly Gayle's *SLIGHTLY TARNISHED*, a historical romance that features the Earl of Gilchrest (Chad) and his American wife (Nicole).

Available from The Wild Rose Press, Inc.

~*~

"Lilly Gayle spins a tale one part suspense and one part family dysfunction. Shocking revelations float throughout the novel…keeps the reader turning pages."

~RT Book Reviews

"Mystery, intrigue, love, and romance all come together to form a…good story with strong characters and a satisfying plot."

~Let's Talk Romance Reviews, July 2011

"This book shows that with the right person you can overcome many challenges and find love and acceptance. I highly recommend this book as a fast paced book, with wonderful characters and an excellent story line."

~The Romance Studios

"Ms. Gayle's plot is full of twists and turns and peopled with vibrant secondary characters that are nearly as interesting as the hero and heroine."

~Night Owl Reviews (a Top Pick, October 2011)

"Ms. Gayle weaves a delightful tale that keeps you entertained and wanting to keep turning those pages to find out what happens next. …you will have to read this enjoyable story that not only captivates the reader but steals your heart as well. A must read!*"*

~Romancing the Book

A word about the author...

Lilly Gayle is a wife, mother of two grown daughters, a new grandmother, and a breast cancer survivor. She lives in North Carolina with her husband. When not working as an x-ray technologist and mammographer, Lilly writes paranormal and historical romances.

You can visit her at:
http://lillygayle.com
http://facebook.com/lillygaylebooks
http://twitter.com/lillygromwriter